HONEYMOON OF HORROR

Trembling, Emily faced Charles in the private compartment of the train bearing them westward to begin married life together. She had confessed to him that she was bearing another man's child, and begged his forgiveness. "I can make you a good wife," she promised. "I know I can."

"Perhaps you're right," he said, and her hopes soared. "Perhaps you'd even be helpful."

"Oh, Charles!" she cried eagerly. "I'd try."

But her heart sank as she saw the avid look in his eyes and heard his icy voice. "I've never had a woman of my own before. One who'd do whatever I asked, who'd explore the possibilities with me. All of them. Everything that a woman could do to give a man like me a good time. Any way I could think of for you to give me pleasure—beginning now. . . ."

For some brides, a wedding night was an initiation into love. For Emily, it was the first step into the abyss.

KINGSLAND

KINGSLAND

By
Deborah Hill

A SIGNET BOOK
NEW AMERICAN LIBRARY
TIMES MIRROR

PUBLISHER'S NOTE

This novel is a work of fiction. Names, characters, places, and incidents are either the product of the author's imagination or are used fictitiously, and any resemblance to actual persons, living or dead, events, or locales is entirely coincidental.

SIGNET, SIGNET CLASSICS, MENTOR, PLUME, MERIDIAN AND NAL BOOKS are published by The New American Library, Inc., 1633 Broadway, New York, New York 10019

First Printing, December, 1981

1 2 3 4 5 6 7 8 9

PRINTED IN THE UNITED STATES OF AMERICA

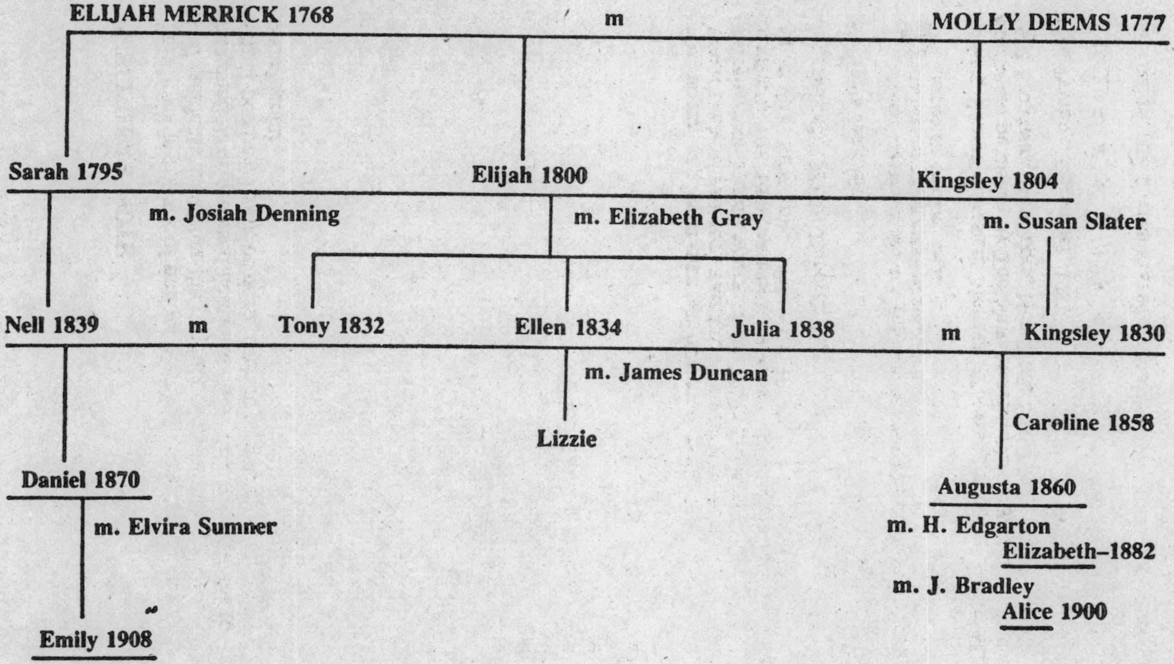
ELIJAH MERRICK 1768
m
MOLLY DEEMS 1777
Sarah 1795
Elijah 1800
Kingsley 1804
m. Josiah Denning
m. Elizabeth Gray
m. Susan Slater
Nell 1839
m
Tony 1832
Ellen 1834
Julia 1838
m
Kingsley 1830
m. James Duncan
Lizzie
Caroline 1858
Daniel 1870
m. Elvira Sumner
Emily 1908
Augusta 1860
m. H. Edgarton
Elizabeth–1882
m. J. Bradley
Alice 1900

KINGSLAND

1928

The American nation, moving into the twentieth century with pride, power, and increasing wealth, survived a war that taught it the bitter lessons known to Europe for centuries, and then grew richer, more populous, more powerful. Cities prospered and the majority of the citizenry moved to them. The rural aspect of America became a thing of the past; the country towns of New England withered. The mountains and their foothills were returned to nature as farms were abandoned, and along the coast the villages in which mariners had been born and bred became only echoes of the days when sail was ascendant.

Such an echo was Waterford, on Cape Cod Bay.

Once Waterford had been in the mainstream of the American epic, because it had been the home of deepwater captains, the hucksters of American commerce. Now the town belonged to the diggers of clams, the tenders of fish weirs, the netters of herring, the growers of cranberries. Its aspirations were humble, its pace steady and slow, though it was brightened by its wealthy summer colony, the antics of which provided the villagers with gossip, the needs of which provided them with work, the style of which gave them the taste of the world outside.

Firmly entrenched in this glittering summer society was the Merrick family, whose roots were deeply planted in Cape soil and whose traditions were part and parcel of Waterford itself. . . .

I

Emily

1

Emily Merrick stood alone in the pantry, peeking through the small crack in the door panel which was known to her from long years of familiarity with this, the oldest of the two Merrick houses in Waterford. On the other side of the door was the dining room, where the pickers of victuals lingered and talked disinterestedly; from the back parlor Emily could hear the noise of music and dancing, though the usual sounds of hilarity and joy inspired by the dancing of the twenties was missing because the party here tonight was fearfully—dreadfully—dull.

But at this moment Emily was not concerned with the party at all, dull or otherwise. Her attention was riveted to the front hallway, easily in view from the crack. Standing in the middle of the hall (large enough to be considered an extra room, all by itself!) where the host and hostess welcomed their guests too loudly, too warmly, was Alice Bradley, distantly related to Emily and anathema to her family. It was in order to avoid a confrontation with this interloper before she was ready for one that Emily had escaped into the pantry in the first place, and now, watching Alice (who'd been accompanied by a very good-looking young man), Emily was dumbfounded to discover that the girl did not possess two heads, nor was she hunchbacked or lame or ugly. In fact, she was tall and straight and graceful (Emily was on the short side), and Alice's eyes, Emily thought (though it was a little difficult to be sure at this distance), were blue, or perhaps green (green eyes ran in the Merrick family), and were a stunning contrast to her dark, becomingly bobbed hair. Emily, whose light brown bob and bluish eyes were not striking at all, recognized competition when she saw it—and that, surely, was bad enough. But God only knew what would happen when she got home with the news that Alice Bradley was present and accounted for on the Waterford social scene! She gnawed a fingernail, considering the situation.

The Merrick family tree had experienced a fork in its trunk some years before. The daughter of its most illustrious member, Kingsley Merrick, had caused Emily's present dilemma by being inconsiderate enough to marry twice. The result of the daughter's first marriage to a wealthy Canadian was a proud, self-centered, perfectly awful old maid—Elizabeth Edgarton—who lived at Kingsland, the Merrick country estate at Waterford. Of the daughter's second marriage, the result was Alice Bradley, standing there in the front hall. And awful old Elizabeth hated the girl so much and was so powerful on the Waterford scene that she'd caused Alice to be cast into social oblivion all these years—from the depths of which Alice now, apparently, was forcing her way to the surface.

Oh, God, Emily thought mournfully. Elizabeth will absolutely turn green.

The door on the back side of the pantry opened and the music from the Victrola became instantly loud.

"Emily?" queried her friend Pris Warden.

"Close the door!" she hissed crossly, startled and made irritable by Pris's abrupt entrance. "You scared me!" she said more pleasantly, by way of apology.

"I couldn't very well knock," Pris pointed out. "I had to just slip in when no one was looking." She came up to the crack, peeked over Emily's shoulder to see the goings-on in the hall. Alice was still there, and her handsome escort too, and a growing number of partygoers.

"Looks like she's making quite a hit," Emily remarked.

"The party's so dull, nearly anything would!" Pris snorted. "Really, have you ever met such incurably gauche people as the Marshalls? I wish your family had been a little more selective about who they sold the house to, Em."

"How could they know?" Emily asked. "Besides, it doesn't really matter, does it? Now that we've had a taste of what the Marshalls have to offer, we needn't bother to come back, do we?"

"Not I," retorted Pris, who had been pursued all evening by the Marshall girls and their mother in an effort to get her to invite them to the Warden mansion east of town. Poor Mr. and Mrs. Marshall had believed that buying the ancient Merrick house (sold to them by cousin Elizabeth, executor for the last decrepit Merrick owner) would entitle them to entry in Waterford society. Well, they'd soon find out that Waterford had no time for shallow nouveaux riches such as they were! But how, in heaven's name, had they come to invite Alice Bradley?

"My mother says that the Marshalls are tacky because they're New Yorkers," said Pris, tossing her head. "She says she wouldn't invite them to our house on a bet."

Mrs. Warden, Priscilla's mother, had done little entertaining for the last five years, due to her preference for sherry over her breakfast orange juice, martinis in lieu of lunch, and bourbon for supper; the chances of her receiving anyone, let alone a stranger in town, were negligible. Still, the point was well made. The Marshalls would find Waterford could not be manipulated.

They watched awhile longer.

"You know, Em, I didn't even realize she existed," Pris said from over her shoulder.

"Who? Alice?"

"Yes, Alice. I realize that old Mr. Bradley isn't exactly a member of our parent's group . . ."

"Hardly!" (Mr. Bradley, in fact, refused to have anything to do with polite society.)

"But how the existence of his daughter was kept a virtual secret really puzzles me."

"In the first place, Mr. Bradley kept her close to home," Emily said. "In the second place, Alice hasn't lived in Waterford since she started college, six years ago. You'd have no way to know her, Pris." Alice's anonymity bespoke the effectiveness of Elizabeth Edgarton's tactics too, which were designed to bury the child of her mother's second marriage permanently. But Emily decided not to say so.

"Who's that dreamy fellow with her?" she asked instead.

"Her cousin Tim."

"Why haven't we seen him before!"

"Newport, my dear," said Pris, imitating the accent of the truly rich. "His family summers at their estate in Newport as a rule. He's only slumming it while visiting his cousin."

"Well!" Emily huffed. "I declare!" She inspected the young

man again. He was truly spectacular. "I wouldn't mind getting to know him."

"That'll be a little hard to do if you insist on shutting yourself away in this closet," Pris said. "How long do you plan to hide here?"

"I'm not hiding," she assured her friend. "I only felt I'd be better off if I could think a bit."

"About what?"

"Well, about Alice. She's Elizabeth Edgarton's half-sister, you know."

"Oh, for Pete's sake," Pris said.

"And Elizabeth hates her. And since I have to live with Elizabeth, I just wanted to approach Alice at my own speed."

"I can understand that," Pris agreed with sympathy. The ferocity of Emily's cousin Elizabeth was well known to her, and to the rest of Waterford as well.

"But I think I'd sooner meet her now," Emily decided. "And her dreamy cousin."

"If Charles gives you the chance."

"Oh, Charles!" Emily said airily, as though it did not trouble her in the least that Charles Sinclaire, a bore, a cretin, and a moron besides, perpetually followed her around. He was a fact of her life she couldn't do much about, after all, like chickenpox and measles, because he and his widowed mother were such dear friends of the Merrick family, and because he possessed all the credentials necessary to belong to Waterford society so that Emily was continually thrown in with him. But Pris knew that Emily heartily disliked him, and loyally she did everything she could to relieve Emily of his presence. "I'll try to keep Charles out of your hair long enough to say hello to Tim Bradley," she promised. "I'll ask him to dance with me, if I have to."

"Gee, Pris, that's really swell of you!"

"Well, kid, I hate to see you shut up in this closet," Pris explained. "I'd like to see you come out."

Through the crack Emily could see Charles talking to the oldest Marshall boy—a good pair: both of them drips. She and Pris had better go out the other way, through the back parlor, she decided. Otherwise she wouldn't get two feet without Charles tagging along.

"Oh, come on, then," she said to Pris. "Out the way you came in."

Those partygoers with energy and interest enough were still dancing when Emily and Pris emerged and considerately everyone looked the other way so as not to betray what they assumed Pris and Emily had been up to: sneaking a forbidden smoke. (Didn't all the boys carry flasks, in defiance of Prohibition? Didn't all couples pet, in defiance of moral standards? And didn't girls smoke, and bob their hair, and roll their stockings below their knees? And more?) Naturally, Pris and Emily were up to some devilment in the pantry!

Alice and her cousin were still in the hall; the group around them had increased yet more.

"Ah! There's Emily Merrick!" Mrs. Marshall simpered. "My dear Alice, you must meet her! Emily, come right here, you sweet thing." Offensively Mrs. Marshall took her arm, drew her into the middle of the throng.

"Emily and I already know one another," Alice said smoothly. Her eyes were indeed green, and very intent. "At least, we know about one another. We're cousins."

"Why, I didn't know that!" Mrs. Marshall effused. "How nice!" She beamed.

"And this is another cousin of mine, Tim Bradley. May I introduce you, Emily?"

"I'm very glad to meet you," Emily said to the tall, curly-haired, cleft-chinned, well-proportioned, utterly marvelous young man who was smiling and looking at her with especial attentiveness. His eyes were blue, very deep, very clear. "And I'm glad to meet you face to face at last," she told Alice, confronting the inevitable.

"You mean you never have?" gasped Mrs. Marshall, astounded. "You mean you're cousins, and you've never met?"

"Rather distant cousins, Mrs. Marshall," Alice put in coolly. "And I've been out of town for quite a long time. You might mention at home, Emily, that I've returned. I've come to stay."

"You have?" Emily asked in dismay.

"Yes. My father is in his eighties now, and his health is failing. I've decided to take care of him in his old age. I'm going to teach school in district number three. So I'll be around Waterford, here and there, and someone at your house might be interested to know it."

Someone like Elizabeth.

Oh, criminy, Emily thought, and could think of no rejoinder to this frontal assault.

"There you are, Emily!" Charles, who had spotted her from the dining room, broke through the crowd, "I wondered where you'd got to. Let's dance."

"N-no, thanks," she stammered. What should she say to

Alice now—Alice, who was watching her so scornfully, she thought, so hatefully. It was not *her* fault that Elizabeth Edgarton had used Alice poorly!

"I'm sorry to hear that your father's ill," she said feebly.

"It'll break the hearts of your family, too, I'm sure," Alice said.

Her cousin gently took her arm, gently shook it. "Hey, stop that!" he said softly.

She glanced at him haughtily, but said no more.

"Come on, Emily," insisted Charles.

"Gee, Charles, I was hoping you'd ask me to dance," Pris interrupted, pouting in pretended disappointment.

"Later, perhaps," he said loftily, as though relegating her to his line of admirers. "Just now I was hoping that Emily—"

"Perhaps later, Charles," Emily pleaded, weak and helpless.

"Now!" he pressed. "You've put me off all night, and I'm tired of waiting."

"Miss Emily has said she doesn't care to dance with you," Tim Bradley said firmly, even a little loudly. "Your manners leave a little to be desired, Bozo." He was twice the size of Charles, who shrank back.

"Well, I certainly didn't intend to be rude," Charles said apologetically. "Excuse me, Emily. Let's not dance."

"Perhaps, instead, you'd enjoy going for a walk to get a little fresh air," Tim offered. He proffered his arm.

"Oh, thank you. That would be nice!" She smiled shakily, very close to tears. Without so much as excusing himself or her to Mrs. Marshall or to Alice or to anyone else, Tim whisked her out of the old house and up to the main road, and along under its elms.

"Well, you've really saved my skin," she said after mastering her shredded self-control. "Between Alice and Charles, I'm happy to leave!"

"My cousin's remark was uncalled-for," he said. "Very unlike her, Emily, I assure you. May I call you Emily?"

"Oh, goodness, yes!"

"Alice isn't really like that. But she's particularly edgy tonight, this being her first opportunity to get back at her sister."

"Is that what she's doing?" Emily asked mournfully. The picture was becoming gloomier and gloomier.

"Oh, yes. When Alice learned that the Marshalls had bought the old Merrick place and were trying to crash the gates of high society, she made sure she accidentally ran into

Mrs. Marshall and let it be known that she's the granddaughter of Kingsley Merrick. The rest fell quite naturally into place. I'm pretty sure Alice would have managed, one way or another, to get herself in a spot to strike—but Mrs. Marshall provided the first opportunity."

Emily sighed and said nothing. The quietness of the evening—there was no traffic this time of night—closed in around them, and Kingsland, past which they were walking now, was nearly indistinguishable in its shadows, its lights low, its windows and doors closed. But its occupants were awake, she was sure, listening to the noise of the Marshall party and knitting and crocheting until her return. And when she did return, with the news that Tim was giving her now—oh, what a scene there'd be!

They approached the Rockford Road.

"Care to walk down to the beach?" Tim asked.

"I'd like to very much," she answered, forcing brightness and gaiety into her voice in order to bely the depression that swamped her. "Tell me about yourself, Tim," she urged. "I could use a bit of distraction at this point!"

"Sure," he complied cheerfully. "I've just graduated from Amherst; I'm supposed to go to work at Dad's factory in Worcester, where we live. But I've talked him into letting me stay here awhile to fix up the Bradley homestead."

"And where is the Bradley homestead?"

"Upstreet. It's the house with peeling blue shutters and a willow out front."

"Oh, that one! The one that's never used!" There were several examples of such houses scattered about town, visible evidence of the exodus of Waterford captains a generation ago. "I didn't even realize that it was a Bradley house."

"Well, it is, even if we never use it. And it needs work. I can save Dad a lot of money, painting it and repairing the putty. It's bad business to just let a house go to pot the way that one is, and Dad knows it. So he agreed that I might fool around with it for the summer. It'll give me a nice break before I jump into the fray at the factory—I'm supposed to learn how to run it, one of these days. So I'm officially on vacation."

"And enjoying yourself, I hope."

"Oh, of course!"

"Partying around and all."

"Well, I haven't been here very long. The Marshalls' shindig is the first party I've been to."

"And so naturally you escorted your cousin."

"Right. Not even Alice had the courage to come alone, considering it's an all-time first for her. And if I may speak frankly," he added, "it does seem very rotten of Elizabeth Merrick-Edgarton to have blacklisted Alice all these years, especially when Alice was too young to defend herself and didn't even have a mother to help her."

"Guilty as charged."

He stopped. "What?"

"You heard me. I agree. It was really rotten." She held her hands out, palms up, to indicate her helpless agreement.

"What makes Miss Edgarton so unreasonable?"

"Miss Merrick-Edgarton, please! Hyphenated, like they do in England."

"How come?" he asked again, undiverted. "Is she neurotic?"

Emily laughed. "Rather!"

"She should be psychoanalyzed."

"Freud himself would run from her in alarm. She feels that she has been so deeply wronged, you see, that she's determined to pay it all back."

"But it isn't Alice's fault that their mother married twice," Tim argued. "Miss Edgarton . . . Excuse me. Miss Merrick-Edgarton's father died, for Pete's sake. Why shouldn't his widow remarry?"

"Well, she did it a little abruptly," Emily explained. "She took John Bradley for her husband only a month after old Mr. Edgarton passed away. You must admit, Tim, that the implication is relatively strong: Augusta Merrick had known John Bradley—and known him well—for some time."

"Humm," Tim hummed. "I didn't quite realize the brevity of mourning."

"Elizabeth was only thirteen when it happened," Emily said. "Her point of view is pretty distorted, but she was simply too young and too inexperienced, and frankly, too spoiled, to be reasonable."

"At the age of thirteen, yes. I can see that. But now?"

She started walking again, pulling him along. "I really don't know, Tim. I can't answer for her. Tell me—why haven't I seen you in Waterford before this, seeing as how your family has a house here and all?"

"Oh, well, that's rather complicated. My father and Alice's father are brothers, you see, but very different from one another. While my dad's keen on making money and running his factory and all, my Uncle John is something of a renegade, living on roots and berries."

"He does not!" she giggled. "He grows cranberries—but a lot of people here do that!"

"A renegade," Tim repeated. "So my father, who is very fond of his brother despite his rather erratic behavior, finds that the whole situation here in Waterford is easier to handle by avoidance. If he joined the portion of Waterford society that he rightfully belongs to—a wealthy man from an old family—he'd be turning his back on Uncle John, who rejected that society years ago."

"But he doesn't want to turn his back?"

"No, he sure doesn't. And with reason. My Uncle John is one hell of a fine fellow, if you'll excuse my language."

They had reached the shore, and the hard surface of the road gave over to sand. "Ugh," Emily exclaimed. "I've got to take off my shoes." They paused while she unstrapped them. "And my stockings," she added. "If you'd turn your back?"

"Oh! Sure!" Dutifully he turned.

She tucked the shoes, stockings, and girdle beneath some sweet peas, their fragrance cloying and clean, tucked her arm beneath his as they began to walk. He was trim and tough, she noticed, feeling the hardness of his muscles beneath his shirt, and the fact registered and Tim Bradley took definition: *Male, tall, strong*. She peered up at his face and added to the list: *very handsome*. The very opposite—the refreshing opposite—of Charles Sinclaire!

"So my dad solves his problem here in Waterford by not coming to visit his brother in the summer. Simple, don't you agree? The summer group disperses in the fall, and then Dad visits Uncle John. Always has, no doubt always will. We've never been here in the summer. This is my first vacation on Cape Cod."

"Well . . . enjoy yourself!"

"I will." He grinned. "Let's talk about you now. Tell me about yourself. Where do you live—when you don't live in Waterford?"

"Outside Boston, in Milton. My father is a stockbroker. He owns Kingsland, our house, jointly with Cousin Elizabeth, which is why we spend so much time here."

"Good grief," exclaimed Tim Bradley. "Your father is in her pocket, then."

"I beg your pardon!" Emily retorted. "Daddy is in no one's pocket."

"Forgive me," he said quickly. "What I meant was that if your father owns that ark with Miss Merrick-Edgarton, then he's surely very sympathetic to her. He'd probably be less than pleased to know you were out here with me."

She frowned speculatively. "It's not that simple. Yes, Daddy is sympathetic to Cousin Elizabeth, but she doesn't own him. She didn't give him half of Kingsland—he inherited it. His father went South after the Civil War, to start a cotton mill on the North Carolina Piedmont. But the mill was in a rural spot and there weren't any other Yankees around. Daddy's family were considered carpetbaggers. They were hated; Daddy was born there, but he never had a friend."

"Wow!" said Tim. "What an awful way to grow up!"

"Well, luckily he didn't have to grow up that way. He and his mother, who was a Waterford woman, spent their summers at Kingsland, which belonged to Julia Merrick, Daddy's aunt. He attended Middlesex Academy and then Harvard. In fact, he was at Harvard when Augusta Merrick came back and married your Uncle John—and got herself disinherited. So there was Kingsland then without an heir. And there was Elizabeth Edgarton, nearly a child, with lots of money that she inherited from her father in Canada—all the money needed to maintain a place like Kingsland—and there was Daddy, without a legacy at all—his father died in debt, it seems—deeply devoted to the Merrick citadel on Cape Cod, carrying the Merrick name. So both of them inherited Kingsland, Elizabeth and Daddy, jointly. And our family is like Elizabeth's family, and naturally Daddy is sympathetic to her. They're like brother and sister. He's the only man in the world she trusts, but he's not her vassal. He only tries to help, to calm her down and make her happy, if such a thing is possible."

"There's always another point of view when you talk to another person, isn't there?" Tim observed. "Alice believes your father is positively wicked—and it's only natural that she would, since he's always on Miss Merrick-Edgarton's side—or appears to be. But actually, he sounds like a very decent fellow."

"He *is* a very decent fellow," Emily affirmed. "Even if a bit conservative."

"Well . . . they're all like that!" Tim laughed. "*My* father doesn't even know I drink. He thinks I'm simon-pure."

"Gracious!" she drawled. "What'll you do when you're working with him at his factory?"

"Educate him." They laughed together conspiratorially. "I suppose you are in the process of being educated, too?" he asked.

"Oh, of course!"

"Where do you go to school?"

"Bryn Mawr. It's just outside Philadelphia."

"So I've heard," he remarked dryly.

She laughed. "I forgot you aren't a Bostonian," she said. "Really, everyone here is so insular. If you don't go to Harvard or Radcliffe, nobody seems to know where you belong."

"I noticed. You'd laugh to see them rearranging their faces when I tell them I graduated from Amherst."

"I have to explain that Bryn Mawr is in Pennsylvania."

They walked, considering the insularity of Bostonians, and then he took her hand.

"Um, I have a very risqué suggestion to make."

"You do?" Instantly her heart, which had until now been behaving normally, jumped a little.

"I'm carrying a little something in my hip pocket. Since we're missing the party . . ."

"There was no liquor at the Marshalls'," she said. "That was one of their problems."

"I think it would be nice to have a little party of our own. If you'd agree," he said politely. He slipped the flask out of his pocket, held it out.

"What's inside?"

"Gin."

"Nice gin? Or bathtub booze?"

"My father has a Philadelphia supplier," Tim said with dignity.

"No wonder you knew where Bryn Mawr was." She giggled and held out her hand, and took the flask, let the gin burn the tip of her tongue, swallowed a little, handed it back. Tim Bradley took a rather long pull.

"Warms you right to the toes, doesn't it!" He pointed to a nearby dune. "Let's sit over there, all right? Then we can really do it justice."

"Sure," she agreed. "That'd be fun." She followed, settled herself comfortably beside him, looked out over Cape Cod Bay, which sparkled at high tide under a full moon. The summer night pushed in behind the gentle wash of low, slow waves.

"How do you like Bryn Mawr?" he asked, passing the flask.

"It's okay," she said. "But I'm trying to persuade Daddy to let me stop and take a job in Boston."

"Sounds adventurous."

"It would be adventurous!" Her spirits rose in consideration of being on her own in the city—even in Boston, which was so close to Milton that living there would be like pitching a pup tent in the backyard. "But Daddy, being conservative, thinks it would be a little too adventurous. I want to get an apartment with my roommate, Pris Warden, who's a bit on the wild side—but so much fun! Together, I expect, we'd have lots of adventures. Lots more than at Bryn Mawr! You met Pris tonight—she was there at the Marshalls'."

"Oh, yes. She was the one who tried to rescue you from the clutches of that, um, fellow. Sinclaire."

"That's her, all right." Emily laughed, her spirits well restored now and the depression of the Marshall fiasco dissipated. "Charles has a crush on me. Has for some time, and his family is close to mine—has been for several generations, unfortunately. At home they think I should be nice to him. So I'm in a bit of a spot, and Pris does her best to help me out."

"It strikes me that you're in a bit of a spot in more than one way," said Tim. "Between your friend, the baboon, and my cousin. Maybe I could help you."

"How?" she asked, thinking that the biggest favor he could perform would be to take Charles's place, squire her around, be her beau. He was handsome, and seemed kind as well. What a combination!

"To begin with, I will tell you the plan of Alice's attack," Tim said. "So that you can protect yourself. You won't be able to stop her from doing what she intends to do—she's very determined! But at least you can get out of the way. And in the second place, I will tell Alice to be more considerate of you, and I think she'll listen. She's not an unkind person, honest! She just needs to be reminded that being unpleasant to you is unfair, since you aren't responsible for her problems."

"Well, that's very nice of you." She smiled. "I'd surely appreciate it."

"And in return, you can dance with me while she goes about hog-tying Waterford."

"What?" she laughed.

"I promised her that I'd take her where she wants to go this summer, so that she doesn't have to worry about getting there—but she made it very clear that once she's got where she wants to be, I'm to keep out of her way. So I'll need someone to dance with."

"Glad to oblige!" Emily agreed instantly. "But tell me how she plans to hog-tie Waterford."

"First she'll lure all the young people to her side—which she's fully capable of doing."

"I'd judge you're right." Emily sighed, remembering the cluster of people in the hall.

"Then she will rearrange their values, so that they'll turn against society as it's presently structured, and of their own free will, dismantle it. Then Elizabeth Edgarton will have no influence on it, you see? And there won't be anything she can do to get it back."

"Elizabeth isn't exactly powerless, you know," Emily remarked, not especially impressed with Alice Bradley's rather farfetched ideas about hog-tying.

"She will be. The values of the group will have changed and they'll no longer honor Elizabeth Edgarton's gods. That's the way Alice puts it."

"Really!" Emily exclaimed, shaking her head. "When did Alice dream all this up?"

"I think it's been growing on her, over the years." Tim lay back on the sand, arms behind his head, regarding the stars. "Alice didn't realize how insulting it was—being blacklisted—until she went away to college. Once she was out from under, she realized she was as good as the next person."

"Better," Emily reminded him. "Since she's the granddaughter of the Great Merrick."

"Hear, hear!" he cheered. He propped himself up long enough to take another snort and offered his flask to her.

"But do go on," she urged, and found her tongue just a bit thick. The contents of the flask were explosive.

Tim lay back again.

"Well, Alice stayed away for six years. Became very intellectual—and did very well at whatever she set herself to do. She found jobs during the summers, taking care of children, tutoring, that kind of stuff. For the last two years, she's been with Gilchrist's in Boston, coming to Waterford to see her father in the winter, just like my dad does. That's really how I got to know her. In the winters, when I visited Uncle John with my father."

Attuned to him by now, sensitized by the gin, Emily heard it. "Why, you're in love with her!" she exclaimed.

"A little, perhaps. But she's my cousin, you see. I can't have her. We don't approve of consanguinity."

"Too bad."

"Besides that, she won't have me because she thinks I'm a philistine."

"She does?"

"Yes, because I'm going to run Dad's shoe factory."

"What would she prefer?"

"Something unmaterialistic." He had a little trouble with so long a word. "Philistine. Doesn't sound flattering, does it?"

"I'm afraid not." She found herself becoming indignant on his behalf. "It sounds a little arrogant, if you ask me."

"Oh, if Alice is anything, it's arrogant," he said readily. "It's only a disguise, though. A role she's assumed while she puts her house in order. Under it all, she's a very gentle, tender person who hurts. She's going to heal her hurt by dephilistinizing Elizabeth Edgarton's precious society. Or so she says." He sat up. "Really, it's a little deep for me. And since according to Alice I'm a philistine myself, I can hardly be expected to understand, can I?"

His feelings had been hurt, Emily saw, and she was sorry. "I don't think you're a philistine," she said, and impulsively patted his cheek. "I think you're nice."

"Gee," he said, catching her hand. "Do you?"

"Yes, I do," she repeated stoutly. "And if you let your cousin bully you around, just because she's a Vassar girl, you're crazy. Running a factory and making money doesn't make you a philistine."

"It doesn't?"

"No."

"What does, then?"

"Your mind." She laughed. "It's a state of mind, is all. Do you think money's more important than anything else?"

"Certainly not."

"There. That proves it. And your father? Does he think money is the ultimate measure of success?"

"I don't think so." Tim considered it. "And even if he does, he's still a good father."

"I'm sure he is," she said softly. "And I'm sure he deserves your loyalty, even if your cousin disdains him and his achievement."

He turned to her then, looking her squarely in the eye, searching her face for verification of her sincerity.

"Thank you, Emily," he said softly, and put a large, gentle hand on her hair. "That's damn sweet of you."

"I didn't say it to be sweet," she breathed. "I said it because it's true."

"Still, you wanted me to feel better. And I appreciate it."

"Well, you're welcome," she whispered as slowly he drew her close, closer and closer until their lips were touching tentatively, carefully, in a get-acquainted sort of way and she was aware of her own heartbeat in her ears, aware of his hand which had buried itself in her short, fine hair, aware of his arm which tightened around her as the kiss deepened, became urgent, binding her to him. Something hot and powerful within her, never stirred before, stirred now, and she put more into that kiss than perhaps she should have done, considering that she did not know Tim Bradley very well, until he released her, his eyes exploring her face, her hair, her lips, which he kissed again.

The night noises of the bay gradually returned from the abyss into which they'd been flung; the water, like a lover, caressed the sand in its quiet high-tide calm. The gulls gossiped, awake and noisy because the herring were returning to the sea; somewhere unseen in the darkness something jumped and fell back into the water, and its unrecorded splash faded away.

"I'm afraid I have to go home," she whispered.

"I was afraid of that, too." He grinned.

Quickly he was on his feet; they started back, quiet now, meditative. Gosh, she just had to see him again. Would he ask, of his own accord? Or should she try to direct the conversation to desired channels? If she waited too much longer, perhaps she'd lose the opportunity. . . .

"The Hallets are having a party next Friday," she said tentatively. "They live in Yarmouth. Everyone in Waterford is going—it's an open invitation, and I'm sure you'd be welcomed there." She waited, hoping he'd grab the chance to see her again.

"How about Alice?" he asked, crushing her. "Would she be welcomed, too? Or does Elizabeth's influence extend even to Yarmouth?"

"I don't know," she said, downcast. "Since it's an open invitation, I shouldn't think Elizabeth would matter one way or another, would you?"

"It'd be fun to see you there, in any case," he said. "What time does it start?" Ah! She became happy again!

"Oh, eight or nine o'clock, I suppose. Parties usually do."

"I take it that it'd be better to meet you at a party than to call on you at your house?"

"I . . . I think I'd better see how the land lies," she stammered. "I'll have to tell them that the butterfly has come out of its cocoon, and see how they take it. I'll tell you all about it at the Hallets'," she added, the thought coming to her as an inspiration. What a good way to ensure his being there!

"All right," he agreed, and they headed back up the Rockford Road to a shortcut known to Emily from her childhood, across a brooklet by means of stepping-stones, through a small meadow with an apple tree in the middle, up to the shadowed hulk of Kingsland and its back door.

"Well, thanks again for getting me out of that awful party at the Marshalls'." She smiled.

"You're welcome," he answered, and smiled and kissed her again, her entire length pressed to his, his lips wonderful. He left her to find her composure as best she could and then to make her way through the darkened kitchen, down the hall and to the library, where there was a light. She peeked around the door, hoping that Cousin Elizabeth wouldn't be in there peeking back, and, sure enough, Mother was alone, dozing beneath the smiling portrait of Kingsley Merrick, Waterford's Great White Father.

"Mother!" she whispered.

Mother started; her face was clouded with concern until consciousness impinged on her and she remembered that Emily was not a little girl who might be calling her in distress. She straightened up in the chair, patted her hair to make sure it was not mussed.

"Hello!" She smiled, speaking softly so as not to arouse the sleepers upstairs. "How was the party?"

"Just wait until I tell you!"

"Well?" whispered Mother. "I'm all ears."

"Alice was there."

"Alice Bradley?"

"The one and only."

"Oh, no!"

Mother was predictably appalled.

"Not only was she there, she was the life of the party."

"Oh, gracious," Mother groaned. "How do you suppose . . . ?"

"The Marshalls are so new, I guess they didn't know. And unfortunately they aren't the kind of people who know enough to ask. Besides, I think Alice tricked 'em into it."

Mother shook her head over the obtuseness of the Marshalls, the treachery of Alice Bradley.

"There's nothing we can do, Mother. The floodgates are open. There's no way to stop Alice, especially since she'd determined to be included."

"Included!"

"You bet!"

"Oh, goodness," Mother sighed.

"Until now, Elizabeth's had it all her own way," Emily said. "She'll just have to move over."

"Sounds like it," Mother nodded unhappily. "We'll have to tell her."

"You can do it," Emily said firmly. "Or Daddy can, when he comes down from Boston tomorrow. I won't! I don't think I could stand listening to her rant and rave. It's all she ever does, and I'm sick of it!"

Mother nodded her sympathy. Elizabeth *could* be very difficult at times!

"What was Alice like?" Mother asked, curiosity getting the better of her.

"Very pushy. Very determined. And making quite an impression on everyone. I was sick, Mother."

"You should have come home."

"Well . . . as a matter of fact, I did leave."

Mother frowned. "You didn't come home early."

"I left with Alice's cousin. Tim Bradley is his name. We took a walk. He was awfully nice, Mother."

"Must be David Bradley's boy," Mother said approvingly.

"Yes."

Mother raised an eyebrow delicately. "Very nice people. Or so I hear; I've never met them."

"They usually spend their summers in Newport, Tim says."

"They'd be quite an addition to Waterford, wouldn't they?" Mother's eyes sparkled at the thought of so rich a plum.

"Tim was really kind. He saw that Alice had put me on the spot, and it was his idea that I leave. And then he told me what she plans to do—to help me figure out how to keep out of her way."

"And just what are her plans?"

"Tim says that Alice isn't going to settle for being blacklisted. She's going to elbow her way into Waterford whether Elizabeth likes it or not. She's going to make it her own. And since our group is old enough to make its own decisions, invite its own friends, and get itself around, I wouldn't be surprised if she succeeded."

"Oh, goodness," Mother sighed. "I don't know. I just don't know. I do feel sorry for Elizabeth, really."

"I don't!" Emily flared.

Mother gazed at her sternly. "I don't blame you for being critical of Elizabeth, dear, but when I tell you what the poor thing has been put through, perhaps you won't be so quick to judge her."

"I know what the poor thing has been through," she said quickly, impertinently. "I've heard it all before."

"Well, perhaps you haven't heard how badly Elizabeth's grandmother played on her hurts and fears and turned her into the unfortunate person she is today."

Emily stopped. Indeed, this was an aspect to "poor Elizabeth" that she had not ever heard. Mother always seemed to think Elizabeth was perfect, as were all the other birds roosting on the branches of the Merrick family tree.

"It was very awkward, you see, when Augusta Merrick developed an infatuation with John Bradley so many years ago. She did so as a young girl—seventeen or so. The Bradleys had fallen on hard times and could no longer keep up with society, and what was worse, John Bradley wanted it to stay that way. He didn't have any interest in Waterford's nicer people, and he had the gall to propose to Augusta and offer to carry her away, to live as he lived, humbly, in his cottage."

"That much I knew," she said, hoping to urge Mother to a faster pace.

"Augusta was very immature, very impressionable, and was willing to live simply, forgoing her father's heritage—this house, the lovely circle of family friends. And so her mother—Elizabeth's grandmother, Julia Merrick—exercised her prerogatives as a parent, demanding a more suitable alliance, and Augusta married an older gentleman instead, a Canadian named Harold Edgarton—Elizabeth's father."

"Yes, yes," Emily said impatiently. Why did adults insist on recapitulating everything, as if you were ever allowed to forget it anyway!

"And when Augusta married John Bradley so soon after Mr. Edgarton died"—meaningfully Mother glanced at Emily, and Emily vigorously nodded, hoping to avoid a description of the awfulness of that lamentably short courtship—"naturally it was to her grandmother that Elizabeth turned. She was distraught to discover that her mother had been carrying on with another man all those years—which was bad enough, surely, but her grandmother selfishly capitalized on this already explosive situation."

Emily looked up, surprised. Never had she heard criticism of a departed Merrick—and certainly not of the wife of Waterford's Great Person.

"Julia Merrick commanded society here in town, and she put Elizabeth into the position of heir apparent, made her feel important, put her at the center—and above all, Julia honed her hates unmercifully. Daddy can remember how cleverly Julia played on the girl's emotions! With results, too! Elizabeth took the Merrick name to add to her own and adopted all her grandmother's attitudes and values, took up her burdens and joys, and rose above her unhappiness as much as she was able—and allowed to! But in the course of time, Augusta and John Bradley produced a daughter of their own—Alice—and Alice became for both Elizabeth and her grandmother the living representation of the initial betrayal and abandonment. They made it clear to their friends that they would appreciate it if Alice Bradley would be considered as just another member of Waterford's year-round population. Like all the other girls who wait table and change the bed linen. And since that was the way she was raised by her parents—a humble daughter of humble people—it was easy enough to forget that Alice was the granddaughter of Kingsley Merrick, same as Elizabeth is. And then Augusta died, and the girl Alice and her father were just forgotten. There was nothing to remind anyone of them, you see, and Elizabeth, following her grandmother's example, made sure the memory of Waterford remained undisturbed. Far as anyone in town is concerned—or has been concerned—Alice is just another chambermaid."

"She's far from a chambermaid," Emily put in. "Elizabeth will have to look sharp."

Mother sighed. "I don't like it," she said. "It means trouble. Elizabeth, I feel very sure, promised her grandmother on her deathbed that she'd carry forward by herself just as the two of them did, making sure that Alice would remain in limbo, just as I know she promised that Kingsland would remain in the family."

"That grandmother sounds poisonous," Emily said waspishly.

Mother waved feebly, as though it were all too much for her. "Julia Merrick was a proud, proud woman, and she was not going to be brought low by her daughter, Augusta. She used Elizabeth's hurt to her own advantage, and she kept the old animosities alive, kept the old wounds from healing, kept Elizabeth from forgetting what John Bradley and Alice stood for. Your father has done a lot to ease Elizabeth's angers, and I've done what I could, too. But, oh! The hurt! The unbearable hurt, and hatred! It'll take a lot to change Elizabeth. Really, I just don't know how she'll react when she learns that Alice is going to be a threat to her."

Emily sighed. There was trouble in the air, unavoidable. And her own concerns to protect. She leaned forward.

"Look, Mother, aside from all this mess, the truth of it is that Alice's cousin Tim is a very attractive person, and I'd like very much to see him again. Do you think all this business is going to make any difference? I mean, will Elizabeth's prejudices make it hard . . . ?"

Mother looked at her sharply. "What about Charles?" she asked.

"Just because you enjoy Mrs. Sinclaire and went to school with her doesn't make me devoted to Charles. I've told you that before," Emily said angrily.

"Oh, of course not, of course!" Mother drew hastily back, wishing to avoid offense, which would get in the way of Emily's appreciating Charles's due worth. Goodness only knew you couldn't force these things! "Although," she added, "you know that I'm confident of your safety when you're with him."

That only went to show you how dumb mothers could be! Meekly Emily waited.

"About Tim Bradley," Mother said slowly, thinking. "Surely he must be a decent boy, if he's David Bradley's son. I'd like to meet him—sometime. But I don't think that just now is the right time, if Elizabeth is going to have to face up to the existence of Alice Bradley. I think it would be unwise for Tim to call here—for a while at least. I hope you understand, Emily."

"Sure, I understand," she acquiesced, understanding only that if she wanted to see Tim Bradley, she'd better be quiet about it.

Well, all right, she thought, bidding Mother good night. Certainly she didn't want to put Tim in an awkward position, which, it would seem, was going to happen if he came to Kingsland. She'd just have to figure out other ways of seeing him, was all. At the Hallets' next weekend, and at Pris Warden's the weekend after that—for she and Pris had already done the initial planning for a party to be held there at the Warden mansion, the main feature of which would be a snipe hunt designed to amuse those in the know at the expense of Charles Sinclaire, Waterford's goat. And because of the hunt, Charles would be out of the way for a while, an ideal opportunity to pair up with Tim Bradley and perhaps, as tonight, steal away with him.

Her toes curled up in her shoes at the very thought of stealing away with Tim Bradley!

Yes, she'd see to it that Pris invited him, and between now and then she'd take advantage of such opportunity as the Hallets' party presented. For Tim Bradley was, by far, the most handsome, the most exciting, the most marvelous man she had ever met, and she meant to make the most of any and every moment she got with him!

2

It was a noisy party. Unlike the Marshalls, the Hallets had no reticence concerning the use of bootleg liquor to loosen up the celebrants—and everyone was making the most of it. Pris fox-trotted by with Jacky Pollard, the two of them, despite the heat of the room, glued flat together. Jacky's hand, which had been pressed to the delicate curve of Priscilla's back, crept downward, cupping her buttocks, and it was a full five beats before Priscilla, reaching behind herself, put his hand back where it belonged. In a far and dark corner Becky Levering was necking with an unknown Yarmouth boy; Evvie Thayer lurched by with a cigarette hanging from her lips. Bob King peered around the pillar on which Emily was leaning, blew a smoke ring and asked her to dance, went away unoffended when she waved him a refusal. Ned Pettingill, polite as always, leaned against the pillar with her for a while, chatting, saw that she did not care to dance, and considerately left, too. Emily looked all around the crowded Hallet living room where the rugs had been rolled up, the furniture pushed into the corner, all lights but one extinguished. Soon that one, too, would go, and then there'd be no way to see Tim if he ever got here—and she was afraid, horribly afraid, that he just wasn't coming.

Her exasperation and anger turned rapidly to despair. If he didn't arrive soon, Charles would come looking for her. And if he did, all her plans would be hopelessly upset. . . . Already, it was nearly too late.

A light went out with a crashing of glass, and the party noise roared to a higher pitch than ever. The girls squealed and the boys laughed, and beside her Tim Bradley's voice said, "Alone in the dark with Emily. Again."

"Oh!" she exclaimed. "Tim!" Her gladness broke loose and flew free over the unhappiness and disappointment of the moment before. "Hello!" she said. "I'd about given up on you."

"Oh? Sorry I'm late!"

"I don't remember any specific time being mentioned," she said with heroic nonchalance. "Did you have trouble finding your way?"

"No," he laughed. "I lost an hour trying to persuade Alice to come. When I was convinced she wouldn't . . . well, I jumped into my car and got here as fast as I could, hoping to find you."

She looked gratefully up at him, delighted he had sought her out. Not even the dimness could disguise the broadness of his shoulders and the narrowness of his hips, the ease with which he moved, belying a body at its peak of tone and prowess. Yes, indeed, he was quite a man, and he had come here looking for her! She clasped her highball glass firmly, controlling the tremor in her hands, leaned against her pillar as though she were entirely relaxed, at her ease, as though she had not spent most of her waking moments since last Friday remembering him.

There was a pause while a new record was put on the Hallets' Victrola. The din of the party roared past like the wind, loud as it wanted to be because Mr. and Mrs. Hallet had abandoned the house so that the young people might enjoy themselves.

"Want to dance?" Tim asked, as the Victrola was wound up. "The Charleston" crashed through the racket and the whole room was instantly alive and in motion.

"You bet!" she cried. tossing her empty glass into the dirt of a potted plant and joyfully jouncing her way onto the floor, bouncing face to face with Tim Bradley, who, for so large a man, Charlestoned beautifully.

"What have you been doing to keep busy this week?" she asked.

The music and the dancers drowned her out.

"What?" he shouted.

"What have you been doing to keep busy?" she yelled.

"Scraping paint. What a job! I'm exhausted!"

"You must be!"

"What?"

"You must be!"

"What have you been up to?" He wasn't even breathing heavily, which was more than she could say for herself.

"Tennis," she panted.

"What?"

She gestured.

"I really can't hear you," he complained, pulling her out of the crush of dancers. "Let's go out to the terrace."

She nodded, so he'd know she agreed, and pointed, so he'd know where the terrace doors were. They wiggled through the crowd and out the double French doors, into the relative coolness of the summer night and the company of other couples who stood around or sat on the low stone walls of the terrace, laughing low and flirting and smoking. It was fresher here—but only relatively. The still night air was suffocating and would remain so until the land breeze, which had held on for three days, changed.

She could see Charles Sinclaire nowhere, which meant he was still hiding behind a curtain somewhere, flask in hand, with a compliant Ginny Porter sitting beside him. How dull he was when sober! How obnoxious when drunk! But since he was getting soused somewhere with Ginny (as Emily had planned), at least he was out of the way and the field was clear to work on Tim Bradley (also as planned). Tim settled himself on the stone wall to converse with her, one long leg swinging time to an unheard, unhurried beat within.

"Why didn't Alice want to come?" Emily asked.

He waved meaninglessly, signifying his inability to understand his cousin.

"She's concerned with overexposure," he reported. "She thinks she did pretty well at the Marshalls' house, and the Hallet revels include Yarmouth people who don't interest her. Pris Warden asked her to a party next weekend, so she's decided to save her ammunition until then."

"She's going to Pris's party?" Emily asked, dismayed.

"Why, yes. She's been led to believe there's going to be a snipe hunt." His smile was mischievous, friendly, but Emily's dismay increased as she thought about the implications of Alice's presence. And most of all, of the fact that Pris must have asked Alice to the party last week, at the Marshalls'—she'd have had no other opportunity. But although Emily had played tennis all week at the Wardens', Pris had not mentioned it.

"By the way," Tim said, "I used your argument against Alice, and it stopped her cold. I wanted to thank you!"

"What argument?"

"About a person's state of mind defining what he is. Actually, I'm very grateful to you, Emily, for giving me that little tool. There's no disputing it, and Alice doesn't try to talk me out of working in my father's factory anymore. Makes things a lot more restful, since I aim to work there whether I want to or not, and own and operate it one day, whether I want to or not."

"Gee, Tim, that sounds grim!"

"It isn't really. I think a lot of my father—I may have told you so the other evening. I certainly don't plan to make a shambles of his plans, just to gratify my cousin. As for myself . . . well, I'm sure I'll enjoy it, once I get into the swing of it."

"Good luck!" she said wryly.

"I suppose that fellow Sinclaire brought you tonight."

"He brought eight of us," Emily said, desiring not to be too closely associated with Charles.

"Do you think he'd mind if I took you for a ride?" Tim asked.

She nearly fell all over herself in her excitement. "There's no reason why he should!" she said, forcing her voice to remain calm. "We don't go together. It doesn't matter whether he minds or not. Where would you like to go?"

"How about the canal? The boat must come through sometime soon."

The fine hairs on her arms stood straight up in alarm. Was Tim Bradley suggesting they park? Canal-watching was a happy pastime for fast couples, who could sit in their cars on the darkened shore and pet in privacy until the ferry came along. Then everyone honked and the passengers waved and the ferry passed, lit up like a floating palace, music and laughter rising from it and the canal lights trailing behind like stars. It was a fine way to spend the evening—but not with a boy with whom you did not have an Understanding.

"The boat goes through at eight-thirty," she hedged. "It must be eleven o'clock by now. We're too late."

"Oh! Too bad!" he declared with a grin, and continued to sit there, wagging his leg, waiting for her to make the next move.

She sat beside him, picked a leaf off a nearby bush,

shredded it, dropped it. "We could just talk," she suggested. "Though if we sit here, we might be interrupted." Nervously she looked around, to see if Charles was in view. He wasn't. "We could walk over to the edge of the lawn."

"Where the shadows are, you mean?"

"Yes . . . that's the place. It looks quite cool, don't you think?"

"And secluded. And so dark that no one would know who you were with."

"Well, it is a little dark. . . ."

"Perhaps you'd sooner no one did know."

"Well, as a matter of fact, Charles . . ."

"That ninny!" Tim said scornfully. "Will he tell on you?"

"He might."

"And will it matter?"

"It's hard to say." She fidgeted.

"Did you tell your family," he asked, with what appeared to be only casual interest, "about Alice?"

"I only told my mother about her," Emily said, wishing there were a way to avoid this mess. "Elizabeth doesn't know yet. Mother's waiting for the right time to tell her."

"Did you ask your mother about me? About whether I could come to your house?"

"Well, of course, until Elizabeth knows that Alice is on the prowl, it might be unwise," she hedged, seeking to soften the edges.

"Is that what your mother said?"

She could only look up into his clear blue eyes, begging his forgiveness because words were hopeless.

"What did she say?" he asked again.

"She thought it would be a good idea to wait," Emily admitted.

His eyes deepened, and his chin became set more firmly.

"Emily dahling!" shouted Charles, lurching up to her, smelling unpleasantly of liquor. He pulled her to her feet, facing himself. "Where've you been, sweet? Everyone wants to go parking." He slipped an arm around her waist.

How mortifying, to be pinned by Charles with Tim looking on! She tried to wiggle away.

"Come on, Emily!" Pris called, hanging on to the draperies by the terrace door in an effort to steady herself.

"Cut it out, Charles," she said, trying to disengage herself. "I'm not going parking."

"Oh, gosh," he pouted, releasing her. "Why not?"

She turned to Tim, to say something that would minimize

Charles's presence, and discovered that he was no longer there.

Oh, God, she cried, and her throat clutched up; she struggled with her dismay. Oh, God!

"I wish you two would cut out the conversation and get going," Pris called, swayed, and with the draperies fell silently into a velvet heap.

"Hey, Pris," called Jacky Pollard, who scurried forward to join the group. "What'd you do that for?"

He fished her out.

"Flimsy." Pris struggled up. "I thought the Hallets had more class than that."

"Emily says she won't go parking," Charles said gloomily.

"Oh, Emily!" Pris sighed. But then, she did understand the cause! "Better luck next time, Charles. Here, let me kiss you and make it well." She clasped Charles to herself in an embrace more ardent in jest than Emily had ever given him in earnest.

"Come on, come on," Jacky said. "Break it up. Unless you let him go, Priscilla, he'll never drive us home."

"He's not going to drive us anyway," Emily said, angry now in her disappointment. "I am."

"What?" cried Charles, forsaking Pris.

"You're drunk," she said flatly. "I can handle the car better than you can."

"I am not drunk," he insisted, pouring his energies into focusing upon her face. "My Gawd, Em, do you think I'd risk precious cargo by driving when drunk?"

She had no intention of arguing with him. "I'll walk, then," she said flatly, heading for the front door as though she would begin this moment.

"I'll drive, if you think I'm a better bet," Jacky offered. "I'm not drunk."

She did not want to sit in the backseat with Charles if she could avoid it, having to fend off his mauling and manhandling, so it didn't matter whether Jacky was sober or not.

"I'll drive, or else I'll walk," she repeated.

"Your parents will think it's very strange," said Charles, trailing her to the door. "My mother will think it's strange, too. Maybe we ought to put the top up, dahling, so no one will know."

She was quite sure that, drunk or sober, Charles would not be capable of putting the top up. "Everyone will be asleep, Charles dear. Just leave it to me."

"Oh, Emily girl, you have got class," he sighed, happy to

let her boss him around, since it at least implied a relationship of sorts. "I wish Ginny Porter did. Dahling, where the hell were you all night?"

He was her passport, after all. So eager were her parents to put her in his company that she could go anywhere if she were with him. It did not occur to the adults of her family that Charles would take their daughter to an undesirable place, like a speakeasy or a wild party, or that a gathering of Cape Cod young people of respectable, settled families might not, itself, be respectable.

She did not answer, but instead linked her arm through his, leading him to the Sinclaire Buick. Draped over its hood was Becky Levering, who had been sick all over the fender, and Bob King, who was patting her back ineffectually.

"If you think I'm going to ride with her, you're out of your mind," Pris objected. "She'll throw up all over me. She'll ruin my dress."

"You can sit on my lap, honey," Jacky said. "That'll leave a little space between you."

"I'm dying," Becky gasped. "And all you can think about is your dress."

"Where's Carolyn? Where's Arnie?" Emily asked. They'd driven over to the Hallets' in Charles's car, hadn't they?

"I think they've left," Pris said vaguely. "Everyone aboard, please. The train is due to depart."

Grumbling, groaning, giggling, they all piled in, and Charles closed the door behind them; she held out her hand for the key and sheepishly he dropped it into her palm. The expensive Buick coughed into instant life.

Pris and Jacky, she saw in the mirror, fell instantly into an embrace from which, she knew, they would not surface until the Warden driveway had been reached. Becky was sleeping already, her head on Bob King's shoulder. Charles sulked in the passenger seat and then himself fell asleep and did not wake up even when she let Becky and Bob out. He was asleep still when they rolled into the Warden driveway and pulled up by the front door, where the porch lights gleamed on the enormous black and shining length of the car.

"Well done," Pris sighed, readjusting the scooped and awry neckline of her dress. Jacky sat in heavy silence.

Pris poked Charles. "Wake up, you slug," she commanded.

"Oh, do let him alone," she begged Pris. She could just leave him to sleep it off in his garage, once she got him home.

"Nonsense. You shouldn't drive alone. Wake up, Sinclaire," Pris called into his ear, pulling sharply at his hair until he stirred. "Wake the hell up."

"I'm awake," Charles mumbled crossly.

"Thanks for the ride," Pris laughed. "It's been so swell."

They left Pris and Jacky standing at the edge of the driveway, waiting for Jacky's erection to subside, and she headed for the Sinclaire garage, only a mile away.

"You can walk me home," she instructed Charles. "If anyone asks, we'll tell them we wanted to walk because it was such a fine night."

"It is a rather nice one. Hot nights are especially delicious, don't you think? I'd be glad to walk. Especially with you, Emily."

"Um," she hummed.

"Did you enjoy the party?"

"Yes. Did you?"

"Indeed. Though I'd have enjoyed it the more if you hadn't just wandered off."

"Tell me you didn't take advantage of it by necking with Ginny Porter."

"I didn't!"

"You did." She ought to know; she'd put poor eager, ardent, ugly Ginny up to it in order to be available for Tim. Oh! And with such unhappy results! Depression swept over her.

She hauled at the wheel and aimed the long, sleek car down the Sinclaire driveway, past the side door with its overhead light providing a focus for swirling insects, past it and around back to the garage, before which she stopped the car and slid out to avoid being pinned behind the wheel by Charles. If his mother were spying from the house, she was well concealed.

He wrapped his arm around her waist and they walked down Main Street toward the tree-darkened driveway at Kingsland. Its porch light was on too, brightly winking through the maples.

"It's a great place, your house," Charles said as he headed her off the driveway to the shadow of a nearby tree. "I like it much better than ours." He would! Kingsland was twice the house that the Sinclaires owned, and would suit Charles's pretensions well. They'd reached the tree by then, and Charles put his hands firmly on her waist so that she'd have to look at him. "I do wish you'd stay with me, Em, when we attend a party together."

"And I do wish you'd stop harping on it. I've told you before, Charles, and I'll tell you again," she said coldly. "We are not engaged. We aren't going together, even, and there's no reason for me not to enjoy myself as I wish—at anyone's party."

Crushed, he only stood there looking sad, making her feel guilty.

"I've told you I'd like to be your friend, and I really don't see why you won't let it go at that."

"I can't," he said abjectly. "I'm so crazy over you, Emily. When I go to Boston, will you write me?"

"Of course," she soothed, wishing he were in Boston this moment!

"Well, that's some consolation!" He smiled and then kissed her, roughly and hard, because Charles was under the impression that passion was crushing, and then he let her go, unwilling to push her passivity too far.

"Good night, Charles." She managed to say it without conveying how much she hated him, left him behind in the dark, shutting off the porch light without looking to see if he was safely on his way, climbed up the circular stairs of Kingsland feeling as though she were dragging a load of bricks along with her.

The bottom had just dropped out of everything, was all, because Tim Bradley had left the Hallets' without saying good-bye. Surely she'd offended him when she'd admitted that he ought not come to Kingsland. . . .

How could everything go so wrong, so fast!

Well, he'd be at Pris's party, more than likely. And hopefully Charles would be out of action. Once again she'd have a chance to talk to Tim, and perhaps when she did, she ought to just put everything on the line—a dangerous thing to do, really, because you never knew what a man was thinking, and it sometimes didn't pay to be candid.

Yet what alternatives were left? Even if Mother spoke to Elizabeth this very night, the chances of Elizabeth's reconciling herself to defeat in one week—to the extent that she'd be nice to Tim if she met him—were unlikely.

No, she'd just have to tell him that she wanted very much to see him—secretly if she had to.

Would the week ever, ever pass so that her opportunity would come?

She cried herself to sleep that night.

3

As usual, Charles had made a mess of things. His white knickers were already dusty and his tie was smeared hopelessly with the grease he had encountered in his haste to remove the jack from the trunk. His fair-skinned face was flushed and wet with the exertion of getting the jack in place; his shirt was already pulling loose, hanging floppily around his belt.

It was not Charles's fault, Emily told herself. He could not be held responsible for a flat tire.

"Well, pals, it seems that we've hit a small impasse," said Bob King. "Do you think we ought to walk?"

"I'd sooner," announced Becky Levering. Knowing Charles, it would take an eternity to fix the tire.

"Me, too." Ungallantly Bob jumped out to hold the door for Becky, and did not offer to help with the work. "Coming?" he asked Emily.

It did not suit her plans at all—hoofing it to Priscilla's, arriving hot and dusty as though, in her eagerness, she could not wait for her escort to catch up with her. Too much that was important required her coolness! The nervousness and uneasiness she'd held at bay all week began to creep up on her now—now that there was too much time to think. But walking was out of the question.

"No, I'll keep Charles company," she told Becky and Bob. "It's no fun changing a flat in this heat."

The land breeze was with them yet.

"I say!" Charles exclaimed. "It's terribly sporting of you, Emily, to stick it out."

She hated it when Charles insisted on being British! Gritting her teeth, she watched Becky and Bob disappear around the next bend as the car tilted a bit in response to the jack. She turned her back on Charles's labors, affecting an interest in the sky and the scrubby little bushes on the far side of the road, both in order to avoid having to talk to him and to hasten his efforts by providing no distractions—and to work on keeping her composure.

It was hard not to urge Charles to greater effort. But it would not help, and yelling at him was undignified, unsophisticated. She must not let herself panic. This was only the beginning, after all.

What would Alice be like? Would she be unpleasant to the daughter of the Merrick house? Or would she attempt to seek favor? If only Pris had not invited her—but Pris had. "You'll like her, Emily," Pris had insisted. "I know it's awkward for you, but the longer you avoid it, the more awkward it's going to get." Pris had offered no further explanation. It was, after all, her house, her party, her choice. Emily concealed her aggravation because, after all, Tim was coming and the snipe hunt was in the offing! And Alice didn't really matter, did she? Only Tim mattered, and Emily Merrick's chance with him!

"There," said Charles with more hope than certainty. "I think it'll hold up at least to the Wardens' driveway." He tucked in his shirt, put his jacket back on, wiped his flushed face with a huge handkerchief that left a grease streak the length of his jaw.

"Oh, Charles, now you've got dirt all over," she exclaimed. "Here, let me see if I can't get it off." She took his hankie and looked for a clean corner. "Your spit or mine?" she asked mischievously.

"Yours. Ever and always!" Charles responded with gallant effusiveness that should have been amusing but was not. He stood happily as she licked at the hankie and rubbed the grease spot off, as though her ministrations were absolute evidence of devotion to him.

"It's coming," she encouraged him, lapping the hankie in a fresh spot. "But you may never be able to use this rag again."

"I'll press it in my scrapbook," he said enthusiastically.

Dutifully she laughed. "You're a hot sketch, Charles!" She knew it would please him—and it did.

"Indeed," he said, gratified that he rated such a billing. He threw the used hankie under his seat; successfully he started the car. At least there was hope they'd get to the party before it ended.

As he had done all week, he began to talk about his new

job. "I do so hope that everything works out," he droned. "I have so many plans, all dependent on this opportunity."

"Yes, I know," she said, straining for a glimpse of the imposing Warden house on its thirty shorefront acres. "You've mentioned it before."

"Have I also mentioned that the company may open a branch office in Ohio? I've been thinking about that office, Em. I've been thinking about it a lot."

Ohio was a remote outpost. Who but a dunce like Charles would even consider it!

He thrust out his arm to signal a left turn into the Wardens' driveway. He swung a wide arc across the road, and in his concentration on what he wanted to say, stalled the car.

"Promise not to tell anyone else?" he asked, oblivious of the fact that he was blocking the entrance.

"Of course." Nervously she looked around, feeling terribly conspicuous.

"It concerns the Mater." (His Latin designation of his parent, an effete mannerism picked up at prep school and never relinquished, was one of his more infuriating habits.) "To tell the truth, Emily, I'd rather there were a little more distance between the Mater and me."

"You mean distant like Ohio?" she asked with asperity.

"Yes. I think it's very important that I be sent there. Since the Pater died, the Mater leans all the more heavily on me. But I'm quite sure she'd never leave New England, and if I were to go to Ohio, I feel certain that she'd never follow me there."

Perhaps there was more backbone to Charles than she had suspected!

"Your mother can always move in with Cousin Elizabeth if she gets lonely," she suggested.

"It would help if she did." Charles nodded. "Take some of the pressure off me, don't you know?"

A car approached, and with horror she saw that it was Tim Bradley's. "Charles!" she cried. "We're in the way. Someone wants to come in!"

"Oh! Zounds!" Charles exclaimed, in what he generally took for British, therefore sophisticated, expletive—another of his unfortunate prep-schoolisms. "I suppose I'd better get the buggy going."

Tim signaled for his turn and brought his runabout up to the rear fender, nudged it gently.

"Something wrong?" he asked. Beside him, Alice watched

impassively while Emily tried to decide whether to laugh or cry. Tim waved. "Good evening, Miss Merrick!"

"Good evening," she mumbled, her heart tumbling inside the cage of her body.

"Going my way?" he asked Charles politely.

"Trying to," Charles said humbly. "I'm going to the Wardens'."

"What a coincidence! So am I! Why not let me push you, then, so we can both get there?"

"Oh! Yes! Of course. Thanks just awfully!" Charles smiled gaily, becoming more and more Harvard and Oxford in his embarrassment. Emily, deep in the pits of mortification, tried to look unconcerned as the Sinclaire Buick rolled into the Warden driveway with Tim Bradley pushing from behind.

"Hey, look at that!" Priscilla called from the conservatory window where the dancing was in progress, the tinny notes of the music competing with her laughter. Everyone else rushed to lean out the other windows, to watch the antics in the driveway below.

Pris would do anything for a laugh, Emily thought, trying to get on top of her anger, and she leaned back against the car seat as though at her leisure with all the time in the world to observe the madding throng.

Charles turned to her. "I'm sorry, Em. They're laughing at us."

"Don't worry," she assured him around her agony. "At least we made it."

Tim Bradley had come over just in time to hear. "A woman after my own heart," he exclaimed over a profuse bow. "Who needs public opinion anyway?"

Gratified, she waited while he opened the door for her, extending his hand. She reached for it, showing her ankle to good advantage as she stepped to the running board from her high perch on the slippery seat of Charles's car.

When she landed, it was Alice's green eyes she looked into, eyes that contrasted startlingly with her hair, eyes that revealed nothing, betrayed nothing that Alice did not want the world to know. She was tall, nearly as tall as Tim in her stylish high heels, slender but not small—built, in fact, exactly like her sister Elizabeth.

Alice held out her hand. "Hi again, Emily!"

The smile she'd practiced in front of her mirror seemed somehow inappropriate. Alice's smile was warm, and it seemed to indicate that she was not going to eat Emily alive.

Tim must have spoken to her on Emily's behalf—and if he had, perhaps that meant he was still her friend!

Her own hand, which returned Alice's handshake, was steady—if damp—and her smile genuine. Then Pris came tearing over the yard, since the group had made no move to join the party.

"Emily!" Pris yodeled, and kissed her cheek. "Your dress is a dream, kid!" she exclaimed as though they had not spent the better part of yesterday together, carefully planning what they would wear.

"And Alice!" She turned to Alice but did not embrace her, since she did not know her well. "I'm so happy you were able to come. Hi, Tim. We're glad you could make it, too! You'll be happy to know that my brother has had a stroke of extraordinary luck," Pris said, leading them around to the back, where the terrace was and where Tommy Warden, like a king on his throne, sat on a white-painted iron chair, his feet resting on a stained, moss-draped packing crate.

"Ah!" they exclaimed reverently, for Tommy Warden had recovered a case of bootleg gin, left on the flats like manna by a rumrunner who, with a federal revenue cutter in hot pursuit, had been forced to jettison his cargo with the hope of finding it later, when the feds and the tide were gone. A futile hope. If a beachcomber like Tom Warden didn't get to it, a thirsty Waterford local would.

"A whole case, Tom?" Charles asked. "None broken?"

"Nary a one," Tommy said proudly, if thickly, well advanced in the sampling of its contents.

Someone unseen revived the flagging Victrola inside; the music accelerated and a roar of protest came from the interior of the Warden house, indicating that the dancers were having a hard time keeping up. The crashing of a glass and a Rebel yell indicated that sobriety was not entirely the order of the evening. It indicated, also, that Priscilla Warden's mother was not present, that her father was still in Boston, along with everyone else's father; it promised to be quite a party, the best ever. They wouldn't even need to hide the liquor.

"May I get you something to drink?" Tim Bradley asked, disregarding his cousin and turning to Emily, bending a little in order to hear her reply over the racket issuing from the house, and it was as though everyone else in the whole world had been shut out.

"A gin and tonic would taste good," she said, hoping it

sounded sophisticated. He'd turned to her! Thought of her comfort and well-being! Oh, Tim!

"I'll get you one," he said. "Alice? Can I get you anything?"

"Not yet, thanks." Alice smiled politely his way. "I told you, Tim. Don't worry about me."

Tim left, and Charles stood there, glued to Emily's side as usual, and Pris stood there, glued to Alice Bradley.

"Some people have all the luck," Charles said to Tommy, still on his throne. "No rumrunner ever dumps anything on the flats when I'm looking."

"How often have you tried?" Pris asked accusingly. "After all, Charles, Tommy spends hours out there."

"I sure do," Priscilla's brother declared. "I even take a shovel in order to dig into suspicious humps."

"Suspicious humps!" Emily scoffed.

"You never know what the tide will do," Tom explained. "Cover something over with sand one day, uncover it the next. I never go out there unprepared. I dig up everything. Usually it's only horseshoe crabs."

"You beast," said Becky Levering, coming outside with Bob King to cool off from toddling. "Probably they're only harmlessly taking a nap out there and you have to go and dig them up."

"Nap, nothing!" Tommy protested. "They're propagating. You can't fool me. And in the name of decency, I believe they ought to go somewhere else, where I can't see them. They'll end up corrupting my morals. The rumrunners are bad enough."

"Hi, Alice," said Becky. "We met a couple of weeks ago, at the Marshalls'. Probably you don't remember . . ."

"Of course I do," Alice said promptly, with a smile even warmer than the one she'd used on Emily. "It's Becky Levering, right?"

"Sure is." Clearly Becky was impressed with Alice's memory.

"You were going to do a lot of sewing, if I remember," Alice went on. "How's it coming?"

"Gosh! Fine!" Becky said, more impressed than ever that Alice had remembered this detail. But Alice, after all, had worked in a department store. She knew all about fashion, to the last stitch, so she'd naturally remember. She and Becky began on it now.

Beside her, Charles shifted. "I think I'd enjoy a small libation, Emily. Will you come with me?"

The prospect of staying here, listening to Alice, was unappealing. Evvie Thayer had joined the group now, listening intently; the interest in style seemed to be moving toward careers in merchandising. But she would stick it out!

"Thanks, Charles," she said casually. "I think I have a gin and tonic coming."

"I trust, Emily, that you will say nothing to the Mater if I indulge?"

"Of course not!" She assured him, as though they did not follow the same routine at every party, during which Charles habitually drank too much in his straining for acceptance.

"Did you find it hard to get into a position of responsibility?" Evvie asked Alice.

"Not once I gave evidence that I was serious about taking responsibility," Alice was saying. "You're Evvie, aren't you? Majoring in English lit at Smith?"

Some people could just open their mouths, Emily reflected, whether they said anything of interest or not, and everyone crowded around to soak up every drop. Probably Alice had boned up on the girls' names, which she could have found out from any villager, and where the owner of the name went to college. There was nothing very remarkable about her knowing that Evvie went to Smith, once you discounted the fact of Alice's troubling to find it out . . . but Evvie watched Alice now as though she was a magician, mystically knowing all things.

"Cut that out!" A high, happy voice from the dining room protested, and the Victrola speeded up again. Yes, it was going to be quite a party, she suspected, and there was only one way, at this point, that she knew how to handle the developing situation. Where was that gin and tonic!

Tim, appearing suddenly beside her, apparently had the same idea. "Might be a little strong," he said. "I thought you might enjoy it that way."

"Why, thanks!" she exclaimed. Perhaps something could be rescued from this mess, after all! "Right around the corner is a screened porch with some tables and chairs, if you feel like relaxing in one of them," she told him. "Perhaps a little less noisy?" She waved a deprecating hand at the house, dismissing its juvenile raucousness. The table was well out of sight of Alice, too.

"Lead me to it!" he said agreeably, and she showed him the door to the side porch where she and Pris had spent many a hot summer's day. At the far end was the little table and two chairs on which she and Pris had sat only this afternoon, drinking lemonade after a set of tennis, and it looked cool and quiet and inviting.

He sat opposite her, crossing his legs to one side of the table because his knees would not fit comfortably under it. From the porch the immaculate expanse of Warden lawn rolled, a soft evening green, and a bird dipped and soared over it. The water far out was turquoise.

"Now, then," she said, settling herself to take advantage of this opportunity. "Tell me about all the progress you've made this week with the ancestral house."

Her drink was nearly straight gin, it seemed. She approached it cautiously, but Tim did not follow her lead. He took a large sip, leaned back in the silly little chair.

"Paint and putty," he said. "Putty and paint. It's all I ever do."

"But are you making progress?"

"Sure I am," he said jovially. "Besides that, I'm learning a lot. About paint."

"And putty."

He laughed.

"Do you stay there alone?"

"Yup."

"Isn't it spooky?"

"Awful," he said. "Drives me to drink." His glass was half-empty, while she had hardly been able to make any inroads on hers. "Something wrong?"

"Wrong?"

"With the gin and tonic I fixed you."

"Well, it seems a little gin-ny."

"It *is* a little gin-ny," he said. "It's supposed to be. It'll make this wonderful party into an even happier occasion."

"You wish you hadn't come, don't you?" she asked softly.

"Somewhat." He finished the glass. "Come on, little girl. Drink up."

"What's wrong?" she asked.

"Nothing's wrong."

"Maybe you're not in the mood for a party."

"Maybe I'm not," he admitted. "Everyone here is going to get smashed. Drunk out of their minds."

"It strikes me that if you keep mixing gin-and-tonics like these, you'll be pretty well oiled yourself in about half an hour."

"Oh, I won't make them *this* strong all night," he explained reasonably. "That'd be silly. We'd get sick. I thought I'd just make them that strong until Alice leaves. Easier for both of us."

"That's very considerate," she said, and finished the glass. The porch seemed a bit tilted in consequence. "When's she leaving?"

"Huh?"

"You said 'until Alice leaves.' When's she going?"

He looked at his watch. "Twenty minutes. Nine o'clock."

"Nine o'clock!" She was astounded. No one, ever, left anyone's party at nine o'clock. Would Tim be leaving then, too? Dismayed, she wondered how to ask, but he answered before she could.

"Alice has a date with a fellow from Boston, who is driving down especially to see her."

"Impressive."

"But of course. Everyone's impressed with Alice." He smiled unhappily, and she saw that he was impressed, too. But she was too tight, on her one glass of gin, to care.

"Then you won't be taking her home?"

"No, sir. I'm not her date, only her chauffeur. One way. Alice made it clear to me that my obligation to her ends at the front door. I was rather hoping that I could adopt you as my date, Emily, once I got here."

"That's a pleasant prospect, I must say." She smiled.

"I haven't quite figured out how to get you home, though," he said, watching her closely.

A shadow passed over her face; she could feel it, and she knew Tim had seen it. She wished she could shoot herself. "There's always the back way. You could leave your car at the beach and we could walk."

"You're willing to do that?"

"Sure," she said carelessly. Now was her chance, and she took it. "Look, I'm really sorry about the situation at my house."

He waved her apology away. "Don't worry about it."

"I was afraid that perhaps it had made you angry."

"Why should it?" He shrugged. "I'll persevere."

"We'll both persevere," she said firmly. "Wait until the snipe hunt. Then we'll steal away and persevere somewhere else."

He laughed. "You're a hot ticket, Emily!" he exclaimed. "You really are. I feel better already."

She glowed.

"Another drink?" he asked cheerfully, conspiratorially.

"If it's light," she said. "It *would* be too bad to get sick."

"Good as done," he promised. "Don't move. Not a muscle."

"I'll sit right here." Comfortably she sat while he disappeared, settling herself into the faraway, yet near niche reserved for alcoholic observers.

Upraisings and outpourings of laughter and shrill conversation came from the patio, where, in the hot evening, young people in groups and pairs posed with the unconscious grace of wealth, which had taught them to never permit themselves an awkward posture. She could see them as they milled around, the girls uniformly pretty in pastel dresses, the waistlines of which encased their hips, hemlines to their knees and stockings rolled below, most with short shingled hair and a few with cigarettes. Young men in summer whites, their hair in high-crested pompadours or plastered down with a part in the middle, like Charles wore his, tan because they were the collegiate sons of wealthy men who need not labor in the summer heat but instead could swim at high tide and at low play tennis on the Wardens' courts. Among them the Warden maidservant, Mary Ann Hall, of Waterford village, passed the trays of canapés, collected empty glasses to return to the kitchen, where her sister would wash and dry them and put them on trays to begin the cycle again.

She wondered if Alice had left yet, where Charles was, and if Pris had remembered the snipe hunt. The evening was definitely getting darker.

A rash of prickles broke out all over her, despite the lingering heat of the day now dying. Remember, she told herself, you asked for it. Whatever happens, you asked for it and planned it all. She contemplated Tim, whom she had last viewed disappearing into the house, moving with easy grace despite the fact that he was a large man. A man! The very thought of being in the company of a man, instead of a boy, thrilled her, made something inside her roll over and wiggle.

"Where've you been?" Charles asked through the screen, his nose pressed to its mesh. "I've been all over looking for you." He hiccuped.

Oh, heck, she thought.

"I've been right here," she said tonelessly, so as not to encourage him to join her.

"By yourself?" he asked suspiciously.

"I talk to whoever happens by." Behind Charles, Pris and Jack and Becky stole up, nudging one another, winking. "I don't think you looked very hard for me, Charles," she said in the patronizing tone customarily used for inebriates. "I feel just a little slighted."

"He's been holding up the bar and crashing around the dance floor," Pris said behind him. Charles jumped and dropped his glass, which broke neatly in two.

"Oh, curses," he exclaimed. "You startled me. Sorry about the crockery, Priscilla. For Gawd's sake, kiss me."

"I can't," said Pris. "Because it's time for the snipe hunt."

"Snipe hunt!" Charles bellowed, falling neatly into line as they'd been so sure he would, and for a fleeting moment Emily had a wild impulse to delay, to postpone the on-marching unstoppable minutes. "What's a snipe hunt? Can I go?"

"Of course," Pris soothed him. "That's why I'm here. To ask you if you want to join everyone in a snipe hunt."

"I do! What is it?"

"The easiest hunting imaginable," Pris assured him. "You take a gunnysack, provided by the house. After dark, which will be soon, you creep to a low, mushy spot and crouch down and hold the sack open, and very, very softly, you whistle. . . . You do know how to whistle, don't you, Charles?"

"Oh, I do. I whistle tremendously."

"Well, then, you just whistle as though you were calling your dog home."

"I don't have a dog. The Mater hates them."

"And if you're good at it, the snipe will run right into your bag. You shut the bag up tight, bring home the snipe, and we'll see who gets the biggest!"

"You going, Em?" Charles asked dubiously through the screen. There were limits to even his credulity.

"I don't think so," she said, putting her hand to her forehead. "I've got a headache. I'd rather take advantage of the peace and quiet and wait for everyone to return. Probably that's all I need—a little quiet."

"Is anyone else going?" he asked Pris.

"Everyone," she assured him. "I'm about to get the gunnysacks now. I think it's dark enough to get started. Otherwise we won't be able to see well enough to find the best spots."

"I'll get the sacks," said Jacky, well primed. Becky clasped her hands in mock ecstasy. "Oh, snipe," she breathed.

"Flashlights," Pris called after Jacky, and they trailed him to the backyard. "On the buffet," she heard Pris say. The voices of the rest of the party came clearly to Emily as they, too, emptied onto the patio, and she heard Jacky going among them, handing out dusty sacks. Everyone was happily giggling, flirting, anticipating the next hour in the bushes, paired off in privacy, listening to Charles whistling, and occasionally whistling, themselves, to lead him on; and the noise of their giggling and guffawing drifted away as the procession wound down to the shore and the marshes that lay adjacent to the Warden place and a little stand of woods that Mr. Warden used for duck hunting in the fall, and when Emily looked up at the door to the house, Tim was standing there, grinning. Rising over the sounds of the fading snipe hunt was the music of the Victrola, dreaming, soft. Tim held out his arms in invitation. Together, alone on the porch, he led her in a smooth two-step until, as the record slowed, they were barely moving. He turned her face to his own and kissed her deeply, and pressed full length against him as she was, after the magic of the dance, she found the kiss devastating.

The Victrola faded to a stop and he whisked in to wind it up; she followed him. The conservatory floor was better for dancing, and they waltzed to another record, which had the same conclusion and left her breathless.

"Ready to leave now?" he asked. "Or would you like another drink and another dance? Or do you want to catch a snipe?"

There was nothing she would have liked better than another drink and another dance, but there was no telling how long the party would absent itself. "A snipe, definitely." She smiled. "A snipe from far away." Distantly she wondered if she were not begging for trouble. Distantly she decided not to ask if Alice had left, nor to mention the difficulty of getting back into Kingsland if Cousin Elizabeth was still awake when it was time to go home.

"I know a good place for snipes," Tim said. "Shall we go and look?"

"Where?"

"I'll show you."

She let him lead her to his car, which—how conveniently!—was parked last in the driveway, its bumper against Charles's. She waited as he got it started, and everything that evening had already accomplished and everything it might yet yield seemed in that moment to flash before her eyes. Beyond the windshield, dusk slid into the velvet arms of night on the bay.

Tim backed down the driveway, onto Main Street, drove well past the tree-guarded hulk of Kingsland and the church and the school and the library, bequests of Kingsley Merrick to the town of Waterford, down the road to a beach west of the old packet landing and breakwater. Tim pulled into a clump of bushes, parked the car, and turned off the headlights. Shadowed in the water were several sailboats, and on the beach were several dories.

"I didn't think anyone ever anchored a boat anywhere else than the breakwater," she observed. "I've never been here."

"Only a few people ever use it," Tim said in the pitch-blackness. There was no moon tonight; a spring tide. "My uncle's one of them. His boat is the second on the left."

The small craft were bobbing freely; there was plenty of water.

He retrieved his flask from the glove compartment. "I'm very glad you came with me," he said, and she could see his smile, vaguely, in the dark. "Will you have a drink? Good for the motion sickness."

"We aren't moving."

"Soon we will be. We're going to Provincetown."

"We are?"

"To look for snipes. They live in Provincetown. If we leave right away, I'm sure we could get over there, bag a snipe, and whisk back. The tide looks about right."

Huh! she thought.

The tide was never right.

"How do you know there are snipes in Provincetown?" she teased.

"I just know it. I know something else, too," he said, leaning near, his nose level with hers as though they were having an earnest, heart-to-heart chat. "It'd be very nice, out there in the night wind, under the stars. You'd like it." He kissed her ear meditatively. "Much nicer than here."

"Sounds like fun," she said. "Let's go."

Instantly alert, he straightened up. "Your dress is awfully pretty for scrubbing about in a boat."

"I'll risk it."

"I have a couple of blankets in the trunk. You can sit on them."

"My hero. I knew you'd come through, Tim."

"If you're wearing stockings, you had better take them off," he said. "You're sure to snag them otherwise." He went around to the rumble seat, opened it and took out two blankets, dragged his little dory to the water and threw the blankets into it while she divested herself of shoes, stockings, and, at the last moment, girdle. She was wearing almost nothing as a result, but it would be unbearable to be trussed up in a sailboat. She'd done plenty of sailing; she knew.

They did not speak as he rowed her to one of the little boats indistinguishable from the others, that swayed, side to side, in the starlight, looking larger than it was. The night breeze was low, nearly nonexistent, and there was a swell that spoke of a distant storm long gone, with only waves to tell of it. The dampness took the edge off the warmth, and she shivered as she hopped onto the bow and crawled over the coaming and into the little cockpit. The floor of the craft was dry, which the Merrick cat that Daddy sailed never was.

She reached for the blankets and a bottle that he managed to produce. Securing the dory to the anchor, he leaped on board and together they readied the sail, hoisted it, and cast off.

"You're a pretty good sailor, for a girl," Tim remarked.

"I'm a pretty good sailor, period," she answered pertly. She'd spent summers in Waterford all her life, after all. If her understanding of the details was a trifle hazy, at least she knew how to tie a decent knot! Tim Bradley laughed appreciatively. Silently they sailed until they were far, far out in the bay; he loosened the lines and released the tiller; the sail swung out over the water and hung there quietly.

"Wonderful," she breathed. "I've never sailed at night. It's just grand." And it *was* grand, remote and quiet, a world with its own sounds and secrets and rhythms, entirely different from its bright and sparkling and cheerful daytime countenance in the sun.

"Come on over here," he invited, and his voice sent chills from one end of her body to the other. "Have a little something from my flask." Obligingly she crawled to his side, and when he reached for her, the privacy and wonder of this secret night world grew greater, his arms around her warding off the chill. They snuggled closely and, in time, emptied the flask, and she did not resist as she felt him press her down onto the blanket and lie beside her. His lips were warm on her throat, her ear, on her mouth to say wordless things, to explore hers in a manner she had never experienced before, to which she could not help responding as though she'd done it all her life, while his hand carefully, but surely, found her breast.

She drew back, as much as she was able in the confines of the cockpit. She had never let a boy touch her without first establishing limits.

He took his hand away, touched the vein in her throat.

"Are you frightened, Em?" he asked softly. "Your heartbeat's fast as a bird's." Her breath seemed caught there, beneath his fingers.

"No. I'm not," she managed to say.

"Good," he whispered, the hand on her throat dropping to her breast again. "I wouldn't want to scare you."

"Well, as a matter of fact," she murmured, putting a restraining hand on his, "it's just that I don't believe in petting on the first date."

"It isn't the first," he protested. "But I won't rush you, Emily."

Oh, damn, she thought regretfully, wishing he was still touching. His hand had been warm and his touch thoughtful, unlike that of inexperienced boys who were rough in their eagerness. How could she get him to do it again, without appearing too forward?

She looked up at him, propped on an elbow beside her, and she looked past his shoulder, trying to think of what to say next. The mast, like a pointing finger, wagged from a star in the east to a star in the west and then back. Her stomach lurched uneasily as, fascinated, she watched the mast again describe its arc. The little boat was lifted, let down, lifted by the swell of which she was only just now aware; her stomach heaved slightly.

"Oh!" she groaned, and rolled over, looked away—but it was too late. She had looked at the sky too long; a vague upheaval crowded everything else out.

"Can we make it back?" she asked feebly. "Is there enough breeze?"

"Back? Do you want to?" He looked carefully down at her, peering through the dimness of the never-dark night.

"I have to," she confessed. She tried to keep her voice happy and lilting, and not heavy like the pit of her stomach. "I'm afraid I'll be sick if we don't."

"Ahah!" He sat up and pulled her upright, too. "You looked at the sky!"

"Afraid so," she apologized. "I forgot not to."

"We'll be steadier when we're moving." He pulled in the rope that controlled the sail. "You won't notice the swell so much then." If he was disappointed, he didn't show it.

"I hope you're right," she grunted, pulling her dress into place, shaking the blanket over her shoulders, hating herself for having ruined her own chances.

Tim stirred the water with backward and forward sweeps

of the tiller, coaxing the sail into the proper spot to take what little wind there was and use it to its best advantage.

"You're a good sailor," she remarked, hoping to divert herself from her increasing misery. "I wouldn't have thought you would have the chance to do it so well, since you haven't been on the Cape very often."

"Once my uncle showed me how, I seemed to get the hang of it. He says I'm a born sailor," Tim said proudly. "We Bradleys come from a long line of mariners. How are you feeling now?"

There was nothing like seasickness for misery, she was discovering. It permeated her whole body, occupying all her thought, commanding the center of all her emotions. But it was growing no worse, now that she was sitting upright and now that the little craft was picking up headway.

"I think I'll make it," she said, cheerfully as she could. "If we're not out here too long."

"Eastham's not too far."

"Eastham!"

"That's the straightest line to shore. Otherwise I'll have to tack."

Eastham!

"I can't go to Eastham! I have to be home by one o'clock!"

Alarm was making her stomach suddenly worse.

"I'd be glad to tack for Waterford," Tim said amiably. "But even if I do, I don't think we'll make it into port. The tide's dropping. We'll be stranded on the edge of the outer bar. Sloshing around. Or walking, of course. We could always walk in—but frankly I'd rather not. It's a terrifically long way and the incoming tide might catch us. People have been drowned doing it."

"I guess I'm more confused than I thought," she said. "I could have sworn the tide was rising when we were at the Wardens'."

"It turned."

It turned and he knew it, and probably he thought she knew it. Probably he figured that she knew exactly what she was doing, coming out here with him, and it seemed quite probable that he knew, himself, exactly what he wanted. Indecisively she waited while they sailed straight along. Unless she said something, they would continue straight to Eastham; they would not go to Waterford, nor would they be able to get there before the turn of the morning tide. She'd be out all night, out all night with Tim Bradley. . . .

The bottom of the boat scraped, bumped, scraped again.

Tim pulled up the centerboard, jumped out, taking the anchor chain with him, pulled the cat boat in as far as he could, dropped the anchor on the sand, stepping on it to set it more firmly.

"We're here," he announced cheerfully. "And it looks like we'll stay until the tide returns to float this tub for us. There's a box under the bow. Can you reach it?"

There seemed to be nothing to say.

She wrestled the box over the side, into his arms.

"Provisions," he explained, without telling her how he happened to be so well equipped. "If you'd bring the blankets?"

She gathered them up and hopped over the side. The wet sand was unpleasant beneath her bare feet, oozing coldness up between her toes. Meekly she walked to dry land, several hundred feet away, and with each step her dread rose, and her excitement too, her fear and her curiosity, jumbled and churning as he led her to a hollow where dunes protected them from the night breeze and the sand radiated heat like an oven. Several unusually large boulders closed them in on either side, creating a small amphitheater with more privacy than Emily had ever experienced in her life. The churning increased, but it was not caused by seasickness.

"What a nice spot," she said, because it seemed as though she must say something. She was nervous, and her fingertips tingled and she could hear her heart racing.

"I thought you'd like it."

"I do!"

"Maybe it'll make you forget about being seasick."

"Maybe it will." Seasickness was far from her thoughts. "How did you know about such a place? How can you find it?"

"A friend told me. You line up Highland Light and another small one, out there near the canal. Follow my finger." He slipped behind her, pointing an arm over her shoulder so that she could sight down its length. Beyond, she saw the little light; she felt his warmth behind her, felt a tugging on her dress and his hand on her breast beneath her bra, which miraculously he had already unhooked. Carefully, with a touch very gentle, well calculated to arouse her, he stroked her unbound flesh.

"Don't," she said, her usual voice trapped in her throat and a different one than she'd ever heard before speaking. She shivered. "Oh, don't, Tim."

"You're afraid, after all," he murmured in her ear, his body's heat pouring into her.

"A little." She was tense and fine drawn and—yes—afraid. Her own heat was increasing, her body filling as though becoming too large for its frame.

"It's too late, you know," he said quietly, his hands more urgent, as though he had sensed her increasing arousal.

"Too late for what?"

"Too late to stop; it's been too late ever since you got into that boat."

"No! It can't be," she tried to protest. "Please, Tim."

He turned her around so that they faced one another, and leaned to kiss her bared breasts. "Don't fight me," he whispered. "Say you want me. Say you want me, Emily, because I want you—so much." In a strong motion he tore open his shirt; its buttons must have flown in all directions, but she forgot about them as she saw the whiteness of his skin in the night and felt it on her own, and then felt his entire warm nakedness against her as somehow he divested them both of the rest of their clothing and rolled her onto the blanket, more and more abandoned to his desire, to coaxing hers; his hands slid to her waist and hips, working her skin and flesh, pushing her restraining hands away, reaching the warm and wet territory between her legs where something opened at his bidding. She could no longer resist but could only lie with him on the blanket and let him do whatever he willed, caught between her terrible intense demand that he not stop and her fear of what would happen if he went forward. "Tim!" she called, her voice weak and shaking as he drove her on and then as he straddled her, hands on her shoulders so that she could not move away from under him. She could not contain her excitement and lust, overwhelming, her clamoring, devouring need. Above the soaring surf in her ears she heard him ask in a voice heavy and strained, "Emily, are you a virgin?" and there was between her legs, suddenly, a stabbing, pushing pain.

"Yes," she whimpered, and tried to move away, away from the hurt, her desire fading fast. "Please, Tim, you're hurting me. . . ."

He was hurting her terribly, terribly, and she couldn't get away!

"I have to, baby." His voice was low. "I have to."

"Don't!" she screamed as her body was rent and torn and he entered her in a terrible, heavy thrust.

She froze, trying to contain the pain. Her silence and tense stillness must have conveyed her agony more convincingly than an outcry, for he stopped and waited, and she suffered, suffered. A small whine escaped her.

"Are you all right?" He was nearly weightless, and he lifted a hand from her shoulder to stroke her hair; she could feel his muscles quivering in his attempt to hold his body away. "Try to relax," he urged. "We'll lie here like this for a while. Just quietly. Try to make yourself float and you'll be able to feel the nice part, and not the hurt part. I'm sorry it hurts. I'm sorry!" His lips traveled over her forehead and temples, ears and throat as he waited, and she waited, and sure enough, coaxed by his concern, she relaxed and the pain subsided a bit and she became aware of a throbbing, a warm vitality that seemed amazingly to increase and become irresistible and she was compelled to reach for it, to meet it, to become one with it.

"Tim!" she whispered. She moved, despite her pain, past it for more of him, astonished and grateful for the presence of this never-before-experienced wanting and its promise of satisfaction as white heat burned and built higher from the depths of herself, from a place she had only suspected before, now unlocked because of loving this warm and passionate man, who even now took himself away from her and then carefully gave himself back, hard and firm, creating an agony of pleasure that inexorably turned to pain.

She could not help crying out, but he did not stop until he too cried out, called something she could not name; gradually his weight fell upon her and he was still. For a long time they lay together, locked, and his manliness withered and fell from her with a soft brushing and he rolled away. The hotness of her pain subsided, leaving instead the awareness of unsatisfied need, leaving an unrelenting quest for its fulfillment, goading her into willingness to sustain pain for its sake. She reached shyly for his hand and rolled toward him, and he gathered her up so that their lengths touched, and like kindling, she burst into flame again, his whispered name on her lips. Tim. Tim. Tim.

She knew she would do anything he asked, anytime he asked it. Her emotion swept her one way and another and another, like sea grass beneath the tide, and the gleaming, starstruck sand of the rapidly uncovering flats breathed and sighed as he took her up again, and showed her the pathways to culmination of love.

The prow of the cat once more scraped bottom. Once again Tim Bradley buried the anchor in anticipation of higher water, and they bound the sail to the mast, secured lines, coiled ropes. Farther toward shore the other boats lay on their sides like beached whales, waiting for water enough to float.

Emily looked dreamily over the bay, at the pinking of things and the brightening blue of the sky and the shining water creeping toward them, speechless at the magnificence of the morning, flooded with the peace of it and the joy of loving Tim Bradley.

"It's often this way early in the day." He leaned against the boat, looking fondly at her. "Sometime perhaps, will you meet me here at dawn?"

"Sometime, and gladly." Her heart soared, swooped, danced—and yet, beneath, lay melancholy, poignant longing for something she could not name.

She had held nothing back from him. All night, each time his vitality had returned, he had reached for her and she had gladly, if painfully, given all she had; and now she was sore and exhausted, an unacknowledged part of herself imprisoned, somewhere, and there was guilt, too, knocking quietly, waiting to be acknowledged, anxiety sneaking around, suggesting that she had been used. And yet, she loved him. She did, she did! Sadness welled up, and she winked back tears.

She dared not look at him; instead she looked over the bay, searing in its loveliness, then leaned on him as he flung an arm over her shoulder, suddenly realizing how terribly tired she was.

"What'll happen now?" he asked quietly. "About your parents?"

"I hate to think!"

"You'll be in for an awful lot of trouble."

"I'm afraid so."

"I can't leave you until we've faced them, Emily."

She tingled happily in response to the "we" and the soaring began again. Perhaps, perhaps. . . . And then she remembered Cousin Elizabeth and the awkward nature of Tim's position, the impossibility of facing her family with him at her side if Elizabeth were present. She was not capable of thinking quickly, just at this moment, but it was clear that she had better begin, soon.

"I think I'd better talk to my family on my own," she said slowly.

"No one worth his salt would let a girl take the blame for what I've done. The least I can do is apologize for keeping you out all night."

"That's the most you'd better apologize for!" she quipped.

Then she looked steadily into his marvelously dark and enigmatic blue eyes. "I have no regrets, Tim!"

"Neither do I," he said softly. "But I am worried about your family." The cat rocked minutely; the tide was lifting it now.

"I'm worried about drowning, too." He smiled. "Let's get moving."

She looked to the distant beach, to which they must make their way, and for the first time noticed that there were two cars there. One was Tim's, she was quite sure. And certainly the other was not.

"Do you see what I see?" he asked.

"Yes."

"What do you think?"

"I think I'm going to throw up," she quavered. "And I think we don't have to face my family. I think they're facing us. Or, at least, one of them is."

"We'd better leave the blankets and booze in the boat," Tim said. He offered her his hand and gratefully she took it. "Somehow I think it wouldn't look good if we walked in with them."

"No," she agreed. "It wouldn't."

Love me, Tim, her heart begged. Love me. Love me.

"If it's your father, I'm glad," he said stoutly. "At least there'll be no question of your talking to your parents alone."

And Cousin Elizabeth wouldn't be there, either, she thought. It could be worse. She took heart as they walked closer to shore.

Yes, surely it was Daddy.

There was a fairly long distance to cover, during which time she must come up with a battle plan. In her fatigued, overloaded brain only one certainty stood out, loudly, clearly: if she had to perjure herself before the whole of Waterford, let alone her own family, she would gladly do it for the chance to lie with Tim Bradley again. Even in her exhaustion and confusion the rise of remembered passion closed off her ability to breathe for an instant and she faltered.

If you're going to lie about it—and you have to, she told herself—do it right. Do it mightily. Do it with conviction. She would! Her weakness fell away and a different Emily took over as she walked with Tim, a self she recognized vaguely as the person she had been before she grew up, a person full of determination, hard and reckless in pursuit of what she wanted, self-serving without a qualm.

"Let me do the talking," she instructed Tim. "It's really easier that way. I can think better if I don't have to worry about you."

"Of course I wouldn't argue with your father," Tim said. "But I can't just stand there and let you take the blame." Of course he wouldn't! She flashed him a grateful smile, tried to reconstruct the scene as her father must see it.

Usually he would not have arrived in Waterford until this evening, Saturday. But the fact that he was here now—here early—could not be related to her antics, even had Mother called him, asking for his help, because he could not have come down so quickly unless he had motored—and the car was at Kingsland for the summer. So he had come of his own accord, probably because of the heat. Since he must have come on the train, he could not have arrived at the house until nearly eleven o'clock; that was when the night train came through, this summer. He would not have known that Emily was missing until even later, when the limits for her being out had been stretched taut and then broken and then, probably, having questioned Pris, having found out who Emily was with, having been out searching, finally zeroing in on this particular beach in Waterford, he was probably in a towering rage, weary, implacable. She had better play her cards exactly right, because the chances were good there would be no replay.

Her walk with Tim was nearly over. It must not be the last. She would press her only advantage—the assumption of innocence, ingenuous innocence in which her father must be made to believe. And if she succeeded, the day would come when she would never have to let go of Tim's hand as she was letting go now to take off his coat which she'd been wearing against the night's chill. They were within hailing distance of the beach now, as she handed the coat back.

"Thanks!" she said loudly, so that Daddy, sitting on a stone near shore, could hear. "And thanks for a lovely sail."

"Um, you're welcome," Tim called, catching on.

"Hi, Daddy!" she exclaimed. "Isn't it a beautiful morning?"

Daddy got to his feet slowly, as though he were stiff, and did not move until they were directly in front of him. The stone upon which he'd been sitting probably had not been very comfortable and it had probably added to the irascibility written clearly upon his face.

"What is the explanation for this?" he asked Tim, his voice cold.

"I'm afraid I misjudged the tides, Mr. Merrick," Tim said. "I'm afraid I'm not as familiar with them as I thought."

"Night sailing is so much fun!" Emily said breezily. "Have you ever tried it, Daddy?"

He looked only at Tim, glaring, as though Emily were not present. "This is inexcusable, young man."

"I'm awfully sorry, Mr. Merrick," Tim said. "I know it looks bad—but believe me—"

"I would consider it a favor if you would keep away from both our house and our daughter in the future." Daddy's face was murderous. "I'm sure your good father would be as upset as I am if he learned such conduct. I assure you that I will inform him, should I see you near Emily again."

Tim opened his mouth, looked at Emily, closed it.

"He's my friend, not yours, Father," she protested. "You can't decide who my friends are going to be."

"Just watch me," Daddy said grimly. "Good morning, sir."

Tim nodded and turned away, walking slowly toward his car. She watched him, his long, loose stride, his lovely shoulders, his sleek hips, his arms, his hands. He had only a little dark hair on his body, and his skin was fine and pure. . . .

She willed herself not to cry, because it would put her at a disadvantage. She must be careful not to skulk about as if she had done something wrong. Skulking implied guilt; she put her chin up and her shoulders back.

"No doubt you're angry," she began coolly. "And I'm sorry to have inconvenienced you, Daddy. But I wish you wouldn't take it out on my friends." She marched past him to the car and climbed in, leaving him to follow. She did not look at him as he slid under the wheel. The beach was a silent, lifeless place without Tim on it—his car had disappeared in a billow of dust now—and she ached with desolate loneliness. I shall get him back, she told herself. I shall fight for him.

"What happened?" Daddy asked, turning to her. His voice was dull and heavy with anger. Whether he wanted to know what had happened on the boat, or how it happened that she had gone out in it, was unclear.

"The explanation should be easy to understand," she said, choosing the less awkward of dilemmas. "Tim Bradley and I didn't want to stay at Priscilla's party. Pris's brother had found a case of gin on the flats, and everyone was making a fool of himself. So Tim offered to take me sailing. Sailing was certainly nicer than staying there, and where else could we go? From a discussion Mother and I had, I gathered it would be a mistake to bring him back to Kingsland."

"Yes, it most certainly would have been." Daddy stared intently at her, searching for the truth. "Charles says you tricked him and escaped from him."

"Charles would. He wasn't my date, Father. Only my escort."

"He picked you up at the house. He was responsible for you. He was supposed to bring you home, and you know it. He knew it even if you didn't. He came to the house with the word you'd left the party, and you can well imagine, Emily, how upset he was."

"Charles is a baboon, Daddy," she said. "Surely you must know that. He believes in snipes."

"Snipes?"

"Pris suggested a snipe hunt," she explained patiently. "A snipe hunt is when you take a bag and hold it open and wait for a snipe to run inside."

Daddy looked beseechingly at the cloth ceiling of the car. "I don't believe this," he said.

"Charles fell for it," she forged ahead. "Someone always does," she laughed. "When a bunch get together who knows about snipes at all, why, they all take gunnysacks and pretend to go hunting, and if there's someone that's never been on a snipe hunt, he generally falls for it and takes a gunnysack too and like a dunce waits for a snipe to run inside. Like Charles did. . . . Can you blame me for not waiting around for him to come back? I mean, Father, Charles is an embarrassment."

"So you went sailing."

"Yes," she said royally. "And if it's an apology you're looking for, I'll be glad to apologize for causing you worry and inconvenience. I've already told you I'm sorry—but I'll say so again, if you want."

"There's more to discuss than that, don't you think?" he asked grimly. He took a bundle from his pocket and handed it to her. It was her girdle and stockings, obviously taken from Tim's car where she had left them. She shook the girdle, smoothed its wrinkles.

"Oh, thanks!" she exclaimed. "I was wondering where these had got to."

He looked a bit disconcerted, and she thought that, after all, she was on the right track.

"If someone else had found them," she said nonchalantly, "I can imagine what they'd think. Thank goodness it was you!" She drew out a stocking, carefully thrusting her hand into it and down to its toe, inspecting it on all sides. "Good as new," she said with satisfaction. "I knew that if I wore them sailing, I'd surely snag them."

"And, of course, no one sails in a girdle," Daddy remarked with uncharacteristic boldness, though his color was deepening.

"It would certainly be uncomfortable," she agreed. "And at least when you saw my things in Tim's car, and saw that his boat was gone and his dory out on the mooring, you must have known where I was."

"How could I know they were your things!" he shouted. "I'm hardly familiar with your underpinnings. Bradley probably knows a hell of a lot more about them than I do!" He collected himself with effort, spoke quietly. "And certainly I didn't know which boat was his. Hopefully, no one else does, either. Everyone watches us, Emily. When the town finds out you spent the night on Tim Bradley's boat, they'll think the worst."

"As long as you and Mother don't believe the worst, I don't care what anyone thinks," she said, hoping she sounded steadfast and loyal. "But, Daddy, I don't think anyone's likely to find out—unless it's you that tells them."

He looked her over head to toe. He did not know what to believe of her, but how could he accuse so ingenuous a child?

"Tim Bradley should have more sense." He started the car. "He should have known better," he grunted, backing around, heading up the sandy, rutted road.

"So should I," she reminded him. She could see Daddy fighting it out with himself, wanting to ask more, probe more deeply, and not daring to—not yet. He sighed, and grimly gripping the wheel, said no more, driving the short distance to Kingsland, into the circular driveway, to the barn, where he parked.

"Needless to say, your mother is upset. We'll need to give her time to calm herself. Don't argue with her, Emily."

Clearly meekness was her best course at this point. She followed him into the house. Mother was waiting, her eyes heavy and underlined darkly. There were lines etched into the flesh of her face that Emily had never noticed before, and she felt a pang of remorse for the worry she had caused—a pang she quelled instantly. This was no time to feel sorry for anyone, unless it were herself.

"Where have you been?" Mother whispered harshly, her face distorted. "I've been out of my mind."

"I went sailing. . . ."

"Keep your voice down," Mother cautioned. "You'll wake someone up." Someone like Elizabeth.

"I went sailing. The tide was wrong, unfortunately, and we couldn't get back."

"We?"

"Tim Bradley and I."

Mother threw her hands up in despair and looked to Daddy at this compounding of their daughter's delinquency.

"I think we'd better go into the library," Daddy said quietly. "We won't be overheard there."

The three of them filed off like Indians, stepping carefully, with stealth.

"I suppose everything would be fine if I'd been with Charles," Emily began the attack. Mother, she judged, had been given sufficient time to collect herself.

"That's enough," Daddy said. "Just don't you get fresh. I gather they merely waited for the return of the tide," he said to Mother. He did not mention her girdle and stockings.

"I only hope no one was up so early that they saw you coming in," Mother said.

"God forbid," Emily exclaimed, in accordance with expectation.

"We must protect Elizabeth." Mother frowned. "She must be made to think Emily was with Charles."

"Charles would never have been foolish enough to sail when the tide was going out," Daddy said. Neither of them seemed to remember that Emily was still present. "Unless she has heard me coming in now, I think we'd just better assume that she's unaware that Em has been gone at all . . . we can just say the party lasted late."

"Daddy told me that Charles came here," Emily broke in. "Wouldn't it be a little difficult? Pretending that I was here when I wasn't?"

"She'd already gone to bed. She might not have been asleep, of course. She might have heard Charles's voice, but probably not what he said. I'm sure we can cover it up. We can say Charles came in to see if they both, himself and Emily, could stay longer at the Wardens'."

"Yes, that's something Charles might do," Emily said scornfully.

They let her remark pass, and quiet edged its way into the library, where the three of them warily awaited one another. The night's exhilaration faded and Emily found herself in the middle of a yawn. As if a signal, her parents instantly launched their attack, which, though not discussed by them, was well-coordinated and directly to the point.

"There's no way we can just disregard your staying out all night," Mother said.

"I've already told the Bradley boy to keep away from her, sweetie," Daddy said comfortingly.

"Well . . . at least we won't have to worry about his effect on Cousin Elizabeth, will we?" Mother glared at Emily. "We'll only have to worry about Alice, when the time comes."

"You haven't talked with her yet?"

"That's right—I haven't. Your father and I decided to let her find out gradually, through the grapevine. Less shocking." Cowards!

"Now," said Daddy sternly, "down to business. You've been out all night! We can't just ignore that. Innocently or otherwise, it is an escapade that must not be repeated," he said sternly, looking meaningfully at her. She understood then that he would not bring the matter of her undergarments into the discussion if she did not force him to. Yet, she couldn't just take it lying down, could she?

"Staying at Pris's would have been worse," she suggested, unwilling to push too hard.

"Perhaps you ought not to see so much of Priscilla," her mother said meditatively, and the discussion, careening like a herd of stampeding buffalo, loped off in another direction.

"Not see Pris!" she cried. "She's my best friend!"

"I've been wondering if you wouldn't be more interested in completing your course of study at Bryn Mawr if Pris weren't egging you on to this lunacy about a job."

Ah. Now they were only using her friendship, threatening it, using it in combination with her indiscretion as a tool to getting her back to Bryn Mawr this fall! There was no end to the perfidy of parents.

"Pris and I have both been reconsidering it, as a matter of fact," she lied, and was rewarded by the little leap of hope in her mother's eye. "And as far as a night sail was concerned," she pressed forward, "I thought it was positively inspirational. I could hardly let Tim bring me home early. And the party was a zoo."

Despite himself, Daddy smiled.

"It isn't funny, Dan," Mother said peevishly. "We need to set limits for Emily, and do it now."

"Yes, of course." He thought about it for a split second.

"From now on, I'll expect you to be in the house by suppertime, and to stay in it."

"Daddy!" she protested, appalled. "For how long?"

Daddy appeared to be unbearably satisfied with this sweeping control over her life. "We'll see."

Good grief! How would she ever get to Tim! Tim! Oh, Tim!

"What about our friends?" Mother asked him.

"What have they got to do with it, sweetie?"

"They'll think it odd that Emily is in, when up until now she's always been so popular. You'll have to explain it."

"She can keep out of sight upstairs," he decided.

"She might keep out of sight," Emily said, trying not to cry. "And then again, she might not."

"And what excuse can we give Elizabeth for grounding her if supposedly she was with Charles?" Mother asked.

Daddy glared at them both, curbing his impatience, his fatigue. Boston had been a furnace all week, exhausting him, and Waterford was giving him little respite. "What do you suggest, sweetie?" he ground out.

"Well . . . something of a more limited nature," Mother temporized. "If she had merely stayed out too late—which is what we plan to tell Elizabeth anyway, isn't it?—then she'd only be grounded for a week or two."

"All right," Daddy acquiesced. "For a week or two you're grounded, Emily. And during that time you may not leave the house except for church. And you may not see the Bradley boy."

She would see Tim! She would!

"Charles is coming to call for her after lunch," Mother murmured, looking sheepish. "He may want to take her out." (It would not do to make Emily inaccessible to the Sinclaire boy!) "He said he would, last night," Mother reminded Daddy. "To see how you are and all," she said to Emily. "He truly was concerned about you, dear."

"Tell him I'm fine. Tell him I'm upstairs, quarantined."

She would not see Charles! She would not!

"You may go out with Charles if he asks you," Daddy barked. "Now, let's go."

But they did not follow her upstairs. She could hear the quiet rumble of their voices as she climbed into bed in the unfamiliar light of morning, and she lay there, wondering what had happened to her girdle. She wondered what had happened to the party—but most of all, she wondered how she could ever, ever expect to hold Tim Bradley if she couldn't even meet with him. She must see him again! She must! The cry volleyed back and forth in her brain as her exhaustion numbed her capacity to think, even to feel, to mourn or even to suffer, and she fell away, away from the morning now in progress, and slept until lunchtime.

"I don't think it was very nice of you, just going off and leaving me like that." Charles's face was taut and grim.

"I'd say it was you who left me," she responded dispiritedly. The afternoon air fanned past the open Buick, leaving her skin sticky and itchy, her head aching. If she thought he could do it, she'd have asked Charles to put the top up. She blinked her eyes, gritty from too little sleep.

What was Tim doing now? she wondered. Was he thinking of her, as she was of him?

"After all, Charles, it was you who went into the weeds with a gunnysack and Ginny Porter," she lashed out in her frustrated longing.

Charles flushed. "Why do they do it?" he asked angrily. "Why am I always the butt of childish pranks? You know what I'd do to them, if I had the chance?" he said fiercely. "I'd tie them up and leave them right in that damned swamp. I'd strip 'em naked and let them get eaten alive by bugs, and I'd listen to 'em moan and I'd watch and I'd laugh. They really used to do that, you know, to Negroes. Tie 'em naked to a tree, leave 'em until they went mad and died." He glanced at her, saw her startled stare, for indeed, he sounded all too earnest.

Shakily he laughed. "They did!" he said lightly. "I read it, somewhere. Oh, well. Next time, I'll know better when someone proposes a snipe hunt!"

"You do take it so well, Charles," she soothed. "You're a real sport—a jolly good fellow!"

They were words calculated to placate his pretentiously anglophilic heart, and they were successful. The pout dissolved, and he smiled.

Did Tim Bradley think of her in every waking moment? Did he dream of her when he got to bed today—if, indeed, he got to bed at all? How could she see him again?

"The point is, Charles, that I didn't know how long you'd be gone. I didn't see why I should wait for you. Here you go off in the bushes with Ginny. Why, what did you think I'd make of that? Everyone knows she's crazy for you."

"Yes," he sighed. "I suppose she is."

"So you must tell me how the party was, after I left." After she left and went sailing with Tim Bradley and made love with him. . . . An insatiable longing swept by, wrenching her.

"Don't you know?" Charles asked incredulously. "Didn't you hear?"

"How could I? I haven't seen anyone."

"Priscilla's Pater came home unexpectedly, that's what."

"Good grief!" The worst, after all, had happened.

"Mr. Warden came down on the train with your Pater."

"I suppose the city was hot," she offered feebly.

"Waterford was hot, too," Charles said. "Pris and Jacky and another couple were skinny-dipping in a tide pool, and when Warden Père happened by, the temperature for miles around went sky-high."

Skinny-dipping!

"Truly," Charles remarked wryly. "Priscilla's Pater was formidable. There he was, ranting and raving, and Pris trying to tell him that repressions are bad for you—that Dr. Freud himself said so—and suddenly I realized you weren't with me." He cast her a reproachful glance.

"I'll forgive you for not noticing before then, Charles, if you tell me what Mr. Warden did next."

"He loaded up his car with the remains."

"The remains of what?"

"The party. Those in attendance, at that point (excluding yourself, I might add), who were not sporting in the tidal pools were lying about in undignified attitudes, so drunk they could hardly talk. Mr. Warden took them home, since they weren't in any condition to drive. I would have been amused if I hadn't been so scared." He giggled. "You should have seen Jacky Pollard trying to get into his clothes when he was wringing wet and not exactly sober." Charles laughed aloud. "Pris has never had such a party before."

"It was that gin her brother found. It's really to blame." Emily watched the passing scene for a moment. "I wonder if Mr. Warden will be unpleasant for long."

"Well," Charles said importantly, "this morning the grapevine had it that he's packed Warden Mère off to a drying-out place, because he holds her alcoholic propensities responsible for allowing such goings-on. But the big news is that Pris's freedom has come to an end. She's getting a duenna."

"A what?"

"A chaperon."

"A chaperon!" she snorted. "Who'd ever be a match for Pris Warden, I'd like to know."

"Why, that new girl. Alice. Alice Bradley."

Charles was driving steadily on, apparently without realization of the disaster he was announcing. "She's free for the summer, and being older than Pris, can probably handle her. I'd judge from what little I've seen of her that she'd be quite capable. . . ."

Alice would be hanging about at Pris's house, accompanying Pris to all the gang's parties. And Elizabeth would surely learn of Alice now, whether Mother could face telling her or not, whether the grapevine operated efficiently or not, and the Merricks would have to stand solidly united until Elizabeth managed to contain herself. And until she did, Mother and Daddy certainly weren't going to defend Emily's right to see Tim Bradley, whom they'd banished already—for the duration. Nor her right to attend a party where Alice would be.

Oh, God, she thought miserably, and suddenly she was appalled by the dimensions of her difficulty, overtaken by guilt that rushed into the space formerly occupied by passion, as her conscience rose up to taunt her: you have submitted to this man in order to hold his affection, and now you will lose him, and you deserve it!

Wait! she told it. Maybe Tim's as desperate as I am. Certainly he wants to see me again—he said so. He loves me too! He does! He'll find a way to my side. He'll see how impossible things are for me and he'll figure a way around them. I know he will!

If worse came to worst and he was unable to break through the barriers erected by Daddy, well, when things had calmed down a bit she could sneak over to Pris's and ask Alice to give Tim a message—a place and time to meet. She'd hate to do it, of course. She was, like it or not, a Merrick, and it would grate sorely to ask Alice for a favor! But if she had to, she would. And in the meantime, she'd just have to sit back and hope that Tim Bradley was inventive.

4

She had not understood what it would mean, to wait for Tim to come to her. She had not understood how painful every minute of every hour could be, how long it could take to pass, how interminable time was. She had not known how much hurt and despair one person could contain as the last light of evening lingered, and the last hope for that day died slowly, agonizingly. . . .

She had never given so much before.

She had never cared so much before.

She had never failed.

But she failed now.

As she'd expected, Elizabeth had been furious when she learned of Alice's presence on the Waterford scene. She'd even gone to Pris's father, to urge him to find another chaperon, but Warden Père had regretfully refused. He'd plain forgotten the relationship, he confessed, so many years ago had the whole thing been left behind. And now, having hired the girl Alice, he could hardly just go and fire her. And the truth of it was that Alice had done wonders for his daughter already, and the further truth of it was that he knew of no one else who could.

Elizabeth fumed; Mother and Daddy cooed and soothed, but Emily was too swamped in her miseries to pay much attention, and certainly she had no sympathy to spare. If it hadn't been for Elizabeth in the first place, she wouldn't be in this spot, dying a thousand times a day. She'd be out and dating Tim Bradley in a normal boy-and-girl relationship.

Oh, where was he! Surely he would lie in wait for her at the library—or Snow's store, or almost anywhere. True, her little sister Celia dogged every footstep, probably employed by Mother and Daddy to report to them if Emily disobeyed—but what difference did that make! They would only see that love couldn't be held at bay, not strong honest love as Emily Merrick and Tim Bradley had shared it. . . . Close, caring, passionate. . . .

She dwelled as little as possible on *that* aspect of things; she'd go crazy otherwise. And when two weeks went by, she tried to close her mind, as well, to wondering when he would track her down. Clearly he did not plan to: Daddy had told him to get out, and he had, and difficult as it was for her ego, knowing that Tim had knuckled under to Daddy's ultimatum, there was not much point lying around dreaming of that wonderful moment when he would pop up from behind a bush somewhere. What she must consider next was the feasibility of giving him a message via his cousin. Its content would be simple: she would meet him at dawn on the beach—she'd already told him she would, after all. She had only to name the day and place. . . . Suffering, despairing, she waited another two weeks, saw no one, went nowhere.

For pride held her back. Facing Alice was bad enough, but there was also the possibility of learning that Tim would not meet her, anytime, anyplace, because he did not want to. And it was a hard thing, an awful thing, to decide whether to chance his outright refusal—or mope about at Kingsland, fearing it. But in the long run, it was Evelina Martin who decided the matter for her.

Emily had slipped downstairs for a cup of coffee this morning, and Mrs. Martin had been in the pantry with her daughter, neither of them aware of Emily's presence.

Assuming a privacy she did not have, Evelina had said to her mother, "I think there's a bun in the oven again."

A bun? Emily wondered. In whose oven?

"It's a little soon for another child, don't you think? Rosie's not yet two!" Mrs. Martin's voice could not conceal concern for her daughter, married to one of Waterford's innumerable Roman Catholics whose forebears, two generations back, had entered Waterford as servants to the wealhty, some of whom had remained to be absorbed by the year-round population.

Evelina sighed.

"Not much I can do about it, Ma. I should have nursed Rosie, is all."

"Maybe you're mistaken."

"I don't think so," Emily heard Evelina say. "I haven't had the curse for three months."

Thoughtfully Emily had gone back upstairs, carrying her

coffee, quietly, so that they wouldn't know she had been there. She rummaged in her desk for a calendar, which, she knew, was pointless, because she never flowed regularly anyway—but perhaps she ought to look.

It had not been marked for four months, though she was sure, very sure, that she had had a period between last May and now.

She opened her nightgown and stood before the mirror, looking critically. Her breasts, pert and pretty, were heavier than they had been, with large blue veins prominent against her fair skin—but perhaps she was about due, and they were enlarged on account of it. Her oven, as Evelina so quaintly put it, did not look any different at all, firm and flat.

But perhaps she had better forsake her pride. Perhaps for all she knew, Tim had been waiting for her to send a message all this time—and perhaps whether he had or not, she had better be sure the channels of communication were open in case . . . in case . . . in case . . .

Quickly she dressed, made her plans. She would pick up colored pencils and paper at Mr. Snow's general store and offer them to Celia (who would inevitably come along), suggesting that they would belong to Celia if she took them right home, right now, and used them. Then she would go up to Becky Levering's house and chat for a while, and then she would ask if she could borrow Becky's bike (Emily's own having a flat tire, she would say), and explain that it had been so long since she'd seen old Mrs. McLaren, who lived in East Waterford, that she'd visit her now, if that was all right with Becky. And she would, instead, ride to Pris's house, and knock on the door, and hope Alice would be there.

Disregarding her qualms and doubts and despairs and fears, she went.

She was hot when she arrived at the Wardens' house. Mary Ann Hall, who opened the door, smiled in welcome, and did not seem to notice her disheveled state.

"Hello, Miss Merrick. Pris is on the porch in back. Go on through, if you'd like to."

"Thanks."

Propelled by her urgent purpose, she forgot to notice that the Hall girl had called Pris by her first name; she strode through the shaded opulence of the Wardens' house and peeked onto the porch, where Pris was sitting on a swing attached to the wooden ceiling by chains, setting the swing in motion with a push now and then, reading a book avidly, oblivious. She was alone.

Sunlight flooded the porch. Its diffused light lit Pris's pink, clean face, and the air drifting through the screens was scented subtly with pine pitch and salt, and Pris looked exactly as she should have, the daughter of a wealthy banker, whiling time away while others did the work.

"Pris!" she called gaily.

Startled, Pris jumped and leaped from the swing.

"Hey!" She closed the book on her finger, which marked the place. "How good to see you, Emily! Does your mother know you're here? Have your parents relented, after all this time?"

"No. I mean, I expect they will, Pris, but just now I had to see you. . . ." She began to say, as best she could, that she needed help, and she paused to phrase it properly, so that she would seem neither stupid nor jilted (the worst of all maidenly states!), and into the pause Pris poured the oil of gushing friendship.

"Oh, I know what you mean!" she exclaimed. "So often I felt that I just had to see you, too!" Her voice was a shade too enthusiastic. "Come right here and sit down. You look hot!"

Pris returned to her swing and patted the empty space beside her, laying the book, the newest one by Sinclair Lewis, facedown on the table.

Feeling awkward, even disoriented, she sat beside Pris, so cool and ladylike.

"Mary Ann, fetch Emily some lemonade, won't you?" Pris had only raised her voice a little, but the Hall girl answered instantly.

"Right away!" It was obvious she'd been nearby, hoping to hear what was going on.

"Well!" Pris clasped her hands in exactly the gesture her mother used. "This is quite a treat! How's everything?" she asked, alert like a bird, her brightness brittle, instantly warning Emily to raise her guard.

"I've got a little problem, actually," she said, aware that something had changed, feeling her way along. "I'd hoped you could help me."

"You know I'd do anything in the world for you, Emily." Pris looked earnestly at her, blinking a few times as though to clear her mind, readying herself for aid to the distressed.

"We have a lot to catch up on, don't we!" Emily made herself smile. "Do you remember when we arranged the snipe hunt a month ago? So I could get away from Charles?"

"Yes, I do." Pris's attention was riveted to her now. She discarded her pose of silly sincerity. "And we never had a chance to talk after that. Charles sure fell for it, didn't he!"

"He sure did. What a success! It was the best stunt we've ever pulled, at least as far as I'm concerned," she said casually, certain that she could no longer trust her friend. Elaborately she looked around. "Does Alice still come here?"

"Oh, yes."

"I don't see her anywhere. Is she still your duenna?"

"Not exactly. She doesn't come here in that capacity. She comes because she wants to." Quickly Pris hurried along. "Alice is actually a lot of fun, Em. She and I have become friends, and I *have* calmed down a lot—even Daddy sees that. It didn't take him very long to realize that I didn't need a watchdog as much as I needed just to be with a person of her caliber."

Pris looked modestly down at her folded hands. "She likes me as much as I like her, even though I can't begin to keep up with her. She's willing to befriend me, even so." Now a great distance lay between them, a constraint that Emily wished were not there. "I think you'd like her, Emily. If you knew her as well as I do." Pris's face lit up eagerly. "But look! I'm going to have a card party Saturday. Why don't you come? If your family would let you. After all, it's nearly the end of the season. If they knew you wouldn't be seeing Alice continually, maybe they'd feel more comfortable about it. Less threatened." She nodded knowledgeably.

Threatened! Emily snorted contemptuously to herself. The Merricks threatened by Alice Bradley? It was laughable. And it was also unlikely that they'd condone a card party if they knew ahead of time that Alice would be there. Still, Pris's card party rather admirably played into her hands. She could ask Alice, herself, to pass a message. Direct contact would be better, in any case, than making arrangements with Pris—particularly this Pris, a virtual stranger to her, a girl she no longer knew.

"A card party," she repeated, as though considering it.

"Sounds dull to you, I suppose." Pris smiled gently. "But it's not. Much as I hate to admit it, Daddy was right. We—all of us—hadn't come in contact with a person like Alice. Only with each other. We didn't have anyone to show us that life could be pleasant without having to break our necks to entertain ourselves. A card party can be more fun than a revel—given the right company. All of us have discovered that now."

There was an implication that life was flowing strongly in its accustomed channels (albeit more sedately), an implication that the gang continued to meet without the presence of Emily Merrick.

Good grief!

"All of us?" she inquired icily. "Has Alice made over the rest of the gang, too?"

Pris stirred uncomfortably. "No," she said. "Not exactly. She's only rearranged it, is all. We've dropped a few, added a few . . ."

The rattling of the ice against the sides of the crystal pitcher told them that Mary Ann was coming with the lemonade.

"Did you bring a glass for yourself?" Pris asked as the girl set the tray on the low table near the swing. "I was just beginning to tell Emily about the card party Saturday."

Mary Ann glanced up with a swift flick of the eye in Emily's direction. "I'll have some later. The kitchen floor needs doing just now." She was gone before Pris could urge her further, and Emily watched her disappearing into the darkness of the shaded house, not quite believing what she had heard. Pris quickly resumed the conversation.

"You see, Alice had Daddy's consent to do just about anything she thought would get me out of the rut I was in, and into a new one. My mother wasn't home; she was at a sanatorium. Alice really was in charge, and it was amazing, Em, how quickly things started falling into place. I don't know how she did it—well, yes I do. First she introduced me to some new people so that I wouldn't be constantly with the kids who insisted on stirring things up just like I did. . . ."

"Like me."

"You weren't in question, since you couldn't come here anyway. But most of all," Pris carried on, "by the force of her personal example I began to see that life was a little different from the way I'd thought it was. Alice—you'll see this for yourself—she has more than we have. She makes our gang and the things we used to like seem so trifling . . . insignificant . . . stupid. Of course, she's a lot older and more mature. . . ."

If she heard another word about Alice Bradley she would scream. And she must not, because Alice must carry a message.

"Alice has everything put together. She doesn't need to find answers to life's questions because she's always had all the answers she needed. And she makes you feel that you can find the answer too, because it's already there, inside you. She makes you confident that it will come through loud and clear if you don't push too hard or do things that will get in your own way."

"What kind of things?" Emily asked suspiciously, her fists clenched.

"Any kind of thing that makes you lose contact with your true self."

"Sounds like Sunday school."

"Well, it isn't. Alice doesn't believe in God. She think He's someone rich people dreamed up to keep poor people in line."

"Is that why I haven't seen you in church? Because you don't believe in God anymore, either?"

"I *am* beginning to wonder a little." Pris was earnest as ever a Bryn Mawr girl could be.

"And you've sat around all summer discussing these lofty things?"

"No," Pris laughed. "We've taken walks and played tennis, and she's taught me how to play bridge."

"You already knew. We played at school."

"College bridge!" Pris scoffed. "Pooh! Compared to the game Alice plays, the bridge I learned at Bryn Mawr might just as well have been gin rummy. You were always better than I was, though, Emily. I'll bet you could keep up with the group here. I do hope you'll come Saturday. Do you think your parents would let you?"

"They needn't know Alice will be here. I'll just tell them that Alice is officially not your chaperon anymore and let it go at that."

Pris frowned. "Deception is always a bad idea," she pontificated. "If you can't do something openly, then something's wrong, somewhere. In this case, Emily, probably with your parents."

The Pris of days gone by would not have thought of such a thing, let alone spoken it. Catching her cue as quickly as possible, Emily spread her hands in a pacific gesture.

"I'll talk it over with them, then. Perhaps, as you say, since it's the end of the summer and there's no danger that I'd see Alice again, they'd feel a little better about it."

They would not, of course. It was conceivable that if she argued long enough and hard enough and skillfully enough, they might reluctantly let her go. But she was not going to risk it. Risk their taking ages to decide, risk losing the chance of seeing Alice on Saturday. Oh, no. She'd just write Charles, was what she'd do. She'd suggest that she'd enjoy seeing him Saturday afternoon. When he picked her up, she'd ask him to just drop her off and pick her up again, and they'd have the whole balance of the afternoon together, she'd explain. Just the two of them.

Naturally, he would cause her family to believe she'd been with him the whole time. Charles would do anything she asked.

That was his function, was it not?

And there could be no question about attending Pris's party. Clearly she had to meet Alice, get her to contact Tim. And she must reestablish herself with the gang, over which Daddy's exile and her own dallying around, waiting for Tim, had caused her to lose control.

"Who all will be at your card party?" she asked. "You mentioned you'd dropped a few people, and added a few. Who's been added?"

"To start with, Mary Ann. And her sister," Pris began, tipping her head in the direction of the kitchen.

"Your maids?" Emily pictured the girls in their black dresses and starched, immaculate aprons, little lace-trimmed hats, sitting primly at the bridge table. She laughed despite herself.

Pris hitched in the swing. "Well, surely you're aware that you can't learn a card game for four people when you've only got two."

"Yes, of course."

"Alice knew the Hall girls, of course, having grown up in Waterford. She's been coaching them already. When she mentioned to Daddy that she needed two people more in order to teach me the game as it ought to be played, Daddy said he didn't mind."

"And now you invite them to your parties?"

"I couldn't see any reason not to. Neither could Alice."

She was becoming more and more impressed with the subtlety of Alice Bradley's mind. Already she'd slipped the less exalted members of Waterford into the youth of summer society. The dephilistinizing had begun, that was clear!

"Don't get me wrong," Emily said. "Those girls are nice girls and their parents are nice people, too, but they aren't your kind of people, Pris, and they never will be. It's a mistake to mix them, thinking that there's no difference."

"There isn't any difference when Alice is around," Pris said pointedly. "That's something else she's taught me. And taught everyone else, too."

"Everyone?"

"Everyone we've included up til now."

Quickly Emily backed up. "Well, of course, if the gang wants them, I certainly have no objection."

"That's a good thing. The gang wouldn't want to lose you on account of it," Pris said, and the truth of things came a little clearer. The dephilistinizing was complete. Alice Bradley had the gang slumming, and the novelty of it hadn't worn off yet. Now she, Emily Merrick, was being tested for suitability.

"Well, I have to be getting along," she said quickly. "If everyone in Waterford plays a mean game of bridge these days, I guess I'd better brush up on mine. Don't you think?"

"They're terrors," Pris laughed warily, still unsure of Emily's bedrock response.

"Thank you for asking me, Pris. What time will the festivities start?"

"Two o'clock."

"Okay. I'll be there." She waved in as casual a manner as she could contrive. "I'll let myself out. Don't bother Mary Ann. She's probably busy boning up on her bridge rules and the most recently published book on etiquette in polite society." It was a nasty crack that she immediately regretted having made, and she cursed herself as she hustled through the living room and the foyer and out to Becky's bike, leaning against the nearest tree.

Nearly the whole gang had reassembled behind her back! That in itself was bad. But what was worse was the fact that not one of them, when she'd seen them, had mentioned it. Probably they had kept silent in order to spare her, just the way Mother and Daddy did with Cousin Elizabeth—and, by God, for the same cause. Alice Bradley. It was perfectly mortifying.

At least she'd have a chance to talk with Alice, and hopefully get back into the swing of things before the whole gang turned against her! Too much hung in the balance to stick to her pride now—for through Alice she could get to Tim. Couldn't she? And if it turned out that her old friends had betrayed her for Alice's sake, what of it? she asked herself defiantly. If that's the kind of friendship they have to offer, you're better off knowing it now.

But it didn't feel better. It just felt worse. The fact was that she would have preferred not to know—and riding back on Becky's bike, her tears dropped, hot and useless, in the dust.

Her vigil continued.

5

"I guess I don't have to tell you that I'm just a bit disappointed," Charles said. The vein in his temple was jumping, and she was unpleasantly aware that Charles had a temper which she had never, ever suspected was there.

"Here I come all the way down from Boston, breaking my neck to do it, I might add—taking Saturday off and perhaps even jeopardizing my progress at Sommerset and King in the process. And what happens when I get here? You want me to leave you at the Wardens' house and cool my heels for two hours while you play bridge!"

Furiously he turned into the Wardens' driveway, so abruptly and sharply that she lost her balance and fell bruisingly against the door. He pulled up to the front door with a flourish of dust and flying pebbles, stomped on the brake and stalled the car, which bucked in protest and then subsided into hiccuping silence.

Never had she seen him so out of control.

"Charles," she said placatingly, picking up his hand and holding it with both of hers. "It's a little too complicated to explain, but I had to get here this afternoon, without my family knowing it. So I thought—what a perfect opportunity! A perfect excuse to see Charles again—surely he'd come to Waterford, surely he'd help me—and I'd get a chance to spend time with him as well as come here."

Desperately wanting to believe her, Charles asked, "Did you really think you needed an excuse, Emily?"

"Of course I did. I know how busy you are, up there in the

city! I know you don't have time for me anymore, Charles, and I understand. Your career is the most important thing in your life just now—as it should be!"

"I always have time for you," he said softly.

"Then, would you pick me up at the stroke of four? We can talk to our hearts' content! You can tell me all about Sommerset and King—I'm dying to know what you're up to, Charles! There!" She kissed his cheek and quickly let herself out. "I'll look forward to seeing you at four."

"Okay," he said, mollified though not happy. "Just see to it that you're ready then."

Quickly she ran for the front door, intent on getting away from him.

"Emily!" Pris enthused. "It's so nice to see you!"

She gritted her teeth in the presence of Pris's fraudulent enthusiasm designed to disguise nervousness.

"Hi, dear." She kissed Pris's cheek. "It's good to see you, too. Hi, Caroline."

"Hi, Em!" answered Caroline King, trying to look casual.

She was instantly aware that Alice was standing quietly near the piano, but she waited for the ball to land in her court instead of going after it.

"Ginny!" she exclaimed. "What a nice dress!" Ginny Porter was no one she need worry about. She began to feel more confident. Ginny waved her acknowledgment of the compliment.

"Emily," began Pris. "Do you know Ellen Shaunessy?"

The young girl she dragged forward was the daughter of the man who delivered parcels and people from the train depot. "Ellen is going to Jackson next year," Pris said. "So we're getting her bridge game in shape."

"If Jackson is anything like Bryn Mawr, she'll need to get it in shape." Emily smiled enigmatically. The girl blushed, tongue-tied in the presence of Emily Merrick, whom she'd seen around town all her life and never once spoken to.

"And this is Amy Stone," said Pris. She had not mentioned either Amy or Ellen before, but Emily was becoming accustomed to the little surprises Pris seemed to enjoy so much these days.

"I guess I don't have to introduce the Hall sisters," Pris gushed.

"No, indeed." She waved to them, sitting on the couch together as though they were Siamese.

"Hi, Evangeline," she said to Evvie Thayer, standing near the couch.

"Hi, Em," responded Evvie, as though she were not truly glad that Emily Merrick had returned to the bosom of their group. Emily decided not to pay attention and turned, inadvertently coming face to face with Alice Bradley, whom Pris was leading to her.

"And you remember Alice," Pris said reverently.

"Yes, of course." She smiled politely at Alice, concentrating on the smile she'd rehearsed for the meeting of the Merrick pariah, a smile that she hoped was disarming and frank, that would cause Alice to believe that Emily Merrick did not share her family's prejudices.

"Well!" Pris said, her words nearly garbled in her excitement. "I think everyone's here. The tables are all set up in the conservatory. Here's the tally cards." Quickly, in case the gathering needed smoothing over, she circulated among her guests with the little folders that told each person who her partner would be at which table. Pris hooked her arm through Alice's.

"Since you're the one responsible for our present interest in Mr. Goren's game, Allie, you can lead the way."

Alice glanced at Emily as if there were more she would say if she could, and then she smiled and beckoned the group forward as though she were starting a regatta.

The tables were set up in the conservatory, and each had a number on it. Emily's tally said number three table would be hers first, and she seated herself there, to discover her partner was Ginny.

"I didn't know you even played bridge, Em," Ginny said. "It makes me nervous. I mean, I don't know how you bid."

"You're about to find out," she said grimly.

Ellen Shaunessy and Pris formed the rest of the table, and with a little nod, Emily fanned the cards for the pick of deal; at the next table her partner was Evvie, and at the third it was Pris, thus eliminating the need to put Emily in close contact with a town girl. Very cleverly arranged, she thought, and she was relieved too, because she would not have known what to say to those girls. Perhaps Pris's new social life was not to her liking, she thought uneasily. Perhaps she wouldn't care to join it, even if she were free to, she thought haughtily. Maybe she would just tell Pris to go jump in the lake. . . .

On the Warden buffet, Pris and Mary Ann, together, spread out the collation—pitchers of lemonade and ice water, cookies, and bite-sized sandwiches—served themselves, and sat in the living room together to eat. "If the rest of you don't want to help yourselves, you can just go home," Pris laughed, totally abandoning the manners instilled in her through the years of her upbringing.

The party drifted into the dining room to fill their plates and eat wherever they wanted to, balancing their plates on their silken knees. No one, Emily noticed, went out onto the screened porch, as though by design avoiding it. She saw that Alice was hanging back, behind the rest of the party, so as to be in the same place as Emily, who hung back too.

"Well, Alice," she said boldly. "Pris has told me what a pleasant time she's had in your company."

"And I in hers. I wished you could have joined us," Alice said. Disregarding the rest of the group, they drifted onto the porch, where Alice seated herself gracefully beside Emily on Pris's swing.

"Pris says that you and she were roommates at Bryn Mawr."

"Yes, we were."

"Pris would certainly like it if you were her roommate again this year, Emily."

"She would?" Emily asked blankly. "She's going back?"

"Yes."

Why had Pris not said anything about this? Surely she'd have known Emily's decisions about school were influenced by hers?

"Well?" Alice challenged. "Have you ever thought about going back?"

"If I haven't, my family has. But I haven't made up my mind."

"Pris says you're so smart! What an opportunity Bryn Mawr gives you to grow . . . to expand your horizons . . . to soar!" She looked at Emily expectantly, probably waiting for Emily to declare herself in favor of soaring. Her hands were folded quietly in her lap, and she would clearly be listening, really listening, to whatever Emily was going to say, instead of merely waiting until her chance came to speak again. But Emily had not taken all this trouble to chitchat idly with Alice Bradley.

"Your cousin Tim told me you worked in Boston," she said, working toward her goal. "Did you soar there?"

Alice shrugged. "I was assistant personnel manager at Gilchrist's. It was a challenge and I loved it—and I'd call that soaring, wouldn't you? And I doubt I would have gotten the job without a college degree."

"But now you're going to housekeep for your father. Your soaring stops, it seems to me."

"No." Alice smiled. "I've only opted for something else for as long as my dad needs me. An option available to me because of that degree—which allows me to teach. You really should go back, Emily," she said softly. "It's important. Otherwise you're pushed around by life, just as women have always been. But I certainly don't want to argue about it. I'd much rather talk about you!" Her face lit up, as though the subject of Emily Merrick were supremely interesting. "How did you learn to play bridge so well? Certainly not at Bryn Mawr, judging from Pris's game before we started working on it."

"Actually," she said irritably, in an effort to head off the small talk, "my parents and I often play with your sister Elizabeth. And Elizabeth is very good. You ought to take her on sometime."

For once Alice Bradley was off balance, apparently startled speechless. Her mouth opened and then closed again, and her face took on a strange, unfathomable look.

"My sister," she said finally. "Elizabeth. And how is Elizabeth?"

"She's fine. I hope I haven't upset you by mentioning her, Alice."

"Certainly you haven't. I was just . . . startled, is all. In fact, Emily, I'd rather like to talk about Elizabeth with you."

Alice's preferences were not her concern. She pressed on, maneuvering toward her own interests. She decided on bluntness. "Tim told me that you were going to weaken Elizabeth's hold on Waterford, so there'd be space for you here."

"Tim told you that? When?" Alice asked.

"Earlier in the summer, when he first came to Waterford," Emily said, searching for an opening, now that the subject was on the right person. "I met him at the Marshalls' party."

"Oh, yes. That party. Did Tim tell you that it was my first battle? And my first victory?" Her eyes sparkled at the recollection.

"Yes, as a matter of fact, he did. And speaking of Tim . . ."

"This is my second. Victory, I mean," Alice said, waving toward the conversational maelstrom in the living room. She smiled—not an especially pleasant smile. "The next will be the Fall Fest."

"The Fall Festival?" Emily nearly fell off the swing.

"Pris has invited me—it's to be held here, I gather."

"Yes," Emily gulped. "It always is."

"And it includes both adults and the young set, I take it—a sort of farewell until the next season?"

"Yes, that's right."

"Well, I'll be here. And so will they." Alice wagged her head toward her town friends.

"Good God!" exclaimed Emily inadvertently.

"In fact, it might be just as well if you told Elizabeth so. Save her from the shock of running into me, and my friends, accidentally, if you know what I mean. But what I'd most like is that Elizabeth join in the spirit of the occasion. The past is dead."

And so, indeed, it appeared to be!

"I really don't care about what is commonly called polite society, Emily. I suppose Elizabeth will never really believe that, since it's so important to her. What I do care about is being shut out without the chance to be judged on my own merits. And what I object to is the exclusive nature of such a society, which is unable to recognize worth—which confuses worth with wealth and breeding. If she decides not to come to the Fall Fest on account of me, you might pass that message along."

"You want me to tell Elizabeth *that*?"

"If you would."

As if she would dare! Quickly Emily marshaled her own plans, which had scattered like sheep as she'd listened to the dephilistinizing of Waterford. "Um, sure," she lied. "Sure, Alice. If the situation develops as you see it, I'll tell Elizabeth what you've said. And while we're on the subject of messages, I wonder if you could deliver one for me."

"Certainly," Alice agreed amiably. "What is it?"

There was a mild uproar of female voices and the sudden carrying rumble of a male one, and Emily thought that surely, surely it must be her imagination, because it sounded like . . .

"Oh, that must be my fiancé," Alice said. "I must be on my way. What message, Emily?"

"Your fiancé?" Emily asked faintly. Her blood had stopped its coursing, and she was feeling distant, very distant from the porch and the swing and Alice, sitting beside her.

"Have I come too early?" Tim asked at the doorway. "I thought you told me four. . . ." Then Emily's presence broke through the intensity of his attention to his cousin, and his face deepened to a dark, dull red and Alice quickly got off the swing and went to him, drawing him forward.

"Tim, you do know Emily, don't you? But of course you

do. Emily tells me that you revealed all my plans to her, right from the start." Alice smiled, gestured. . . .

She had no breath with which to speak, no will, no power, and Tim, equally speechless, turned to avoid having to look at her. He mumbled something to Alice, who stood so close to him in a proprietary way, who answered him low, so that no one else could hear.

Onto the porch burst Pris. "Charles is here, Emily. He wants to take you away—now!"

"You bet I do!" Charles followed Pris closely and crowded onto the porch behind her, taking charge of the moment so effectively that it was easy to pretend that Tim Bradley and Alice did not exist. "Did you win the bridge?" Charles asked, sliding into the swing beside her, making it bounce.

"No," she heard herself say, aware that the Bradleys were waiting, watching from the doorway. "I'll talk to you about it later," she heard herself say to Alice, carefully avoiding Tim's eyes, herself so fragile, like porcelain, ready to shatter.

"Okay." Alice nodded, then looked up at Tim, and in the wordless agreement of people finely tuned to one another, they walked away.

Inanely Pris sighed. "Handsome couple, aren't they? They've been in love for years, really."

"Years?"

Pris looked at Emily directly, and spoke directly, too. "They've tried to get involved with other people, but it just never seems to work. They can't get each other out of their respective systems, no matter how many other people they try to love." Thus did Pris tell her erstwhile friend Emily that Tim Bradley had only sought refuge from an insoluble difficulty when he'd made a play for her; thus did she tell her former friend Emily that the difficulty had been overcome. That Alice came first now, first for everyone. That Alice had taken Pris away, and Waterford, and Tim, too. It was not possible to know when it had happened or how it had happened or if Tim had only deceived her in the manner of fickle men everywhere—nor did it matter.

Because Tim was gone.

She stood up so quickly that she nearly tipped Charles out of the swing.

"Well, it's all been simply charming," she said to Pris, hating her. "But unfortunately, Charles and I must leave now."

"We sure do," Charles agreed happily, rushing along to catch up. At the door, in the distance she saw Tim helping

Alice into his car. Tim, who had tried to forget his cousin with the help of Emily Merrick.

She must escape! She must somehow flee to the safety and privacy of the Buick, where all she had to do was contend with Charles, and would no longer be assaulted by such impossible, untenable hurt. She allowed Charles to help her in, and sat, absymally silent, while he backed the car onto Main Street and drove toward the western end of town.

She had lost him.

All that she had to offer, he had discarded.

She could hardly make herself breathe, and her torment writhed and tore at the edges of her consciousness.

He can't, she told herself, panic-ridden. He couldn't just . . . drop me! He couldn't. He couldn't.

But he had.

"Are you in love with that fellow?" Charles asked crossly.

"What fellow?" she asked dully.

"The Bradley fellow, who else? You were watching him rather intently, it seemed to me."

"I didn't either watch him. I was watching his cousin. Who is also my cousin."

She didn't think she'd been so obvious, but it didn't matter if she had, because there was nothing she could have done about it.

"Quite lower-class," Charles grumbled. "I can't imagine why Priscilla's Pater picked her as a companion. I'd forgotten she was your cousin, too, until you reminded me. I say, Emily, that must have been a bit difficult for you, having to play bridge with her and all."

It would do. It would account for her obvious depression; it was a better excuse than the truth, the truth she could not bear but must. "I . . . I guess it was," she said. He will never love you, she told herself. He is in love with her. And Alice was not lower-class, for all her upbringing. Not a bit. The girl was a Merrick, Emily reminded herself. She was undeniably a Merrick in a way that Emily was not. She was a descendant of Kingsley Merrick, Waterford's Famous Person, same as Elizabeth was, but she was worth a half-dozen Elizabeths, and her impact on the lives of others was past calculating. Her impact on Tim had been lifelong. Pris trailed her with devotion. The gang had reformed because of her. And Emily Merrick had lost just about everything that counted, because of her.

"If you're not in love with that fellow, then I'm glad," Charles said shyly. "Because there's something I've been wanting to speak to you about, and I can't very well speak of it if you love another man." He pulled the car to the side of the road, past the little bridge that carried the overflow from several ponds above, installed when Main Street was paved a few years ago. Nearby was the site of Waterford's old mill, the foundations of it barren, deserted; the houses that had once formed West Waterford were gone now, as if they never were, dismantled stick by stick and burned in the stoves of Waterford's poor during the winter, or used by them to enhance their own dwellings or those of their pigs and chickens. West Waterford was only a memory now, and a convenient location for discussion of intimate sorts.

With a sigh, Emily resigned herself to hear Charles out. Of course she knew what he was going to say. In that tone of voice it was impossible not to know. She did not want to hear, because she did not want to have to cope with it now, not now . . . but he was launched already.

"They're talking more and more of sending me to Ohio," Charles said. "They're opening a branch office in Port Huron and they want me to go because, of course, men who are already settled in the Boston area are loath to pull up stakes."

"Yes, I suppose they are," she said, wondering how much more she could take of this afternoon, of her hurt, of her aching need for Tim, her hatreds, her agonies . . . and of Charles Sinclaire, mumbling along about Port Huron, Ohio, and his prospects.

"Now that I've been away in Boston, on my own, it's become even more clear that I do need to get away from the Mater, and I see no way to do it but to accept this assignment."

"That's probably wise," she agreed, as if she cared.

"And I'm hoping, Emily, that you will do me the honor of coming with me—as my wife."

Numbly she heard him, and no matter how hard she tried, she could not make herself respond. Dumbly she looked at Charles and felt the start of tears, and wished, somehow, that she could sleep, and stay asleep, and not wake up until the sun was setting and the birds were calling in an afternoon far, far removed from this one.

"Emily, darling, what have I done?" Charles, in a twitter of distress, took her cold hand. "Emily," he begged, "surely asking you to marry me can't be that bad!"

She tried to laugh, but it came out a sob, and she covered her burning face to evade the necessity of speaking.

"I didn't realize you were so wrought-up, my dear,"

Charles said stiffly. "I gather you don't want to discuss marriage just now."

Tired. She was excruciatingly tired. And yet the instinct to preserve herself stirred, stretched, reached out to pluck at her consciousness. . . . Was there, after all, a bun in the oven?

Charles was here. Now. Oh, Jesus, Christ Jesus, he was here, and Tim was not. . . .

"Maybe you'd just let me rest here, with my head on your shoulder," she said. "Maybe I'll feel better in a minute."

"It would be an honor to have you rest your head on my shoulder," he said pedantically. "And it would be an honor to have you be my wife. I'll be going to Port Huron in four weeks, if I accept this job; I realize that you couldn't very well go with me then. But at Christmas, perhaps. That would give you enough time."

"Time for what?" she asked helplessly, still hidden on his shoulder.

"To get your trousseau together. Have the little parties women seem to love so well," he said patronizingly. "Assemble silver and china and all. You know."

"Oh. Yes. I know," she said feebly, and pulled herself upright. She must go home. She must go now. She could not think, she could hardly speak. "I've never considered marriage very concretely, Charles," she stumbled. "I hope you'll give me a while to think it over."

"Of course! Of course! But, Emily, surely you must care about me a little, if you're willing to consider it."

"And surely you know I care about you, Charles," she sighed.

He moved closer. "Sometimes you seem to put me off—hold me afar."

"Sometimes you rush me," she fumbled. "I don't like being rushed, Charles. It confuses me, and frightens me."

He smiled, as though the idea of frightening her appealed to him, made him masculine and powerful. Swiftly he bent and kissed her, heavily, harshly, a kiss that lingered for an unbearable amount of time, which she dared not put off, nor did she dare to stop his hand, which he pressed heavily on her breast and squeezed—too hard.

It was an awful price to pay, and she surely did not want to pay it. She wanted nothing to do with him at all, but she made herself pay for a decent interval before she gently disengaged herself and persuaded him to drive her home. It was all she could manage to say good-bye to him in a composed and civil manner, letting herself into the vestibule at the base of the tower, sliding behind a portiere that kept drafts out of the hall during the winter. She leaned against the cool woodwork behind the heavy curtain, and the hot tears that she'd held in were released in the privacy of the musty velvet, running freely down her face and dripping onto her pretty party dress, staining it.

"Emily!" exclaimed Cousin Elizabeth. "Good grief, child! What in heaven's name is wrong!"

The surprise at unexpectedly hearing Elizabeth's voice brought her up short, just before she fell over the brink of hysteria. "Oh!" she choked.

Cousin Elizabeth, sizing up the situation, led her to the library, the heavy doors of which would muffle any sound they made.

"Your mother is meeting your father's train. No one's home," she said. "You can speak here, if you want to."

Elizabeth was not the right person! She was absolutely the wrong person, because the Bradleys were never, never supposed to be mentioned in her presence. But Emily's unbearable hurt drove her into the arms of this inappropriate person.

"I've lost him," she choked.

"From what I saw, out the parlor window, I wouldn't judge you'd lost him at all. Why, the look on his face—"

"Not Charles!" she cried. "Not that stupid clod! I mean Tim. And can you guess, Elizabeth, who I've lost him to? No, you never will. Never. Not in a million years."

"So tell me," Elizabeth urged indulgently, without realizing whom Emily was talking about.

Helplessly Emily mopped at her still-free-flowing tears. "Alice," she hiccuped. "I've lost Tim to your sister Alice."

Cousin Elizabeth was ordinarily a striking woman, tall, dark-haired and imperially beaked, poised of carriage and demeanor. Her inbred sense of dignity did not desert her now, though all of her features, her chin and lips, the lines that ran from her nostrils to the edges of her mouth, the creases between her eyes, became stark, as though sketched in charcoal, and she was a caricature of the woman she'd been a moment before.

"Alice?" Not even her voice was the same. Instead it rasped, as though there were not enough room in her throat for it. "I wish you'd start at the beginning, Em."

There was no point hiding now, was there? Elizabeth was due for a head-on collision with Alice at the Fall Fest anyway.

"I met Tim Bradley earlier this summer," she explained over her pain. "And then Mother said he mustn't come here, because it would upset you. So I met him at parties, until Alice became Pris's chaperon, and I couldn't go to parties at all because she'd be there. But I'd fallen in love with Tim by then."

"This Tim would be David Bradley's boy?" Elizabeth queried.

"Yes."

"Go on. Go on!"

"I'd hoped to marry him—I love him so! But . . . but now I discover he's been seeing Alice—that he was really in love with her all the time and only using me in an attempt to forget her."

"The Bradleys were always two-faced," Elizabeth said, her voice hard. "Go on."

"They're engaged, is all," she said, her voice tinny.

"They're cousins."

"Apparently that's not stopping them—although Pris says that Alice has put Tim off for a long while because of it."

Elizabeth sat motionless, and Emily's crowding, searing anger was born in the space of waiting. "She's taken Tim from me, and she's going to take Waterford from you, Elizabeth."

"Oh?" Elizabeth asked coldly, as though she did not care. But she did care; her clasped hands were so tight that her fingers were white.

"She's going to the Fall Festival."

"Alice Bradley? To the Fall Fest? At the end of August?"

"Accompanied by her retinue." Cruelly Emily named them, the Shaunessy girl and Amy Stone and the Halls—all of them—and the expression on Elizabeth's face changed from anger to illness; she shut her eyes tight and was quiet for a long, long time. When they opened again, Emily saw that they glowed, like a cat's watching a bird, waiting for it to hop a little closer, a little closer. . . .

Then they cooled. "She must be stopped. And I shall stop her."

"You mean Alice?"

"I believe she is the subject under discussion?"

Emily quailed under the severity of Elizabeth's gaze.

"I must see her before the Fall Fest. Can you arrange that?"

She shrugged, her anger dissipated and her despondency returning.

Elizabeth's eyes changed again, keen with calculation. "It would be to your advantage," she said. "After all, if Alice tells the young man that she is no longer interested in marrying him—why, wouldn't he return to you? Apparently he must have found you attractive once. . . . Can't you see, Emily? Why, the situation speaks for itself. All you need to do is to remove Alice from the picture! And since it seems that a lot of your troubles have been brought on by me—why, I'll help you fix everything."

It was humiliating to think that she, Emily Merrick, had to scheme and plot to capture a man—she, who had always enjoyed boys, had always had girlfriends, too, and now seemed to have lost her ability to hold the affections of either. "How can you help?" she asked humbly.

"Just get Alice here, and you'll see," Elizabeth said firmly. "Tomorrow being Sunday, there'll be no appropriate opportunity. But Monday afternoon, perhaps, when we all tuck in for our naps—that, I think, will be a good time."

"I'm not sure she'd come, Elizabeth. I mean, just because I ask. . . ."

"Come upstairs with me, dear, while I write a little note. You deliver it Monday afternoon, and I think you'll find she'll be as interested in seeing me as I am in seeing her."

"I'll give it a try," she agreed. But short of hog-tying her, she could not imagine Alice doing anything she didn't care to do.

Elizabeth bounded out of the library, upstairs to her bedroom, moving more briskly than Emily could ever remember.

From the window in Elizabeth's room, which faced north, the bay sparkled at high tide. To the west, up Main Street, the tops of the trees were so dense that she could see nothing but the steeple of the church, which poked up past them. She stared at it, working at the hardening of her emotions, of her heart, of her soul, so that she would no longer bleed and suffer, so that she could at least survive until she knew whether Cousin Elizabeth's plans would work out.

"Here you are," Elizabeth said from her escritoire. She held out the stiffly embossed paper with "KINGSLAND" printed at the top.

> Miss Elizabeth Merrick-Edgarton requests the honor of your presence at the library of her house Monday at two o'clock.

"Think that might whet her appetite?"
"We'll find out, won't we?" They smiled at one another over, above, past their separate hates, and Emily smothered the small, insignificant quickening of guilt, of shame.
The responsibility, after all, was Elizabeth's.
Wasn't it?

6

Out over the low-lying bog the foliage was turning russet. Birds in the bushes sang and the sun sowed contentment. Looking over it, watching it, Emily was poignantly aware of the absence of peace within herself, saw that her inner turmoil prevented her from truly understanding such a day, such an hour; miserably she looked over the several acres. The Bradley bog swarmed with pickers. It was portioned off into alleys by lines of twine running front to back, and the pickers —men with large tined scoops and women with small ones, little children crawling along behind hunting for the berries that had been overlooked—labored along their respective lanes, chattering and laughing. From the road which overlooked the acreage, Emily searched for Alice at the ladies' end, nearest to where she stood—but Alice was dressed like any rural woman, with a sunbonnet and a long apron, and it took a while to identify her. At the men's end Tim was gamely though inefficiently slinging his scoop. Behind him five gleaning children picked their buckets full.

Emily was quite sure he would not see her, since he was quite far away, down the bog. She hurried past the little barn where the screens were set up over barrels; the elderly sorted and picked out bad fruit, and old Mr. John Bradley himself sat at a desk made of a board suspended between two square-cut stumps, keeping tally sheets and dispensing money. Beyond the barn, on the slope running up from the bog, was the Bradley house, a small Cape cottage with a low-eaved roof that caught the sun in winter, uncluttered and clean in the clear afternoon, simple and pure as all true Cape houses were.

Hoping that she could approach Alice without being obtrusive, Emily made her way down the rough and dusty path to the end of the twine-marked aisle where Alice was laughing with Amy Stone over some trifle Amy thought funny. Now Alice was telling Amy something equally amusing to them both.

"Alice!" she called softly, but it was Amy Stone who heard.

"Alice," Amy said, glancing Emily's way. "Someone wants you." The Stone girl knew perfectly well who Emily was, of course, having been introduced just two days before, but she forbore to say so. Village people were like that, referring to summer people as "them."

"Emily!" Alice's face lit up in genuine pleasure, through the fatigue and dust that had accumulated on it. Without hesitation, she rose, lithe with youth though she had been crouching for a long time. Between them lay ten feet of unpicked bog over which Alice dared not walk. "I'll have to come around. Otherwise I'll squash the berries. I'll meet you." Instantly she turned away, walking rapidly to the end of her aisle, making comments as she went to other pickers with whom, apparently, she was on the best of terms. Quickly she came around, scanning the men's end to see how Tim was doing, shaking her head as if in despair over his slowness. Emily backed up, putting the barn between her and old Mr. Bradley, who might recognize her—beckoning Alice to follow. Alice did.

"Now! What is it?" She smiled.

"It's Elizabeth. She wants to see you." She handed over the invitation.

Incredulous, Alice stared at it. Suspicion hardened her mouth. "I wonder why."

Emily shrugged. "She didn't tell me."

"How much of my message did you deliver?"

"Well, naturally I softened the edges a bit. I only said that you were coming to the Fall Fest."

"Hm." Alice thought about it. "So in effect, she doesn't

know what I'm doing or why I'm doing it. She only thinks I'm a gate-crasher. Determined to find a place, et cetera, et cetera."

"Well?" Emily challenged. "Aren't you?"

"That's only half of the story, Em. You know that."

"Oh, yes." Emily nodded. "All that business about being exclusive and all. No, I didn't tell her that."

"It's important that she knows." Alice hastily untied her apron, removed her bonnet, shook out her hair. "Otherwise I appear no different than any other social climber, and without any more moral justification than she has. I'll have to freshen up. Come with me if you like." She turned, hastened up the path toward the little house, and then took an even more beaten trail to the back. She opened the kitchen door and waved Emily inside.

It was a pleasant room, with a black iron stove in the middle and a soapstone sink with a pump under the windows, a table at one end and an icebox at the other, fresh gingham curtains and rag rugs and a gleam and shine that made it seem warmly loved.

"I'd better wash my face and comb my hair. I've never even spoken to my sister, and I want to look decent before I do. But I think I won't change my clothes," Alice went on stubbornly, taking the kettle off the stove and pouring some warm water into a basin, carrying it to the sink and rinsing her face and hands, dipping a towel into it and scrubbing vigorously, raising blotches on her fair skin. "It'll do Elizabeth good to know that there's a Merrick who isn't afraid to get her hands dirty." She snatched a comb from a shelf below a small mirror and started to work on her hair. "We'll have to hurry," she exclaimed, tugging at a snarl. "I don't want Dad and Tim to know where I'm going."

"Why not?" Emily asked.

Alice threw the comb down and headed for the door, and Emily hurried behind. "Well, let's put it this way," Alice said as they took another path that would connect with Main Street farther up and out of sight of the bog. "My father is the cause of all this fracas—or at least, its starting point. My mother loved him so dearly, and had loved him for so long, that she sacrificed her family—all of it—once she had a chance to marry him. He's about the greatest fellow that ever was, but he has his pride. He'd never allow me to brawl with my sister for his sake."

"Brawl?" Emily gulped.

"In a manner of speaking." Alice smiled. "What I'm doing, I do for his sake—and my mother's, too. I'm just carrying the basic argument a generation further. People like Elizabeth need to be shown that value lies beneath the surface—and if she's too obtuse to see it, then she needs to be coerced."

"Which is what you've done by becoming intimate with Pris Warden?"

"It accomplishes what I mean to do, yes," Alice said grimly.

"I'd better warn you, Alice, that Elizabeth is far from stupid. She has a few preconceived ideas, I'll grant you that—but dumb she is not."

Alice's voice became fierce in its intensity. "My mother loved Elizabeth, Emily, even though she was willing to risk losing her for the chance to live here, in Waterford, with my dad. She and my father would happily have given everything they had to Elizabeth—shared it all—desperately wanted to, both of them. I'd like to tell Elizabeth that. I'd like to tell her how much our mother loved her, and I will, if the opportunity comes up. Maybe it'll help loosen those preconceived ideas."

They had, by now, reached the driveway to Kingsland, where the maples, so gold in the sun, reflected a nimbus over and around themselves in the clearness of the air and sky.

"I've never been inside," Alice said. "You'll have to show me the way."

"Sure."

"My mother grew up here, but I've never seen the things she had or the room she used. I've always wanted to. Do you think Elizabeth would mind if you showed me around?"

"I'll find out," Emily said without even a tremor, knowing perfectly well that whatever Elizabeth's intentions were, permitting Alice Bradley to poke around the house of her ancestors was not one of them. "There are people napping upstairs, so we'll have to be quiet as we can."

"Oh! Sure!" Alice agreed, her eyes dancing, her color high, her shoulders straight as she followed Emily through the parlor and the hallway, to the library. The door was open, and Elizabeth was seated at the desk, waiting, looking Spartan and forbidding. Emily stood back and motioned Alice to enter. From the hall she could see Kingsley Merrick's portrait, the painted curtain behind him parted to show a Concord coach on the horizon of a strange country. In his hand was a tome entitled *Australian Annals,* both the book and the coach designed to let the onlooker know that Merrick had done well down under. The library was liberally walled with books in handsome leather bindings which Emily could not recall anyone ever reading, and the wide, broad surface of the desk where Elizabeth waited was bare except for one slim book which lay open.

"Hello, Alice," said Elizabeth from behind the desk. She neither got to her feet nor smiled in welcome.

"Hello," Alice said from the doorway. She waited, forcing Elizabeth to show her hand, and Emily was reminded that she was Kingsley Merrick's granddaughter the same as Elizabeth was—and clearly shared many of the characteristics that legend attributed to him: shrewdness, swift intelligence, that ineffable stamp of strength that is called presence. Now for the first time together in the same room, it was easy to see that Elizabeth and Alice were sisters; neither of them much resembled the man in the portrait, but both were tall, with dark hair, and the modeling of their faces was vaguely similar.

"Well!" said Elizabeth. "This is indeed an unexpected addendum to the summer. Will you be seated?" She gestured to a straight-backed wooden chair beside her desk, as though Alice were a pupil—a naughty one who needed talking to.

But Alice rearranged the scene by pulling the chair away from the desk, setting it at an angle, giving a more intimate impression of the interview.

"Sit over there, Emily," Elizabeth commanded, and returned her attention to Alice. "I hear you're going to the Fall Fest."

"Yes," said Alice, her voice even and strong.

"No doubt the prospect pleases you."

"Not particularly," Alice said calmly. "I'm not especially interested in parties and the dull people that attend them. But this is different, isn't it? When you can't have something, your appetite for it is whetted. Don't you agree?"

"It can happen that way, I suppose." Icily, Elizabeth appraised Alice. "But in this case, my dear girl, your appetite will have to remain unappeased. You are not going to attend the Fall Fest."

"Tell me why," Alice said softly. "And then I'll tell you why you're wrong."

"Indeed." Elizabeth waved at the open book on the desk in front of her, pushed it toward the edge, in Alice's direction. Alice did not move or look at it.

"This small volume is a record of the burying ground of the old first parish church—the one that's gone now, though, of course, its cemetery remains. Thirty years ago, when genealogy was so much the rage, Waterford's historical society looked up and recorded the inhabitants there—and this book is the published result. Our great-aunt Hetty Merrick was responsible for it. She organized the whole thing brilliantly—dividing the cemetery much as you divide a cranberry bog, and each member of the society was assigned a strip, the idea being to find out as much about the deceased people within it as possible. The first person I'd like to call your attention to is here." Elizabeth pointed to the opened page; being upside down from her vantage point, she could not read it. But obviously she did not need to.

"It says, 'David Bradley. Died 1818. Princes Island, South Africa,' " Elizabeth recited.

Emily perked up—remembered that Tim's father was named David Bradley, too. Obviously not the same one!

"David Bradley," Elizabeth said to Emily, who, being seated across the room, obviously could not read the book, and would have to be told its contents. "David Bradley has only a memorial stone in the cemetery because he is buried in Africa. Directly after the War of 1812 our men were trading there, and a plague struck—so badly that our ancestor Elijah Merrick was ruined when so many members of his crew were stricken that the Boston Port Authority condemned his ship and sank it. And this poor soul, this David Bradley, never made it home at all."

Mesmerized, Emily nodded as though it were news to her—which it wasn't. At least, not the part about Elijah Merrick, mutual ancestor of them all.

"And here's yet another Bradley memorial marker." Flipping expertly through the pages, Elizabeth pointed to a particular spot for Alice's benefit. "The Bradleys, it seems, had a rather tough time of it. This one, a later generation, was lost at sea after the Civil War, when Cape mariners, if they wanted to sail at all, freighted coal around. This poor fellow, Sears Bradley, was burned up when his cargo of coal ignited spontaneously. Sometimes coal did that." Elizabeth nodded knowledgeably. "In his youth, Sears Bradley married—you can see her name here, beside his—married a young lady whose name was Angelina Winslow, and a fetching young thing she must have been, as you'll see. Of this marriage there were three sons—the eldest of whom is your father, Alice. Am I not correct?"

Alice did not dignify Elizabeth's performance with an answer; in fact, Elizabeth had not expected one.

"The youngest of the three sons is the father of your cousin Tim. Am I not correct?" Elizabeth's eyes were steady on Alice. This time she waited for an answer.

"Yes, of course you are," Alice said firmly.

"Now to the subject at hand, the lady who was your Uncle David's mother, and who was also your father's mother—the mutual grandmother of yourself and your cousin Tim—Angelina Winslow. Do you remember her?"

"No."

"It doesn't matter. Because in any case, I am quite sure you are unaware that she was Kingsley Merrick's mistress."

For an instant Alice neither moved nor breathed, and then she sat back in her chair, her composure unbroken. "My grandmother was my grandfather's mistress?" Her smile was sardonic. "Really, Elizabeth!" she laughed.

"I see nothing very amusing about it," Elizabeth said grimly.

"I see nothing believable about it," Alice said calmly. "It's probably just village gossip."

"It isn't gossip, and I can prove it."

"Go ahead," she said carelessly, her control superb. "If you think it matters."

Elizabeth elaborately looked in a desk drawer. "I have a document here, written by *our* grandmother, yours and mine. Julia Merrick. And her signature is witnessed, too, in case doubt should ever arise as to its author. In it she states unequivocally that Angelina Winslow and Kingsley Merrick were lovers. She states that the result of this liaison was a bastard son—raised by Sears Bradley, who was naturally unaware of the child's paternity—and she further states that this information was given her maliciously by the child's own mother, Angelina Winslow, whom she considers a rather reliable source, all things considered." Elizabeth smiled. "Julia Merrick wrote this document because she was afraid that someday someone might need to know about its contents.

Waterford, after all, is a small town, and its inhabitants tend to intermarry." She skewered Alice with a piercingly significant stare. Alice was noticeably pale now. Elizabeth shifted her gaze to Emily. "You were aware that Kingsley and Julia Merrick were cousins? Consanguineous marriages were not uncommon in an earlier day, though naturally, among the enlightened, it is never practiced now. But Kingsley and Julia Merrick learned the hard way. Their eldest daughter, Caroline, certainly proved that the Merricks have intermarried long enough. You do know about Caroline?"

"Stop," said Alice. "Just stop."

"Who was Caroline?" Emily asked, confused by this new family member of whom she had never heard. "What does she prove?"

"She was feebleminded." Elizabeth pressed forward relentlessly. "And the point is that she was a product of the marriage of Merrick cousins, and the weakness she demonstrated could well show again in another consanguineous marriage. The possibility certainly exists. And so it is my duty to make sure that such an eventuality never comes to pass. It is my duty to point out that the bastard son of Kingsley Merrick and Angelina Winslow is Tim Bradley's father, the respectable David Bradley of Worcester and Newport."

David Bradley—a bastard!

"And that as a Merrick, David Bradley may have passed to your cousin Tim certain undesirable traits."

She impaled Alice with her cold, cruel gaze.

"That's none of your business," Alice said. "It's none of your filthy business. Just leave me alone, Elizabeth!"

"But, my dear!" exclaimed Elizabeth in mock surprise. "However can I? There's just about only one way you and young Timothy could be more closely related than you are, and that is if you were brother and sister. It would be positively unclean if you were to marry—but perhaps you ought to read this document, which Julia Merrick commissioned me to show to whoever required it. So you will understand, once and for all, that I haven't dreamed up all this."

Alice held out a less-than-steady hand and took the document, broke the seal. Silence gathered heavily as she read, and the sun splashed on the rugs and the gold-lettered book bindings. There was a pause in which Emily was virtually certain that Alice was no longer reading, though her eyes were still glued to the writing of Julia Merrick.

"Do you really think anyone would believe this garbage, Elizabeth? Do you really think anyone would credit it?"

"I believe that when he learns that he is Kingsley Merrick's illegitimate son, Mr. David Bradley will be extremely disturbed and upset. I believe when everyone else learns it, he will be ruined. When your own father, John Bradley, learns of this, his disappointment and distress will be profound—and his health is none too robust these days, I understand. And then there's David's son, isn't there?" Alice looked up from the damning document. "Not a nice thing to learn about your father, is it? And I understand that Timothy is fond of his sire?"

"You just cut that out," Alice said fiercely, on her feet now. "Tim isn't bound by convention like you are. He understands his father's worth."

"How noble," remarked Elizabeth. "I'll be interested to know how he feels should it turn out that David Bradley can't stand up to the truth. I'd like to know how he'd feel should any harm—self-inflicted or otherwise—occur as a result of public sneers or private qualms. Victorians being so . . . so sensitive about such things." Alice was backing toward the library door as one would back away from a snake. "Make no mistake, Alice. Should it come to my attention that a marriage between you and Tim is going forward, I will be compelled to show this document to anyone who has any interest in seeing it. And should I see you at any—I repeat—any gathering of which I am a part—I would name the Fall Festival explicitly—why, I'll show it to all and sundry upon that occasion, too. And don't make the mistake of thinking I wouldn't do such a thing. I would, without a qualm. Emily, would you show Alice to the door?"

She could not make herself look at Alice, but blindly led her away, back through the parlor and off the porch, too ashamed and stunned to speak, unable to tear herself away from Alice's side.

"I always did oppose the marriage of cousins," Alice said tonelessly. "Any educated person opposes consanguinity. I should have stuck to my guns."

"What changed your mind?"

"Tim did." She smiled despite her obvious distress, and at the sight of that smile Emily hastily changed the subject.

"Was Caroline Merrick really feebleminded?"

"Yes, she was. She ran off with the coachman's son, just to prove it."

"I should have thought you'd believe that evidence of intelligence. Mixing with the lower orders, I mean, seeing their true value."

Alice did not hear the sarcasm. "The coachman's son married her for her money," she said, stopping by a tree, reaching out as though to anchor herself. "He left her as soon as her mother disinherited her, and the poor thing died in the birth of her child—and the child died too. And that was that." Leaning on the tree, Alice closed her eyes, but the tears she was trying to hold back escaped. "Uncle David really is a Victorian, just as Elizabeth says. And so is my father. Did you know that Daddy and my mother weren't lovers? All the years that their friendship stayed alive and they met one another secretly, they weren't lovers. Trite, isn't it? I mean, who cares?"

She looked up at the sky between the tree branches. "Who cares?" she repeated, and then looked at Emily. "They care, damn them. They care. Awfully. It's so important to them. All that stuff—virginity and chastity and fidelity and the sacredness of marriage. God knows what it would do to them if they thought that their own mother had sported about with the honorable Kingsley Merrick."

Helplessly Emily stood there, watching, and Alice's eyes changed, and became cold, hostile. "Please excuse me, Emily," she said icily. "I must go home and fix supper for my father and my cousin. I trust I won't be seeing you again soon. I hope not, anyway."

She turned and walked away and did not look back, and Emily, besieged with conflicting emotions, could only watch as Alice became smaller and smaller.

So. Elizabeth held the whip hand, after all, and did not hesitate to use it.

An exercise of the rawest sort of power. Unpleasant to watch; yet even now, as Alice disappeared, Emily's disgust at Elizabeth's wickedness was fading in favor of hope—hope that with Alice firmly, inexorably out of the picture, perhaps Tim would come back of his own accord. That would be far preferable to presenting him with the unpalatable possibility that he'd got her in trouble, using his decency as a weapon, forcing him to marry her. Besides, she wouldn't know for sure whether she was pregnant for yet another month. So she would wait, and in that interval hope—hope that he would come to her.

For surely Tim Bradley must care about her—care deeply, despite his involvement with his cousin, which, after all, had been in existence long before he had met Emily Merrick. But once Alice returned to her former place, unattainable, untouchable, Tim would surely turn to Emily and he would marry her, because whether he knew it or not, he loved her, and she would make him happy because she loved him, better than Alice or any other woman could.

And if he didn't, and if, indeed, she had conceived his child . . .

She did not care to think about it. The prospect was too horrible, too impossible; she put it right out of her mind, into the limbo of the untenable.

And waited.

7

" 'Board!" the conductor bawled. " 'Board!" His voice was hollow, long-carrying, the word drawn out to its fullest. Outside the windows the milling crowd moved even more vigorously, as though stirred with an invisible spoon, and among them redcaps strove to swim upstream with their baggage carts. In the crowded compartment, Mother tearfully reached out to embrace Emily, and Daddy's long arms embraced the two of them together; Mother embraced Charles next, and Charles's Mater switched places and embraced Emily, and Daddy shook Charles's hand. A porter appeared with a basket of flowers to add to the rest and a bucket full of ice which was conspicuously devoid of any bottle. The porter winked at Charles.

"You folks will have to go now," he said apologetically to

those who were obviously parents. His gleaming black visage wrinkled into a smile of subservient joy. Such a happy occasion as the sending off of a newly married couple ought to rate a considerable tip; carefully making sure the smile was firmly affixed, he assisted the ladies to find the little metal steps to the platform, their last link with the puffing, flatulent train, raising his red boxy cap to each, happily pocketing the five-dollar bill Daddy gave him.

The train shook a little as it fired up to even a steeper pitch, poised and ready to leave South Station. With an enormous snort it rolled an inch, paused.

There had been an east wind as they'd driven to the station, smelling of salt and clams and wet pilings and seaweed, and it brought home to Emily forcefully the fact that she wouldn't smell an east wind for a long while, nor see the darkened, old and twisted city for a long time. Desperately she looked out the window, hoping for a last glance, but no part of Boston could be seen from the trainyard here. Below on the platform her parents smiled bravely and Charles's Mater blew them kiss after kiss and the train lurched, shuddered, and then, shouldering the yoke, leaned into it and steadily pulled. The home folks, waving frantically, slid to the right, and over her shoulder Charles waved gaily, breathing down her neck, and then they were gone, and she was alone with the husband she had chosen.

A discreet knock at the door, a murmur; Charles went to it and received the proffered basket, tipping lavishly, and brought in the hidden champagne.

"Oh, Charles, what a treat!" she exclaimed. The wedding and the reception had been abysmally dry because of Mater's insistence on observing the law, and Emily was as grateful as Charles to have a little something to oil the ways.

"I though a bit of the bubbly would hit the spot just about now," he agreed, sitting beside her on the red plush seat, drawing the ice bucket up between his legs and working the bottles into it so that they would chill. Reaching into a basket of fruit, he withdrew two champagne glasses, knocking them together so that they gave a clear ring. Ribbons were tied to the stems of each, and a corkscrew lay among the bananas and apples.

"Why, Charles, you've thought of everything," she said admiringly. "Just everything."

"Indeed I have," he said proudly. "In that basket over

there is cheese and crackers and anchovy paste and sardines, too. All arranged by me, my dove."

"Well!"

"I thought we'd get hungry sometime," he said. "And the thought of lurching around in the dining car wasn't very appealing."

Clearly she was going to be stuck in here with him for the duration! "The redcap can bring us anything we need," she said bravely. "I think it's a fine idea, Charles."

"Do you suppose that champagne has got any chill to it at all?" he wondered wistfully.

"There's only one way to find out."

"Right!" He withdrew a bottle from the ice. It took considerable fussing to extract the cork, which boomeranged off the ceiling, its explosion by now nearly unnoticeable over the racketing of the train, its squeals and clatters and groans. He poured a little for himself, testing it with concentration, swishing it around in his mouth, swallowed it.

"Very nice," he said. "But definitely not cold."

"Maybe it is, farther down."

"Good show! We'll try." He poured her a full glass and one for himself, set it and the bucket to one side. "To you, my dearest. To us." They touched the glasses, whose ring was muted this time because of the wine, and she drank hers without stopping. "More?" She held out her glass, and he filled it and again his own.

"To you, Charles," she said, her glass bumping his. "To the future, the years together." She was beginning to float a little; if she drank the champagne judiciously, she'd float all evening. And she'd need to! She leaned back against Charles's chest.

"Ah, Emily," he breathed. "At last." He set his empty glass on the floor by the bucket, drawing her nearer. Champagne from her glass slopped onto her silk traveling dress. "I can't even begin to tell you what it means to me, that you should be my wife."

"Dear Charles," she murmured, taking a sip of the champagne so that he wouldn't kiss her. He's just a boy, she told herself, and eager like a boy. Relax.

"I know you must be tired, sweeting," Charles murmured, working on the top button of her dress. "But I've gone along with this abstinence business just as long as I can. Though it seemed silly—I mean, since we've already been lovers—I was willing because I'm so crazy about you, Em, and want to make you happy. But I just can't wait anymore."

Yes, the silly ass believed that they'd already Done It! That was why he consented to marry her now, in October, instead of waiting until December, as he'd originally planned. Consented? Insisted, because he'd found her naked beside him in the car, weeping with what he'd believed to be desolation at losing her virginity—the fool! The fool!

She'd been willing, God knew. They'd parked in the woods with a bottle of gin, to celebrate their impending engagement, and she had it all figured out. She'd wait until he got tight, she'd allow him all the liberties he'd always clamored for and that she'd always denied him. And what came naturally would take care of her dilemma—and the unwanted pregnancy brought on her by Tim Bradley, who had not come to her, upon being turned down by his cousin, but who instead had run away to sea on a tramp steamer so that there was no way she could get word to him. The pregnancy, therefore, would have to be screened by Charles Sinclaire, who would insist on marrying her immediately, once he'd had his way with her, because a gentleman always married a lady whom he believed he'd deflowered.

And she'd made him believe it!

Her dress and undergarments were down to her waist by now, and he was happily squeezing her breasts, fingering her nipples and kissing them while she drank the champagne, and in between maulings, poured more, hoping to make herself numb, hoping to anesthetize herself. For she must not hold back. After all, Charles believed that all this had happened before, and she must make sure that he continued to believe it.

And indeed, the scenario was the same, the same offering of the preliminaries, the same joyous acceptance of them.

"Emily, darling, sweeting, my dove," he had sighed. "You've never been like this before."

"I've never been engaged to you before," she had said, wishing she were more drunk as she accepted the stroking of his hands. "Why do you think I've been so prim before, Charles? Surely not because I didn't like you!"

"Sweeting," he said, "I just never could tell what the hell you had in mind." He put his lips on hers again, heavily, and continued to press, knead, and fondle freely, because it was his right; they were engaged to be married, and on the morrow would announce it. She was unsure of how long she should allow it, or of how long she could stand it. Probably nature would take care of itself, if she were patient, she thought, and she waited.

"Emily," he said shakily, "since we're engaged, darling, may I take the rest of your clothes off?" He hiccoughed.

"Why, no!" she exclaimed coyly, drawing away. "I'd catch cold."

"But I have a blanket. In the rumble seat."

"The rumble seat is out," she said firmly. "It'd be much too cold in the rumble seat, and that is that."

"I didn't have in mind sitting there," he said carefully around his thickened tongue.

"What did you have in mind?"

"I'll show you." Somehow he extricated himself from under the wheel, letting himself out into the cool October night, supporting and guiding himself by leaning on the car, feeling his way to the back of it. Then he maneuvered himself into the backseat, dragging the blanket.

"Come on, right here," he coaxed, patting the leather seat beside himself.

She would not have to persuade him at all. She would only have to fall into his arms as though he were impossible to resist. With an ego like his, he'd easily believe she was so crazy about him she was unable to restrain herself.

"All right." She took an enormous gulp of liquor, and could feel herself floating as she swallowed it, the world becoming smaller as though seen backwards in a telescope, and she handed the bottle to Charles and then climbed over the seat and into his lap.

"Ah hah!" he smirked, and put a hand on either breast, squeezed. She smiled, made herself go on smiling as though she liked it.

"I really feel you ought to have your clothes off," he said, sweat breaking out on his forehead. He pulled the blanket around her like a tent, and she took its edges and wrapped him in it, too.

"Maybe we should rest a bit, first?" she invited, to get him prone and that much closer to where he'd need to be.

"All right," he said with a crooked grin, and fell over, pulling her down beside him. "Tuck that blanket around my chin, won't you, sweet?" he slurred, and instantly his breathing was deep.

"Charles?" she whispered.

There was no answer.

"Charles!" she called, but there was only a snore, indicating that he was alive. She held a tight rein on her panic, considering the situation from all angles while she huddled beneath the rough blanket.

The moron! Given his chance at last, it was just like Charles to flub his lines. It was more than annoying, though. In this case it could be disastrous, for he must—he must!—have sexual intercourse with her, and he must do it tonight, drunk or not.

Whether he knew it or not!

Whether he remembered it or not!

Perhaps he could be made to believe he already had?

After all, even had her plans gone according to schedule, he still might have passed out afterward and woken up without recollection of anything.

As gently as possible she unbuckled his belt, undid his fly, untucked his shirt; as gently as possible she lay back, covered them both with the blanket, and waited for him to revive, to discover the dismayed, deflowered virgin (herself) weeping, inconsolable, rescued only by marriage. Marriage now, to redeem her honor. . . .

As she lay there beside him, she could not help but feel satisfied with herself. You got off easy this time, she told herself. One day you'll have to go the whole way with him—one day very soon—but not now. Not now, and not for a while, for surely she could coax him into abstinence.

Their marriage would be more meaningful, she insisted, if they entered it as chastely as possible. Just one slip in the height of passion didn't justify connubial arrangements whenever they felt like it. Didn't Charles agree?

Reluctantly he did.

"But the great day has finally arrived," he was saying, trying to conceal his eagerness. "There's no reason to put me off any longer, is there?" Rural Massachusetts flashed by.

"Oh, no, Charles, none at all," she agreed, finishing the champagne in a gulp. "But perhaps we ought to rest a little," she temporized. "If you're tired, sometimes things are difficult. Particularly if you're nervous," she added desperately.

"Who's nervous?" he asked.

"You'd better pull down the window shade, then," she murmured, her hands sweating. "And lock the door."

He complied, and the afternoon light, shining in only at the bottom of the window, became dusky and the rattling room intimate. He turned back to her, staring at her breasts that hung free and jiggled a bit with the motion of the train, and she tried not to feel self-conscious.

He reached for her hands with both of his. "Won't you stand up?" he asked, his voice polite, strained. "I can get your dress off easier if you do."

She stood, braced against the sway of the train with a hand on one wall of the compartment, the other on the bulge that was the upper bunk, while Charles fumbled at and peeled off her dress and slip and then stopped in dismay at the more complicated fastenings of her girdle and garters. "Perhaps you had better do the rest." He grinned sheepishly while she removed her girdle, her stockings, and her step-ins, he gazed in approval and then he unbuttoned his shirt and removed it, and his undershirt too, which had narrow straps over his shoulders.

He is your husband, she told herself. He has the right to look at you, and she smiled as he came to her, to kiss her lips hard as he always did, because he thought kissing should be passionate, and then, because he was her husband, he stooped to kiss her breasts, too, raking their nipples with his teeth. It hurt, because he had been too rough.

"Be careful," she whispered. "You're hurting me, Charles." But the clacking of the train covered her whisper so that he did not hear, and she held herself still until she could stand it no longer, edging away with a little smile that she hoped was encouraging, that would, perhaps, indicate that she was ready to try the prickly couch.

He stripped off his trousers, revealing his thin, white legs with garters that twisted around his calves to hold his stockings up; he kicked away the trousers and took off his undershorts and approached her once again, to gather her close, rubbing her skin against his.

"You are so lovely!" he declared. "Your body is flawless, Emily."

"Not really," she demurred in an attempt at modesty. "It's only because you think so, Charles. But I'm glad you do!" In wifely fashion she put her hands on either side of his head, drawing his lips to hers and kissing them lightly, and felt the cold metal wall against her back as he pushed her nakedness against it, his mouth clamped tightly against hers and his whole body grating against her, his groin grinding harder, harder, as though he could press from her what he wanted and needed. The hardness of the metal hurt, and the hardness of his boniness hurt.

She had no idea he was so strong, and knew she would have to tell him he was too rough, even at the risk of wounding him, because he was just too vehement, nearly brutal in his eagerness.

He released her abruptly, stepping back, looking down, and she followed his gaze: the flag of his manhood drooped listlessly, flaccid, waving with the sway of the train. Transfixed, her thinking stopped, her being paused, a moment of time escaped her notice.

"You've duped me," he said.

She tore her gaze from his profoundly uninterested member, to his face, to his burning, blazing eyes.

"You tricked me, didn't you?"

She was not able to understand, nearly incapable of speech.

"You . . . you must be tired, Charles. You're nervous," she fumbled. "You need a good night's sleep, is all!"

His open hand hit her face so violently that her head bounced hard against the metal wall behind her, and sparks whirled up, as though a log had been thrown on a night fire.

"Charles!" she cried.

He hit her again, his lip curled in fury, his face terrible, and then he seized her wrist and twisted it and pain ran up her arm to her shoulder. He twisted it farther, forcing her to her knees.

"We never did it that night in my car, did we?" His voice revealed nothing, its very tonelessness terrifying, and she knew she was in trouble, terrible trouble. Her face and lips throbbed where he had struck her, her arm nearly numb, until, impatient at her hesitation, Charles wrenched it and the periphery of the compartment went black. "Answer me, Emily."

"Yes," she whispered, swamped in torment. "Yes. I tricked you."

He released her, straightened up, steadying himself against the wall of the car, and clad as he was, in only his stockings and garters, there was no denying that which she had never suspected.

Charles Steven Sinclaire was impotent.

Slowly, slowly, she stood, backed up to the door for support, daring hardly to breathe, certainly not daring to take her eyes off him. She held her right arm with her left to ease its aching, waited, tense, terrified.

"It never occurred to me to doubt you." There was hatred

in his face. "There you were, moaning and groaning about your virginity. So naturally I reached the only possible conclusion—the one that I wanted so much to be true. And, I'm sure, the one you counted on." Shame and despair covered her; she closed her eyes, turned her face away.

"Will you please look at me when I'm talking to you, Emily?" His voice dripped patience like acid; the absurd boy she'd known all her life had disappeared entirely, and she saw a Charles she'd never known before, cold and calculating, fearless and formidable. Reluctantly she looked. Her heart was pounding, her blood racing so fast through her ears that it was difficult to hear as he said, "I've loved you a long time; you excited me more than any other girl had ever done—though God knows I've tried enough of them. And tried hard enough! I always thought that with you things would be different. I never had to pretend to be excited when I touched you—I was so sure, so sure." He paused, and she knew his despair and disappointment were deep.

"I'm sorry," she whispered, but he did not hear over the rattling train.

"I think I have the right to know why you made such an ass of me. Don't you?" he asked conversationally. He reached for a small suitcase beneath the window and laid it flat, sat upon it so that he could look up at her in comfort. She had never stood naked in front of anyone before, and she longed for concealment. Her thighs were trembling, their muscles burning with fatigue and tension, her arm setting up a violent ache, her face throbbing. It was a nightmare of a proportion she had never known could happen.

"Are you going to answer my question?" he asked.

"I needed you to marry me because . . ."

"What? You'll have to speak more loudly. I can barely hear you."

"I needed you to marry me because I'm going to have a baby," she made herself say more loudly.

"Speak up! You're mumbling, Emily."

"I'm going to have a baby," she called, trying to meet his eyes and failing.

"Whose baby?"

She could not bring herself to answer.

"Whose baby?" he repeated mercilessly.

"Please," she whispered, her eyes smarting because of the hot tears filling them.

"I'll ask only once more," he said, and she dared not provoke him further.

"Tim Bradley's," she said around the obstruction in her throat.

"Ah." He leaned back against the wall beneath the window, where daylight flickered and leaped behind the drawn shade. He looked her over slowly, with deliberate rudeness. "I thought you loved him. I asked you if you did. Do you remember?"

"Yes, I remember." She was weeping now.

"Did you tell him he had fathered your child?"

"No."

"Why not?"

"He . . . he left Waterford before I got the chance, and no one knew where he'd gone."

"Left you high and dry, eh?"

"Yes," she whispered, the hurt of it riled up by his probing, as he intended it should.

"So you turned to me, because you knew I was more than eager to marry you!"

There was no answer that would not offend him, and her tears dried in the face of the immediate present, the immediate problem—Charles Sinclaire, who had turned out so differently from what she had ever dreamed. What could she say to him that would make things all right?

"Is that it, Emily? You turned to me because you figured I was a pushover?"

"You'd already asked me," she said shakily. "All I needed to do was get you to marry me right away, instead of waiting for the usual engagement."

"And so you staged that production in my car."

Her mouth was so dry she couldn't even swallow. The train lurched around a bend and flung her against the seat, and thankfully she sank onto it, less visible—and less vulnerable, she hoped.

"What did you plan on doing when your pregnancy became so far advanced that even I—dunce that you take me for—would catch on?" he asked, pivoting on the suitcase in order to face her.

"Charles, I never—"

"Stick to the subject at hand, Em. What were your schemes?"

"I . . . I knew I couldn't hide forever, Charles. But I'd be gone from home and from everyone who knew me. I wouldn't have to face my parents—or the future as an unwed mother, the shame and ridicule. . . . I thought I could count on you to be understanding. To help."

He said nothing.

"Charles, Charles, I'm sorry I stooped to such shabby behavior," she pleaded. "But I knew you were . . . attracted to me, and I believed I could make you a good wife. I still believe I can, regardless of . . ." She could not prevent her eyes from straying to that part of his anatomy which had betrayed them both. When she looked up, he was watching her.

"Perhaps you're right," he said.

Was there a chance he would accept this apology, this offer?

"After all," he mused, "you are very attractive, Em. Any man would be proud to claim you as his wife."

The hope that bounded irrepressibly must have shone from her eyes, for he smiled then.

"Perhaps you'd even prove helpful, given time," he speculated.

"Oh, Charles!" she cried eagerly. "I'd try!" Perhaps there *was* hope!

"I've never had a woman of my own before. One who'd do whatever I asked, who'd explore the possibilities with me. All of them." His gaze sharpened, and she felt her eager relief draining away.

Instinctively she drew back. He was virtually unknown to her. All along he'd been disguised as a bumbling boy—but he wasn't. He was a man whose temperament and basic makeup were so foreign to her and so alien to her experience that she had no way of predicting what he would want or need or demand.

"Whores have ways of giving people like me a good time. Would you be willing to do what whores do, Emily?"

"I don't know what it is they do," she said shakily.

"Oh, I'd instruct you. It would be my pleasure, instructing you. There are things that a woman can do to a man that are just about guaranteed. And there are things that a man can do to a woman which tend to be somewhat exciting to him." Indeed, there was evidence already that Charles found it so even in the contemplation. She wrenched her eyes back to his face. He was watching her minutely from his suitcase. "I think exploring the possibilities together might be a fair exchange for giving Tim Bradley's child my name—don't you?"

Words were not possible. She could only stare.

"What about it?" Charles asked.

It was hideous, devoid of love or kindness, far from the tender, unfettered sharing she'd known with Tim Bradley, and it would always be. It was like being turned out of the Garden and into the desert, to burn and suffer and labor—and perhaps she deserved it.

"I'm waiting," Charles said.

Was it possible? Could she live with it? It was as blatant a proposition as anyone could make. There was a graceless gap between what was going to happen if she agreed and what it would politely be called, a gap she could not get around but would have to face day after day. Yet the alternative was going home to public scrutiny and judgment, living with the consequences until she died.

"Well?"

She would have to do it. She would have to in order to keep her child and Tim's, to avoid the horrors of illegitimate pregnancy, of giving birth to a child in a place where unwed mothers went, of having to give it away—a part of herself wandering alone in the world, unprotected.

She'd just have to live in the desert as best she could, was all. She'd have to take it and be thankful that Charles had provided a way out, even if that way was not to her liking. She'd have to take whatever comfort she could from the fact that no one would ever know—about any of it.

"All right," she heard herself saying.

The corners of Charles's mouth upturned, and his face grew flushed in the anticipation of his every salacious dream fulfilled in a manner unhurried, enjoyed to the last drop.

"Ah," he breathed, and slowly he reached for her. "Well, then, first things first, don't you agree?" He met her eyes levelly, without apology or shame, and pushed her legs apart. "Let's see what you look like."

Raking, searing mortification washed over her, and appalling dread rose up. "No!" she cried, and struck his hands aside.

He did not rush her, nor did he raise his voice.

"The first discipline you will have to accept," he said steadily, "is the discipline over yourself. When I ask a thing of you, I expect your cooperation. If I indicate"—he waved in a spreading motion—"that I want you to open up, you will do it. And anything else I ask." The smile had gone. The lust of his fantasies gleamed in his eyes, and his face was lewd. "I'm waiting," he said softly, and she knew he would not wait much longer.

She closed her eyes tight, forbade herself thought, and made herself comply. Somehow she would find a way to hide her sentient being, to inure her inner self, find a way to endure.

Tim . . . oh, Tim, she thought. See what you have done to me.

The child within her stirred.

II

Steven

8

The stairs turned back on themselves, and Steven peeked carefully around the corner, past the banister and through the carved wooden spindles. Below stood his father going over the day's mail, and now Father had reached the report card, which Steven himself had slipped beneath everything else in an effort to delay this dreaded moment. He watched, his anxiety gnawing at him, hands sweating. Would Father come upstairs after him, determined to have it out now? Or would he wait? . . .

The expression on Father's face did not change; he turned the card over to read the remarks written on the back and then placed it deliberately on the mahogany desk, picked up the Camp Quivet folder that had also come today in Mr. Wood's huge leather pouch, turning to the window's light to better see the picture on its cover. His glasses with their gold frames flashed, and, panic-stricken lest he be seen, Steven quickly ducked back, out of sight, waited until his heart became calm again, and again took up its usual uninterrupted, mindless trotting through life.

Your life depended on your heart beating, beating, whether you thought about it or not, Steven knew, and there wasn't any way, in the year 1939, to make it start again once it had stopped. Sometimes people came to life again, when their heart stopped—like on an operating table. They said God had made them live again, but once they had met Him (they said), they'd have rather stayed dead. . . .

Father was in the kitchen now, where Mom was fixing dinner, their mumbled conversation rising, falling, Mom's voice high and Father's low. Either they were discussing Camp Quivet, described in the brochure, or the report card, or both, and the thought of discussing them, either one, of having to wait until Father made up his mind about them—the very thought of it sent Steven's heart to his shoes, where it thumped on undisturbed, regardless of his dismay, beating its own time like the metronome on the Sinclaire piano which challenged him to keep up with it when he practiced that hated instrument.

Now that his parents were in the kitchen, their voices would hide any noise he might make. He hung on to the railing, treading at the farthest edge of each stair step, a maneuver that would keep the treads from squeaking, and like a shadow slipped into his own room. Quietly he closed the door, and the distant murmuring from the kitchen was abruptly stopped as though a radio somewhere had been snapped off. It was a large house, sixty or seventy years old (which, for Port Huron, Ohio, was old indeed), and it was more sturdily built than houses being constructed today, Father said (although no houses were being built that Steven knew of), and because it was old and sturdy, when you shut a door you shut out everything else, too. The house had high ceilings and massive amounts of dark woodwork, and had a grace that the bungalow of today simply could not compete with (Father said), but, of course, if you'd lost all your money in the depression, like some people he knew, you'd be glad of a doghouse to live in.

He was referring to Mom's father, Grandpa Merrick, when he said such a thing. Grandpa had jumped out of a window a long time ago, when Steven was a baby, because he had lost all his money in the crash. Grandmother Merrick had been required to give her house in Milton to the bank, and she had moved into the big house in Waterford with Cousin Elizabeth Edgarton, and Father sent her money—Steven knew about that, too, because Father always made quite a production of it. Father's own mother, whom he called Mater, had been supported by him, too, but he did not support her now, because she was dead. She had died before Steven could remember her, and now there was only Grandmother Merrick to whom father gave money so she would not have to live in a doghouse, or here, in Port Huron, in this large and sturdily built house equipped with heavy solid doors that shut out distraction and noise. . . .

And because the doors cut out distraction, Father said, there could be no excuse for not concentrating when you were doing your homework. And therefore no excuse for a C in arithmetic (which Father knew about now because he had Steven's report card). He would not like that C! Oh, hell, he whispered daringly. Oh, hell . . . oh, hell . . . oh, hell!

The tightrope upon which Steven walked day by day, hour to hour, stretched endlessly into the days that lay ahead, and miserably he tried to steady himself in order not to fall off. Tonight he must cope with Father—tomorrow it would be Spike McCloskey, with whom he had competed all his life in order to avoid being cut off from the other kids. Spike McCloskey resented him and always had, and had tried to erode the allegiance of those Barton Elementary boys who were willing to accept the fact that Steven Sinclaire was a little different from everyone else, different, at least, from children born and brought up in Port Huron, Ohio.

Tomorrow he had to meet Spike at the base of the Maple Street bridge. The kids would watch while he and Spike climbed up the pylon that supported it, remaining crouched at the top until a truck rolled over and shook everything, and everyone would enjoy the show except Steven Sinclaire, who was unhappy at heights—who, in fact, was afraid of them. Had Grandfather Merrick really, of his own free will, jumped out of a window, falling, falling like a star in the August sky, knowing he could not back up?

He tried not to think about Grandfather Merrick. He tried not to think of the bridge, either, because it really proved nothing; the bridge was only a training ground for the huge trestle by the high school, which the bravest would tackle when they were old enough. But Steven had accepted the challenge of Spike McCloskey so that no one—including McCloskey—would know of his fear of heights. And because they would not know, they would continue to respect and admire him. They would continue to like him even though his grades were usually good and he took music lessons and his clothing was too neat for any self-respecting boy and his parents spoke strangely, differently from anyone else's parents, removing R's from some words, replacing them on others where they did not belong, doing strange things to A's. No, the kids would overlook this and other alien customs. They would continue to like him and they would not tease and torment him as they did Ronald Goetling, who wore glasses and lisped and once had wet his pants at school, the puddle beneath his chair damning him ever since.

On Steven's desk in his quiet, silent bedroom were the twenty arithmetic problems upon which he was supposed to be working. He slid into the desk chair hoping that they would not be as formidable as they had seemed when he'd left them to spy on Father—but they did.

Father was an engineer. He was not the sort of engineer that ran trains, but instead one that built bridges upon which trains ran, or figured out how they should be built, and he was excellent at arithmetic. Anyone could do mathematics, Father declared. All you had to do was put your mind to it. Whenever Steven received a C (which was not often), that was absolute proof that he was not putting his mind to his work. And Father always had a ready remedy for the repair of one's concentration.

Ah! His dread overtook him for a moment, and in despair he looked at the ten multiplication problems he'd done already. Four numbers on the top, three on the bottom. He'd done them carefully—as carefully as he could. Hidden somewhere in them were mistakes, and the ten left to do wouldn't be all right, either. There would always be errors on his arithmetic papers, for all the arduous, unsuccessful effort at concentration on the operations and numbers that grew vague whenever he attempted to bear down on them. And—as was the case now, when the result was a C on his card—Father would discuss everything very, very carefully, meticulously, going needlessly over the same old ground, and then the two of them would go upstairs where the broadside of Father's razor strop would be applied to the backside of Steven, and Steven would try harder. . . .

He twisted in his chair, made himself stop thinking about it, instead tried to multiply. Nine times five was forty-five, carry the four. Nine times seven is sixty-two. Carry the six. Or was it seventy-two? No, that was nine times eight, which came next in the tables. If nine times five was forty-five, then nine times six was nine more (he counted on his fingers), or fifty-four. And nine more than that (he counted again) was sixty-three, not sixty-two. But there was something to carry, wasn't there? And your answer would be wrong, if you didn't carry properly, even if your multiplication was right, and Father would get his strap, which cut and burned.

He turned away, clenching his fists, trying not to cry, and the image of the beasts in the nearby Toledo zoo rose up in his mind, lions and tigers and their kin, who paced vigorously, back and forth, the same measured three lunges, as though they would one day discover a loose bar that they had overlooked before in their frantic haste to be free. Frantic—like himself.

Desperately he skewered his attention to the remaining ten problems. If he tried with all his heart, maybe he could do enough of them now to be able to complete the assignment later, in time to listen to Amos and Andy, whose humor provided a happy respite from the rest of the week.

The glaring white damask cloth was soiled. His bread-and-butter plate had been placed a bit to the left in order to conceal the spot, and when he automatically adjusted the plate, there it was. Quickly he slid the plate back again, to its position of camouflage. His mother, he instantly understood, had hoped to get another night out of the cloth, because washing and ironing it was tedious and burdensome. Yet it was necessary.

The spotless silver, the spotless cloth (well, almost spotless) was all part of the way the Port Huron Sinclaires dined, in accordance with Sinclaire tradition, because Father wanted his son Steven to be acclimated and comfortable in the presence of gracious living. It was true that they lived in the cultural wilderness of Ohio, Father said, but that was no reason to become barbaric. Steven would one day encounter correct people doing correct things, and it would be important for him to know how to be correct, too.

If Limoges china and Tiffany silver and damask were correct, the Sinclaires were the only folks in Port Huron who were. And as a result Steven never, ever invited a friend in for dinner unless Father was away on a business trip engineering something. Upon these occasions Mom agreed to call dinner "supper" and she served it in the kitchen, like ordinary people in Port Huron did, and such friends as he had came and ate meat loaf and chocolate pudding and afterward played gin rummy with Mom at the kitchen table, and drank Coca-Cola out of the bottle.

Steven was quite sure that Father was unaware of these Sinclaire "suppers." They were a carefully guarded secret which Mom, he knew, would never betray. And they were very important in taking the curse off his Boston-born parents, both of whom, as far as Port Huron children knew or understood, had attended the Boston Tea Party, at which codfish and baked beans were served.

"If you're through, Charles, I'll clear," said Mom, and

waited for Father to indicate that she should. She slid out of her Duncan Phyfe chair and moved gracefully about the table, taking her own and Father's plates, returning for Steven's and the bread-and-butter plates, setting them down on the enamel drainboard in the kitchen, where they made quiet crashes.

"There's a spot under Steven's plate," observed Father.

"Why, yes, so there is," said Mom with surprise in her voice, as though she had not noticed.

"How'd you manage that, young man?" Father demanded facetiously. "Better launder it, Em," he said, without waiting for Steven to answer.

"I will."

She came back, reseated herself, poured Father a second cup of coffee from the gleaming percolator that sat always close to her right hand, passing the cup to Steven to give Father. The moment had come, he knew. The crab that lived in his vitals reached out with its claw and pinched sharply, cruelly, and he looked to the left of Father's place, where the report card and the Quivet envelope lay, sprinkled with rainbows that fell from Father's carved crystal goblet.

Father picked up the card. Although he'd seen it already, he pretended that he had not, turned it over, inspected the back with its deportment marks, and turned it over again.

"It's a good card, Steven. I'm very pleased." He opened it. "Except for this math grade. What seems to be the trouble here?"

"I don't know," he said, his voice carefully attentive.

"Your teacher says you seem not to care about your arithmetic."

How could a teacher know whether you cared or not! How could a teacher know how many hot tears you'd cried in the privacy of your own room because of not being able to add, subtract, multiply, and divide with the rapid ease required to finish the assignment in the correct amount of time. He looked down at the fine white threads of the damask cloth, at the now revealed spot, at his mother's coffeecup banded with gold. There was nothing he could say.

"What about it?" Father said.

"Charles, he really works hard at his arithmetic," Mom said. "You can't fault him for not trying."

"I am only faulting this grade," Father said coldly. He disliked Mom's interference. "I am trying to see that it is raised to a B next time, so that there'll be no question of the boy's entrance to Harvard." (Father always used that reason, because he wanted Steven to be an engineer, like he was. And go to Harvard as he had.)

"I'd like to get to the bottom of this. What's the difficulty, young man? You got a B last quarter. Clearly you're capable!"

"We've been doing long division," Steven offered up. "I just never can do it right."

"Do you check it by multiplying?" Father asked.

"There's never enough time."

"That," said Father, "rather depends on whether you're using your time well or not. Doesn't it?"

It was unfair! It was untrue! He did try! He did! He did!

"Doesn't it?" Father asked more sharply.

Helplessly Steven looked back at him, begging to be understood.

"Well," Father said, laying the card down. "Let's postpone your grades momentarily and discuss camp." He slid the contents of the Quivet envelope onto the tablecloth, looked at the application form, the letter that accompanied it, telling Father how much the Quivet staff looked forward to the return of Steven Sinclaire.

At the foot of the table his mother folded her hands, her face frozen into an expression of indifference, pretending that it did not matter whether Steven went to camp in Waterford or whether he stayed home. But it did matter, he knew, because she hated for him to be gone four whole weeks. He guessed Mom believed he did not love her enough to stay with her, that he betrayed her by his willingness to leave Port Huron. She did not really understand that attending Camp Quivet required a lot of sacrifices.

There was the difficulty of maintaining his position here, in Port Huron, while the kids played baseball and kick-the-can and held roller derbies on the neighborhood pavements and formed and reformed their allegiances and Spike McCloskey tried to turn everyone against him.

There was the eternal uproar at camp over merit points, earned in the pursuit of excellence and the acquisition of the bronze arrow, or a silver one, or gold (all of them phony, he'd discovered, all of them only a base metal covered in bronze, silver, or gold). Achievement, competition—he had not enjoyed that—and there was the lack of privacy, too, which he particularly minded because he was accustomed to so much of it, and the loneliness he recognized as a need for the quiet sustaining presence of his mother, who believed he did not love her enough.

Yes, attendance at Quivet was not the pleasure it appeared to be! In fact, it involved a lot of strain, but he desperately wanted to go there.

For there was the sea. And Kingsland.

The sea, or at least part of it: Cape Cod Bay, dancing in the sun and sulking in the rain and breathing deeply, creating the tide. Cape Cod Bay, which always called him out into the deep past the flats and onto its black depths, where it swelled and reached farther, farther, and the voices of boys and men at camp fell away into the distance, and his woes and worries here at home became small and time was measured by the briskness of the breeze on the sail, the tide, the currents, the wake behind, the turmoil of the water on the hull.

And before he reached camp, and upon leaving it, he would spend a little time at the big old Merrick house, which had a tower, with windows all around from which you could see the town lined up along Main Street, the trees spreading to the south and the Cape itself, its sandy north shore holding the bay like a great cup, and blue water way, way out, out to the end of the earth, so beautiful that it hurt you just to look at it. Kingsland, with its huge old trees and its high-ceilinged cool rooms and its assurance that it would remain right where it was, forever.

"Well!" said Father. "I don't see, quite, why your mother and I should spend all this money to send you to camp, when you haven't earned that privilege."

He meant the C, of course.

"I got the bronze arrow last year," he reminded Father. "You said that I could go again if I earned that."

He should not have said so, because Father did not appreciate being reminded of anything. "Your job is to do well at school, Steve, and I don't call a C good. Not at all. With a C in arithmetic, I don't think you really deserve a reward, like camp. Do you?"

"Charles," Mom said hesitantly, sitting tensely behind the coffeepot. "Perhaps the fault lies with the teacher."

"I doubt that it does, Emily," Father said. "I think the fault lies right here, with Steven. Though I'd be glad to go to school and inquire about the methods this . . ."—he looked at the card—"Miss Meegher uses. I'd be glad to discuss it with her. Would you like me to do that, Steven?"

Oh, gosh, it would be murder! It would get Miss Meegher down on him and she would harass him in those silent sneaky ways of teachers, assigning unnecessary work, making him recite more often in class, keeping him after school for the least of reasons.

"She teaches all right," he said quickly. "She tries real hard, Father. But so do I. Honest," he begged.

"She must be pretty poor at teaching grammar, if your last remarks are any example of her ability," Father remarked, leafing absently through the Quivet brochure, which had pictures in it, showing the campers in their blue shorts and white shirts and white sox and sneakers, crafting things and shooting arrows, swimming and riding and sailing, with the sea and the sky meeting in a long, endless line.

He waited.

Father put the camp brochure back, beside his fork, and picked up the Barton report card. "I'm still not sure how to find the balance here. A boy of your obviously outstanding ability ought not to be getting C in arithmetic."

"Oh, Charles!" his mother burst out. "Stop badgering him."

"I'm not badgering him. I just don't want to fall into the trap of causing Steven to think his C is being rewarded by being allowed to attend camp. I'm inclined to punish him by keeping him home this summer. That's all."

He hung his head, despairing, looked down at his hands, clasped tightly in his lap, his feet hanging just above the floor, one twisted around the other—when it came to him in a moment of certainty as swift and as sure as lightning that bolted down the Ohio sky in summer. When he knew what he would have to do, because suddenly he understood what Father wanted. His heart stopped trotting for an instant as he swallowed, feeling a little sick.

Was Quivet worth it?

He had only a few seconds more to decide; the camp brochure, lying on the table where Father had left it, turned its own stiffly bound page and revealed another picture, with white clouds reflected in the bay. The bay, that laughed and scowled and threw a trick at you, now and then, to keep you on your toes, holding freedom out there somewhere, just past the horizon.

As suddenly, his decision was made. He looked up. "I'm sorry about the C," he made himself say.

"Do you think you can improve it?"

"I don't know. But Miss Meegher is right." Something tasted bad, rising up in the back of his throat. He swallowed, fighting it, and said in self-abnegation, "I know I should have tried harder." He was committed now.

Gratified, Father relaxed. "It's a question of discipline," he said righteously, "as I've explained to you upon those other occasions when you haven't been bothered sufficiently to maintain your grade. I've warned you before that we must remedy such a situation whenever it crops up."

He said nothing, because nothing was required. Father had what he wanted now, and this night Steven Sinclaire had seen what it was.

"Go get my razor strop, and wait for me in my room."

"Yes, sir." He rose from the table and pushed his chair into its proper place, his body feeling feeble, his feet heavy, as though the soles of his shoes were cast iron. There was no need to hurry, because Father would take his time, letting the dread build up. Behind him he heard his mother say, low, nearly whispering, "Is this display necessary, Charles?"

"Of course it is," he heard his father say in his even, cool, unflustered voice. "It takes no time at all for a boy to get out of control. Pater, when he was alive, always maintained that you saved everyone a lot of grief by nipping disciplinary problems in the bud—and that you could expect to find problems in disguise nearly everywhere. In this instance, shirking math. The boy has admitted it, Emily. You heard him."

In the bathroom cabinet hung three leather straps, slick from endless honing. Father, like all the other men in Port Huron and the world, used a straight razor that could be closed into its own case, looking like the clam that had been named for it. He selected the thickest strap, because if he didn't, Father would make him come back and get it. Once he had believed that Father used the heaviest in order to make his point more forcefully, but now he knew better. . . .

His shame made him hot, as though he had demeaned himself and then shown his shame to the whole waiting world. But there was no changing it now. He took the strap to his parents' room, which was very large and had two beds, two massive dressers, two chairs. There were imposing fixtures on the wall that had been used for gas lights, once, but were not connected to anything anymore, since the house had been wired for electricity. His mother's chair was placed by the window so that she had plenty of light when she sat there and mended, and between the dressers and the chair there was plenty of space left over for the swinging of a razor strop.

"Now, young man," said Father, closing the door behind him. "If I could have that, please?"

He came around the end of the bed, his hand extended, and Steven gave the strap over.

"Well?" Father, his face set in stern lines, caressed the leather, waiting and watching while Steven turned, his whole body feeling heavier and heavier as this dreaded terrible moment rushed down on him. He unbuttoned his knickers and pulled them down to his socks, and pulled his skimpy cotton drawers down too, and leaned over to grasp his ankles, keeping his knees stiff because that was the way Father liked it. The mortifying moment had arrived in which he presented his white, bare bottom for Father's discipline.

Help me, he cried soundlessly to the faceless deity whose power had never intervened in his behalf. The blood rushed to his head and swished in his ears, and the strap whistled as Father brought it down smartly on his exposed buttocks, and he lost his grip on his ankles.

The first one was always hard.

Quickly he grasped his ankles again and felt the strain on the backs of his knees and clenched his teeth as the strap whistled again, the second blow landing beside the first, smarting, burning, cutting.

Make it be short, he begged wordlessly, without hope. Make him stop. The strop whistled again, and hurt him again, burned and cut again, and he knew what he would have to do: with the next stinging slap he fell forward on his hands and knees as though overpowered by Father's might. He folded his arms and hid his face in them, his rump high in the air, ignominiously offered in an attitude of the most abject servility, which had always brought these episodes to a quick close and which was the most loathsome aspect of the punishment. The strap whished and struck, whished and struck, whished and struck, and stopped.

He did not move. There was always a minute or two before Father told him he could get up, and this time was no exception.

"All right, then. On your feet," Father ordered at last.

Steven pulled his pants and his trousers over his smarting buttocks, and Father stood aside so that he could pass sorrowfully by, the lesson learned (whatever the lesson was). He reached the bedroom door, opened it.

"I'll fill out the Quivet application," Father said behind him. "I'll mail it in the morning."

It rose again in his throat, unspeakable and vile, but he held it back as he turned to Father, made himself smile through his tears, made his tremulous voice properly eager. "Oh, thank you, Father. Thanks a lot."

He closed the heavy door to his own room, and carefully

lowered himself, stomach down, onto his bed. His tears were soundless, pouring out as though they could wash him clean and free, but they did not cleanse him now, because his knowledge made him guilty—and he would remain guilty for as long as he remained party to Father's secret. For now he knew that Father liked to inflict hurt, that Father waited, like a spider, for the situation that would give him the chance to wound, to humiliate, torment, as this one had—that Father had always done so.

And tonight Steven had invited it, in exchange for Quivet.

He thought about tomorrow, when he'd have to sit all day on those hard desk seats at school, and about the bridge pylon and climbing it, made more difficult because he'd be sore from sitting, stiff from Father's strapping, and afraid, besides, of climbing so high. But perhaps it served him right, a just reward for inviting Father's punishment in exchange for Quivet. He would grit his teeth and he'd take it—all of it—and perhaps it would redeem this betrayal of himself.

He thought about the arithmetic that lay on his desk, where he'd left it. Painfully he edged himself off the bed and stood awhile looking at his homework. The completed problems were messy, the columns of figures were smeared with erasures, and the answers, many of them, were probably wrong. But he would do no more. The struggle that always went on, hour to hour, day to day, to balance the conflicting forces of his life and to keep them balanced had used up what he needed to finish the assignment, let alone do it correctly. He would get an F or perhaps a D depending on how many problems of those he'd already finished he'd done correctly. But there were times when a boy had to act as he saw fit, and Steven saw that he must assert something of himself now, before it was too late. What it would be too late for, he did not know. But this did not diminish the certainty that to complete the paper, to comply, was more than he could afford to do.

He snapped off the desk light and crawled back onto his bed and waited for Amos and Andy.

9

Cousin Elizabeth glared up at the smudged train windows, looking for him, waiting with her arms folded, her foot tapping as though she'd been there all morning. She was wearing a hat with a veil that tied tightly around her head and a black dress that was too long, and thick-heeled shoes that laced up, like librarians and teachers always wore. Clutched under her arm was her pocketbook, held tightly as though she were afraid someone would snatch it, and she did not flinch as the train stuttered to a stop, spraying soot and ashes and leaving her one hundred feet in the rear.

Steven retrieved his overnight bag from beneath the seat where he'd hidden it. The conductor was hauling the rest of his gear onto the platform, and Cousin Elizabeth had spotted him now, the severity of her face stretching into a tart smile as she unfolded her arms and began walking briskly toward the train steps in order to be at the bottom of them when he came down.

"Camp Quivet!" the conductor called with a grin.

Of course it was not Quivet at all; it was Yarmouth Depot, which was as far as the train went anymore, but he had held many conversations with the conductor on the connecting trip down from Boston, and the conductor had gotten him to talk a lot about camp.

"Welcome, stranger!" Cousin Elizabeth called from the bottom of the steps. "You can put his bags right over there, red cap," she instructed the conductor, who winked at Steven. The duffel, the footlocker, the tennis racket joined his overnight bag. The conductor tipped his hat, but Cousin Elizabeth did not give him any money. Instead she dismissed him with a brisk nod, motioned imperiously to the station agent to come and put the camp gear in her Model T. The agent, forsaking his other duties, came over instantly, but Cousin Elizabeth did not give him money, either. These services, apparently, were due her; the agent saluted, as though happy for the opportunity to help, and Steven climbed up onto the slippery upholstery of the car, watched Elizabeth do all the wonderful things she knew how to do with the levers on the steering post and the pedals on the floor. He waved to the conductor, who, still standing by the train, waved back. Cousin Elizabeth gripped the wheel with both hands, aimed the car onto its proper course north to route six, Cape Cod's principal highway.

"How was the trip?" she asked.

"Fine."

"I hope you aren't too tired."

"Not too," he acknowledged.

"I've got your room all aired out and ready for you," she said kindly. "If you feel like lying down for a while this afternoon, feel free to do so."

"Do you think I could spend some time up there even if I'm not tired?" he asked. Last summer, when he'd come to Quivet and had stayed with her, she had allowed him to furnish the room at the top of the tower for his very own, and had assured him that only he would ever sleep there. The room, apparently, was still his.

"Spend as much time as you like in the tower," Elizabeth said. "I'm glad you like it, Steven."

"Oh, I do!" he exclaimed, wishing there was a way he could tell her how much.

"How are your parents?" she asked quickly, so that he would not have time to thank her. Cousin Elizabeth hated sentiment.

"They're fine."

"Are they still planning to drive out at the end of the month, to pick you up?"

"They sure are." Father would not miss such an opportunity to visit Cousin Elizabeth and spend some time in the big old house which he coveted. Father considered the acquisition of Kingsland a shining goal, like the Holy Grail, in pursuit of which he always went out of his way to be cordial to Cousin Elizabeth, because his best hope of owning Kingsland was to inherit it.

It was pleasant to think that here, at least, was one thing that Father wanted and could not have for the asking, that here was one person—Elizabeth Edgarton—who controlled

Father instead of the other way around. Steven's heart always warmed at the thought of it, and his feeling toward Cousin Elizabeth was always warm, too, in consequence of this knowledge, adding to his gratitude over the tower.

The intersection of route six rushed toward them. Cousin Elizabeth turned the corner, heading east to Waterford, without looking to see if the coast was clear. She never looked. She barreled through Waterford intersections the same way, as though they had been constructed expressly for her use, and everybody in Waterford watched out for her passing. Apparently they watched in Yarmouth, too; no one was coming. The village with its old houses, small ones and large ones that were identical to Waterford's, passed sedately by as the Model T picked up speed, hit thirty miles per hour, and stayed there.

"Your grandmother is very much looking forward to seeing you," Cousin Elizabeth said, reminding him that he had forgotten to ask about her.

"I'm looking forward to seeing her," he responded politely, having forgotten her completely. "How is she?"

"Just fine. Right now she's entertaining your cousins. Otherwise, of course, she'd have come with me to meet you."

"My cousins?"

"Yes. The Long Island family is here. They'll all be looking forward to seeing you, Steven."

He would not be looking forward to seeing them, because his cousins were spoiled Easterners who looked down their noses at his gauche Midwestern ways. They were nearly rich, and even though their mother was his own mother's sister Celia, he did not like them; they would sail their boat, which they stored in Cousin Elizabeth's barn, without inviting him to join them, and, being girls, they would giggle whenever he entered the room, in order to make him feel unwanted.

But dislike them though he might, he would not let the Long Island family bother him. They were insignificant, of no consequence at all, because to his left, suddenly, just there behind the buildings that were thinning out, behind the towering old New England elms reaching successfully for one another overhead, beyond the brilliant green of the sun-splashed marshes, was the bay, spread out with gentle power to the straight, limitless horizon, omniscient, calm.

It was out there, same as it had always been, and he could not keep his eyes off it nor slow down the beating of his heart, which did not trot, but raced and ran and jumped for the joy of it, for the thrill of seeing the sea again. Yes, it was the same as it had always been, steadfast since the last time, and his soul, his whole being was emptied of all the things that persecuted and tormented it, and he was filled instead with a rising, flooding benediction that stilled him and made him strong. It was there, and it was his.

It had been worth the price.

III

The Allies

10

They watched casually, stoop-shouldered and long-armed, their knees jabbing the students in front of them. The afternoon air was crisp on their faces; the clarity of the sky bespoke autumn, and on the field the high-stepping majorettes of Morrison High School strutted, batons twinkling in the sun, flashily uniformed in deep blue outfits with gold buttons and braid.

Steven had not paid attention to girls until this year, but now, going on sixteen and large for his age—now, with his body changing fast and his voice sliding down and his daydreams fluctuating rapidly between enemy aircraft which he shot down single-handed and the girls on the calendars at the local filling station which he admired at a shy, inarticulate distance—now Steven Sinclaire was well aware of women. All this past summer he and his best friend, Ed Lamson, had discussed the merits and drawbacks of female people and had even taken one or two to the movies. At this very moment, he knew, Ed was admiring the second majorette from the left, whose curves were very apparent even at this distance. Then the band filed into the two rows of bleachers allotted for it behind the goalpost; the loudspeaker at the end of the field echoed incomprehensibly. A roar from the whole stadium went up as the teams spilled out from their respective places beneath the grandstands where they hid between halves and the cheerleaders—all girls—lined up in front of the student section. Instantly he and Ed watched them, and especially their bulky white sweaters with a large letter M on the front that bulged interestingly—and differently—on each.

"Morrison!" the cheerleaders called through their megaphones. "Morrison!" They sank to their knees, their arms outstretched as though worshiping the sun, and the students obediently yelled and clapped in unison.

"M! M! M-M-M!"

Clap. Clap. Clap-clap-clap.

The cheerleaders rose a little.

"O! O! O-O-O!"

Clap. Clap. Clap-clap-clap.

They rose a little more with each letter, then threw themselves sideways in a cartwheel on the full yell "MORRISON!" and happily Steven and Ed watched the display of revealed legs.

The cheerleaders ran back to the bench placed for their use at the base of the student section, and the teams lined up on the field. The referee's whistle blew and the spectators hooted and shouted and cheered for the squad, and the opposition scored again, lined up to kick the point after touchdown.

Steven yawned. Football was not his favorite game, and Morrison's trailing so far behind eliminated any interest he might have had in watching for its own sake. He cared only about basketball, and Ed was hooked on it too. They practiced arduously in the gym at the Congregational church after Pilgrim Fellowship, and they practiced on the Lamsons' driveway, which was concrete and smooth, and on rainy days when Father wasn't home they practiced in the Sinclaires' basement, and they went to all the Morrison games to study the strategy, the setups, the skills they would need to make the team. Tryouts would start soon, in a couple of weeks, and they had picked up three other kids to practice with them, and all five of them would show the world how basketball should be played! In the manner of boys everywhere, Steven pictured himself scoring spectacularly, playing wisely, the model of sportsmanlike conduct, admired, emulated, trailed by girls, sought after by men. . . .

"Want to get some popcorn?" asked Ed.

"Sure," he said, relinquishing his daydream. "Let's go." He leaned over Ed so that the rest of the gang could hear. "You guys want any popcorn?"

Shakey and Sam and Neil did.

Down in the bowels of the stadium an ascending howl from the spectators told them that the kicker was running to the ball. The bass drum bumped and everyone cheered, but the sounds of life above were muted and remote, as though he and Ed were under water. They ordered the popcorn, waited for the bags to be filled. A crowd of Negro boys came down, and Steven's stomach tightened in an instinctive defense against something alien to himself. Deliberately he did not look at the black boys, whose teeth flashed as they laughed, whose voices were slurred and soft as they slid snide jokes back and forth between themselves, their contemptuous glances, their mocking falsetto laughter an indictment that Steven only vaguely understood.

Their hands full, he and Ed made their way back, up where Shakey and Sam and Neil were saving their seats. In the tiered student section the social makeup of Morrison High was laid out before them like a huge Dagwood sandwich: the Negroes at the top; the tough white kids of Port Huron in the rows just below, both boys and girls, whose expectations in life were not high, who were not in college-prep classes and who took no interest in school affairs. Below them sat kids not unlike Steven and his own gang, kids who might, if life were kind, amount to something; and in front of them, the golden ones—the ones who were sure to succeed, who led clubs and who participated in school-oriented activities like the yearbook and the newspaper, and who were very smart and whose parents were well-to-do, whose fathers worked for Sommerset and King, Port Huron's largest business, and who were bound for great things when they grew up, assuming the war didn't get them first.

One of these days, Father was going to discover that Steven was not part of that golden group. If he ever got around to staying home for a while, Father would find out that Dave Farmington, and Dick Van Teassel, and Tom Beckman—all of them sons of prominent S & K personnel—were not calling the house to ask for Steven. If Father were home instead of representing Sommerset and King at the Pentagon, he'd find out soon enough about Ed and Shakey and Sam and Neil, and he wouldn't like it. He'd complain that they weren't good enough, not smart enough, not suitable companions for his son Steven. He'd disdain Ed, whose father was a supervisor at the glass plant and whose mother was an Ohio farmgirl brought belatedly to the city; he'd make Ed feel so small and uncomfortable that he'd leave and not come back. And Sam and Shakey and Neil? Why, one glance from Father and they'd scatter like leaves in a hurricane, and that would be the end of the only friends he'd ever had.

Until now, World War II had been on the horizon of their lives for so long that it seemed permanent, like a movie perpetually playing at the Paramount. But one day—perhaps soon—the announcement on the marquee would change. It would read "ALLIES VICTORIOUS," and Father would come home to stay and Steven would once again have to toe the mark—an obligation nearly forgotten since the war's beginning, because Father was gone so much of the time.

Steven did not look forward to it.

Father would demand to know why he wasn't on the newspaper or yearbook staff, why he was not the president of a club or indeed even a member of one. He would be unhappy when Steven told him that Beckman and Farmington and Van Teassel made him uncomfortable. They formed a clique when they had come into Morrison from the same elementary school and they deliberately made anyone else feel unwanted, bumbling, inept. He could hardly tell Father that he'd prefer to avoid at school what inevitably had come his way, all his life, right here at home. . . .

Mom had always helped, as well as she could. She never mentioned Steven's friends to Father, either in the letters she wrote or during Father's brief trips home. She never told Father that Steven didn't take music lessons anymore, but instead was learning junior lifesaving at the Y. Not that she and Steven had any spoken agreement about such things. Indeed, the fact of the agreement's being unspoken bound them even more closely. . . .

The opposition scored another touchdown and attention to the game waned and the adult spectators began to leave. The students stuck it out because there was going to be a record hop after the game, and along with the rest, Steven waited, and watched, and wondered about the dance and if Pam Thompson, sitting behind him higher up in the bleachers, had really meant what she'd said to him in study hall.

They had both been at the pencil sharpener.

"Going to the record hop Saturday afternoon?" she had asked.

"I don't know," he'd answered, stupid with embarrassment and self-consciousness.

Perhaps she wanted to be friends? He gambled on it. "I might go if you'd dance with me. All right?"

"Maybe." She smiled seductively, and he smiled back, trying not to glance down at her little pointed breasts that rose up under her tight sweater like twin cones. Then she was off, back to her seat before Mr. Larsen could catch them talking. Bemused by the prospect of dancing with her, he ground his pencil right down to the eraser while he considered it.

She was more wise in the ways of the world than he; any jackass could see that. She was also a little fast—or, at least, had a Reputation. She'd been going out with boys for at least a year—he'd seen her at the movies, last summer, with Spike McCloskey; and she was a good dancer—he'd watched her at other hops. He was not especially light on his feet unless he was on the basketball court . . . probably he'd step on her.

Yet if he could somehow make a good impression on her, get her to go out with him, probably she'd let him kiss her—and maybe more. If she had a Reputation, and all.

At sixteen, having dated a little and thought a lot, he was ready for more!

The score was 48–12 when the final gun popped and the crowd dispersed, the student section surging toward the school building and the gym doors. In the crowded foyer the students milled around, waiting for the members of Philodendron, the girls' literary society who sponsored the hop, to finish arranging the records, to station themselves at the door for the collection of the twenty-five-cent admission charge. The girls who were not members of Philodendron (the majority) clustered in the ladies' room, peeking around the doorway every now and then to see how many boys were there. When the first record began, they marched out en masse and into the gym, and Steven saw that Pam Thompson was among them.

A Glenn Miller record started, and the floor filled quickly. The girls, who'd clustered tightly on one side of the gym, spread out a little, making themselves more accessible, and Pam became visible. It was now or never!

It was unfortunately similar to diving off the high board at the Y, which Steven hated, because once you were airborne, you could not turn back.

He was terribly conscious of himself, marching up to Pam as if walking the plank, not daring to hesitate lest he make himself ridiculous.

"Would you like to dance?" he asked hoarsely.

She glanced around, as though hoping there would be an alternative. "All right." Her voice revealed neither pleasure nor eagerness.

She was, as he'd feared, a better dancer than he. But she knew what a girl should do and did it without waiting for his lead, twirling herself at every provocation so that her skirt swooshed out and up, revealing pretty legs. Their dancing looked good, he was sure and he was very relieved. When the record stopped, he was winded and wondering what to do next. Should he take her back to the girls' end? Turn and walk away before she beat him to it?

"Thanks for the dance," he managed to say.

"Sure thing."

"I hope I wasn't too bad at it," he apologized.

She glanced around again, then turned back to him. "Oh, you were fine." She smiled at last, but it was not possible to tell whether it was genuine or merely polite.

He wondered if he dared to ask for another dance; he didn't see Spike McCloskey approaching from behind as the introductory measures to "Heart and Soul" blatted from the loudspeakers high in the corners of the gym.

"Can I have this dance, Pam?" Spike asked.

"No," she said rudely. "This one is definitely taken." She moved a step toward Steven.

"By him?" Spike glanced his way contemptuously, his voice incredulous, as though he did not believe that Steven Sinclaire could even walk, let alone dance.

"Who'dja think?" she drawled, and held her arms up to Steven so that he could assume proper dance position. Spike threw them both a dirty look and walked away.

Pam's smile was warmer now. "I hope you don't mind," she apologized.

Mom and he had practiced ballroom dancing a lot, and "Heart and Soul" was a good number to use it on. He executed a quick turn, and Pam followed him easily, through another, and another.

"I don't mind at all." He smiled. "Especially since you dance so well." That sounded good, he thought, confident, suave.

"Gee, so do you!" she exclaimed, apparently impressed with his accomplishment. Wait until he made the varsity basketball team! She'd be positively carried off her feet!

"I guess you don't like Spike, huh?" he asked inelegantly.

"He's a creep," Pam said flatly. From the pack of tough kids, Spike was watching, and Steven was careful to dance particularly well at that end of the gym. Then he guided Pam to the other end, where they would not be so closely observed. "Do you know him?" she asked. "Because if you do, you know yourself what a creep he is."

"We both went to Barton Elementary," he told her. "I know him as well as I need to."

She laughed. "So do I," she said fervently.

"You used to go out with him, didn't you?"

"Yes, I've gone out with him," she said disdainfully, as though it was a mistake of immaturity that she did not intend to repeat. "But he's a creep. I don't go out with him now."

"Heart and Soul" wavered to a stop, and he walked Pam back to the girls' side.

"Thanks again."

"You're welcome." They turned from one another simultaneously; to do anything else would be an expression of too much interest for so new a friendship.

Eager to find Ed, he nearly mowed Spike McCloskey down. "Oh!" he exclaimed. "Sorry." He moved to the left, to go around, but Spike moved that way too.

"That's my girl you were dancing with," he said unpleasantly.

"That's not the story I heard," Steven said, stopping short, no longer attempting to avoid Spike or get away from him, a move that Spike would take as cowardice. That much he knew. After all, he'd been in competition with Spike McCloskey most of his life, up to the time he entered Morrison, anyway, when Spike had been put in the vocational track and their lives had mercifully diverged.

At a distance, Pam Thompson watched.

"Let's discuss it outside," Spike said.

"There's nothing to discuss." He was certainly not going anywhere in the darkening afternoon with this boy!

"Why, Sinclaire! I never knew you were chicken!" Spike jeered softly.

"I'm not and you know it." He wanted to speak with quiet and firm authority, but his voice cracked a little.

"I'll just bet you are, Steve-boy. I'll bet I can prove it."

Oh, cripe, he knew what was coming next. "How do you plan on doing that?" he asked scornfully, somehow pushing his voice past the sudden clutch of fear.

"Suppose you meet me at the trestle Monday after school and we'll just see who's a chicken and who's not. Okay?" Spike challenged.

"Okay," he said with valor. "If you think you're up to it, McCloskey."

Climbing the trestle was unavoidable. If he refused, he'd lose every ounce of self-respect that he'd ever had, and his friends, besides—even Ed.

But the high board at the Y was nothing in comparison.

"What did he want?" Pam asked, coming over from the girls' end.

"Nothing much," he said. In the corner Spike was watching, and it occurred to him that by accepting his challenge he had earned the right to ask Pam for another dance. "Shall we?" he asked as a particularly fast number loudly blared from the loudspeakers.

"Sure!"

He grabbed her left hand in his right and backed away as she also jived back, then toward him, ducking under his arm, twirling.

"Perhaps you'd like to come home with me after the dance," she suggested as she zipped past, her right hand in his left. "I'd get you a glass of milk and a sandwich or something."

He'd made it! He'd scored! She'd probably go out with him if he asked her now! "That's real nice of you," he said as they closed in on each other, and backed away. "But I'd rather take you to the movies. Tomorrow night. And come back for a sandwich after that," he continued, thinking that he sounded pretty smooth. "I hear John Wayne is at the Paramount."

"Yeah. I think he is."

"Would you like to go?" They moved out of the melee and into a calmer pocket where they could talk.

"Sure," she said.

"We could pick you up at seven-thirty."

"We?"

"My Mom and I."

"Your mother?"

"She can drive us," he stammered, feeling his face going red. "Unless you'd rather go on the bus. I mean, I don't have a license."

"Oh," she said shortly.

How in hell did Spike get around this impasse? he wondered. Double dating, he guessed, with another, older couple. But Steven knew no older couples, and Mom was all he had to offer.

"We'll pick you up at seven-thirty," he said doggedly.

"Okay." She turned and walked back to the girls' end, and Steven searched out Ed, hiding in the shadows of a far corner.

"What did McCloskey want?" Ed asked.

"Says Pam Thompson's his girl."

"What does he plan to do about it?"

"You can guess."

"The train trestle, huh?"

"Yeah. After school Monday."

"Are you going?"

"Sure."

"I'll go with you," Ed announced loyally. "Is it okay if the other guys come too?"

"Why not?" He shrugged, wishing he were braver, wishing there were alternatives. But there were none, he knew. Aside from the fact that physical combat was severely punished by school authorities, he did not have the courage to slug it out with anyone, let alone Spike McCloskey, who was far more practiced, let alone skilled at such things. No, it was the trestle, and he wasn't sure he had the courage for that, either. Unhappily he watched as Spike approached Pam again.

She was standing with her group, and she turned her back when she saw him coming, leaving him with no choice but to walk away, humiliated and angry.

"Gosh," muttered Ed, who had been watching too. "Is she worth it?"

"I don't know yet." Steven laughed hollowly. "But I'll find out soon, because I'm going to take her to the movies."

"You are!"

"To see John Wayne."

"Hey, man!" Ed grinned and turned to Sam and Neil and Shakey, slouching nearby. "Can you beat that?"

"Beat what?"

"He's taking her to the movies."

"Whew!" said Sam admiringly. "Hubba hubba!"

And thus was Steven Sinclaire launched into the pursuit of womankind.

11

The sky behind the high classroom windows was uniformly overcast, sliced into ordered segments by the metal-mullioned lights of glass. A wind was starting; Steven could see the bare treetops dip, rise, dip in a soundless sigh. The trestle would be bad enough without a breeze trying to blow him off it, without the wind sending spasms through the metal network of crosspieces and spans and lattices. He looked away, tried not to think about it, glanced furtively over at Spike. Spike stared back, arrogant, sure of himself. Steven could only hope that he, himself, looked arrogant, too, as he returned to his biology notes. On their margins was doodled weaponry used by the American fighting forces this October day, 1944, accurate in all the detail dear to the hearts of boys, well known to a people who were generally unmartial. But war and its accoutrements were present everywhere, like an unwanted in-law, even here in the Midwest, where the danger of invasion did not exist.

Across the aisle Ed coughed and glanced significantly to the front of the room, where the teacher in charge of study hall was on his feet, frowning, scanning the assembly, on the watch for people reading comics, and Steven flipped over the page with his tank on it and scowled at his notes on phylum Chordata as though extracting life's juices from them. Mr. Larsen walked to the rear of the room, where he suspected the back-row boys of hanky-panky (a term Larsen used generically, to cover anything he didn't like), and Pam Thompson, across the aisle and up one, took the opportunity to slip him a note.

I heard you're going to meet S by the bridge.

Please don't. You're too nice to end up in
the river.

Gratefully he glanced over to her and smiled, and on the back of her note he wrote:

If I come out of it alive, will you let me
walk you home from the next dance?

"Maybe," she wrote in big letters in her notebook, holding it up for him to see, and then turning the page as Mr. Larsen returned to the podium.

Hah! He guessed that Saturday night at the movies hadn't been a washout after all. Ever since he'd left Pam then, he'd been wondering what she'd thought of him and if he'd compared favorably with Spike.

She'd seemed interested in his conversation, hadn't resisted when he held her hand, nor, later on in the evening, when he'd put his arm across the back of the theater seat. She'd introduced him to her parents when they returned to the Thompson house, and he thought he'd impressed everyone favorably as he sat in the living room discussing the war news until Mom arrived, tooting discreetly from the car.

Perhaps Pam had expected him to kiss her. He had not planned to, not on the first date, nor, as it turned out, was there an opportunity. But an opportunity could be made, he knew, and he hoped he had impressed her enough that she'd see to the details of arranging one.

And now?

Why, her "Maybe" was an affirmation of the best sort!

He guessed he hadn't done so badly after all! It was a comforting thought—just when he needed one.

Over the teacher's desk a large clock told him that in ten minutes he would be released from the study hall. In ten minutes he and Ed would go to the locker they shared, select the books they needed to take home, collect Sam and Shakey and Neil, and go down to the river, where they would meet Spike and his gang. There would be other kids, too, watching what was by now a well-publicized contest, information of which was passed along the teenage underground, kept carefully secret because if adults found out about it they would put a stop to it. Adults always broke up anything that was fun or exciting or dangerous. But this time he'd have been relieved if someone did break it up, because surely he did not want to climb that trestle, with the now rising wind whistling through it, Spike waiting for the train on one span and himself on the other (assuming he made it to the top).

Think about something else, he counseled himself. You'll throw up if you keep on like this.

He would think about Quivet, instead, which the war had taken from him because traveling was so difficult, the trains crowded and so consistently off schedule; he had not been back to Waterford since the summer of forty-one, when he had won the golden arrow at Quivet and had been voted the best all-around camper. When camp was done, he'd spent a week at Kingsland that year, wandering aimlessly over its fifteen acres, climbing its enormous trees, poking around in the carriage barn where Elizabeth's ridiculously old car was kept, breathing in the peace-and-quiet solidity of the Merrick heritage which he shared with his mother. Now lost to him for the duration of the war.

He climbed into the cat boat, and its sails bellied and snapped in the gale-force wind, and smartly he tacked out to deep water, the little craft dancing on the waves like a filly ready for the race, and then he came about and raced back to the shore, where Pam Thompson waited to be rescued. . . .

The bell shrilled through the study hall and everyone instantly flipped books shut and flung up the hinged desk seats with vigor so that there'd be as much noise as possible, and like cattle stampeded from the room.

When he and the gang reached the river, twenty or more boys were waiting to watch the show. None of them were the school's sterling leadership, and Steven was relieved because there were no sons of Sommerset and King employees present, and therefore the possibility existed that Father would never learn of this exercise in futility.

Casually he gave his books and jacket to Ed, who took them proudly and followed him, like a spear-bearer, to the bottom of the steep bank and the river, which was gray and glassy now with the approach of winter. Above him the bridge rose up, its gleaming arches bounding across the water in three parallel leaps.

"Well, look who's here." Spike grinned. "I was afraid you wouldn't be able to make it, Sinclaire."

"I wouldn't want to let you down, McCloskey." He tried to smile, but nothing happened.

"We'd better hurry," Spike said. "Or we'll miss the three-fifteen. Unless you'd rather just forget about it."

Of all the trains in the whole of America, the three-fifteen was generally on time, or close to it, because it started in Toledo, only thirty miles away, and a successful climb to the top of the trestle included perching up there while the train slammed past eighteen inches above the croucher's head.

"Forget about it? Oh, no," Steven said with exaggerated politeness. "I've been looking forward to this all afternoon, pal."

The metal was cold, numbing his clammy hands and causing the trestle to seem even more alien. Glancing up to the top of the arch that he must climb, it seemed to him that there was no end to it, that like Jack's beanstalk it just kept growing and growing, with a giant at the top, in the form of a train. Was the river deep enough to keep him from being pounded to a pulp on the bottom if he fell? He did not know, and at that point, it seemed not to matter much.

The arches were built in X's of steel lattice, and he put his left foot in an angle of the lowest X, swung himself up. Across from him Spike mounted the corresponding arch and hitched himself along easily, quickly, like a monkey climbing a palm tree.

Christ, he couldn't do that, no matter what the cost to his reputation. He'd be lucky to even get as far as Spike had gone now; doggedly he placed his right foot in the next angle of the next X, his knees touching the rising lift of the curving arch. If he kept his eyes on his hands, and only his hands, which were so cold that they felt nothing and were nearly useless, concentrated on their placement and only on that, maybe, maybe he could do it. . . .

Spike, across from him and higher, was laughing, proudly waving at his friends below. "Scared a little, Sinclaire?" Without waiting for an answer, he scrambled up another ten feet. "Hurry, Sinclaire," he jeered. "You'll miss the train. You wouldn't want to do that, would you?"

He knew better than to look up at Spike, and said nothing, because he needed all his concentration to set his left foot in a slot . . . right hand; right foot . . . left hand; his head was cold from the breeze fanning his sweat, and below him he could see stones and branches and tin cans and trash in the bottom of the river, and the upturned faces of the kids, which were small, their features all alike at this distance, their clothing fluttering slightly in the breeze that sang in the spans. The bridge seemed to sway . . . He quickly looked back at his hands, which were frozen in their grasp, and his legs were locked and stiff.

There was no power on earth that could loosen them.

And then he knew: his real problem would be getting down again.

From the top of the span across the way, Spike's voice floated down. "Aren't you coming, Sinclaire? You chicken, man? You a little yellow around the edges?"

He hoped no one on the ground could hear, though what difference would it make? It would become abundantly clear very soon that not only did Steve Sinclaire not have what it took to climb to the top, he didn't have what it took to climb back to the bottom, either. Soon everyone would know that Sinclaire was a sissy. He grasped the arch tightly and then was horribly aware of the distant, then distressingly nearer roaring and whistling of the train, and he wrapped his arms around the span, his cheek on the metal, his teeth aching from the coldness. Oh, Jesus, here it came; the train's ponderous entrance onto the bridge shook the trestle like a dog punishing a shoe. Soot poured down; the horrendous crashing burst over him, and he opened his eyes just in time to see Spike hurtling by, the black contorted hollow of his mouth soundlessly screaming as he fell down and down, his arms and legs flapping in futile effort to catch at a strut, until he hit the water nearly flat, shivering and splintering it with the impact of his body.

And surfaced, facedown.

Without thinking further about it, Steven jumped as he'd been taught to do from the high board at the Y when he practiced junior lifesaving, arms stretched wide out and legs set in an open scissor so that when he hit the water he could snap them together, push down with his arms. If he did it right, his head wouldn't go under. He'd stay at the surface, and if the water was at least six feet deep, he would be safe. It had to be that deep. It must be!

It was. He brought his legs together and his arms down as he'd been taught to do, and stayed on the top, the way the manual said he would if he'd done it right, the breath nearly squeezed out of him by the shock of the water. He went for Spike, who was floating listlessly downstream, while the train, indifferent to the scene below, crashed and roared and stomped off the bridge.

The instructions in the manual came readily; hand cupping victim's chin, forcing head up and out of the water; arm supporting spine, sidestroke to safety. The current was stronger than he had expected, but Ed followed him, and the spectators trailed along to help pull them both out. Ed, who was taking the lifesaving course too, put an ear on Spike's chest.

"Steady and strong," he said. "Probably the impact just knocked him out."

The pages of the manual seemed to flutter before his eyes as though ruffled by the breeze, men in black bathing suits with tops like underwear doing the correct things to save people, and he wondered what artificial respiration would do to Spike if his ribs had broken. Ed busied himself arranging the boy's arms and face properly, when, mercifully, Spike stirred and coughed and then threw up water, followed by his lunch. Everyone who had crowded around politely turned away, and when they turned back it was Steve Sinclaire at whom they respectfully looked. Steve Sinclaire, who had saved Spike McCloskey by a spectacular lifesaving leap and a very professional lifesaving carry; Steve Sinclaire, strong, bold, brave, and no one thought to ask if Sinclaire had made it to the top of the bridge, thereby meeting Morrison High School's test of manliness, because it no longer mattered.

He looked up. Now, from this vantage, the train gone and the river quiet, the bridge didn't look as high or as menacing as before; he looked down at Spike, retching and groaning. "Probably he should see a doctor," he said to one of Spike's gang.

"What are we supposed to tell the doc?" sneered the boy. "They'd nail us if they thought we was climbing this bridge."

"Just say he fell in." He tried to speak kindly, but it was difficult, because the shock and the cold were getting to him now, and it was hard to control the violent shaking. Someone threw a heavy coat over his shoulders, and he acknowledged it with a grateful smile. "He should see a doctor, honest," he said urgently to Spike's friend. "The river's not clean, and he's swallowed half of it."

"Go screw yourself," muttered Spike's friend, and turned away.

He shrugged at Ed and looked up at the ring of faces that watched him with admiration. Admiration! Him! Steven Sinclaire! All of them closing ranks around him, walking back up the bank with him, leaving Spike and the four boys of his gang alone by the water.

He grinned at them, loving them all. "Well, so long," he said awkwardly. "I'd better hurry home and get into dry clothes."

"Yeah, go, man."

"Hurry."

"See you tomorrow."

He and Ed and Shakey and Sam and Neil set off then in a

hard run in an attempt to scare up some heat. The breeze blew dried leaves ahead of them, and whirlwinds of dust rose up in front of them, and Steven hardly felt his feet touch the ground.

12

Not even his wildest dreams of glory prepared him for the following day. Dozens of kids at Morrison High School spoke to him by name, some of them walloping his back or shoulder in comradely respect—even upper-classmen who had, until now, seemed infinitely remote and uninterested. At the student bookstore a pimple-faced youth in the instant adolescent response to notoriety circulated a petition nominating him (him!) for Student Council.

And Pam. Well! Pam was wonderful—that was all there was to it. In the hall, she casually drifted past his locker.

"Would you like to continue our discussion about John Wayne? After school?" she asked.

He was so pleased that he nearly choked.

"My mother and I baked a batch of cookies last night. Perhaps you'd like one, and a glass of milk."

An open invitation to walk her home, that's what it was! "Sure!" he managed, with a little more sophistication this time. It took all his self-restraint to walk sedately into the study hall that afternoon, with Pam at his side as though she belonged there. With Spike McCloskey looking daggers at him. With all the kids watching while they pretended not to.

Wow!

Usually he practiced basketball down at the Congo Church with Ed and the gang after school, but he could meet them there, couldn't he? He could walk with Pam and then backtrack while the guys were warming up. Perhaps they wouldn't mind.

"Wants you to walk her home, huh?"

"You won't need a warm-up anyway, Sinclaire. You'll be plenty warmed by the time you get to practice!"

"Hubba hubba!"

He didn't have the courage to carry her books, because he didn't know her well enough to do such a proprietary thing, and valiantly he talked about another movie he'd seen John Wayne in, wondering if she was really listening but feeling obligated to fulfill the terms of her invitation. After an endless monologue they were within a block of her house.

"I'll show you a shortcut," she said, and led him down an alley that divided the backyards of the houses on either side of the block. "And then, through here," she instructed, and they cut in between two garages, and there, before them, was the back side of her house, with a small fenced-in yard that had been converted into a now frost-nipped victory garden.

She led him to the kitchen door and peeked beneath a loose shingle where a key was hidden.

"Isn't anyone home?" he asked.

"My mother works," she explained.

"Oh." His disappointment was profound. He would have enjoyed her company longer, but no one went into an unoccupied house with a girl. Even he, in his inexperience, knew that.

"Don't worry," she assured him. "It's okay if you come in for a few minutes. I told my mom you were coming for a snack."

He didn't know what kind of a mother she had, who agreed to letting her daughter entertain a boy alone in the house, but he knew what kind of a mother he had.

"I'm sorry. I can't come in."

"You can't?"

"No." He said it firmly.

"Tell you what, then." She brightened, as though inspired. "I'll go in and get the cookies and you can eat them right here."

"Sure! That'd be great." He was elated at her thoughtfulness, watched her unlock the back door and let herself into the Thompson kitchen and then come out again with a napkin-wrapped bundle in her hand.

"Let's just duck into the garage, instead," she suggested. "It'd be more comfortable." This was it, he was sure—the opportunity he was hoping she'd make! She backtracked to the garage and opened a small door at its side. "Come on!" She beckoned impatiently, and closed the door firmly after him and locked it, too, he noticed.

It was a garage in which no car was ever parked. There was a derelict couch nearly hidden among three-legged tables and broken chairs, lamps without shades, newspapers stacked up, rakes and shovels propped against the walls, a cracked mirror and a rusted lawnmower and a heap of old leaves that had, no doubt, crept in on the crest of last autumn's wind. Neatly Pam spread a blanket so that leaking innards of the couch wouldn't get lint on their clothes, and she sat, patting the space beside her. Like a glad lamb he followed her lead, munched a cookie self-consciously, and wished he knew what to do next. It was hard to make conversation with his mouth full and with Pam watching him expectantly.

It occurred to him that she was waiting for him to kiss her! Golly, that must be it! And why not? They were well-launched into a relationship of sorts, weren't they—between last Friday's dance and Saturday's movie, and her invitation this afternoon.

He put the cookies to one side and picked up her hand. "You're so little," he said, comparing her hand to his. He had not reached his full size yet (he hoped), but even so, her hand seemed only half as large as his, fragile and delicate. He felt large and strong as he held so small and warm a thing.

"I haven't really had the chance to thank you for taking me to the movies Saturday." She smiled.

"Oh. You're welcome."

"Your mother came pretty quick, as I remember."

"Mothers are like that," he agreed. "And the worst part about it was that I never got the chance to kiss you good night."

A drop of sweat rolled down his ribs as he waited for her to give him his cue.

"Yes," she said softly. "That was too bad."

"We could try again," he suggested. "Saying good night, I mean."

"Not a bad idea."

"Well, then, good night," he said, and pulled her carefully toward him and pressed his lips against hers, softly, gently, as he had done before, the few times he'd kissed girls last summer, but nothing prepared him for Pam now, whose mouth opened slightly, her kiss an invitation instead of a culmination of an evening shared. He felt the faint moisture of her tongue, and put out his own tongue, just a little, to meet hers, felt her lips with it, and discovered more—a good deal more—than he'd bargained for. He released her before he made a fool of himself, and hoped she didn't know how deeply she'd moved him.

"I guess I have to go," he fumbled.

"Not if you don't want to."

"Yes, I do. My friends are waiting at Pilgrim Congregational Church. We practice basketball there."

"Basketball?" There was a speculative sort of look on her face. "Basketball, huh? You never told me about that. How often do you practice?"

"Every day."

"Every day!"

"We hope to make varsity," he explained.

"Are you that good?"

They were very good. "We hope so," he said modestly.

"Well, then! You'd better get moving! I hope your friends won't be angry with me for making you late!"

"Of course they won't. But if I don't get there pretty soon, they'll be plenty mad at me."

"Well, thanks for walking me home."

"You're welcome. Do you suppose I could do it again tomorrow?"

"Maybe."

Was it a refusal? Dismay crowded out all his newfound pleasure and happiness. Maybe she was angry at his rather abrupt departure? "Well, then." Slowly he backed out the garage door. "I'll meet you at your locker." Perhaps if he didn't give her a chance to refuse outright, she'd go along with it.

"Okay," she agreed, and his hopes and joys soared again. He jogged to the church, considering the prospect of walking with her again, and talking with her, and sitting in the garage with her, and . . .

In the echoing gym his friends' voices called distantly back and forth, sounding hollow as though they were shouting at the end of a long tunnel. He threw his jacket on top of the jumbled heap of theirs and ran onto the court.

"All warmed up, Sinclaire?" they teased.

"Go to hell." He grinned, and played harder than he'd ever done before.

Her hand was warm, insistent, and he burrowed his burning face in the curve of her neck and hoped he would not unman himself by crying out.

Then she took her hand away, leaving behind an enormous pulsing, a throbbing ache that tormented him.

She kissed his sweating forehead.

"Did you like that?" she whispered. For three weeks now he'd walked her home; for twenty-one days she'd slowly taught him the progressions of petting, and she could bring him to this point now almost without preliminaries.

"Yes, baby," he whispered back, unable to find his full voice. He pressed her softness, lifted her sweater, kissed her small, pointed breast which, by now, was always accessible to him, once the privacy of the garage was reached.

"I guess you know now what comes next," she murmured.

He laughed in embarrassment, found himself nearly paralyzed with lust. "I guess I do," he said thickly.

"But usually a girl doesn't do that with just anyone," she explained.

"I hope I'm not just anyone!" He was beginning to recover his normal self now.

"Silly!" she murmured, kissing his ear.

"Gosh, Pam, I'm crazy about you. You know that!"

"I like you a lot too," she said satisfactorily.

"So, then, will you go to the dance Saturday night with me?" It was a night dance—a fairly serious affair—and when he'd mentioned it yesterday she had not answered.

"If I do, everyone will think we're going together." She smiled. "Nobody else will ask me to go out."

"Nobody else had better!" he declared.

"Maybe I'd like it if they did."

He was stunned. "What do you mean?"

"Well . . . if I see you a lot, and no one else, then everyone will think I'm out of circulation . . . and I don't have anything to show for it . . . well . . . that seems a little foolish to me."

"What do you want—to show for it, I mean?"

"I'm not sure." She smiled, running a finger around his mouth, encouraging him to kiss her again. "We'll just have to think about it." They kissed, and he thought of nothing at all.

"About the dance . . ." she said.

"Yes, the dance."

"I'd rather your mother didn't drive us."

He could understand her feeling, but there wasn't much he could do about it.

"If a guy in our gang doesn't drive, he gets a ride with someone who does," she suggested.

"None of my friends is older than I am, if that's what you

mean. Most of them don't even date girls yet." He hated to say it because she might be disdainful of someone like himself whose friends were so immature that they didn't like girls. Still, that was the truth of the situation, and they were both stuck with it. "I'm sorry," he said unhappily. "We can meet at school, if you'd rather."

"Oh, no," she said quickly. "That's not what I meant."

"Well? What's the alternative?"

"The bus." She laughed. "In case you haven't discovered it."

"Oh, sure! I'll take the bus here and we can walk to the dance, and I'll take the bus home from here afterwards. Is that what you meant?"

"It sure is," she approved. "And we can come back here early, if you want. Early enough to make sure that we have a little extra time before the last bus. It'll be dark, too. We won't be able to see each other. It's apt to be kind of interesting that way."

She glanced up at him, and he went hot and cold all over, all at the same time.

Oh, Christ!

They kissed again, touched again . . .

"I have to leave." His voice was unsteady.

"Yes," she said without evidence of concern or disturbance. "You'd better." She did not get up from the couch, but only sat there watching. "I'll miss you tomorrow," she said softly. It would be Saturday—a whole long day. "So I'll look forward to tomorrow night even more."

"Me too."

"Student Council election Monday. Everyone says you're going to win."

He shrugged as nonchalantly as he could. "Seven-thirty?"

"Okay." Her smile was one meant especially for him, private, sharing their own secret, their own intimacy, and it was sufficient to set him off all over again. If it weren't for basketball, he was quite sure he'd explode!

He didn't tell Mom he was taking Pam to the dance. Nor had he told Mom that he'd walked Pam home from school every day for three weeks. He was not sure of the reason for his reluctance. It was true that the Thompsons were not the same kind of people as the Sinclaires—and it was true that Pam wasn't exactly his type, either. But it was not the awareness of this rather intangible difference that had stopped him. More realistically, he thought, it was because his aspirations with regard to Pam were not the most straightforward, and you couldn't very well say so to your own mother, could you?

In any case, he did not correct Mom's impression that he was going to the dance stag, an impression she could hardly avoid, since Ed and Shakey called at the door and the three of them went off together. He told himself that he did not mention it because of Mom, herself, who had received a letter that day, with the disappointing information that Father would be coming home for a week or two, and Mom (it had not escaped Steven's notice) was usually testy and high-strung at the impending presence of Father. Much as he was, himself, since it was so difficult to work his way around Father's imposing personality. But he did not let himself dwell on this unfortunate prospect. For once he was able to relegate Father to the back burner of his mind, because he was absorbed by the expectations of the evening, which he could not let himself think about but which prevented his thinking about anything else as he set off with Ed and Shakey and then as he picked up Pam and approached the school with her beside him. *That* was a moment to be savored, and he indulged himself fully in the enjoyment of walking grandly into the gym, hand in hand with Pam, watched by everybody there because he had saved a boy's life, and because he was up for Student Council, and because he had burst from oblivion to the pinnacle in just three weeks and had a girl. It was too good to last and he had no intention of not enjoying it while he had it, of not enjoying the heady well-being that it brought to him as he took Pam out onto the floor to dance and knew everyone was looking. He curled her hand into his own and twined her arm beneath his (he had practiced this with a broom handle) and pressed her up against him as "Stardust" played, and as the evening progressed and they danced with more and more secret intimacy (in such a manner as to escape the notice of the chaperons), he wondered if he would ever, ever get enough. . . .

"He's here," muttered a boy he hardly knew. He glanced over Pam's head and saw Spike near the door, with two members of his gang flanking him.

"Who's here?" Pam asked.

"Santa Claus." He grinned crookedly, much as John Wayne might have done in a similar situation.

"You must mean Spike," Pam said.

"Yes."

Her face was impassive. "He'll probably ask me to dance."

"Probably."

"What should I do?"

"Whatever you want, Pam."

"Don't you care?" she asked, disappointed.

"You bet I care. But if I tell you what I want and you do it, I'll never knew if *you* care. Will I?"

"You think you're so clever," she mocked.

"No." He laughed shortly. "If I was clever, I'd have figured out how to avoid a situation like this."

"He won't challenge you again."

"Don't count on it."

She was delighted to be the focus of so much attention. Everyone in the gym was watching now. The record ended, but instead of the usual hum of conversation and laughter that rose up after a dance, the whole place was silent as Spike walked across the floor.

"I'm cutting in," he said. "Scram, Sinclaire."

"Get lost," Steven said, stepping between Pam and Spike McCloskey.

"Listen, buddy. Pam's my girl, and I want to dance with her."

"Sorry, Mac," he said promptly. "She isn't your girl. If you want to dance with her, you'll have to ask her."

For a moment Spike stood there and looked hungrily at Pam. "Well?" he said roughly.

She stared back, her chin high, but said nothing, and the moment lengthened.

"Don't say I didn't warn you." He turned quietly to Steven. "You'll be sorry." He walked out of the gym, and "In the Mood" was next. The gym became noisy again and everyone backed and filled according to the requirement of the beat.

"You never answered him," Steven said dully. Pam still liked Spike, he thought to himself. She still likes him, or she would have said something.

"Answer him!" she exclaimed. "Why should I talk to that creep? Besides, words are so shallow. Action speaks much louder, don't you think?"

"Depends on what it is," he answered, and the unintentional innuendo, her giggle in response to it, was sufficient to give him his cue. Only a few minutes later Pam was pulling him gently toward the door and out into the cool night air. Trying to stroll casually so that no one would understand the urgency of their leaving, they hastened to the alley behind her house, slipped into the garage, feeling around in the darkness for the couch, finding it, finding each other.

"I'm glad I had a fight with Spike, back then when I first danced with you at the football hop," she said close to his ear as they embraced. "Because if I hadn't, I'd have missed the chance to get to know you."

"What did you and Spike fight about?"

"He wanted to go steady," she said seriously. "And I just wasn't sure. Now I'm glad I didn't take his ring! He's not like you, Steve. You're going to amount to something. Pretty soon you'll be on the Student Council, and the basketball team—I'll bet you're even going to college—and Spike McCloskey isn't going anywhere, and he never will."

His pride, his joy, swelled, and in the darkness she moved closer, kissed his ear and then his mouth, and something else swelled too.

"I think a lot of you, too." He swallowed.

"Enough to go steady?"

"Gosh!" he exclaimed. He had never dreamed that she'd consent to such a thing—though now, as he thought about it, perhaps it was what she'd been suggesting all along and he'd been too stupid to understand it, too insecure to believe that a girl like Pam would take such a novice as himself seriously.

"Sure," he croaked. "I'd be really happy if you'd go steady with me."

"Well, then," she said softly. "Let's consider it done. Um . . . usually people who go steady exchange jewelry or something."

"Here's my class ring," he said, taking it off and folding her hand around it. "I'd be real pleased if you'd take it."

"It fits my thumb." She laughed. "I'll wind thread around it and put nail polish on the thread to seal it, and then I can wear it."

Wow! Proud of his conquest, he could hardly wait to confirm it; he drew her close, and she offered herself up, helping him to loosen her clothing and his own, her breast soft against his lips, her fingers trailing shiveringly across him, and the prelude to climax gathered, grew stronger, hotter, more insistent, but instead of drawing back, as she always had before, Pam divested herself of her underpants and hiked up her skirt, and it was very, very clear what going steady entitled him to—and enormously clear to him that he would be able to deliver. Like a migrating bird, he knew where to go without even thinking, knew to spread her legs and crawl on top of her. Beneath him she squirmed, upthrust her hips, presenting the best possible entry past her hot threshold, and when tentatively he prodded, she gasped with the pleasure of even that limited contact and guided him into herself, moaning as though deeply in pain. His own sensuality burst into even greater dimension.

"Are you all right, Pam?" he whispered, hardly able to hear even himself over the pounding in his ears.

"I'm dying," she panted, moving her hips. "Oh, God, I'm dying. Oh, Steve, lover, you are great. Just great."

The beating, throbbing, swelling of his groin stretched him taut over the wheel of his body's imperative; his whole being was centered in this hot, finely drawn, and exquisitely expanded pleasure that was rooted deeply, deeply in himself, moving him closer and closer to orgasm. He could hardly breathe.

"Lover," Pam murmured, her hand caressing his hair. "Have you got a safe?"

"A what?"

"A safe." He paused. "A condom. So I don't get pregnant, lover."

He opened his eyes, though he could not see much, only the vague outlines of her face, and struggled to understand her. A condom. Yes, a condom. That was what she'd said.

And there was only one way she could have learned about condoms. For the instant that he hovered, his attention diverted to this probable aspect of reality, to a consideration of the lineup of boys that went back into her still-brief past, the last of whom had been Spike McCloskey, the lineup which no doubt would extend into her much longer future, the first of whom was himself, and in this moment the urgency of his lust let up long enough to give him a chance to choose.

He drew back, away from her, climbed off, turned while he refastened his trousers and tucked in his shirt. Within him pent-up needs raced and scrambled, seeking an escape from the bond of his body—yet he knew. He knew.

"What's wrong?"

"Nothing, honey," he said. "I'd better be going, or I'll miss my bus."

"Why did you pull out like that?" she demanded.

"I don't have a condom," he said. An answer that would satisfy her, he thought—but he was wrong.

"Well, then, you can pull out, like you just did—but later, just before . . ."

"I have to go, Pam," he said, firmly as he could. "I have to go now."

"Okay," she said, clearly mystified.

"Let me walk around to the front of the house with you, as

though we've just come back from the dance. Then your parents won't think anything's been going on."

"Okay," she said submissively, and without saying anything more he took her around to the porch and left her there in its bright light.

He started off down the street toward the bus stop.

There was only one thing, really, that would cause Pam to regard with favor the pursuit of a boy as inexperienced as he had been. Only one thing he had that would interest her. It was well illustrated by the kids at the dance tonight, by their attention, respect, which Pam shared while at his side. Which he would share with her as long as they had a claim on each other, and she'd guaranteed that claim by dispensing her favors so as to bind him to her. Yes, she must have been very gratified tonight, when the gym hushed and Spike McCloskey walked up to them, and like John Wayne himself, Steven had stood his ground, spoken quietly; and there were additional trophies in the offing—Student Council and the basketball team, if he made them. No doubt when she'd met him at the pencil sharpener she was only fishing in untapped waters, without knowing what she'd draw, but then Steve Sinclaire emerged as a hero—thanks to her—and she'd made sure, ever since, that he stayed close by.

In the night he blushed in his humiliation. Yes, sir, he'd let her lead him, all right! Couldn't wait for her to lead him! And got McCloskey mad at him, besides—a person it didn't pay to have mad at you.

And then he remembered: Spike promising revenge. *Don't say I didn't warn you.*

Christ! Why hadn't he arranged for Ed and Shakey to follow him, just to be on the safe side!

Because you wanted your chance with Pam, he answered himself. And God knows who might be following you now.

The smite of fear was like cold water poured onto a warm, happily napping body, and he was instantly alert, his hearing more acute, every sense tingling as he strode forward, from one pool of streetlight to the next, without hurrying, so that if anyone was watching, no one would know that he was tense and waiting. He tried to lengthen his steps gradually so that he would not appear to be fleeing; then, behind him, like summer-swept rain, running feet bore down on him in the darkness and he broke into a run, and then saw that someone was coming toward him. A car pulled alongside and stopped. From behind and now ahead he was crowded over, and the unseen inhabitants of the car pulled him in, and vaguely he heard Ed and Shakey yelling somewhere in the darkness, and the car tore away as someone pushed him harshly onto the floor on the backseat and sat on his head, crushing his face into the worn carpeting. There was, for a moment, only the smell of oil from the old car, and the smell of sweat from his captors, and the panic of not being able to breathe. Desperately he tried to move; the car threw itself around a corner, and the weight on his head shifted a little.

"Watch him!" said a voice. "He's trying to get up."

"Pin him," he heard Spike say. "And get off his goddamned face. I want some of it left."

Mercifully the weight lifted and a foot was put carefully on the nape of his neck. The car picked up speed, and beneath the floor the tires on the road whispered and hummed. He lay motionless, numb, hopelessly desperate. Soon the car would stop and he would have to face Spike and his gang. He thought of prisoners in the camps of the Germans and Japanese and the torture done to those men. What if he, too, were in a stalag and was subjected to systematic abuse? Would he have what it took to stand up to it, or would he give information to the enemy in exchange for the cessation of pain? Whether he could take it or not, there would be no exchange tonight. Nothing to use in his own defense or to trade for mercy. His enemy was not after information but only revenge, retaliation. His only option was to take what was coming, without outcry. Because the alternative was to scream his head off—and sure as hell there'd be no one around to hear.

Jesus! He was sweating like a pig now, trembling from head to toe, and he bore no resemblance to the manly G.I. of a prison camp. And with reason. No one, after all, knew better than he what it was like to be on the receiving end of the wrath of someone more powerful than yourself.

But Spike was not more powerful, was he? Not taken alone. None of these boys, by themselves, were any larger than he, nor any stronger. There was no rule here that said he could not fight back, as had always been the case when he confronted his usual adversary—Father. Father no longer used a strap; he used words instead, and the revocation of privilege, but Steven still had to stand there and take it mutely, pretending to accept his chastisement. But now—this night—he didn't have to take anything without giving as good as he got.

A vestige of strength stirred. There were, of course, four

kids in this car, as far as he could determine. Four-to-one odds weren't so good, and there was little hope he could escape into the blackness of the night, but he sure as hell could break a nose or two, couldn't he, before they got in their licks? It felt better, anyway. If anything could be said to feel good at all.

When the car stopped, he went slack. The shadowed, featureless boys, believing him paralyzed with fear, dragged him from the car, marched him carelessly toward a nearby tree, part of what appeared to be a woods, and they were unprepared when he wrenched himself loose. Doubling his fist as he'd seen John Wayne do it, he drove it into the face of the nearest boy, his whole hand in the grip of sudden agony as it connected with something spongy that cracked. Blood spurted, warm on his knuckles, and he turned to the next boy, in a frenzy to reach him, and the one after that, and Spike himself. The giving of pain, the lashing back, fed upon itself, and he was no longer the person he'd known all his life, but a stranger doing alien things. He hit and kneed and kicked and did not stop until it was over and they all had him pinned against the tree, holding his arms back around it so that his shoulders were wrenched in their joints, forcing him into immobility. They were all breathing hard, their faces bloody, and he guessed his own was bleeding, too, his nose swollen, throbbing, his shoulders an awful agony, pinned against the tree.

"I guess we've all got a score to settle now," said Spike. "Who wants to go first?"

"I might as well," said the fourth boy, standing beside him. "And then I'll take an arm and Joe will be free, and then Joe can take Art's place . . ."

"Okay, okay," said Spike impatiently. "I get the picture. Go ahead."

The boy hesitated.

"Afraid?" Spike jeered.

"I might hurt my hand," the kid complained.

"Get out of the way, then, and let Joe—"

"Hell, no." The boy approached Steven's helplessly exposed self. He drew back, appearing to aim, and Steven watched in an appalled haze as the boy hit him, just below his ribs, and then watched no more as the boy hit him again, lower this time, and again, and he was caught in the racking grip of pain that left no room for anything else.

The boys exchanged places, and his shoulders were further wrenched in their sockets as the new shift tightened its hold.

The new tormentor did not hesitate, but punched hard, ramming agony deeply, sharply, unmercifully into his innermost self, and the world narrowed down to a black, soundless hollow where everyone, everything receded and he was unaware of who hurt him or even how until he heard Spike say, "Turn him around."

The pain in his shoulders as they lowered his arms and turned him was abrupt, and the world exploded in bright light and he heard himself scream.

"I knew we could get him bawling," he heard Spike say. "When I'm through, he'll be bawling plenty."

And Steven, his cheek pressed against the rough, scratchy tree bark, heard the slapping of leather against the palm of a hand, and then the too-familiar whistle of the belt whipping through the air, and he locked his teeth to prepare himself for what was coming next, and heard himself scream again as the belt's buckle ripped into his back.

"Jesus, McCloskey," one of the boys said nervously. "Not with the buckle."

"Want to stop me?" Spike struck again, and there was a distant moaning which Steven took to be himself, but which must not have been, because the boys dropped him where he stood, the tree bark scraping his entire length as he crumpled to the ground, alone with his agony as they ran for their car, the gravel thrown by its wheels spraying him in a final spitting insult.

He waited with his intolerable hurt, unable to breathe because of the obstruction that was his nose and because of the inability of his ribs to expand, all his hurts pounding as though the beating were still going endlessly on, on, on. The circling light of the squad car blinded him; he could hear Ed's voice but could not see him. There was a press of people, shadows in the night, a blanket tucked around him where he lay.

"Steve!" Ed cried wretchedly. "Steve!"

He did not try to speak, to comfort Ed, because he could not. It was a relief to let everyone else do the work, to have decisions decided for him, to coast, suspended, over them all as he was lifted into the back of the ambulance that arrived from an unknown source, as he waited for the next hideous moment and the one after that and the one after that, until, in a time uncounted, he would no longer hurt and could somehow resume the masquerade of the person he had been an hour ago.

* * *

Patients in private rooms were not bound by visiting hours. His interrogation by the police moved forward without disturbance and was soon done to their satisfaction. He did not bother with the heroics; by Sunday afternoon, when he could speak comfortably, he had told everything he knew or could think of, and so had Ed, who had, with Shakey, followed from the dance, waited behind a bush, who had seen Spike's gang pull Steven into the car, and, unable to prevent it, who had called the cops, and who guessed that Spike's gang would head for the river and the woods that lined it. Spike and his pals were in custody, all of them admitting complicity, and now it was Monday. Ed and Neil and Sam and Shakey had bumbled in after school, shuffling and poking around the room, staring at his bandages and trying to amuse him.

"They're all on probation now," Ed said cheerfully. "They can't drive anymore, and they have a curfew, and the next time they get in trouble, they'll go to reform school."

"McCloskey won't be getting in your way for quite a while," Sam said, drawing the rope controlling the venetian blind at the window so that the room grew dark, slowly opened it again. The room became light.

"You and your girl are free to pursue whatever it was you were after." Shakey grinned from the foot of the bed.

Pam! He blushed beneath his bandages. "I don't have a girl. I mean, she's not mine."

"Maybe she wasn't before, but she is now," Neil reported. "At least, everyone thinks Pam Thompson and you are going steady."

"They say she has your ring."

Oh, shit—his class ring. He'd forgotten about that. Frustration arose, though he was unsure of its source, and tears were close to the surface. He'd been very moody during his stay in the hospital—a normal response to shock, the doctor said. It would pass, given time. The only thing left would be a slight off-centering of his nose—nothing to worry about. He compressed his lips and worked at making the tears go away. His bandages effectively disguised any trouble he was having.

"Now for the big news," Shakey said proudly. "Are you ready?"

"Sure."

"Well, in case you're interested, you were elected to Student Council today, Steve-boy!"

All of them watched to see how he would take the news. Their faces shone with pride and loyalty, and his gratitude nearly overwhelmed him.

"When you get back, all the girls will be following around waving palm branches," Sam laughed. "You can have your pick, if you don't want Pam Thompson."

"Dancing girls." Shakey shuffled around the room as though he were performing in a minstrel show.

"Roses tossed at your feet."

"Without thorns."

There was a stir by the door, and the atmosphere of the room changed, like the surface of a placid pond ruffled by a sudden breeze. All of them, at the same time, sensed an alien presence, and looking up, Steven met the hard, pale blue of Father's eyes.

Oh, Christ.

Mom came breezily into the room, throwing her hat on the dresser, her smile wide so as to put everyone at ease. "Well, Ed!" she said cheerfully, perching on the edge of Steven's bed, sending a ferocious knife blade through his gut. It took all of his concentration not to cry out, and for a moment he forgot that everyone was there, that Mom was speaking to each of his friends, calling them by name, showing Father that she knew who they were, acknowledging the special relationship they all shared.

But she could not undo Father's cold silence, which cast a pall on the group, and uneasily the gang shuffled its collective feet, its arms too long, its posture awkward, its hands too large.

"We were just leaving," Ed mumbled. Under Father's imperious gaze, everyone in the room was small, insignificant, unhappy.

"Steve was elected to Student Council today," Sam said to the dresser that held Steven's thermometer and Mom's hat. "We just came by to tell him."

"It's a terrific honor," Neil said earnestly to Mom. "And he didn't even have to take out nomination papers. Other kids did it for him."

"Our hero won by a landslide."

"Terrific!" Mom exclaimed, rising from the bed to see the kids out, again jostling him, sending sparks across the back of his brain. She patted Ed's shoulder, said good-bye to everyone as the gang melted away quickly, self-consciously stumbling over things that weren't there in their effort to skirt Father, jostling a nurse in the corridor, apologizing loudly, their voices farther and farther away until their exodus was a muttered shuffling. The elevator doors opened and shut again, pinching off their noise, swallowing them up. And then there was just the three Sinclaires left, a little group that should have been close-knit and was not, that should have belonged to one another in the special ways of family units, and did not. Thankfully Mom did not return to the bed, but leaned instead against the dresser.

"Hi, Father," Steve said through the hole in the bandages left for his mouth. "Welcome home."

It occurred to him that Father could not see his facial expression any better than the gang could, because of the bandages. It was the first time that he'd ever had anything to hide behind in any confrontation with Father, and considering his rather delicately balanced emotional state, he was grateful. Very grateful. Father would, no doubt at all, want to know how he'd gotten into his present situation, and God only knew where his interrogation would lead.

"I heard about your little fracas," Father said. "How in heaven's name are you?"

"Better," he answered, trying to sound alert and unhurt. "How are things in Washington? Did you get a chance to visit Cousin Elizabeth?"

"I did. I had a fine visit." He put his coat over the rail at the foot of the bed. "Elizabeth has got enough food to feed all of Waterford in her bomb shelter. And jugs of water, which she changes for fresh every week. You'll be glad to know that she and Grandmother Merrick are prepared to withstand an enemy attack of sizable proportion."

Steven smiled at Elizabeth's readiness, though it was a fact that people on the East Coast were much more war-conscious than folks in the interior, where German and Japanese planes could not reach. On the East Coast they watched out for submarines. Cape beaches were patrolled with dogs. People had blackout curtains at their windows; in the cities, older men who couldn't serve in the army patrolled with flashlights and helmets to see if any light was visible under doors and at the edges of windows and watched for aircraft in the menacing sky. The gold dome of Boston had long since been blackened so that it wouldn't be so obvious a target.

"Elizabeth sends you her best, Steven," Father was saying. "And so does your grandmother. Naturally, at the time they sent their felicitations, they were unaware that you were in such dire need of them. Perhaps, sir, you would be so good as to tell me what happened."

Steven stirred, though it hurt to move. He hated like anything to tell Father about Pam, but the police already knew there was a girl involved, so it stood to reason that Father knew it, too. Father seated himself in the room's lone chair.

"I was walking a girl home from a dance."

"You were at a dance? Emily, did you know that?" Father asked Mom.

"Certainly," she said coolly.

"I thought that since my friends were at the dance, too," Steven went on, "Spike wouldn't try anything. But I was wrong."

"Spike McCloskey, do you mean? That barbarian from Barton Elementary?"

"That's the one."

"Huh!" Father snorted. "Were those boys, the ones who just left, the friends you mentioned who were going to protect you?"

"Yes."

"Not much use, were they?"

"Not much," he agreed, waiting to see if Father was sufficiently diverted from Pam.

"They're nice boys, Charles," Mom pleaded in their behalf.

"They don't look nice," Father said. "They don't look as presentable—not by a long shot—as Van Teassel's son, or Beckman's boy, or Farmington's. Why in heaven's name have you chosen such riffraff, Steven?"

Beneath the bandages, Steven grew hot and sweaty, and he thought it was not possible, after everything that had happened to him, that he should be right back at the beginning, under Father's thumb.

"Ed Lamson is my best friend," he said apologetically.

"Is that so?"

"Yes."

"And for how long has he been your boon companion?"

"A year and a half."

"A year and a half!" Father exclaimed.

"Now we're taking junior lifesaving at the YMCA."

"Did you know that, Emily?" Father turned to Mom.

"Of course I did!" Mom said. "Steven hopes to get a job on the waterfront at Quivet, once he's old enough and the war is over. He's doing what he can to prepare himself. Besides, Charles, he needs recreation and friends of his own choosing."

"But does he need those boys? The ones who just left? That down-at-the-heels, shambling example of manhood that recently walked out of here?" The expression on Father's face was similar to one he would wear at the monkey house at the Toledo zoo, trying to be tolerant of the odor of the inmates and their occasionally gross behavior. "It's a good thing I came home just now, I can see that. Perhaps I'd better arrange for a replacement for me in Washington, so that I can get things better organized here in Port Huron!"

Behind the protection of the bandages, Steven tried to think. Surely Father did not want to be replaced at the Pentagon; he gloried in his importance as Sommerset and King's representative there. It was an empty threat.

But one day Father would be home for good, and this scene would be replayed, the same attempt to diminish Ed and Shakey, Sam and Neil, and the same attempt to force Steven into doing what Farmington did, and Beckman—what, in fact, Father decided was right to do. This battle would have to be fought without the screen of bandages that would prevent Father from knowing whether or not he was hitting where it hurt. It might as well be thrashed out now. Like facing Spike McCloskey, it was better for your battered self to come out fighting, rather than whimpering and hoping for the best. Taking as deep a breath as his bruised ribs would allow, Steven began.

"Ed and I have done a lot of practicing with the other three kids who were here. We plan to try out for Morrison's junior varsity basketball team later this winter." Surely Father would be happy at the thought of Steven's being a member of the Morrison team?

But Father was unimpressed. "It would be difficult to maintain a top-flight grade average if you're playing games at the same time. And you must have good grades to secure your admission to Harvard. It's important to order your values, Steven."

So much for Father's pride in the team. He would have to approach differently. He must fight back, openly. Now, while the issues were so clear. Now was the time to tell Father, not ask.

"I have ordered my values," he said as firmly as he could. "And playing basketball is very important to me."

"More important than Harvard?"

"Yes," he declared steadfastly. So much for Harvard. And yet wasn't it possible to play a sport and get decent grades? "Harvard has always been your idea, Father, not mine."

"My gracious!" Father exclaimed with exaggerated emphasis. "You've thought it all out, have you?"

"Yes, I have," he said flatly, trying to still his quaking, which must be rocking the high hospital bed. "Ed, and my friends, are more important than just about anything else."

Father snorted. "Has it ever occurred to you, Steven, that your youth and inexperience disqualify any judgment you might make? Has it never occurred to you that if I, who am responsible for guiding you, decide that playing basketball works to your disadvantage, all I would have to do is inform the school authorities that I am opposed to such a waste of time, and you would not be allowed to play? Surely you're aware of that."

And if Father did it, and Ed and Neil and Shakey and Sam made the team, he would be very effectively separated from them. He would have little access to them for as long as the basketball season lasted because of the long hours of practice. He would lose touch with them and eventually lose their friendship. Father, in one sweep, would take care of everything. Everything. Defeated, he picked at a piece of bandage. Quickly Mom moved between them. "If Steven has no chance to do at least some of the things he likes, his grades could suffer more than if his schedule were too full," she said softly. She took Steven's hand, though she turned to Father. "I'm sure he can do better in school if he's able to see boys he enjoys—and I expect his grades wouldn't suffer if he played basketball. But they might slip if he were bottled up, without outlet for his energy. Mightn't they, honey?" She turned to him guilelessly, her eyes urgent as they searched his soul, to see if it was strong enough, steadfast enough to take the opportunity she offered.

Suddenly he understood her, and he squeezed her hand gratefully. Why in God's name hadn't he seen it before?

"Well, I guess it's true enough," he said to his mother, as if Father wasn't there. "People usually do well at nearly everything they try, if they're happy." He listened to himself carefully, trying to gauge his timing to get the best possible effect from this one weapon given to him by Mom. "And they don't do well at things they don't enjoy doing. Their grades slip badly. They don't get into any college then, and especially they don't get into Harvard." Then he risked it all: he swung his eyes from Mom's face and met Father's gaze squarely, unflinchingly.

The room was filled with stunned silence. It was a standoff; permission to see his friends, play ball if he was good enough, lead his own life at Morrison, in exchange for grades good enough to get into Harvard. Around the pain in his temples everything was fuzzy. He hung on to this one certitude, this one chance to maneuver Father instead of letting Father maneuver him, and willed himself not to look away. It was Father who gave away, rising from his chair, dusting his trouser legs as though sitting in this room contaminated him. "Well, we certainly wouldn't like to see your grades slip! I see you're quite fatigued, my boy," he said smoothly, as though nothing troubled him. "And since I've only just this day come back to Port Huron, I'm a little tired myself. Perhaps it's time to go home, Emily."

Reluctantly Mom let go of Steven's hand, picked up her hat, backed up to her coat held by Father, who pressed it heavily, firmly onto her shoulders, looking down at her with an enigmatic smile that made Steven profoundly uncomfortable. Then Father turned back, as though just now, at this very moment, remembering something he'd forgotten. "How is it that those ruffians wanted to injure you?" he asked.

Startled, strung tight, and worn out by the effort to win, letdown now that it was apparently over Steven forgot to watch his step. Quickly, incautiously, he improvised so as to avoid mentioning Pam. "There's a railroad trestle over the river," he fumbled. "Everyone considers it a challenge, and every once in a while someone dares you to climb it. If you don't, you're a chicken. Spike McCloskey challenged me, a few weeks back, to climb it."

"Did you?" Mom asked, hearing about it for the first time, same as Father.

"Yes, I did. But Spike slipped and fell into the river. I pulled him out, and between falling in the first place and being rescued by me . . . well, I think his attack was his way of evening up the score, making up for his loss of face. He's not top-heavy with brains, anyway."

"You saved Spike McCloskey's life?" Mom exclaimed.

"Laudable," Father remarked in rare approval. "How did you know what to do?"

"Because of my lifesaving course. They teach you how to jump so as to keep your head out of the water. So you don't lose track of the victim."

"And so you jumped."

"That was very brave of you, honey!" Mom's pride and admiration shone from her face.

"But was it necessary?" Father asked, tapping a foot.

"What do you mean?"

"Did you have to jump?"

"Well, the kid was floating facedown."

"Could no one have reached this unfortunate hooligan by wading in from the riverbank? Wouldn't that have been more sensible than your jumping from the bridge?"

"Well, I was glad to jump, actually," Steven blurted, flustered.

"How was that?"

"It was the only way I could get down." He laughed weakly, deprecatingly. "When I got halfway up the trestle, I froze. By jumping in after Spike, I could at least get back down again in one piece."

"You mean you discovered you were afraid of heights?"

"I've always been. What I discovered was that fear can paralyze you."

"So you jumped, thereby avoiding the difficult position of being stuck?"

"That's about the size of it." He grinned uncomfortably.

"And I suppose everyone thought you were brave, just as your mother here does." The words were brittle, sharp. "Your friend, who just left, made reference to your being a hero."

"Well, you know kids." He squirmed.

"Indeed. Your escapade worked to your advantage, didn't it?"

"What do you mean?"

"I heard one of the young men—one of your friends—say you were elected to Student Council without even seeking the office. The preparations for such honors don't take place in a day. The moving force behind your election—an honor indeed!—must have begun before today."

"As a matter of fact, it did."

"At about the time your lifesaving endeavor was made known, I expect."

"Yes."

"As if no one else could have waded in and pulled the fellow out."

"Charles!" protested Mom.

"As though any of you had any business down there at the river, to begin with," Father persisted.

Steven said nothing.

"And of what did your heroism consist? It looked like a spectacular leap brought on by mercy, but it wasn't. It was inspired by desperation. You were driven to jump because you couldn't get down any other way. Isn't that right?"

"Charles! Stop!" cried Mom, agonizingly distressed at watching Father flay the cover off Steven's masquerade.

"Isn't that right?" Father demanded, ignoring her. "You jumped to save yourself, not Spike McCloskey?"

All the joy of his newfound popularity collapsed, and he

guessed he deserved it. He'd been riding the wake of a dream—the dream of the loner—and it all had been an illusion, a fraud, self-induced.

He waited for Father to finish with him.

"And now you are a member of the Student Council, no doubt voted into office by the misapprehensions of your fellow students. Let me congratulate you, Steven. A splendid sleight of hand."

There was nothing more to say, nor any need to say it.

"Well, Emily, I think it's time we left. I think we've accomplished just about all we're going to. Good night, Steven."

"Good night," he whispered.

Poor Mom couldn't speak at all; she let Father take her out of the room and away to the elevator, their footsteps fading and then disappearing while Steven lay suffering beneath his bandages, his victory gone, his fighting spirit reduced to a feeble flicker, nearly demolished.

Well, he'd won, hadn't he? The right to freely choose his friends? To play ball if he and Ed and Shakey and Neil and Sam made the team? He'd been elected to Student Council, hadn't he, and if, as Father said, he'd won today on the strength of a fraud, he could still be a good Student Council representative, couldn't he? Father couldn't take that away! He couldn't!

Yes, he thought bleakly, and tears blurred his vision as he fought back the rising urge to weep. He could.

The fact was that Father had won, hands down, simply by taking all the joy away.

Don't let him! He told himself fiercely.

Don't let him! Concentrate, Sinclaire, on the things he can't take away—not on the things he's already dismantled.

Think.

Think!

And then it was there, blessing him, soothing him, restoring him—Kingsland in its fastness behind the maples in the yard, Kingsland with its tower and the room in it especially his own, Kingsland and the carriage barn with its bronze weather vane on its mansard roof, a horse reaching for the road, the sun setting it on fire in the summer afternoon. Kingsland and the bay upon which he would sail again once the war was over, when he'd be able to get back to Waterford and Quivet—the bay and the shore, the salt breeze, the tide

—it all would be his again, the things that were really important.

Yes, there were some things that not even Father could destroy.

IV

The Quivet Summer

13

"Julius Thayer's will provided money for the town of Waterford," Cousin Elizabeth said to Sam Hall, chairman of the Waterford selectmen. "The point is to get the best use out of it—a use that Mr. Thayer himself would have been proud of. He would not have been proud of a town dump, Mr. Hall. I'm sure Mr. Thayer had in mind a project that would edify and enlighten the public—not provide for its conveniences."

"Oh, good one!" crowed Father. "Score one for you, Elizabeth!"

Dinner at Cousin Elizabeth's grand table was over, and the August evening was cooling fast, its shadows drowning the details of Mary Deems Merrick's portrait in a gray mist, with only the lady's face, alight and delighted, showing from her niche in the parlor where they all sat.

Sam Hall, perspiring and uncomfortable in his Sunday suit, cleared his throat. "The public good can be interpreted more than one way—don't you think so, Miss Edgarton?" he persisted gamely.

"Apparently the public good *is* being interpreted in more than one way," Cousin Elizabeth said. "And I think it's up to me to preserve, to the best of my ability, the intent of an old gentleman who loved Waterford dearly and whose concept of the public good embraced more elevated concerns than the disposal of garbage."

"If Waterford doesn't have a new dump soon, the one we've got now will be a public menace," Sam pleaded.

"Then the public should purchase a new one," Cousin Elizabeth countered briskly. "Not Julius Thayer."

"Mr. Thayer would have thought it awful to buy a dump," contributed Grandmother Merrick, sitting beside Mom on the velvet sofa, its feeble springs permitting her to nest deeply in a pocket. "At least, I believe he wouldn't have approved of it. But Elizabeth," she asked with excessive innocence, knowing perfectly well the answer to her question before she asked it, "exactly what do you think Mr. Thayer would have wanted done with his money?"

Steven manfully suppressed his urge to throw the nearest vase on the floor and stomp on it.

"Why, that money would be sufficient to buy the old mill property, and there'd be enough to dig out the foundations of the old mill my grandfather, Kingsley Merrick, built there in the days of the Civil War. It would be a splendid start toward a project I've had in mind for a long time—to build a museum on those foundations and set up mill machinery so people could see what went on out there. The mill site is part of Waterford's past, and I think we ought to honor that past."

And honor as well Elizabeth Edgarton's illustrious grandsire, of whom she was so proud.

Mr. Hall wished he could smoke like Miss Emily (now Mrs. Sinclaire) was doing, but he knew better than to assume such a privilege for himself in Miss Edgarton's house. And he knew, as well, that he was beaten. Julius Thayer's will left the money to the town of Waterford, to be used at the discretion of the Historical Society. And everyone knew that rich old Miss Edgarton ran the Historical Society.

Besides, Waterford would happily sell the mill site it had so enigmatically acquired. Old towns often acquired land without knowing how: deeds might be casually kept, old ones destroyed by fire at the courthouse many years ago, sometimes got lost, often were never recorded at all. No one knew, now, how Waterford had acquired the property, but one thing was certain: the town did not want it. It would much rather have the money, and if there was anything left over from the Thayer bequest, rich old Miss Edgarton and her pals would build an eff-ing museum that no one but her and that damn Historical Society wanted, putting up any extra cash needed out of their own pockets because they were wealthy enough to do it, while everyone else in Waterford had to scratch just to keep going.

"The land we hope to buy for the new dump is one of Barney Stone's woodlots," he said futilely, knowing full well that stingy old Miss Edgarton didn't give a shit about Barney Stone. "What with a willing buyer and all, ol' Barney could pay for a person to help him care for Mrs. Stone instead of having to send her to the county home, and we'd get a new dump besides, which we need."

"In view of such a good cause, Waterford's town meeting, I'm sure, will vote to purchase the land out of tax money." Elizabeth nodded. She rose grandly from her chair; Father, too, got up, commanding Steven by the lift of his eyebrow to do likewise. Gentlemen did not remain seated when there was a lady standing. Ashamed of himself for his compliance, Steven rose, waiting for Sam to catch on that he was being dismissed. "So pleasant of you to have called, Mr. Hall." Cousin Elizabeth extended her hand, which Hall, belatedly getting to his feet, took in his own and dropped as quickly as possible, as though its texture or temperature surprised him.

"Steven, you may show Mr. Hall to the door," Cousin Elizabeth said, and rudely turned her back, saying to Mom, "What did you think of Mr. Edmund's sermon this morning, Emily?"

Thus was Mom drawn into her rudeness, just as Steven was, and just as unwillingly, he knew. But there wasn't much either of them could do about it. He walked with Sam Hall to Kingsland's parlor door, ushered him through, and followed him out. Behind the door was his mother's muffled response about the sermon the family had endured this morning while Steven had been at Camp Quivet helping Howard Ware to lead a worship program for the kids, the last of the season, in which awards had been presented and all the camp songs sung, a benediction for the winter to follow given.

"Will the town meeting vote to buy Mr. Stone's land?" he asked Mr. Hall.

"No," said Sam Hall. "I don't believe it will. The Stone land will come up for taxes soon and the town will acquire it because Barney hasn't paid on that land in years and can't start now. We were just trying to stop it from coming to that, is all."

"I'm sorry," Steven said, mortified, that he should by default be on the side of the pharisee, who, reciting the prayers of tradition, would not lift a hand to help. Sam Hall saw the distress on the young man's face and tried to smile. "Something will work out," he said heartily. He did not clap Steven on the back to confirm his words, because Steven Sinclaire was the Merrick scion and unclappable (for all he seemed like a decent lad), but his handshake stood for the same thing. "Don't worry, boy. Something always works out."

He climbed into his elderly car, parked in front of the Sinclaires' Pontiac, started the engine with a roar, lurched out of Kingsland's driveway in a cloud of blue exhaust. Its sound, rough and uneven, died away, and still Steven lingered, loath to return to the stuffy, impossible parlor, to the people in it—his people, who shamed him, humiliated him, infuriated him, rendered him helpless by the habit of years, by their expectations, and by necessity as well, dammit. Who, after all, paid the bills?

If he'd had an ounce of gumption, he thought unhappily, he wouldn't have just sat there listening to Elizabeth cut Mr. Hall to ribbons, listening to Father applauding her effort. He'd have stood up for Mr. Hall. But he had not. Father would have been infuriated at this vexing of Elizabeth, and the prospect of Elizabeth's acid tongue (let alone Father's) was enough to cause the devil to pause. And besides, it was important to keep the tenor of the afternoon as even as possible, so that if a moment for escaping presented itself he would be able to take advantage of it. For he needed badly to be elsewhere! He needed to be in East Waterford, where the family of his counselor-in-training were waiting for him to join them for an evening of canasta.

He was due a half-hour ago.

He clenched his fists, subdued the need to escape on the spot. He didn't want to hurt Mom's feelings, so longingly did she look his way, eager to talk to him and unable to do so because of Father and Cousin Elizabeth, whose monopoly of the conversation, whose very presence, created inhibition. Mom would want Steven to herself—but if the right moment presented itself, he'd take it, whether it hurt her feelings or not. Because he must get to the cottage in East Waterford! After all, he'd endured a whole afternoon at Kingsland, trapped in the family circle, which contrasted so stridently with the warm and loving, easy and comfortable companionship of the family of his CIT at Quivet. The thought of which made his loneliness nearly unbearable, his disappointment at perhaps missing the evening more and more intense with each moment, like that of a penniless child who watches the other kids at the amusement park, unable to join the fun, unable to tear himself away from the agony of watching.

"What are you loitering about?" Father called from the parlor window. "Here we travel halfway across the country to see you, and you aren't even here."

"Just admiring the fresh air," he called back. "After so much wholesome living at camp, it's hard for us boy scouts to be confined to a smoke-filled room with a ceiling."

Father chuckled, pleased with this evidence of the Sinclaire expertise with words, and with its implied disparagement of Mom, which Steven had not intended and for which he was instantly sorry.

"Well, come in anyway," Father instructed. "You're being rude to our hostess."

If he asked for the car, Father would want to know where he wanted to go with it, and Steven dared not tell him, because everything Father touched tarnished. Reluctantly he slunk back into the parlor.

Mrs. Blake was passing a miniature tray with cordials on it, and everyone was drinking a demitasse of coffee, which Steven declined. Camp was officially closed, but Howard Ware was still there, in his cabin, and perhaps Steven could invent something that he'd left behind, that he needed the car to go back and pick up, that he could fetch because Howard was still around. But Father might come along, messing everything up, or everyone else might decide (God forbid) to come too, so that they could tour Waterford once the phantom article was recovered. Cousin Elizabeth and Grandmother dearly loved to ride around town, viewing places that were only ceremonial markers now, commemorating things that were dead and gone or had simply moved away. The depression had wiped out the summer society, and with it, Waterford's cash crop. Of the former days, only the Leverings used their house in the summer, in the manner of former days. As for the rest of it, the war had delayed any restoration of Waterford's former glory. The grand houses of the rich weren't looking very grand anymore, some approaching dereliction; the population of Waterford was an even five hundred.

But Kingsland, the great Merrick house, was not derelict. It stood proudly among the ruins of Waterford, comparison with its shabby neighbors honing its grandeur to an even finer edge, and, unless Steven were very much mistaken, whetting Father's appetite for it more and more acutely.

"Now, Elizabeth," Father was laughing, "now that you've belabored Sam Hall with it, what do you know about Civil War woolen mills in West Waterford?"

"Almost nothing," Elizabeth snapped tartly. "The point is, Charles, that very few people know about mills. But they represent a whole way of life in our American past. They can be reconstructed, and I think they should be, along with a means of describing the kind of operation my grandfather, Kingsley Merrick, ran out there in the cause of the Union Army . . . the merino sheep that Waterford raised for those mills . . . the sheep gates—a whole way of life, Charles, that no one knows about anymore. Why, the sheep cropped the grass so closely that all the topsoil blew away, and that's why the land here is so poor. I think that little tidbit is very interesting, don't you?"

Apparently Father did not care to bring up the observation that sheep could hardly account for all the poor soil everywhere on Cape Cod—poor because it had been farmed without understanding of its fragility many years before anyone even heard of a merino sheep. Father never did anything, if he could help it, that would antagonize Cousin Elizabeth and cause her to leave Kingsland to Aunt Celia instead of to Mom (and to himself).

"What kind of a mill do you suppose Kingsley Merrick had out there?" Father asked politely, to please Elizabeth, sucking up to her, the freak, and scornfully Steven watched him falling all over himself. No question about it: Father was a pompous, conceited ass, and suffered horribly in comparison to other fathers he'd met this summer—notably that of the counselor-in-training who'd served under him at Quivet this year. Why, Doug's dad made his own look mean and without any saving grace whatever—in fact, Doug's whole family, warm and happy, made this one, sitting here in the parlor at Kingsland, seem pretty paltry, despite his mother's efforts to give it the spark of love. If it was disloyal of him to deem her efforts unsuccessful . . . well, he had to live with it, was all, because compared to Doug's family, his own was dead.

He'd liked his CIT instantly, the boy's open, frank friendliness happy and gentle; and everyone else had liked Doug too, when he invited as many of the Quivet staff as could fit into the family car to raucously play badminton or croquet or miniature golf on a course the family had rigged up at their rented cottage farther east. There was Kool-Aid and Coke and popcorn and lemonade, and a more adult refreshment was proposed for those old enough to take advantage of it.

"Would you like some beer, Steve?" Doug's father had asked as they watched the Quivet staff milling around the golf course, trying to shoot balls through open-ended tin cans.

"Sure I would," he'd answered.

"Me too. Let's go up to Orleans and get some."

"Right!" he agreed, glad to leave the whooping and hollering for so splendid an errand. And instantly responding, as well, to the companionship Doug's dad offered so easily, as though he considered Steven a man equal to himself. An individual, therefore worth knowing. The result was exhilarating, particularly to one such as he, whose own father had not ever recognized his individuality, let alone his growing manhood.

"You're the waterfront director, they tell me," Doug's dad commented as they rode.

"Yes. I was one of the instructors last year, and this year I got promoted."

"You must have done a good job."

"The guy who used to be director quit. We all moved up," he said. "Otherwise I'd still be teaching Tadpoles I and II, like Doug will do if he gets through the training program. And I'm sure he will."

"Do you like teaching on the waterfront?"

"Oh, yes. I'd rather sail, but swimming's fine."

"Why aren't you part of the sailing staff, if you like it better?"

"I didn't have the chance to get good enough. The war stopped me from coming back to Quivet after I was eleven—I lived in Ohio—so I never got past Intermediate Mariner."

"Too bad. I'm pretty keen on sailing, myself."

"Have you done much?"

"I used to." They pulled up in front of the liquor store, went in to fetch a cold six-pack, returned to the car. "Help yourself, if you want," Doug's dad offered, and he did, the freedom and nonchalance of the moment heady as they rode along, the beer in his hand, the wind blowing through his hair. Doug's dad pulled up at one of Waterford's bay landings and turned off the car motor, opened a can of beer for himself.

"Hope you don't mind," he apologized. "Sometimes it's nice to watch the water without screaming hordes of little girls—like mine—jumping up and down in the backseat."

He laughed. "Doug did mention that his little sisters are a handful."

The father of the little girls cast his eyes heavenward, looking for strength to keep up, grinned, swigged his beer briskly.

"Yep," he said. "I did a lot of sailing, once, right here on Cape Cod Bay. That's one reason I wanted to send Doug to camp at Quivet when he was little. We lived close enough to get him here during the war, for one thing. What mattered to me most was giving him a chance to sail, too, so he'd love it as I did. But you can't dictate these things! As it turns out, Doug really likes swimming better."

"He teaches it well," Steven confirmed. "He's a good CIT, and one day he'll be a good counselor. Waterfront director too, maybe, when he's old enough."

"If you aren't there."

"I can't stay at camp forever." He smiled. They watched the bay companionably, and he thought how strange it was, and wonderful too, to feel so comfortable with an adult. This is what it could have been like . . .

"Well, whether Doug likes to sail or not," the father said, "I have a good excuse to come and stay while he's at Quivet. And I've enjoyed coming back. Once you've become addicted to the Cape, you always return."

"I'm addicted to it, that's for sure," he agreed.

"You were a camper at Quivet quite a few years?"

"Yes, before the war."

"I hear you collected the Outstanding Camper trophy—back before the war."

"Yes." He felt himself going hot in happy embarrassment.

"I hear a kid has to be pretty good to get it."

"Well, you have to work pretty darn hard, that's for sure," he said as casually as possible.

"It's a pleasure to meet someone who doesn't need to blow his own horn, Steven," the father said quietly. "Glad to know you."

"Thanks," he said, grinning foolishly—glad, very glad, that he'd met a man like Doug's dad, and glad he'd have a chance to spend time with him, off and on through the summer, for he needed the company of a man such as this one, he knew now. Needed it much more than he'd ever realized; Doug's father, without trying or understanding what he did, somehow smoothed over the awful, hateful sore places that Father invariably left behind.

They talked all the way back with the beer, about sailing and Steven's first year at Harvard, just completed, and the imminent prospect of the second, and how they might take a Quivet boat out sometime and see if they were as good sailors as they thought they were. Age fell away and there was no difference between them. And when they returned to the cottage, there was Diana. . . .

Elizabeth was still going on about overshot wheels and undershot wheels and ones with little buckets attached to them, and turbines, too, although she was not certain just which of these sorts Kingsley Merrick had used in West Waterford.

Steven, protected by the curtain of concentration he'd learned to lower at will, switched his attention to the most urgent reason he must get to East Waterford tonight—Diana. For tomorrow the family would leave, and Diana, a senior in high school, would go with them, and while he was pretty sure she understood that he planned to visit her this winter, and was surely going to write, and while he was pretty sure she wanted him to—still, he must! he must!—see her one more time, reassure himself that she liked him as much as he liked her . . . and, oh, God, kiss her one more time.

His urgency increased. . . .

When he'd first met her, that night of the staff party, he'd thought her pretty; in the next three minutes he knew she was beautiful. Her light brown hair was cut shoulder-length and curved under in a gentle pageboy, and it held the sun with gold and red lights. Her eyes were a brown-and-green mixture (mundanely called hazel, a name which did not convey their loveliness). She had an unusual voice, like a calling bird's, pitched somewhere between two notes, rich and vibrant. She was slim and finely built, and shortly after he met her he found himself dreaming about her and found that he wanted very much to put his arm around that slender waist, press her against himself because it seemed that he'd be able to feel every bone she had, every muscle, every pleasant curve, all of which would perfectly fit the contours of his own body.

On his earliest available Sunday off he'd taken her out for a session in the camp boat, which he and Doug had rowed down to the cottage. Everyone had been lounging on blankets, eating sandwiches and drinking Coca-Cola, basking in the sun, and after sitting awhile together, Diana had left the group and pushed the boat into the water, scrambled over the side, placed the oars in their locks, dipped and pulled. The boat went in a circle and scrubbed against the beach.

He waded out. "Would you like a lesson?"

"Well . . ." She squinted at him doubtfully. "I would if you aren't too bossy."

"I'm not bossy." He hopped in over the stern. "But I will have to instruct you to face me."

"Oh!" She looked at either oar. "That would be more convenient, when you get right down to it. Since the paddles are behind me."

"We call them oars," he said as the boat grated on the pebbles and sand again, making a wrenching sound.

"I'd just like to remind you," said Doug, coming to push them out, "that this boat is camp property, and it doesn't do anyone any good if it doesn't have a bottom." He gave it a shove, and they floated seaward.

"Try it now," he urged. She did, and the boat moved. Quickly she took another stroke, splashing him.

"Sorry!"

"It's okay."

"How do you know where you're going?"

"It's within the rules to look over your shoulder."

"It seems hard to row and look at the same time."

"Once you're satisfied that you're pointed where you want to go, then you set up a landmark, relative to the stern—in this case, me. If you keep their relative positions the same, you ought to stay on course."

She stopped rowing and looked, started, stopped, giggled. "I seem to be somewhere else," she laughed.

"Keep trying."

Her tongue poked out of the corner of her mouth as she concentrated. If his watching her made her self-conscious, she hid the fact very well. "We aren't going very fast," she said, comparing their position with the shore.

Nice as it was to watch, he had other ideas. "Two people are better than one. You could move over and take one oar, and I'd move up and take the other. Then we'd go faster."

Doubtfully she looked at the oars and then at the seat. "There's enough room?"

"Sure. In the old days, when you chased a whale you nearly always had two rowers to a seat."

"Okay, then," she agreed. "Let's chase a whale."

She moved, and the boat rocked. She paused, waiting for him to tell her what to do about it.

"Together. We have to shift together, counterbalance each other." They did, and he settled himself beside her. The sun's accumulated warmth seemed to emanate from her, and on the beach he could see Doug, watching, lounging on an elbow, talking to his mother. The younger sisters were trying to fortify a sand castle against the tide and had shanghaied their father into lugging stones for it.

"It must be nice to have so many people in your family,"

he remarked, watching the castle builders as he and Diana headed out.

"They're a pretty good family," she said. "Are you an only child or something?"

"Yes," he admitted.

"I almost was, myself."

"Oh?"

"I was a year old when my mother married Daddy, who is only my stepfather, really, but who is so great that no one—including me—can see any difference between the way he cares for me and the way he loves the others."

How wonderful, to know your father cared for you. Quickly he veered away from the sore spot that he knew could not be healed.

"Your own father died, I guess," he asked shyly.

"Yes. And my mom was working in the office of the Port of Philadelphia when Daddy, who was working on a tramp steamer, sailed in."

"He told me he likes to sail."

"Working on a tramp steamer isn't exactly sailing, but it's deep water, which, he says, is the real lure."

"It's part of it, that's for sure."

"However, I myself, not being truly his daughter, have no love for deep water at all. Do you think we might turn around?"

"Oh! Sure," he apologized. "I didn't realize you were uneasy. Hold your oar steady and deep, at right angles from us."

She did, while he continued to work the oar on his side, and instantly they reversed directions.

"How about that!" she exclaimed. "You really do know how."

"She doubted me!" he exclaimed to a passing gull.

"Sorry," she laughed. "I didn't mean it quite the way it sounded. You have a golden arrow, don't you! And no one wins a gold arrow at Quivet without being proficient at everything Quivet has to offer."

"Oh, quite!" he said blithely.

"And you must have a bronze and a silver one, too, because you can't earn a gold one unless you've already got the others."

"It's only bronze and silver paint."

"What difference does that make?" she demanded. "They stand for something. For something you achieved."

"They stand for carrots," he said modestly. "They're

dangled in front of campers to keep them ever striving, onward and upward forever."

She laughed again. "You're hopeless."

"Actually, they're very useful. I have them tacked up on the wall where my bunk is, to serve as an inspiration."

"Do they? Inspire the kids, I mean?"

"Into frenzies of admiration and cooperation."

"I'm sure I'd admire them properly, too. Someday you'll have to show them to me," she said shyly, and was interrupted by the scrunching and then the jolt of the boat, which they'd run up onto the beach. . . .

"A museum would be a fine contribution to West Waterford. The locals have very little appreciation for history," Elizabeth was saying. "They're so very . . ."

"Local," contributed Grandmother Merrick, and they all laughed.

"A practical group, to say the least," Cousin Elizabeth drawled. "Their appreciation of life's finer things pretty much centers on the activities at the grange hall, and a museum would enlighten them."

"You must have been pleased, then, to hear that the Pettingills have decided to live here in town," Mom said. "Nicer than the locals, I expect."

"I'm delighted," Cousin Elizabeth said. "They'll be excellent company. And I'm quite sure they'd be happy to help in building a museum at the mill site too." Significantly, she stared at Father.

"Tell you what," he proposed jovially. "I'll match whatever you can squeeze out of old Everett Pettingill."

It was his bid for Cousin Elizabeth's favor, and it was appreciatively received.

"Fairly said," Cousin Elizabeth approved. "And fairly done. I shall follow your fine example myself!"

"And now tell us, you two, about the Sunday dinners you've shared while Steven's been at camp. I'm sure you've had a grand time," Father beamed.

Steven held his breath. If Elizabeth wanted to complain about the free Sundays he had not spent at Kingsland this summer, here was her opportunity to do it.

"Why, we've had lots of fun." She smiled blandly. "And just think, when the Pettingills are here permanently, they can join us for Sunday dinners—it'll be a little like the old days!"

Steven sank back in relief as the conversation veered away to the subject of the old days. They would sit around interminably, he was sure. They always did, finding endless uninteresting things to talk about. . . .

He and Diana had walked the flats, the tide dead low, the shimmering sand appearing to reach to the horizon. They walked all the way up to Quivet, where the canoes were stacked like firewood, the rowboats overturned, one leaning against the other like spoons in a drawer, the flotation dock like a beached sea serpent, lying immobile on the floor of the bay. The gulls keened, and sandpipers chittered; the waterfront was empty because camp was deserted. It was a changeover, and the old boys were gone, the new not yet arrived.

They sat a few minutes by the buddy-board, resting, talking, observing the vast flatness before them. He glanced at her out of the corner of his eye, hoping that she would be receptive. It was, after all, the perfect opportunity . . .

"About those carrots," he began.

"Carrots?"

"Silver, bronze, and gold."

"Oh, yes! Those."

"I could show 'em to you now, if you like."

"Sure," she said easily.

He led her up and into his cabin, hoping that he was not breaking a rule by bringing a girl here. Bunks lined the cabin walls, the broom leaned behind the door, the light bulb hung, unadorned, from the rafters. The counselor's bunk was closest to the door so that in the night he'd be more likely to hear a camper leaving for the latrine, and be watching for his return.

The bronze, silver, and gold trophies were visible if you stooped slightly to look under the bunk above.

"Just see those wonderful carrots." He grinned, and she stooped, as he knew she'd have to. His heart began to pound because he knew what he was going to do next, and knew he could not stop himself. He put a hand on the rail of the top bunk, and when she straightened up again, it was there to prevent her from leaving. She looked at it, and then at him, past his arm to the freedom of the open door, and when she looked back again he was waiting for her. Their lips met sweetly, without haste, without demand, and when he stopped, he saw her eyes were still closed, her lashes long and dark against her cheek, her face peaceful.

"I didn't plan that when I brought you here," he lied, and when she looked up, the green and brown in her eyes were intense, a quick smile lighting them.

"You must be more pure than I am," she laughed. "I had it in mind all along."

Her smile deepened, and his body felt weightless, as though it were joyfully taking off in a striped and brilliantly colored balloon, lifting and soaring, free in the wind. They stood a moment longer. Into the essential quiet of the moment the sound of sneakered feet patted by on the path outside the cabin. Camp would soon be coming back to life.

"I guess we'd better get going."

"I guess we had," she said, and waited for him to take his hand away. But he slipped it around her waist instead, and pulled her closer. Sure enough, he could feel her delicate bones and the muscles of her thigh and the softness of her breasts against his chest, and he kissed her again, carefully, because she was young yet, but fully, so that she would know how he felt.

And then they left the cabin. . . .

"Old days and old ways are all well and good," Father was saying, "but many modern improvements really are superior—for instance, oil heat as contrasted to coal."

It was not the first time such a topic had come up for discussion.

"An oil burner wouldn't take up as much room downstairs," Father persisted.

"I don't live in the basement," Elizabeth pointed out. "So I don't care how much room the heating plant takes. But since it's a capital improvement and since you might stand to benefit by it, Charles, in time to come, perhaps we should take a look at the best place to install one. If I decide to do it someday."

"How about the far corner, where the coal bin is now?" Grandmother suggested.

"Come along with us, Elvira," Cousin Elizabeth urged. "Give us the benefit of your opinion. But I'm warning you, Charles. I don't intend to buy one. Not now, anyway." Their feet clumped heavily on the cellar stairs.

"How about if I helped you with the expense?" Father offered, no doubt hoping to earn her gratitude and be rewarded in her will.

"It's not money I worry about. But a little help would be acceptable," she said.

Perhaps Elizabeth disliked Father, Steven thought. Maybe all she wants from him is money.

The door at the bottom closed, and their voices were no more than murmurs.

"Well!" sighed Mom, putting down her cigarette. "How are you, honey?"

There was a gentleness in her voice that was never there when Father was present, as though Mom did not want Father to know that any bond was shared between herself and her son.

He smiled genuinely for the first time that afternoon. "I'm fine, Mom."

"And Harvard. How do you really feel about it?"

"It's okay. I have to work pretty hard. No time for fun. But I'm passing." Quickly he crossed over to the couch. "Mom," he said urgently, "I have a date in East Waterford. Could you take me over there?"

"East Waterford?"

"Now? Could you take me now?"

The light in her face faded as she realized he had not come to the couch simply to be near her, but she struggled to conceal her disappointment, and smiled conspiratorially. "Sure," she said instantly, reaching for her purse. Well did she understand that Father would massacre such a request.

They let themselves out the front door and hastened to the Pontiac with its Ohio plates. Mom slid in behind the wheel while Steven climbed in on the other side. Neither of them slammed the door until the engine caught and Mom had shifted into first gear, and the car was already moving. Like the great gal she was, Mom asked no questions. "I hate having you so far away," she said, continuing their conversation. "You've completed a whole year, after all. I wondered if you wanted to transfer, after this coming year. Then, at least, I could see you at holidays. Perhaps Father would consider it; you'd have half your college education at the alma mater."

"Fat chance!" He had traded his friendship with Ed Lamson and the chance to play varsity basketball in exchange for attending Harvard, and going to Harvard didn't include any halfway measures, he was quite sure. "I don't think Father would go along with it, Mom, and I don't think he'd pay tuition anywhere else, either. And my Quivet salary wouldn't quite do the trick."

"You've seen something of Elizabeth this year. Perhaps she'd help," Mother persisted.

"I doubt it. Not in opposition to Father," he said, and dismissed the whole discussion because the lane to the Bradleys' cottage was coming up. "Turn here," he directed, and pointed to a sandy, bumpy lane on the bay side of route six. As soon as they bounced into the backyard of the cottage, Doug came running, and Diana followed behind slowly, a little shyly.

"Gee, we were afraid you wouldn't be able to make it," Doug called.

"This is my C.I.T.," Steven said to Mom. "And his sister Diana."

"Please come in, Mrs. Sinclaire." Diana smiled. "You can meet Mom and Dad. And our aunt." She turned to Steven. "My aunt is visiting for Labor Day." Her smile for him was special, more intimate than for just a casual friend, warming him right to his toes.

Doug opened Mom's door invitingly.

"If you're sure I won't be intruding," Mom said, throwing Steven a little glance that told him to relax, that she would not stay so long that he'd regret it. Willingly she let herself be led into the kitchen, where the little girls were mixing Kool-Aid. They stopped long enough to acknowledge Doug's introduction, resuming their measuring and pouring as Doug led everyone through and into the living room, where the table for canasta was set up and waiting. From the group of comfortable chairs by the fireplace Doug's father got to his feet and started to approach, and stopped, his handsome face awry with shock and amazement. From her own chair by the fireplace a lady whom Steven had not seen before struggled slowly up and leaned on the chair back as though she lacked the strength to stand alone, and when he turned to Mom, to make sure he was not in her way, Steven saw that she looked incredibly old and incredibly young, all at once, and that her skin was terribly, terribly white.

Doug's mom was the only one capable of speech. "Is this your mother, Steven?"

"Oh, yes!" he said awkwardly, made clumsy in the presence of so much tension. "Mom, I'd like you to meet Doug's mother, Mrs. Bradley."

Mom turned her whole self as though her neck were stiff and she was unable to turn just her head. "How do you do, Mrs. Bradley?"

"I'm so glad to meet you, Mrs. Sinclaire," Doug's mother said warmly. "We've enjoyed Steven so much! Thanks for bringing him tonight."

"You're welcome," Mom said tonelessly.

"This is my husband," Mrs. Bradley continued valiantly on against the utter silence into which the stirring sounds in the kitchen filtered. "And his cousin, Alice. Steven, this is Doug's aunt, Miss Bradley."

"How do you do?" he said politely.

"Hi, Alice," Mom said wearily. "Hi, Tim."

"Hello, Emily!" exclaimed the lady cousin. "How amazing to see you!"

"You know one another already!" exclaimed Mrs. Bradley.

Mr. Bradley, who so far had said nothing, suddenly came to life. "A long time ago," he exclaimed, perhaps too heartily. "I had no idea, Emily! The Sinclaire name threw me off."

"Probably you remember Charles," Mom said. "He ran around with our gang sometimes." She took a step backward, toward the door.

"You mean the fellow whose family lived in the old Denning place?" asked the lady cousin. "The one who had an English accent—or what passed for one?" She was having a hard time to keep from staring at Steven, while Mr. Bradley had a hard time not staring at Mom, and Mom was covertly sizing up Mrs. Bradley.

"We could start the game in the kitchen," Diana offered. "In case you all would like to visit a little."

"Oh, no!" Mom exclaimed, heading for the door. "No, I must be running along."

"We'll bring Steven home later, then," Mrs. Bradley said cordially.

"Fine. I can let myself out," Mom said as the three adults and Steven simultaneously moved toward the back door with her. "Really, please don't bother," she said, her voice a little shrill, and then she was gone.

"Well, can you beat that!" Mr. Bradley said happily. "Emily Merrick! After all these years!"

"Hm," said the Bradley cousin, who did not seem especially pleased, one way or the other. Then she smiled at Steven. "I'm so happy to have a chance to get acquainted with you, Steve. Your family and mine have known each other for a long time. Won't you call me Alice?"

The tension in the room broke.

"Well," said Mr. Bradley expansively, "who wants to get whipped at canasta?"

The game over, the family in the kitchen consuming snacks and discreetly turning their backs, Steven and Diana walked out onto the beach and silently went up to the next point.

He stopped, pulling her to a halt beside him.

"End of the line," he said, and put his arms around her. She leaned against him, nestling her face into his throat. They stood together, clinging, which he knew they couldn't do indefinitely because Mr. Bradley was waiting to take him back to Kingsland—yet he didn't have what it took to separate himself from her.

"I'll come to Worcester," he said despairingly.

"Yes."

"When do you want me?"

"Tomorrow."

Sorrowing, they laughed.

"How about the first weekend in October?" He'd have saved enough of his spending money by then, he hoped, to pay for bus fare.

"If I last that long," she said. "The first weekend in October would be great."

"And I'll write you."

"Yes."

"And you'll write me."

"Yes. Yes, you know I will." Her voice shook, and he was close to tears himself; he kissed her, the aching, trembling kiss of departure, and frantically she tried to prolong it, hopelessly reaching up for him, following his mouth when at last he ended it, because . . . Good Christ, they had to stop sometime.

He looked at her lovely face in the moonlight, memorizing it. "I'll see you soon. Right?"

"Right!" She shook her head, willing her tears away, and they went back to the cottage and into it and he said goodbye to the little sisters and to Mrs. Bradley, and Aunt Alice, and to Doug.

He left Diana by the door and got into the Bradley car without looking back.

"Well, I won't go into another song and dance about how nice it's been," Mr. Bradley said as they bounced over the ruts and turned onto Main Street. "But you know it has."

"Yeah," he agreed inarticulately, suffering.

"You know," Mr. Bradley said, "we never did get that chance to take out a Quivet sailboat, and I'm sure sorry. I'd like to see if you sail as well as I think you do."

A ray of light shot up out of the darkness of his misery—a reprieve! "My aunt and uncle have a cat boat anchored on the flats," he said. "It's an early tide. If it won't delay you too much, I'll bring it down first thing and we can get a sail in after all."

"And you can see my daughter again, right?" Mr. Bradley laughed.

Hot with embarrassment, he did not answer.

"Well," Mr. Bradley went on, "I don't think your cousin Elizabeth would like the idea, your borrowing that boat to sail with me—now that I know she is your cousin! And while I don't personally give a damn about her preferences, I'd rather not involve you in any unpleasantness."

"You know Elizabeth already?"

"Her reputation preceded her many years ago, when I was young and first heard of her."

"It's true she's apt to be stingy." Steven smiled. "But perhaps, since it's Aunt Celia's boat and not hers . . ."

"I'm sorry, Steven. I think it unwise."

It felt like a rebuff, and not knowing what to do about it, he said nothing. Apparently Doug's dad sensed the hurt he'd inadvertently caused; pulling into the driveway, he said kindly, "All right, then. I'll just leave it up to you and your mother, instead of making a decision for you. I didn't mean to be so dictatorial. If you arrive at the cottage before eight o'clock, fine. If you don't, I'll know you ran into trouble. Okay?"

"Okay." He smiled. He'd be there by eight o'clock if it killed him!

"Good luck to you this year at school." Mr. Bradley held out his hand.

"I'd like to visit you in Worcester," Steven said. "I hope that's all right with you and Mrs. Bradley."

"Renewing your acquaintance with Doug, no doubt."

"Um, no doubt."

"Diana, of course, has nothing to do with it," he teased, and then laughed. "It'd be great, Steven, to have you with us."

How wonderful—to anticipate the continued friendship of this great guy—and that of his beautiful daughter, as well!

Warmed, the parting ache eased, he got out, waved to Mr. Bradley, who, turning around, sped away.

He turned toward Kingsland, a waiting hulk silhouetted by a harvest moon that scattered blue insubstantial light everywhere.

She was waiting for him, sitting on his bed. The small desk lamp threw long shadows on the tower walls and made her seem more petite than she was, made her face seem lined and bleak.

"Hi," he exclaimed softly, so that no one would wake up. "What are you doing here?"

"I had to talk to you. Before someone else does."

He sat on the edge of his bed, beside her. "All right. I'm here. Is Father mad at our taking off without asking him?"

"No. It's not that."

He waited to find out what it might be.

"You enjoy the Bradleys very much, don't you?" Mom asked finally.

"Yes."

"All of them."

"Sure, all of them."

"The boy, Doug?"

"We've been good friends this summer. He's younger than I am, but it doesn't seem to matter. We hope to meet at camp again next year. He's a good egg."

"And Diana? How well have you gotten to know her?"

"Pretty well," he hedged. "I expect I'll get to know her better this winter, because she and her family have invited me to come to their house in Worcester whenever I can make it. I'll just have to see what happens."

"So you'll be visiting them?"

"Why, yes. I'd sure like to, anyway." Perhaps his enthusiasm for the Bradleys hurt her feelings? Perhaps she didn't like Diana? "Not too often, of course," he hedged, hoping to hide the fact that Doug's family gave him what her own efforts could not. "We've more or less set up the first weekend in October. I'll take it from there."

She stared at the floor.

"They're fun," he explained lamely. "They don't mind if I share their good times, and I'm grateful. After all, being so far from home . . . it's nice to have a place to go."

"How about Mr. Bradley?" she asked strangely, as though she had not heard.

"Mr. Bradley?" In the region of his heart something fluttered briefly downward, an autumn leaf swirling to the earth.

"Do you expect to see him, too, while you visit?"

"I don't see how I can avoid it, do you?"

She did not answer.

"In fact, we hope to go sailing tomorrow, before the family has to leave. We talked about it tonight. Contingent on Elizabeth's letting us borrow Aunt Celia's sailboat. It's anchored on the flats; no one's using it. Do you think she'd mind—Cousin Elizabeth, I mean? Mr. Bradley is a pretty good sailor—at least he says so. I don't think any harm would come to the boat, or anything. I told him I'd sail to the cottage in the morning and pick him up, if everything was all right. Otherwise, we'll just forget about it. I'll see them all in October, anyway . . ."

Mom turned away from him and covered her eyes as though the light were too bright. "Oh, God!"

To his horror her voice was trembling, and tears were running over her fingers. "Oh, God! Oh, my God," she wailed brokenly.

He stared, paralyzed by this display of distress, dismayed at Mom's loss of control. Beside him on the bed she was shaking, her hands pressed to her mouth now, as though to hold in her cries, and within him instantly rose the recognition of catastrophe.

"The boat's not that important," he said quickly. "Mr. Bradley will understand, I'm sure."

"Steven," she wept, utterly defeated, her shoulders slumped abjectly. "Steven. Steven, this has got to stop. Tim Bradley is your father."

The distance between them increased, and a void separated him from his inner being. It was clearly a mistake—a monstrous mistake—and clearly he had heard it wrong. He burst into a cold sweat and waited because there was nothing else he could do.

"I don't know how to tell you," Mom struggled. "I've never known how—but I always meant to, someday. I owed it to you. Now . . . now, of all the freakish things that could have happened, you've met the Bradleys. . . ."

"Old families often come back," the man Steven said, his voice steady. *Once you become addicted to Cape Cod, you always return,* the boy Steven heard Mr. Bradley's voice say.

"And, perhaps, becoming really serious about Diana."

"I *am* really serious about her. But it's okay, she's Mr. Bradley's adopted daughter," he argued, as though it made any difference in the sum total of this disaster.

"And with your planning to continue seeing them . . ."

Yes, that had been his plan, hadn't it?

It would be great to have you with us.

"It's just impossible, is all, and I can't put it off anymore. I'm sorry, Steve. Oh, honest-to-God, I'm sorry."

It was unreal, as though the room were a painted stage setting and the two of them, the actors, were pasted flat to it like paper cutouts, gutless, lifeless.

"Perhaps you'd better tell me everything," he said stiffly, his voice as flat as the pasted image.

"Yes. Yes, I'd better. I . . . I hardly know where to begin. I . . . I met Tim Bradley twenty years ago, right here in

Waterford." Her voice was thin, wavering. "And I was crazy about him. The friendship got a little ahead of us, is all, and I'm afraid I . . . I conducted myself unwisely. I got pregnant . . . but, of course, you never know you are pregnant when you get that way." Her weeping overcame her, and she looked away and he looked away, too, unwilling to witness this exposure of his mother's vital, vulnerable private self. He got up from the bed, to put some distance between them.

"Go on," the man Steven instructed his mother.

Within himself the boy had withdrawn, stung, appalled, into a corner somewhere, from whence he looked out at the world, out at the consequences of his mother's foolishness.

"The trouble was that I didn't know I'd gotten pregnant until after Tim had left Cape Cod, and I couldn't find him when I needed him. He'd gone to sea . . . and I was alone, alone with the penalty." Mom's mouth started quivering again. "I'm sure he'd have married me, if he'd known about you. He was a decent person, he really was."

"Yes," he managed to get out. Mr. Bradley was, after all, decent still.

Oh, God, he cried silently, the pain starting to build as he realized what he had missed in that terrible turn of fate that had put Tim Bradley beyond his mother's reach when she needed him, so that Steven himself (whoever he was) had barely missed being claimed by the very person who had so recently, so generously filled the emptiness of his youth.

It's a pleasure to meet someone who doesn't need to blow his own horn.

Oh, God, his inner being railed in senseless protest against abandonment, against injustice, against the dying of innocence, and he knew it was the last time that the Lord would ever enter his mind as a refuge or a source of peace.

"And so I was on my own," Mom said, her voice toneless now that she'd gotten past the hard part. "There was no question, of course, about bearing an illegitimate child. Occasionally you hear about it being done, of course, but not by a girl of a certain type, who upholds a certain standard. A respectable girl didn't have a . . ." She met his eyes unwillingly.

". . . a bastard," he filled in for her from his man's strength.

"She didn't have a child out of wedlock then, not if she wanted to continue to be respected. No more than she does now." It was true. Nice people did not beget children out of wedlock. Women who did that sort of thing were women like

Pam Thompson, no doubt, would turn out to be, buying and selling to get what they wanted.

"I didn't know about abortions. There were only two choices for a girl in my position. I could go away and have a baby and give it away, secretly. But I'd have needed my family's help for such a thing, and telling them was unthinkable. I never, not even once, considered it. Besides, I didn't want to give Tim Bradley's child away. I wanted to keep it if I could. It was all of Tim Bradley I was going to get."

A bastard. He was a bastard! The result of a sweaty, secret, panting liaison, a mistake, the consequence of an accidental spill of sperm, of the insatiable lust of male-kind.

A slip of the dick, and there stood Steven Sinclaire, who should have been Steven Bradley, he thought bitterly. And knowing it was an awful burden, separating him from other people, isolating him. He turned away from his mother, looked out the window, seeing only his own alien reflection and hers behind him. The crab that once lived within his depths came to life, grabbed, held hard, hurt. Hurt a lot.

"So how did you happen to marry Father?" he asked. And then it came to him that he had labored under Charles Sinclaire's heavy hand all these years, believing himself unworthy of parental approval, and all the time, why, Charles Sinclaire was only giving his name to a bastard—and probably giving it unwillingly.

His mind reeled away.

"I'd known Charles for years," she said apologetically. "His family had been friends of the Merricks, and my family wanted me to marry him, and Charles had been after me for some time. So I married him."

"What happened when he found out about me?"

"He was pretty upset. But he agreed to raising you as his own."

"You never had more children."

"Charles isn't very . . . he isn't interested in that sort of thing."

"He enjoys beating little kids more, is that it?"

"Steve!"

"It was more fun to whip a child than to screw you, I gather. What was wrong? Couldn't he get it up?" he asked roughly.

Her silence told the answer.

"So he rescued your reputation and fed and clothed you these twenty years, and in exchange you let him do whatever he wanted. To me."

"He abused me, too," she said slowly. In the reflection of the window he saw her tense face, rigid mouth stiffly opening, closing as she spoke. "It was an agreement we reached, when he found out. His right to his pleasures, such as they are, in exchange for protection."

"Was it worth the price?"

"Steven," she pleaded, "I loved Tim Bradley, and you are his child. I certainly never regretted the chance to keep you by me—you've been a wonderful son."

"How swell for you." Coldness pervaded him.

"Isn't it better than being adopted?" she cried.

"You've got to be kidding." His sarcasm was brutal, and he regretted the hurt that it inflicted. But it was too late to take it back, too late to care, too late for a lot of things. In the window he stared at her tormented face.

Ah, this inexplicable, this unutterable, this irradicable pain. Tearing at his throat, getting worse all the time as the enormity grew on him—that Tim Bradley, whom he'd enjoyed so much this summer, was untouchable now. That he had lost Diana because he could not accept the Bradleys, any of them—not even her. That he would have to hide the truth about himself, always and forever, because there would be few, if any, people with whom he could share such knowledge. That he was stuck with Charles Sinclaire, who had ever crippled and maimed him, tormenting the bastard child who was worth nothing to him, a mere mote in the eye, a piece of humanity without value. The totality of these disasters was overwhelming—yet he must bear up under them. There was no choice.

"I don't want to discuss this any longer," the man Steven told his mother. "Please go."

"Steve . . ."

"Please. Now," the man commanded over and above the impossible begging of the boy to be comforted. He turned to face her, face the expression in her eyes that was so overwhelmingly sad, and he met it coldly, hatefully, and watched her shambling, stumbling exit from the room. He turned off his light and stared out the window again without seeing the strangely lit land, and wrestled with the tearing wound that was working, like a rip in his very flesh, deep, deep, its edges grinding together.

What difference would it have made if he had always known?

None.

So why the pain?

Ah, why the pain!

Why not anger in the face of that which was so utterly beyond his control: the lack of judgment, the surrender to passion so many years ago that had brought him into being by a father who had left him at the mercy of that bastard Charles Sinclaire.

No, he told himself. It's you who's the bastard, not Sinclaire. And he has always known it.

He stilled the impulse to put his fist through the window, to smash something, throw something. He had to do something! He could not lie supine under the weight of his mother's mistakes. He must take charge of the situation, of himself, his future, in such a way as to nullify mistakes of the past. But how?

He leaned his hot forehead against the piercing coolness of the glass and suffered—for he had lost it all. He thought about Diana, of her lips and of her body, her clear, honest face; he thought of Doug, who was his brother; he thought of Tim Bradley himself, whose praise had kindled bonfires on the otherwise barren moonscape of his heart—his father! His father! What he could have been and done with a father like that! Oh, Jesus, he must turn away from this before it destroyed him with its frenzy and wild railing against so unjust a fate—yes, he must turn away and instead concentrate on that which was possible. . . .

The annihilation of Charles Sinclaire, whom he had hated for years and now must banish from his life—for good. His annihilation as though he'd never been, his influence demolished, his power denied. And the instrument of this reduction lay not far away, was so simple that as he thought about it now, he could not understand why he hadn't done it before. And perhaps, by the time he accomplished it, this hurt, this pain, this loneliness and twisting hatred would have subsided to manageable levels and he could live again. Must subside, else he would be lost forever in it.

He would begin right away.

V

The Annihilation of Charles Sinclaire

14

The maples in the curving driveway had not yet turned gold, and the greenness of their leaves was as a veil of clouds, obscuring the face of a mountain. But basking in the sun, Kingsland shone through the minute gaps and interstices as though it had an inner light, and Steven paused on the edge of Mr. Snow's steps, across the intersection, and looked over at the distant object of his pilgrimage, listened to the sounds of Waterford in early autumn.

This morning, he'd hustled his belongings—all of them—to the bus station in Boston and stuffed them in lockers. With only an overnight bag and a small duffel, he had come to Waterford.

It was quiet, freed at last from the persistent buzzing of its summer visitors. The usually continuous passing of traffic was gone, and an unhurried quiet had reasserted itself; within the old store, Mr. Snow was stocking shelves. He nodded his head in greeting as though he had seen Steven every day of his life and certainly expected to see him here, in Waterford, only one day after his parents had ferried him and his stuff to Boston. Casting a glance at the duffel Steven had left outside on the steps, Mr. Snow continued stocking the shelves. "That yours?"

"Yes," Steven replied.

"A little late going up to college, aren't you?" Mr. Snow asked cautiously, carefully skirting the issue of Steven's presence so as not to appear to be prying—the cardinal sin of the countryman.

"I've been there, and now I've come back." Steven smiled at Mr. Snow's caution. "You wouldn't happen to know of any jobs around town, would you?"

"Not offhand," Mr. Snow said. "What kind of job?"

"Any kind, as long as its unskilled."

Mr. Snow stepped back from his shelves, eyed Steven's height, breadth, and stature. "You mean, unskilled like a college boy could do?"

"Yes. Something like that."

"Painting, perhaps? Carpentry?"

"More like hod carrier." He laughed. "I really don't know how to do much, Mr. Snow."

"What makes you think someone would want you, then?"

"Because I'm cheap, and I'm anxious to learn. That must be worth something."

"Expect it is," Mr. Snow said. "Young Bob Casey's just starting out on his own. Probably be happy to know where he could get cheap labor."

Steven frowned. "Do I know Mr. Casey?"

"I expect you would, if you saw him. Matter of fact, he's working on the old Pettingill place, replacing slates on the roof. You could just run up there and see what he looks like, if you want."

"That'd be great! Can I leave my duffel here for a while, Mr. Snow?"

"Expect so," Mr. Snow agreed, without asking why young Sinclaire couldn't lug it over to Kingsland, where it belonged. But, of course, until Elizabeth agreed to letting him stay with her, it did not belong there. Would she agree? He remembered that she had not given his absences at Sunday dinner away . . . he was banking on her cooperation!

The pavings of the sidewalk were uneven, like teeth that needed straightening, and the lovely old trees dappled the dust on the road's edge. The Pettingill place was square, and hip-roofed, as all the oldest places in Waterford were, with a pretty fan of glass over the door and a lilac bush on either side of the stoop. The paint on the house was old and unpromising; the grounds had not been kept up, but mowed only perfunctorily, probably by one of the Stone kids, who did that kind of thing for fifty cents an hour.

On the roof two men were laying tar paper. Broken slates and nails lay on the ground, and surely needed to be picked up. By someone.

"Mr. Casey?" he called up, shading his eyes from the sun. One of the men looked over his shoulder to see who was calling. "Mr. Bob Casey?"

"That's me," the man said. He had not raised his voice, but Steven had no trouble hearing him.

"Can I come up and talk to you?" Certainly it would not do to ask Mr. Casey to come down.

"Help yourself." The man turned to his companion and said something Steven couldn't hear; he gripped the sides of the ladder and started up. It bounced and rattled and was unpleasantly reminiscent of climbing trestle bridges. He made himself go to the top, and knew better than to look down.

"My name is Steve Sinclaire, Mr. Casey. Mr. Snow, down the street, said you might be interested in a hired hand that didn't cost too much and was willing to do anything."

"Anything?" Bob Casey smiled, sweat-stained and dirty from the old roof, and his face was the kindest that Steven had ever seen. He was probably in his thirties, well built but not especially tall, as far as Steven could figure out from his necessarily hunched position on the roof. Mr. Snow was wrong; he could not remember seeing Casey before. "What can you do?" Casey asked. "Aside from anything."

"Not much, I'm afraid. I've been a counselor at Camp Quivet for a couple of summers, and I play basketball. That's not worth much to you, I know, but at least it proves I can run, and take responsibility."

Casey laughed. "I guess it does, at that."

"I need to learn a lot, Mr. Casey. If you'd even let me work with you for nothing, this fall, just so I could learn, I'd be willing to do that." It would take a long time to get anywhere, working for nothing, but he had to start somewhere, didn't he? At the moment, after all, he was nowhere.

"Well," said Casey, "right now, as you can see, we're roofing this house, and it takes a little know-how to do it."

"I'm sure it does," he said quickly. "But it doesn't take any know-how to pick up your mess."

Casey looked down onto the littered yard. "You willing to pick up that crap and throw it on my truck?"

"I sure am! I'll start right now, Mr. Casey!"

"Bob. The name is Bob."

"Okay, Bob!" He slid down the ladder and began on the old shingles, working as fast as he could. When he'd finished, he took the rake, leaning against Casey's pickup truck, and cleaned up the tar-paper scraps and splinters and nails, and suddenly the sun was low, the afternoon over, and he remembered that his duffel was at Snow's and that Cousin Elizabeth still didn't know he was in town and he could no longer put off facing her. Casey and his pal climbed slowly down the ladder, both of them stiff from crouching on the roof, stretching appreciatively when they were on land again, grunting, glancing around at Steven's efforts. Casey was a man in his prime; his companion was old—in his sixties at least. They were an oddly assorted pair, though plainly well-suited to one another, attuned to the thoughts of each other as now, when Bob turned to his cohort. "Wouldn't hurt my feelings to have someone toting shingles up the ladder. How about you, Hubie?"

"Wouldn't hurt my feelings, neither." Hubie grinned. "Just like it don't hurt my feelings to have that junk in the truck already."

"And if the Pollard job works out, we'd need help with that, too."

"I wouldn't mind someone else lugging for that contract. Someone younger than me," Hubie agreed, both of them assiduously ignoring Steven's presence and the gratitude on his face. "Maybe we could get him to do the shingling with us."

"Depends on how good he is with the hammer, I expect."

"Well, I could kind of show him," Hubie suggested.

He hoped he wouldn't cry, that was all!

"I can't pay you much. Would seventy-five cents an hour be all right?" Casey asked.

"Great." He swallowed.

"That settles it, then. Would anyone care to join me at the Ace-High on the way home?"

"Why, you might convince me," Hubie drawled.

"Sure," Steven agreed, gladly postponing his interview with Elizabeth. He climbed into the truck beside Hubie, silently accompanied the men to the roadhouse, unfolding himself from the cab of the truck and following Bob in. The interior of the Ace-High was not elaborate: booths on one wall, bar on the other, a small space for dancing at one end of the room, and a few tables and chairs at the other, where the jukebox was. It was well-populated, though not packed, with men in work-worn overalls, pungent faded blue workshirts, their hands rough, their faces invariably smudged, their quiet voices buzzing and mumbling and occasionally breaking out in a rash of laughter. Refreshment, apparently, was all they were after; several were leaving, and at the bar, where he seated himself with Bob, several more were finishing a bottle of beer, staying to talk but refusing a refill.

He had very little money, and was glad to see that the men had a one-beer limit. He nodded as Bob asked, "Draft?" and gratefully drank half when it arrived.

"So . . ." Bob grinned, leaning back to observe him. "Can you do the same tomorrow?"

"Pick up trash, you mean?"

"Yup. That's what I meant."

"Sure," he said casually. Were they waiting for the city kid to whine? Well, they'd have to wait a long time!

He took another sip of beer and glanced at the clock: five-thirty.

The barkeeper came by. "Another?" he asked politely.

"Maybe we should," Bob said expansively. "Celebrate Steve's arrival in Waterford."

"I don't need another," he put in quickly.

"Do you know Steve Sinclaire?" Bob asked the barkeeper. "This is Ed Slater, Steve."

Ed Slater reached across the bar to shake hands, in the manner of countrymen looking elsewhere as he did so.

"Steve is old lady Edgarton's nephew," Bob said.

"Yes," Ed said, indicating that he knew it already.

"He's helping me shingle old lady Pettingill's roof," Hubie chimed in.

"That so?" Ed remarked wryly, as though he did not believe it. "Did any of you want another?"

"I will," Hubie said.

"No, thanks," Bob said, and turned to talk to a man who had come up behind him. Ed Slater moved on down the counter to serve another customer, who, from what Steven could gather, was asking who the new young fellow with Bob Casey was. Hubie and Bob continued to talk; Steven waited patiently while everyone ignored him.

Going to the Ace-High was less than pleasant, he reflected, if you didn't belong. He worked hard at keeping his face impassive and thought for a while about his upcoming interview with Cousin Elizabeth. He was counting on the rapport he'd had with her ever since he was a boy—if anyone could be said to have rapport with Elizabeth Edgarton! Yet she had always been kind to him, in her way, and unless he missed his guess, she was less than thrilled with Charles Sinclaire. She might even enjoy being part of Steven's rebellion against him, even though she would not know its cause.

"This is Arnie Stone, Steve," Bob was saying. Apparently introductions were performed selectively in Waterford.

"Business going pretty good?" Arnold Stone asked Bob, signaling Slater for a mug of beer.

"Can't complain."

"Casey here has went on his own just this summer," Arnold Stone said to Steven. "In case he didn't tell you."

"He didn't. Mr. Snow told me," Steven contributed.

Everyone nodded, and Steven suspected that this indirect endorsement had done him no harm.

"Takes guts to go it alone," Stone continued. "But we all have to do it sometime."

Bob had evidently decided it was time to leave. He slid off the bar stool, signaled Hubie, nodded at Steven, and walked away. Wearily Steven hurried behind and climbed back up into the cab of the Casey truck, hanging on to the dashboard as Bob bumped over the potholes of the parking lot to Main Street.

"Nice fella, Arnie Stone," Bob remarked.

"You know him well?" Steven asked politely.

Hubie, sitting between them, laughed.

"Used to work for him," Bob said with a smile.

"You'd think he wouldn't be so friendly. You're his competition now, after all."

"Well, we've got to hope there's enough business for two," Bob said easily. Apparently Waterford men did not despise competition. "Which reminds me to tell you that things generally come to a stop here around Christmas," Bob added. "And don't start up again until early spring."

"I see," he said around his dismay. What was he supposed to do all winter?

"But for as long as I've got need for a man to haul shingles, you're welcome to the job."

"Okay," he gulped.

"I expect someday Hubie'll see that you get a chance to show your stuff with a hammer. If I get the Pollard job."

Ah! There was some hope! And he could always offer his services to Kingsland during the winter months. Painting woodwork, perhaps, and ceilings. Wash windows. Repair or refinish furniture. Things that would pay for his keep.

"Thanks," he said, determined to measure up if it killed him. "You can let me off here. I have to get my bag at Mr. Snow's."

But he did not cross the street to confront Elizabeth. He needed more time—he was not sure for what—and hiding his duffel beneath a bush, he jogged down the Rockford Road to the beach, to the bay and the western sky, where banks of clouds were hurrying to witness the setting of the September sun, their underbellies flushing, their tops darkened. The sky and the sea became deep and lustrous as the sun touched the rim of the world. The wind of the fall season, coming now from the northwest, blew its warning across the beach. Far, far up, a line of ducks was stitched in the sky, and he watched as they reversed themselves and dropped closer to the earth, heard them calling, calling until they coasted to a feeding ground beyond his vision.

The sun was gone.

The clouds, having seen what they had come to see, now dispersed, and the bright star of evening watched from the cold, clear sky, and Steven, also watching, was somehow made pure, too, emptied for that moment of his angers and hurts and poisons, an empty vessel into which the peace and benediction of the evening and of the season was poured.

And then he was ready to face her.

15

"I'll miss this boy, I really will," said A. Lincoln Sears loudly, and everyone in the booth at the Ace-High looked away, embarrassed by Linc's sentiment, which they themselves were too reticent to express.

In fact, they all had become fond of the Sinclaire boy.

"Well, I'd like to toast his success," said Don Slater. "Long as success'll make him rich enough to retire to Waterford when he's old like us." Don was all of thirty.

"I'll drink to that," agreed Casey.

"And we'll do all your repairs for you, Steve, because you'll be all thumbs by then, and lazy too," Greenleaf Stone said. "And we'll charge you a fortune."

"Hear! Hear!" said Ed Slater.

"Thanks," Steven laughed. "What pals you are." Most of them were older than he—some by quite a bit—but, by God, they were pals; they'd been good to him; they'd made him one of their own.

"He'll be able to afford it," Linc Sears assured the group. "College people always end up rich."

Much as they envied the opportunities that wealthy people from the city had, opportunities that, as country people, they rarely got themselves, they neither envied nor despised Steven Sinclaire in his determination to go to college. The boy had worked shoulder to shoulder with them this past year and a half, and had earned enough money for two semesters at a school in Ohio, and they admired spirit like that. They'd miss him when he was gone.

Roly Hall, Waterford's law-enforcement officer, poked his head around the doorway of the Ace-High, located the celebrants, pulled up a chair while declining a beer.

"Can't drink on duty," he explained. "I might get relieved of my situation if I had alcohol on my breath whilst telling off them summer people." For years Roly Hall had been Waterford's policeman and dog officer; since neither of these positions was full-time, he comfortably managed them from the office of his gas station, where he smoked cigars, gossiped with his cronies, and listened to his police radio, pride of his life. Summer traffic caused him to put on his suit about five o'clock; now he pointed to his official badge, winked at the laughers, refusing to take either them or himself seriously. "Heard this is your swan song, Steve," he said. "Wanted to wish you luck."

"Thanks, Roly."

"And if you ever want a job pumping gas, you come talk to me—hear?"

"Sure thing."

"He's going to be rich," said Bob Casey. "He won't need you, Roly."

"Wrong!" declared Steven. "One of these days I might forget myself and drive too fast. I'd need him then, wouldn't I? To fix my traffic ticket."

They guffawed, because they could not remember Chief Hall ever fining a Waterford native for speeding through town. In fact, Chief Hall never issued tickets to anyone; it was against his principles. They drank a toast to Roly and his nonticketing propensities, and Steven watched them fondly: simple men, poor men in comparison to city standards, yet men who had befriended him—a boy related to Waterford's Merrick family and presumably high above them in the social order of things. But they had chosen to disregard that gulf and he was grateful to them now, and hated like hell to leave them. He would miss them and their town, which he had come to know so well and had made his own. Waterford and these rough men had made the struggle for survival possible, and the struggle had been a mighty one!

To his relief, Elizabeth had agreed that he might live with her, a year and a half ago, when he'd proposed an exchange of his labor for room and board. But she had driven a stiff bargain, the old scrooge, and he had reputtied all the storm windows, dug up every blade of grass around the house and reseeded the lawns there, planted flowerbeds and tended them, painted all the ceilings in the dingy house, rebuilt sagging piazzas. It was a stiff price to pay, and Elizabeth was no fun to live with, either. Still, in her he'd acquired an unexpected bulwark against the furious Charles Sinclaire, who, understanding nothing, had come fruitlessly ranting and raving to Waterford, intending to drag Steven back to Harvard.

He did not succeed.

"A young person has to make his own decisions sometimes, Charles," she'd said coldly. "Apparently you've pushed this boy around long enough. He's on his own now." Majestically she excused Charles from her presence, and had not, since that time, invited him to return.

What she really thought, there was no way of knowing. As far as Steven could see, she believed she'd got the best of his defiance of Charles—cost-free maintenance and repairs. And she made it clear that under the terms of the present agreement he might stay indefinitely. And why not? He was a bargain! So wonderful a bargain that she simply ignored the fact that he was working for an Irish carpenter of humble descent, working because he wanted to, and she had said nothing about his frequenting the Ace-High every evening, where he got to know the year-round population of Waterford. Perhaps she saw that, too, as part of his rebellion.

Was it possible that she enjoyed the discomfiture of Charles Sinclaire?

If so, Steven was certainly glad of it, because it had given him the chance to know these people who made no apologies for themselves, who accepted the rhythm of life close to the soil and sea and who had made their peace with it. Men who weighed one another's worth in a balance of their own devising. Men to whom it would make no difference, should they learn he was illegitimate. Sinclaire a bastard? So what? they'd ask. Is he afraid to work? Is he any good with a hammer? Is he honest?

Content, he listened to the latest saga of Greenleaf Stone (whose mother had so admired the Quaker poet of the last century that poor Leaf had got stuck with his tag).

"So there I was, digging," Leaf told the assembly. "I'd taken this heap of dirt out of the hole, and it was laying there between me and the far edge of the property. I hear voices. I look over the edge of the pile—I see 'em. A whole clutch of 'em."

"Of what?" they demanded.

"Of bird-watchers!" Leaf crowed. "Like a damned army, binoculars hung around their necks, books under their arms, all slicked up in their best city bird-watchin' clothes—slinkin' along the edge of the woods. I couldn't stop myself, boys. I just couldn't."

"Well?" they urged.

"I call. Hidden behind my dirt pile. I call like this. . . ." Fingers in his mouth, Leaf melodiously whistled a bird-song—rich, beautiful, impossible.

"They dropped their books and whipped out the binoculars, pointed this way, that way, all directions, talking, excited as hell. I made their day, boys! And I thought it was a shame to just stop, let 'em down. So I crawl outta my hole and go around to the far side of the woods, call 'em all over there, and then lead 'em toward the Warden place. Last I seen, they were thrashin' around in the swamp, binoculars at the ready."

Steven cheered with the others. City people were always the butt of Waterford humor, and soon enough he'd take on all their trappings. Trappings he had learned to laugh at—yet he couldn't stay in Waterford forever. There were things to do, and things to learn that could not be done and learned here (although he did not know, yet, what they were), and over the past year and a half he had gathered the spunk and gumption to go out and find them. He had put the past in its place: he had not written to Diana, nor answered the few letters that had been forwarded to him before she'd caught on that he was not going to pursue their friendship. He had responded to the letter Doug had written a year ago in February, to find out what Steven's plans for Quivet were. He had written back: no plans. Quivet was for kids. He was through with it, he told Doug, and he was sure they'd gotten the idea, all of them, that Sinclaire had been bitten by the bug of college pseudo-sophistication. And now they were out of his life.

He had negated Charles Sinclaire, reduced him to a cipher, damn him, and he had not contacted the Port Huron folks even once. He'd held up under the grueling hours of labor, the lessons, sometimes hard ones, taught him by Bob Casey. He'd earned money to start college and had gained the confidence that somehow he'd be able to earn the rest when he needed it. He was his own man now; a year and a half in Waterford had given him that, and it was time to move on, to measure himself against the world outside, the one that Waterford disregarded utterly except for making fun of, and money from in the summertime. For like it or not, the world outside was where the action lay.

"Well, sir," Linc Sears was saying, "we took off the old plaster, exposin' the beams, and he looks at me and I look at him, and he hands me his pocketknife, and I do it."

"Do what?" they chorused.

"I carve the date 1760 in the beam, and I rub old ashes on where I carved so it looks old, too, and then we cover it up. It's only an old beach cottage." He chuckled. "My old man built it for a family God knows how long ago—thirty years, maybe. One day someone from New Jersey is going to decide he wants to do that place over—the paneling we put in is cheap stuff, it'll look like hell in ten years—he's gonna take it down and he's gonna find that date, and believe me, boys, he'll swear his house is pre-Revolutionary. He's going to paint a little white sign with little black numbers on it—1760—and hang it up beside the door. That man'll be pretty excited, and pleased with himself, and I only hope that I live long enough to see it."

"To men from New Jersey," Ed Slater proposed, his stein high. "And to their women."

They drank with gusto and prepared to leave lest Linc be tempted to get another beer. Alcohol was becoming an increasingly insurmountable problem for him, and the men, knowing how hard it would be for him to leave if the party was still being celebrated, pushed their chairs back, shook Steven's hand a final time, a few of them clapping his shoulder, pointedly not saying how nice it had been but, instead, muttering that they hoped to see him when he vacationed on Cape Cod next.

They left, and only he and Bob Casey remained in the booth; Ed Slater resumed his vigil at the bar.

"You can level with me now," Bob said. "No one will hear what you say. I'd just sort of like to know, Steve, if your cousin's dying had anything to do with your leaving day after tomorrow. Seems a little hurried, to me."

"I was planning to leave at the end of the week anyway," he told his friend. "It doesn't matter."

"I wondered . . . if you're being thrown out of your house . . ." Bob looked down, embarrassed at what appeared to be prying. "If you'd rather not leave so fast, you're welcome to stay with Barbara and me."

He shrugged; not for the world would he embarrass Bob by letting him know the strength of his gratitude.

"Thanks. But I'm all set to go now."

"If you stayed those few extra days, we could sail."

It was a passion they both shared.

Regretfully he shook his head. "Another summer, I guess."

"Sure."

It was a tribute to Cousin Elizabeth's basic alienation from Waterford that not one of the men gathered here today had mentioned her dying. Probably it would take another day before the word got around, because her life did not touch theirs. Elizabeth Edgarton, who considered herself so important, historian par excellence, curator of Waterford details, knew nothing about Waterford itself or the people who lived in it and ran it, the people who had taught him so much this past year and a half. For them, Elizabeth Merrick-Edgarton did not exist.

For himself, unfortunately, the fact that she no longer lived did pose a certain problem—that of room and board. Aunt Celia and Mom were Elizabeth's only family. Should his aunt and uncle take possession of Kingsland, they would not care for his presence there, and should the place go to Mom . . . well, he was not staying in anyone's house with Charles Sinclaire.

Thank God for summer school! Attending it moved his schedule forward twelve weeks and made his financing a little tighter, but he'd work it out, of that he had no doubt. It was one of the things he'd gained here in Waterford: optimism.

"You want a ride?" Bob asked. "Or are you going to stay here?"

"Hell, I'm staying," he said. "Everyone will be at the house sooner or later, so my grandmother will have company. And she's the only one who needs it. She set a lot of store by Cousin Elizabeth."

"Well," Bob said politely, "Miss Edgarton has been a fixture around Waterford for a long time. The town just won't be the same without her."

"For all you know"—he grinned—"it might be improved."

His mother would be there, waiting for him. She and Charles would have arrived sometime this afternoon while he and Bob were working, and even though he did not intend to cause his mother pain, he would not spend an evening with Charles Sinclaire if he could help it. Aunt Celia and Uncle Joe would be coming tonight, and all of them would sit around talking to their hearts' content about God knew what—Elizabeth, probably. They did not need him, nor did he need them. He'd have to get through tomorrow in their company; services for Elizabeth would take place Monday. Monday night he'd be gone; tonight he would stay away.

"Why don't you come home and have supper with us?" Bob asked. "As long as you aren't going to your house."

"No, thanks." That he had learned, too. Countrymen never imposed on one another, and they never gave excuses.

They sat in silence—for silence, he'd learned too, was an integral part of the conversation of Waterford people. Then Bob put down his empty stein. "Well, then, I'll be on my way. See you later. Around nine o'clock." He turned quickly, before Steven had a chance to speak, and walked away as fast as he could without giving the appearance of hurrying, and Steven understood that Bob would return to the Ace-High and did not care to discuss it, one way or the other. He would return, and he would stay, whiling away as much time as Steven need while, and he would ferry his friends back to Kingsland whenever he wanted to go there, or stay out all night with him if he preferred, and he would not ask whether Steven wanted his help or not.

For that was the way your friends looked out for you, in Waterford.

Now the long, long afternoon stretched ahead, to be followed by an equally long evening, in which everyone would be polite. And Mom, when she looked his way, would beg him to love her again. And Steven would disregard all innuendo.

Charles was in the library going through Elizabeth's papers

and the women were in the kitchen making sandwiches, their subdued chatter weaving a counterpoint with the Attwater Kent radio in the library, where Uncle Joe fiddled with the knobs, coasting from one burst of static to the next.

The older folk had spent the morning in church, from which Steven had briskly excused himself; now he puttered around in the rose bed he had dug and planted under Elizabeth's dictatorship. The garden would keep him busy, keep him from being required to join the conversation, and besides, it was coming into bloom now, and he had learned to appreciate the beauty of roses. He was truly sorry that Elizabeth hadn't lived to see it. Trying she was, utterly impossible at times, still he'd grown fond of her and the outmoded pathetic things she championed so fiercely, so convinced of their rightness and her own.

Things sure wouldn't be the same without Elizabeth to supervise them!

Uncle Joe snapped off the radio and came out into the rose garden, too. "They just announced it," he said.

"Oh?"

"The North Korean army has crossed the thirty-eighth parallel."

Korea! For Christ's sake, he didn't even know where it was!

"They're calling a meeting of the Security Council at the United Nations," Uncle Joe said. "I think we'll end up fighting."

It came to him, harshly, stridently, devastating in its implication: Uncle Joe was talking about another war.

"We just got done with one," he argued stupidly, the labor and care and thrift and struggle of the last year and a half suddenly clear in his memory, and of infinite value.

"It was just plain stupid to withdraw our troops from South Korea in the first place," Uncle Joe was complaining. "The writing was on the wall a couple of years ago, when the Russians wouldn't allow elections."

His mind scrambled, frantically running from one side of the trap to the other. What if he were drafted, for Christ's sake! What if he went to Korea, and died there. Nothing he'd ever hoped to do would come to pass. Everything Waterford had taught him, everything he'd learned about himself, would be rendered meaningless. Everything would be swept away, broken and lost, because Steve Sinclaire was young and strong and nonessential: draft-bait.

Charles stood in the doorway looking cool and calm, and

in possession of himself and everything else. He nodded. "I'd like to see you in the library, Steven."

"All right," he agreed, without caring. He had not spoken to Sinclaire in a year and a half, and now that this moment was upon him, his moment to match his wits and his self-confidence against Charles, it seemed not to matter very much.

Nothing mattered, did it?

Of course, just because you went to war, that didn't mean you'd die in war. Did it? And wasn't there at least some possibility that America, having finished one war, would refuse to fight another?

"So," Charles said, closing the library door, seating himself at Elizabeth's desk. "You are, I understand, planning to go to that godforsaken school . . . Clinton, is it?"

"Yes." Maybe. If America did not go to Korea.

"And what did you tell me you planned to study? If and when you get there."

"History."

"Ah. History." Charles contemplated it for a while. It was as reasonably far from math as a person could get, and Steven was reasonably sure that Charles understood it as such. "Yes. History. I've been listening to history happening—on the radio." He smiled. "Unpleasant news, to say the least. It would be pretty hard to study history in Korea, wouldn't it?"

"Yes," he said stolidly. "I suppose it would be."

"Naturally, I suppose you're very eager to go and bleed and die for . . . for whatever it is you're supposed to bleed and die for in such a godforsaken place. Not the defense of the homeland, certainly," Charles toyed. "Not the assaulted honor of our country, surely. But something worthwhile, I expect. War is always such a worthwhile thing. Or do you think otherwise, Steven?"

He tried to swallow past his despair.

Charles's face hardened. He gestured to the chair nearby. "Sit down."

He did not move.

"Sit down," Charles said again, his voice deadly and quiet, and Steven sat, not taking his eyes from him. "It's in my power to get deferment for you. Never mind how. I worked in Washington, in the Pentagon, through the late lamented war, and I know a lot of people in positions of responsibility. Take it from me, I can do this for you if you want it."

He need not go!

He could be released from this enormous obligation! He could tackle the world!

Charles smiled, his eyes coolly appraising the hopes and ambitions now nailed to the power of that gaze.

"Needless to say, I would have to take care of the matter instantly, before the selective service gets into gear. There's a chance, I suppose, that we won't go to Korea, in which case tinkering with the records would be unnecessary. The odds are ones you'll have to figure out for yourself."

The odds were not good.

"But few things in life are certain," Charles went on. "You'll have to make your own decision about that. I can arrange a deferment for you, as I said." Charles cleared his throat. "But not without strings attached."

Suddenly he knew. Yes, with certainty.

"I've been over Elizabeth's papers. Over her will. Incredible as it seems . . . unbelievable, really, she has left Kingsland to you."

Distantly a dish clattered; a car horn honked somewhere on Main Street; a gull called in its passage through the sky.

He could not even think, let alone talk. Kingsland was his! That cantankerous, unfathomable old lady had given it to him outright—him!

Charles scowled. "The fact is that I'd always assumed she would leave the house to your mother and me."

Kingsland. This absurd house, with its ridiculous tower, its drafty rooms, enormous lawns that required endless care (who should know that better than himself?). What in God's name would a twenty-one-year-old boy do with it? An albatross, if one ever existed, yet he loved it, and needed it; it had stood for the solidity of the sea and had been his childhood refuge, and even now, in his encroaching maturity, it was his bastion, his fortress—his claim to himself. And Elizabeth had trusted him with it. And she had used it, too, as an ultimate weapon in the annihilation of Charles Sinclaire, making his own rebellion the mere act of a mere child—ineffectual.

"Now, then," Charles was saying, his fingertips pressing gently against one another—his hands, Steven noticed, steady despite his distress. "I think you have been aware, over the years, that I have worked hard to secure Kingsland for your mother and myself. It's extremely unfair of Elizabeth to simply ignore all my contributions to its maintenance—but she was always a silly old fool. So I shall have to approach through this alternative direction. Through you, Steven. I want Kingsland, and I'm prepared to offer you your life in exchange. The house will be yours sometime. You are my only legal heir, after all. Assuming you outlive me, eh?" He stared malignantly, his hatred nearly showing, and then he leaned back in the chair, smiled in his belief that he had the upper hand despite his setbacks.

Jesus, how he hated this man! Who would return Kingsland to him, in the fullness of time, a bequest he had no right to give.

"No," he said into the silence.

Charles's eyes widened in surprise. "No, you say?"

"That's what I said." His voice sounded calmly quiet in his ears, covering the tumult within.

"The house means so much to you?"

"I've lived here for a year and a half. I've become fond of it." And more, that he could not tell Charles or anyone else: Kingsland had given him a sort of legitimacy. "You want too much," he told Charles. "I might as well be dead as give in to you. Besides, just because I'm drafted doesn't mean I'll die. It just changes the odds."

Charles looked quickly down at the desk, shuffling the papers there, trying to hide his aggravation—and, yes, his fear that Steven was not able to be manipulated. Superciliously Kingsley Merrick, from his portrait on the wall, sneered vacantly in Charles's direction, and Steven found himself remote enough, detached enough, to think it amusing.

It was nice to have something that amused you, and he hoped it would continue to make him happy when he found himself in a Korean foxhole.

"So I'm not for sale, you see," he said without rancor. "And neither is the house."

Charles's icy blue eyes became harder yet. "Oh?" His voice became sharp in the way it always did when he was about to deliver a fatal blow. "Are you sure? Everyone has his price, Steven. Let's see if we can't find what yours is. Let's see if a different avenue of exploration will help. Answer me this: do you know the circumstances of your birth? Or, shall we say, your begetting?"

There was no possible answer, of course. Clearly Charles believed that he was going to spring the ultimate surprise and use it to bait the ultimate trap, and there was no way to stop him.

"Well?" Charles asked sharply. "Do you?" He was annoyed, no doubt, that Steven had not asked him what in hell he was talking about.

He made himself speak quietly, without bravado. He could beat Sinclaire to the draw on one issue, at least.

"If you're referring to the fact that I'm Tim Bradley's illegitimate son, you're a little behind the times, Charles. I've known it for quite a while."

Not a muscle twitched as Charles considered it.

"For a year and a half, I gather," he said, putting the pieces together with his usual rapidity.

"Yes."

Charles's disdainful face was full of hate. "Since you've chosen a course of discreet silence, I must gather that you are very much aware of the difficulty you would experience, trying to make your way with the known fact of your bastardy dragging along behind you. And since you force my hand with your stubbornness, I shall tell you outright and frankly that if you balk me now, any man you interview for any job higher than ditchdigger shall get this information—though he will not know its source. Assuming, of course, that you survive a war in Korea . . . eh?"

He had not experienced despair for a long time; renewing its acquaintance was unpleasant, but there was no choice. Difficult as life might be with Charles poisoning the very air he breathed—as endangered as it might be if he got drafted—he could not give him Kingsland, which stood for so much.

"You do understand, don't you?" Charles asked, rubbing his nose in it, with relish. "I will tell the world you are a bastard unless you play the game my way, according to my rules."

The door had opened so quietly that they hadn't heard it.

"No, I don't think we do understand," Mom said. Instinctively they both jumped up as she came in.

"This is a private conversation, Emily. I'll thank you to leave," Charles said loudly.

"It's not private anymore." She seated herself in the chair Steven had just vacated. "You aren't the only person around here with interesting information you might—or might not—disclose, Charles," Mom said. "My feeling is that people would reject you even faster than they might reject Steven, if they knew the truth about you."

"Me?" Charles was white, Steven saw as he stared at one and then the other, a spectator in a verbal tennis match.

"And no one knows the truth better than I do," Mom pointed out. "I'd like to remind you of that. How do you think your career at Sommerset and King would fare if your habits and pleasures were public knowledge? Which they will be when I tell the court why I am divorcing you."

Charles brought himself under wooden control. "I doubt that you'd have the nerve to tell anyone, since you've been a willing participant for twenty years," he said menacingly. "Willing because you were pregnant out of wedlock. Your own reputation would hardly come out unbesmirched, Emily."

"It's a funny thing"—she smiled unpleasantly—"what you do to people, Charles. I've been listening out in the hall for quite a while. I've just heard Steven tell you that life is literally not worth living under your thumb. You've backed him into such a corner that you can't bluff him anymore."

"Believe me, Em, I'm not bluffing."

"Nor I," she said evenly. "I am suing you for divorce, Charles. I'll get one in Nevada, and you will pay for it, because if you don't, I will give my real reasons for not ever living with you again, exposing you for what you are. Divorce isn't exactly regarded with favor. It'll make things a little awkward to S & K for a while, but it beats their knowing about perversion, don't you think?"

"And the deferment?" Charles asked haughtily. "That means nothing to you? This boy's life means nothing? And his education, Emily! I'd even be willing to pay for that."

"I don't believe, for a moment, that Elizabeth has left Steven the house without means of maintaining it—without income. She's just too shrewd." Charles glared. "You weren't going to say anything about that, were you! You must be more desperate than I realized, Charles. How long did you think you could keep it from him—that not only does he have the house, but the money too, plenty for college, to invest for taxes and upkeep, to use as he wants to use it, go where he wants to go."

"He won't be going far if he's in Korea," Charles spat.

"He won't be going to Korea. He'll be going to college. He will have an automatic deferment because of it, and should he encounter any unexpected difficulty relative to the draft, you will fix it." Coldly she stared at Charles Sinclaire without moving so much as an eyelash, settled back in her chair, playing her cards superbly as only twenty years of living with such a man could teach a person to play.

They waited while Charles weighed it; they waited while he stared at them, rudely, haughtily, and then came out from behind the desk, crossing through the library and out without looking back.

Mom sighed. "Well." She smiled shakily. "That, I expect, is that." She looked up. "I hope it'll help, Steven. I knew he couldn't defend himself against my knowledge of him—I only hope I've done the right thing, picked the right time, so that both of us are rid of him for good. And rid of the past."

It was hard to think or even to know what to feel, having seesawed back and forth between such extremes all afternoon. He wondered if he would cry, and he stared at his mother, who had done so much for him over the years, in so many unobtrusive ways. Now as he stood looking back through the distance of those years, he saw that the power of her devotion had been far more present than he had realized, even when their lives did not touch, that she had kept her love for him involate, and he wondered if she had fled from Charles Sinclaire even as he had himself, escaping into the depth of experience where Charles could not follow.

"It'll be easy for you now," she said. "Elizabeth has made everything you wanted possible, hasn't she? You don't have to worry about college or anything." She was right, of course. But he could hardly conceive of it—so long, so hard had he worked. It seemed that there must be more he should do—a lot more—but he could not remember what it must be, nor what his plans had been. Everything seemed out of focus somehow, dislocated.

She misunderstood his silence, and her eyes filled. "I've missed you this past year and a half," she said. "I know I hurt you when I told you about Tim Bradley. You hated me then, and I didn't blame you. But can't you try to forgive me now?"

He pulled a chair up close to hers and made himself speak, despite the clamping pain in his throat. "I should have written you, Mom, but I couldn't. It's you who'll have to forgive me."

"I won't bring this up again," his mother said. "I'll only mention it now: if there's anything you want to know . . . about your father . . ."

"There's nothing."

"But if it troubles you, honey, if you think about it a lot . . ."

"Believe me, Mom, I don't think about it at all."

"Not at all?"

Christ! Was there no way of making her understand that he had started over and had no need of anything but the right to continue what he'd begun? But what have you done? he asked himself. What have you started that Elizabeth didn't finish for you? Or that Mom didn't put together with the glue of blackmail!

"Not a bit," he said abruptly, "and I'd an awful lot rather not argue about it."

"All right," she said hastily. "We'll consider the subject closed. Let's talk about student deferment instead."

Oh, yes . . . deferment. War. Clinton. He tried to consider them.

"Perhaps you ought to leave first thing in the morning," Mom said. "So that you're already there, on campus, when and if the president declares war . . . or the United Nations does."

"The funeral . . ."

"I don't think Elizabeth will mind if you don't hang around for it."

It didn't seem right, somehow, but he was unable to get a grip on the reason. After all, he could do nothing for Elizabeth now. What was the point? "All right." He stood up, kissed her cheek. "I suppose I'd better get going, then. Do I need to do anything? About the will?"

"Not right away. I'll keep my eye on that. But you'd better decide what you're going to do about the house. Since it's yours to do with."

Unaccustomed as he was to owning houses, he had not once thought of it. Stupidly, he shook his head.

"If you don't have any other plans, would you consider letting me live here?" she asked.

"You?"

"Me."

"It's a big house for one lone lady."

"Your grandmother is here, and has nowhere to go. Nor do I. You'll need someone to keep an eye on it. Someone to take care of it until you're in a position where you can do it yourself."

It was the perfect solution to a problem he didn't even know he had. "Please," he begged. "Please live here!"

"I'd be delighted to," she laughed.

He must start packing. How much should he take? he wondered. Not much, he decided. Mom could send him what he needed. She'd be here. At the door he turned back to tell her; she was still sitting there as though being interviewed by the invisible occupant of the desk's chair. Somehow it was too complicated, just now, to explain. "I'll write," he said.

"Good."

"And, welcome home, Mom," he said, forcing a smile.

"Thanks!"

Slowly he climbed to the tower, looked about it, looked out each window, to the bay, to the town, up Main Street and down, at the newly leafed trees below, and realized that it would never be the same again. Kingsland would never be what it had been, because it was his, its responsibilities and its cares as well as its shelter and warmth.

No—nothing was the same, at all.

16

Smokey Joe's was filled to the brim. Located near the Clinton campus, it was exclusively inhabited by college students; in fact, it was packed, and Steven Sinclaire, jammed into the booth with his date and three other couples, looked over the smoke-filled room with the jaded eye of an old man, detached from the miseries of youth and its pleasures, its earnest appraisal of itself and its bravado, all of which occupied every booth, the bar, the crowded aisles, the very air.

"Just what is right, and what is wrong," Ray Johnson rhetorically asked at top voice, barely making himself heard above the din of a Friday night. "It seems to me a person has to decide that for himself, and then stick to it. What's right for you isn't necessarily right for me." Ray's date, a pretty girl in a red sweater, did not bother to answer, looked instead at the swaying drinkers closest to their booth, who held themselves ready to occupy it at the first hint of availability. Perhaps she was smart enough, Steven reflected, to know that Ray was leading up to the ultimate, usual conclusion of such discussions: that it was all right for him to indulge in sexual intercourse whenever he wanted to, regardless of the fact that the girl he did it with would lose her reputation.

But the double standard, an interesting exercise in ambiguity, did not interest Steven just then. Nor Ray, nor the girl in the red sweater. Not even Ed Lamson, sitting across the table from him, watching him closely while pretending not to—not even Ed mattered. They'd worked out in Clinton's gym this afternoon, just the two of them, presumably hoping to get Sinclaire in shape again, but both of them knew it was too late. They'd known it all fall, though neither of them had said it—yet it was more than simply not having the quickness anymore. He'd lost his drive as well, and there was no way to know if Ed had seen this, too. Pretty soon he'd have to say something, relieve the pressure they both felt. Ed must somehow be told that his friend Steve Sinclaire no longer cared about basketball, without also being told that Steve had lost the ability to care about anything. Anything at all.

He did not care!

Jesus! It was lonely, achingly lonely, and he was lonely in a way he'd never experienced before, not even among Waterford's laborers with whom he had so little in common. He turned away from the group at his booth, looked again over the crowd, lost, isolated. Yes, isolation—that was it. More than being lonely, he was isolated. After all that work, all that effort, all the months of laboring in Waterford, the luster had simply faded from all his dreams and plans, and he himself was drained, weak, without enough energy to care, one way or another, about anything. It had seemed important that Ed be kept in ignorance, as if the refusal to acknowledge his lassitude kept it from gaining the upper hand, taking over his whole life, his future, destroying him. Often evasion had worked for him before; why didn't it now? he wondered.

Perhaps I am just tired, he thought, let down after all that struggle with Sinclaire. Maybe I just need a little time.

He drank long and thirstily of his beer. Beside him, his date (arranged by Ed) looked up and smiled. "Tell me about yourself," she said, by way of breaking the conversational ice. "Ed says you grew up in Port Huron with him."

"He's right." He nodded, winked at his friend.

"And now you live in Massachusetts?"

"My house is there. But I live here," he pointed out beerily.

"*Your* house."

"Mine."

"You own a whole house, all by yourself?"

"I do indeed. In fact, I inherited it. From a cousin. Would you like to hear about it?"

"Sure," she encouraged, believing herself successful in drawing him out. In order to be heard, he had spoken loudly, and he noticed that Red Sweater, snubbing Ray Johnson, was listening too.

"My house is on Cape Cod. It's a ridiculous mansion. It

has a tower that looks like a misplaced toadstool, and it has lots of porches that make everything inside so dark you can't see your way around. It's filled with ugly Victorian furniture that no one wants, and it's surrounded by acres of grass that have to be mowed every week until August, when everything dries up and the lawn looks like Shredded Wheat."

"Gosh," said his date.

"It's got horsehair chairs and buttoned-down chairs and chairs with fringes around their bottoms and tables with bowed legs that have claws on their feet like a chicken."

"I think it's supposed to suggest an eagle," giggled Red Sweater, "or at least *some*thing more dignified than a chicken."

They all laughed, making the booth sound like a happy one, to be envied by the swaying hubbub in the aisle.

"Another beer?" he asked. "Everyone? Beer!" He slid a five-dollar bill across the table toward Johnson. "Be my guest, Ray, 'ol buddy."

"Sure," said Johnson. It was one of the advantages of double-dating with a big spender: you were likely to get free beer. And one of the disadvantages: you were stuck fetching it. But Ray Johnson did not voice his observation, because, all things notwithstanding, the fact was that Sinclaire had a car as well as cash. Johnson left, shouldering his way to the bar.

"I'll have to go to the little girls' room," said Steven's date. "Otherwise I won't have room for more beer." It was a risqué remark for a Midwestern girl in the year 1950, no doubt intended to amuse him, and he guessed that she was well on her way to drunkenness. He saluted and let her out into the aisle, where she was swallowed up in the mob.

Across the table, Ray Johnson's date was watching him. Her red sweater was pleasantly filled; she had shining brown hair and pretty blue eyes and high color, smooth skin. He found her suddenly very, very attractive. Why, he wondered, did she look so familiar?

"Hi," he said to Red Sweater. "My name's Steve. What's yours?"

His introduction was, truth to tell, not necessary. The girl must have been introduced to him and he to her, since they'd both been sitting in the booth God knew how long. Surely Ray had introduced them, or Ed—but in fact, he was too drunk to remember.

"The name is Marian," she announced, a knowing smile of amusement on her face. "But you can call me Mari, if you want to. Pronounced as in 'to mar a piece of furniture.' Mari."

Mari, short for Marian. It became her, gave her class and distinction, and it pleased him. "Mari Crawford." He nodded. "How the hell are you?"

"Great," she answered briefly, still sizing him up.

"I know I've seen you before. It doesn't sound very original, but could you tell me where?"

"Psychology." She smiled. "When you're there."

It was true he was inclined to skip classes. Top-flight grades didn't matter, since he wasn't on scholarship; Clinton, respectable though it was, could not compete with Harvard in academic standard. It was not difficult to pass an exam in a course you had not attended, not at Clinton, and it had been a while since he'd been at Professor Benson's psych lecture.

"Where are you from, Mari spelled with an 'i'?" he asked. "Are you an Ohio farm girl?"

"No," she laughed. "I'm an Illinois girl."

"Illinois, for Gawd's sake!"

"Illinois. Springfield. You must be from Columbus."

"What makes you think so?"

"Oh, you just have that Columbus look about you," she teased. "We Springfield, Illinois, people can spot it a mile off."

He shook his head. "As a matter of fact, I grew up in Port Huron, Ohio, north of here. Beautiful Port Huron, beside stinking Lake Erie, filled with garbage and iridescent with oil." Perhaps he ought to forsake the study of history and write poetry, instead. Iridescent with oil, he mused. Splendid.

"But you are also an absentee landlord, if I've heard correctly. Which I may not have, considering the noise in here."

"Right. Or an absentee house owner, at least. My mother lives in the house and I'm not the sort of man who'd charge his own mother rent. Actually she does me a favor by living there. She keeps an eye on everything for me—like the plumbing and mice and stuff."

"How'd she get there if you grew up in Port Huron?"

"Why, she just got divorced, is how," he explained. "She went to Reno, Nevada, for six weeks in order to be divorced, and then she came to Cape Cod. She's been my caretaker ever since."

Mari Crawford's face was carefully blank. "I never knew anyone who got divorced," she remarked.

"You will. It's the wave of the future."

"I hope your cousin left you money, besides her house."

(Was it true that Steve Sinclaire from the East had his own car?)

"She did. And she financed Mom's trip to Reno, too. It's swell, sometimes, how things just work themselves out." He had let bitterness creep into his voice without intending it to, and she looked at him closely. So did Ed, listening alongside her; then Ray arrived with the beer mugs and Steven's date fought her way back through the crowd and the party staggered forward.

"I think, after we've finished here at good ol' Smokey Joe's, that we ought to take a little trip to Observatory Hill," Ray announced loudly.

"I love the way Ohio people think a lump on the ground is an elevation, don't you?" Mari Crawford asked Steven. "We Illinois people don't have these crazy misconceptions."

"A lump!" Ray exclaimed. "It's no lump."

"It's no hill, either."

"It's private—don't knock it."

"There isn't room for four couples in Steve's car," Ed protested. "Some of us will have to gracefully bow out."

"Why, I'd be glad to," Mari said sweetly.

"What?" Ray asked, his face and throat going purple.

"Are you interested in touring Observatory Hill?" Steven asked his date.

"Sure." She smiled agreeably, her eyes praising his face and shoulders.

"Well, then! Here, Ray, you take my keys and this young lady. I'll see that Miss Crawford gets home safely."

Even Ed, loyal as he was, could not hide his incredulous dismay at this breach of collegiate etiquette. "Gee, Steve," he murmured.

"Go!" He waved his hands at them all, as though flapping at gnats. His date, understandably angry, eyes flashing, said to Ray, "You can just drop me off at the Delta house."

"All right," Ray said unhappily, pointedly ignoring Mari Crawford.

"We have a television set."

"You do?"

"Sort of small, but you're welcome to come in and watch Milton Berle. If you can see him through the snow."

"Why, sure." Ray brightened, handed the car keys to Ed. "We can walk to the Delta house." They disappeared into the smoke and darkness of the outer reaches of the bar.

"I hope you're satisfied," Ed said, edging his way out with his date.

"I'm satisfied." He shrugged. "Are you satisfied?" he asked Mari Crawford.

"Awfully." She smiled.

"Mind if we take the other side of the booth, since it's empty?" asked a boy.

"Help yourself." Steven gestured, and five people slid in opposite them.

"When you're through with your beer, I'll walk you home," he said to Mari Crawford.

"That's very nice of you. And nice of you to rescue me from Ray Johnson."

"My pleasure."

"He's a bit of a creep."

"Why'd you go out with him?"

"I didn't know he was a creep until we got here."

"I'll have to be careful, so that you don't think I'm a creep, too."

"Oh, I have a feeling about you, Steve Sinclaire."

"You do?"

"Yes, I do."

"A nice one, I hope."

"Quite nice. In fact, very nice. Would you like to go for a walk?"

"It beats sitting here," he said agreeably.

Quickly she drank up and they swam upstream of the jumpers for their side of the table.

"Your date will hate you forever," she said, once they'd beat their way out. "It's just not done here—dumping your date."

"If she and Johnson find out they were made for each other, they'll think I'm wonderful," he pointed out negligently, sloshing in his every pore with beer. "Where shall I take you? Do you live in a sorority house?"

"I live in Warner dorm. Only upper-classmen can live in sorority or fraternity houses."

"That must mean you aren't an upper-classman."

"Sophomore," she explained briefly.

"Will you live in a sorority house next year?"

"Oh, yes!" she exclaimed. "The Omega house. It's beautiful. The best Clinton has," she said proudly. "Because Omega is the best sorority. The girls are just wonderful. What fraternity will you pledge?"

"Hadn't thought about it."

"You haven't?" Clearly, not having thought about such

matters was unbelievable. "How could you have lived on campus these two months and not thought about it!"

"Four months. I went to summer school."

"Question remains unanswered," she noted.

"I haven't thought about what fraternity to pledge," he told her, "because I think I won't pledge any."

"But you've got to! You'll be out of it if you don't. And you have so much on the ball! Don't be silly, Steve. Of course you'll pledge a fraternity." Her vigorous directive was like a cool, refreshing breeze, clearing the fog that had followed him from Waterford. He laughed.

"I'll look dumb in a beanie." All pledgees wore them, he'd been told, a ridiculous red cap with a letter "C" on it.

"It's worth it," she insisted. "Nearly everyone on campus goes Greek. You'd regret it always if you didn't. You'd be lonely and miserable."

"I could accelerate my course program and graduate early. If I kept busy enough, I wouldn't notice being miserable."

"Why hurry?" she asked.

"I'm two years behind as it is."

"Two years? How old are you?"

"Twenty-one."

"Gosh." She was impressed, being with an older man, and steered him toward the outlying districts of the campus, a hand tucked under his arm. Their footsteps echoed in the frost-nipped night; the even, unhurried cadence was pleasant and relaxing.

"How is it that you're two years behind?" she asked.

"I lost time fighting with my . . . my father. He wanted me to go to Harvard."

"Harvard!" She was impressed even more. "Did you?"

"Yes. For a year. But didn't want to stay there, so I took some time out to earn my own tuition for Clinton. Then, just when I had enough to make a start, the rich cousin I mentioned died and there was more than enough to come to college."

"And buy a car, et cetera, et cetera."

"Et cetera, et cetera," he agreed.

"Must have taken the wind out of your sails, speaking nautically," she observed, "to have made all that effort—and then find it all done for you." The girl was not stupid.

"Hm," he agreed.

"Doesn't the Midwest seem a little . . . well . . . unsophisticated, after living in the East so long?" (The image of Mecca rose in his mind as she said it.)

"A lot of the time I lived in the tiny town where my house is. It's not a very sophisticated place."

"From the sound of it, the house is very imposing."

"It is. A member of my family built it nearly a hundred years ago, when he made a fortune in Australia."

"No kidding!"

"No kidding."

"Tell me more."

He told her more while they circled the campus, ending back at Warner dorm twenty minutes before curfew. On the broad shadowed porch the vague ghosts of closely locked couples inhabited nooks and crannies and he was reminded that it had been a long time since he'd kissed a girl, and he remembered that Mari Crawford had a nice body, beneath the red sweater, and he wondered . . .

He glanced down at her, and she smiled. "I see an uninhabited tree over there on the lawn," she said.

"Perhaps you'd like to get a closer look at it?"

"I wouldn't mind," she said softly.

On the other side of the tree a couple were happily necking; he and Mari Crawford took another maple, farther away, and on its far side he put his arms around her and pulled her close.

"I really think you ought to reconsider," she said, offering no resistance to his arms, locking her hands around the back of his neck, looking up at him earnestly. "About not pledging a frat."

"I'll take it under advisement."

"And about finishing early—why, that wouldn't be any fun at all," she said, and smiled. "Wouldn't you like a little fun before you face life, Steve?"

"In fact, I'd like it very much," he said, suddenly forgetting that he had not enjoyed Clinton even for a moment since his arrival. "If I wore a beanie, though, you'd be embarrassed to be seen with me. Everyone would think you were dating a freshman—that is, if you'd consider going out with me?"

"I might consider it," she said, and held still while he approached her tentatively and kissed her in a friendly manner, to let her know he thought her pretty and fun. Her response was equally friendly. Beneath her light coat her body was pleasantly warm, and he was aware of a need to hold it closer, to draw nearer to her, know her well.

"Would it embarrass you?" he asked softly, in the intimate voice a man reserves for a woman he wants to know better than he does.

"Would what embarrass me?"

"Being seen with a person that everyone thinks is a freshman?"

"No one thinks you're a freshman," she laughed. "This is a small school, and everyone knows exactly what you are, Steve."

Well, maybe not exactly, he thought, kissing her again. But maybe they knew all they needed to. The kiss developed nicely, and the balance of the twenty minutes passed more quickly than he'd have liked. When he took her to the door of the dorm, he secured her promise to meet in the student union Monday before Psych II.

Ed was waiting for him on the steps of the men's dorm.

"Back so soon?"

"Damned curfew," Ed growled. "Here's the damn keys."

"A little upset?" He grinned.

"I must say you're not."

"No, I'm not. In fact, Ed, I've been thinking."

"What about?"

"That play we were practicing today. I think I could do it if I set my mind to it. Takes a while, is all, for the patterns to sink in."

"You haven't been trying," Ed grumbled.

"Well, maybe in the morning we could try again."

In the darkness Ed tried to read his face, gave up. "You want to?"

"Yes, I want to."

"You really want to?"

"Hey, I told you I do. If you'll help."

"Glad to oblige." Ed grinned. "It's about time, big shot."

"Yeah," he drawled, and then laughed. Yes! He wanted to! There were lots of things he wanted to do! He would, in time, tell Mari Crawford what they were.

And he would do them. All of them.

VI

The Caretaker

17

She had never been especially fond of Kingsland when she'd spent summers here, long ago. But now it felt like home, familiar and without surprises, and it was a fortress too, protecting her with its dignity, shielding her from the stigma of divorce here in Waterford. And it provided a strong and binding link between Steven and herself, ensuring a continued mutual interest between them. Yes, Emily thought, she liked Kingsland very well, indeed!

She poked the mop under the bandy-legged, claw-footed sideboard in the dining room, overcoming the fat, fluffy dust balls that had been growing there all week, and carefully carried the loaded mop to the kitchen door and onto the porch. She watched the dust float away as she rapped the mop on the nearby pillar, smelled the dampness of the warming earth, and then, because spring had incontestably arrived at last, and because the air was soft and tender as a new shoot, she sat on the steps and breathed it in.

I'm tired, she thought. No matter how well I like Kingsland, the truth is that its too big for me. It would be better, in the winter at least, to live in only one part of the house. The billiard room, perhaps, if anyone could ever be persuaded to cart away the pool table. The billiard room, the library, the kitchen—she would not need more. She must speak to Steven about it this summer, ask him if the heat could be diverted into just that section of the house—and the plumbing, she reminded herself. Whether the pipes in the unheated part could be drained. There was a lavatory just off the kitchen—could it be made a little larger? Well, she'd talk to him, see what he thought. He'd be here for two weeks—plenty of time to work on it. But, perhaps, considering that two weeks was all he had, he'd rather not be bothered? Don't fill the boy's time for him, she counseled herself.

He's not a boy, she reminded herself. He's a man, thirty-one years old. And you are . . . fifty-one? How ridiculous, she snorted, letting herself back into the kitchen. Fifty-one is old, but I'm not. Except for my legs tiring easily, I'm not old at all!

The silence of the huge house closed in on her, once the door was shut. She disliked those silences, and the more years she accumulated, here at Kingsland, the more she minded them. Perhaps it's good that you do, she pointed out to herself in her usual interior dialogue. (She suspected it would become spoken when she reached senility.) Perhaps if you mind enough, being lonely, you'll do something about it.

Not that she had exactly moldered away here in Waterford—she would not permit that! She'd kept busy enough, once her mother no longer needed her. She'd volunteered her time at the library so that it might remain open to the public an extra day, attended boring meetings of the Garden Club, cooked up enormous batches of fudge (her one claim to fame in the culinary arts) which Mr. Snow sold on consignment at his store, and shared an occasional glass of afternoon sherry with Mrs. Boardman, who ran an antique shop in the parlor of the Pettingills' house. All those mundane things were enjoyable enough, once she'd gotten over her mother's death. Her relief at being rid of Charles Sinclaire, and her newfound happiness in the house of Kingsley Merrick, took the edge off having to live there alone.

Yet, just lately, she'd become more and more aware of her essential isolation in Waterford. The summer society that had once glittered here was gone now, of course. Of the old houses, only Kingsland remained in the hands of the family who'd built it, and the Warden place. The other houses that had made Waterford lovely and gracious once were antique shops now, like the Pettingills', sold to the Boardmans when old Mr. Pettingill died.

There were at least a dozen Boardman-type people in town now—nice enough, to be sure, but not very interesting; there was no question of becoming close to any Waterford native, naturally. Such a person would not be comfortable around a Merrick, though Steven had made his way with them pretty well, when he'd been young. . . . Still, men were more able to accept differences between themselves—their companionship did not require the kind of closeness that friendship between women did.

No, the fact was that now, well settled after ten years of freedom, comfortable with herself and her fortress, Emily Merrick was becoming restless. The exhilaration of independence was no longer enough to keep her content—in fact, she was just a little afraid that independence had become a burden. She had not really been aware of it until last month, when unexpectedly Tom Warden stopped in. Checking up on the old Warden place, he'd said; Mr. Snow at the store had told him Emily Merrick was in residence at Kingsland, and he'd hopped right over, had Tom, hugged her joyfully, accepted a highball, and told her all about himself and as much about the old gang as he could remember. When he left, she had experienced, for the first time in years, a real melancholy, and she had not really shaken it yet.

Maybe you *are* old, she told herself crossly. For ten years you've lived here happily, willing to sit at the edges of Waterford and observe its comings and goings, and now it's not enough. Why? she asked herself—yet she knew the answer before she asked. The present was not enough because Tom Warden had brought back all the warmth and gaiety of her youth, its hope and zest and resilience . . . and had served to remind her that life was passing her by, just as it had when she was married to Charles Sinclaire.

She returned the mop to the broom closet under the stairs and took out the antique carpet sweeper, launched her attack on the faded Aubusson carpet that had covered the thirty-foot parlor for as long as she could remember. But the sweeper trailed as much trash as it picked up, and her exasperation rose as she set about picking up the litter it left behind. Stubbornness alone kept her from accepting Steven's offer of a vacuum cleaner. She knew he could afford it—he was doing very well at Bronner, and she knew he truly wanted her to have one. God knew *she* couldn't afford it. Her alimony did not go as far as once it had, and never could she sell enough fudge, not even if she cooked and stirred twenty-four hours a day. Yet, she would not—would not!—give Mari Crawford cause to complain or feel that Steven was too generous to his mother. Any such complaint (stated or suggested) only masked Mari's basic envy of the closeness that

Steven shared with his mother—as might be expected. Surely Mari was threatened by it—and so Emily had consciously tried to keep it out of sight. Just as now, she would not accept a new vacuum cleaner, even though she needed one, because Mari would regard it as evidence of affection that rightfully belonged to herself. She would not see it for what it was—a tool in the maintenance of her husband's property, a relief for the rigors of the cleaning lady. Mari was apt to take everything rather personally—bah!

There was really nothing wrong with the girl, Emily told her inner being as she proceeded with her lint-picking. There was nothing wrong with her at all—except that she wasn't right for Steven. It had not been apparent at first. On the contrary. Mari's vigorous bossing around had seemed just what Steven needed. He pledged and joined a fraternity because of this girl's persuasion, played basketball on the Clinton team in order to impress her, had enjoyed school thoroughly—and Mari could rightfully take the credit! Emily had been glad then. Steven had worked so hard here in Waterford that he had become rather withdrawn, she thought. He needed someone to show him how to have fun. God only knew he had not had much! Mari, she'd hoped, would show him the way. Make him happy. If she seemed a bit superficial . . . well, perhaps that wasn't as important as it might seem. What mattered was Mari's involvement with life, her energy, and enthusiasm, which well might give Steven the chance to live as other people lived, and as the Sinclaires had not.

Steven! So sweet a son, unspoiled by Charles, unspoiled by herself. Who had, in fact, kept her from succumbing to bitterness at the unfairness of her life, who had tempered her pain with joy and so forged it into strength she would not otherwise have had, creating the Emily of today—a wise woman, one able to take and sustain life's burdens, one able to love Steven completely—and able, as well, to let him go, give him over to Mari, who, she hoped, might fill the hollow spaces left by the boy's struggles within himself. Now she knew that Mari could not fill those spaces. She'd been good for Steven when he was young, and she'd loved Steven and been a fine wife to him, and she was a good mother for Kathy and Rick. But her love, real as it was, sincere and earnest, had not been able to grow and change, because Mari had been through growing at twenty. Her love would not be tempered by time, nor would she deepen and strengthen, because there was no steel in her. And unknown to them both,

Steven had. He was pursuing the path of success he'd begun in the early fifties and doing well with it, encouraged by the American environment of achievement and nurtured in it by his wife—but now Steven had fallen into a hollow space of a different kind, lived in it, worked in it so hard and so well (so far!) that he hardly noticed he'd outgrown it. But he would, one day, and what would Mari Crawford do then, I'd like to know, Emily demanded as she returned the carpet sweeper to its lair under the stairs. And how about yourself? Analyze Steven all you want, but you, too, live in a vacuum. What are you going to do about it?

I'm going to open a shop of my own, she announced to her inner self, to her inner surprise. I'll earn extra money and I'll travel. I'll meet people that do interest me. I will collect them, like charms on a bracelet, and then I will visit them and they will come here. The house will hum again, as it once did, and I'll hum too; I'll be thinking of so many different things at once that I won't worry about life passing me by. No, sir! It'll come to my door.

She wandered into the kitchen to heat up water for tea. A shop. First of all a shop. It would be fun! Already she could feel the stir of anticipation as she thought about it. What to sell? Pot holders?

Pomander balls?

Stuffed toys?

The phone rang.

Home-baked bread?

No, it needs to be something Cape Coddy, she thought, walking into the library to answer.

Beach-plum jelly?

It will never jell for you, she thought. Except for fudge, you're a menace in the kitchen. She picked up the phone.

"Hello," she said meditatively. Artistic arrangements of driftwood? Shells?

"Emily?" A familiar voice she could not place spoke to her from the receiver.

"Yes."

"This is Priscilla, Em. Priscilla Warden."

"Pris?" she gasped. Good grief, the past was really catching up!

"Tom called last night and told me he'd seen you, Emily, that you'd been there in Waterford for ten years! Really"—Pris's voice became reproachful—"how could you be there so long and not let me know!"

She had not let anyone know—in fact, had deliberately dropped out of sight. . . .

"I didn't exactly announce it, because it was part of working out my divorce from Charles." There. Maybe that would satisfy Pris.

It did.

"Oh! Of course, Em darling, I understand . . . but surely you must understand how I felt. You knew how fond of you I was—and then, it was as though you'd just disappeared from the face of the earth! And now you've divorced Charles Sinclaire?"

"That's right," she said into Pris's expectant pause.

"He was such a creep, Emily." Pris giggled. "I never did understand why you married him, to begin with."

The old memory of the old friendship, its happy secrets and delicious mischief, tantalized her—and yet it was Pris Warden, actually, who had betrayed her long ago, forcing her into marriage. . . .

"Why, Pris, it was all on account of you," she said mildly, though the old anger was still there, beginning to beat against her temples. "You and Alice Bradley squeezed me right out, if you remember. Then you left me high and dry and went back to Bryn Mawr and never said a word. So when Charles came along and asked me to go to Ohio with him, I went." She'd had this answer at her fingertips for years, in case anyone from the old days ever asked.

"That's what I heard!" Pris exclaimed. "But I could hardly believe it when they told me. Ohio, of all places!"

Emily did not ask who "they" were. She did not care.

"Your brother mentioned that you lived in New York State," she offered as an alternative to discussing her disastrous marriage to Charles Sinclaire. "Olney, did he say? Where is it?"

"North-central," Pris said. "We've been here for years."

"I'm afraid I don't know your husband's name."

"Why, it's Darion. Darion Hunt."

"How distinguished, Pris!"

"Oh, Darion is very distinguished. And unfortunately away quite a lot, just now. He got let go, five years ago, and the job he has now requires a lot of traveling!"

"Good grief! Let go?"

"His company congealed."

"Congealed!"

"Or is it conglomerated?" Pris wondered. "It all seems a

little vague. My daughter thinks it's like putting a Band-Aid on the jugular—perhaps that's where I get lost."

"You and Darion have a daughter, then?"

"Two," Pris said. "Married, living in the New York City area. I wish I did. There'd be more to do. Say, Emily, you wouldn't be interested in coming to Olney for a week or so, would you?"

"To Olney?" The very thought, so unexpected, was downright startling! "It's very nice of you to ask, but I . . ."

"I really do get lonely here, Em," Pris said, and over the flatness of telephone wire came the echo of despair. "I'm terribly sorry if something I did so long ago caused you to marry Charles. I'd never have done it if I'd known what would happen—you were so dear to me. Please forgive me and come to Olney."

"Honestly, Pris, coming to Olney and forgiving you aren't part of the same thing. Besides, you didn't really make me marry Charles. You only dug a hole and I fell into it, is all. Of course I forgive you!"

"We've known each other so long . . ." Pris's voice trailed out thinly, and Emily suspected that tears had overtaken her.

Would going to Olney be so difficult? she asked. It sounds as though she needs you. What if she does! Why should you care? she demanded. Doesn't sound as though Pris has changed an iota. Self-centered, a trifle dense—and she knew perfectly well what she was doing when she chose Alice Bradley over you.

Emily! she urged. That was thirty years ago! And perhaps Alice Bradley represented, then, a way for Pris to avoid the rut of being a Warden . . . and speaking of ruts, are you so deeply entrenched in your own that the mere thought of leaving it throws you? It does not! she protested testily. It just takes time to change. And going to Olney requires money, too.

"I can't decide right this moment, Pris," she said. "Money is a little tight, and I'm not sure I can afford it. Can I call you back after I've thought it over?"

"Oh, sure, Em," Pris said quickly. "It's been just great, talking to you. If you can't come, let's do keep in touch anyway, okay?"

There was barely time enough to say good-bye before Pris hung up.

She thinks I'm putting her off, Emily thought. She didn't even bother to give me her phone number. She believes I'd never call her, that I'd never come to Olney, New York.

Thoughtfully she steeped her tea, throwing the tea bag into the overflowing trash basket, carrying the whole offensive mess out to a waiting garbage can which Mr. Gray would collect on his weekly rounds. She went back to the kitchen, sugared the tea and stirred it, and sat at the table and lit a cigarette and thought of Pris and Alice Bradley, of mean old Cousin Elizabeth and Daddy, who had never met Steven—of pain and despair and the weight of young love—and suddenly she was plunged into a free fall of thirty years, back to the days when she and Pris had been young, back from life here at Kingsland, past the nightmare of Port Huron, and into the daylight of the twenties and the summer society of Waterford. . . .

Where, waiting for her, were her memories of Tim Bradley and all the agony he'd brought her and all the love she'd felt for him and had never experienced since, rising like a monster from an ocean fissure, troubling the waters for miles around until she was able to master it and command it to return to the deep, from whence it came.

Her hands were shaking.

Suddenly she did want to see Pris again. Suddenly it was imperative. Through the years she had learned to curb her impulses, control her emotions, deny her wishes. But now she need not. Now she could make decisions, without considering who might or might not like them, and right now it was her wish to see Pris, talk about old times, perhaps even reminisce about Tim Bradley if she could do so without tipping her hand—for she had loved him, had she not? He was part of her, a part of herself that she needed to regain, to make real again, in order to somehow stanch the flow of the years so rapidly now passing her by.

Yes! It would be good to see Pris! It would be good to get out of Waterford for a while. Good to be a girl once more.

Quickly, before she changed her mind, she dialed O. "Olney, New York," she directed the operator. "The residence of Darion Hunt, please."

18

"Emily, it's so good to see you!" Enthusiastically Pris emphasized her words with a series of small hugs. "You're so good to come!"

"It's just . . . great to . . . see you . . . too!" she said around the squeezes. Stepping back, out of Pris's range, she looked at the friend of her youth, now well-launched into her middle age. Around them milled the mob peculiar to airports—busy, important, smartly dressed.

The truth was that Pris appeared unwell: loose gray flesh puffed beneath her eyes, her skin was pasty and toneless. Middle age, relentless as a glacier, had removed her contours and left her figure a featureless column, draped with a navy-blue suit tailored to fit a differently proportioned woman. A balding fur stole did not disguise the fact that the suit was ten years out of style.

You don't look particularly marvelous either, kid, she reminded herself. No one at fifty is the girl she once was, no matter how she feels, and your clothes are reprehensible too, because you haven't done anything that required new ones. You, too, are ten years out-of-date.

"It's really very exciting to come to Olney," she assured Pris with a hearty smile. "I don't get out of Waterford much—I feel as though I'm on an adventure!"

"You are, really," Pris said more wisely than she knew. "An adventure into the past, Emily. Oh, I'm just so glad to see you."

"I only hope I won't be a nuisance to your husband," Emily said politely.

"He's not even home." Pris waved the apology away. "He won't be in until tomorrow night, and in three days he'll be gone again, to Albuquerque, I think. It's very tedious, I assure you! Let's get your bags."

They made the pilgrimage to the luggage conveyor.

"Have you eaten anything?" Pris asked. "Did they serve dinner on the plane?"

"Oh, yes. It was a fine meal, too. There's my bag."

"Just one?" Pris asked, her disappointment obvious. "I thought you promised me you'd stay awhile, Em!"

"I did no such thing. Promise, I mean."

"Well . . . you will stay a little while, won't you?"

"Of course! I didn't come all this way just for a cup of tea!"

"Oh, Emily! I always did like the way you express yourself!" Pris gushed. "Let me take the bag."

"Don't be silly!"

"I insist!"

The bag was light, and Emily refrained from further protest, accompanied Pris to the airport parking lot and to a rust-encrusted Chevrolet.

"We're going to have to replace this car, and that is that," Pris said breezily, throwing the bag into the backseat. "They have to use so much salt on the roads here that cars get eaten alive." She pulled out onto a highway without signaling. "Let me point out the brighter lights of the city. Tomorrow, when it's daylight, I'll take you on a guided tour. That beacon over there is the radio station. Next to it the Astor, Olney's finest restaurant-hotel."

It was an atrociously flat, drab city, and there was no bright or happy remark she could make about it.

"If you're thinking that it's unattractive, you're quite right," Pris said, driving in an obviously affluent suburban direction of narrowing streets, expanding lawns, double garages.

"How did you happen to end up here?"

"The inventor of Hatfield spark-testing equipment—Phil Hatfield, in fact—lived here. Darion was his salesman—one of the first, and most definitely the last. Hatfield was so crazy he couldn't sell hip-waders to a trout fisher! He relied on Darion absolutely, as well he should have! The company grew and grew, but Phil Hatfield was happy here in Olney, land of his birth. So we had to live here, too."

"Well, I'm sure it has its good points."

"I never found any," Pris said. "We have a nice house—Darion made a lot of money when he was with Hatfield—but what's money? This is it," she said, pulling into the driveway and then into the attached garage of a large, rambling ranch that peered out from behind untamed shrubbery.

"How nice, Pris!"

"Like I said, Darion had a good job. Before Hatfield congealed."

"Where'd you meet your husband?"

"In Philadelphia. When I was at Bryn Mawr and he was at Penn. Wait till you meet him, Em. He's still handsome!"

"I'll bet he is."

"Was Charles every much the drip he seemed?" Pris pried, pulling out the suitcase.

"Absolutely."

"I'll get the garage door. That door over there leads to the kitchen. Go on ahead," Pris directed. "Do you get lonely for a man after living by yourself ten years?"

"Well, I don't get lonely for Charles Sinclaire, if that's what you mean. I've rather enjoyed the freedom of being single."

"Huh," Pris remarked, following her into the darkened kitchen. "I didn't get around to the dishes today," she said. "Excuse my mess." She snapped on the glaring overhead light, which starkly revealed an accumulation in the sink far greater than could have gathered in a day.

"Well, now, let's just mix ourselves a little drink," Pris said, clasping her hands in the gesture her mother once used, peering around in a cupboard. "What'll it be?"

"Scotch, if you have it. And water."

"Great. Scotch is my drink, too." Drawing two streaked and detergent-spotted glasses out from the back of a cabinet, Pris splashed Scotch into them. "If you want ice in yours, help yourself."

She found the freezer compartment well-filled with frost and ice trays and nothing else. Pris led the way into the spacious, graciously proportioned living room, where bookshelves covered one wall, the fireplace another; deep brocade-covered furniture was grouped invitingly. They settled for the couch, one at each end; across the room the blankly staring television set kept a disapproving eye on them.

"What was Tom really doing in Waterford?" Emily asked, tasting around the edge of a rather strong highball. "He said he was checking your old house, but I think he was up to something more." She lit a cigarette, which helped kill the drink. Her fourth, out of her daily allotment of ten.

"Oh, he was! He's thinking about developing it."

"Developing it!"

"He's had conferences with builders and architects and engineers; he thinks the property would make a swell housing subdivision."

"So it would. But who does he think is going to live in it?"

"That does seem to be a problem, doesn't it?" Pris laughed. "For some reason, Tom had the impression that Waterford was growing. When he got there, though, it wasn't exactly the metropolis he thought it would be."

"Well, it's bigger than it was. Somewhat. Probably eight hundred people live there now."

Pris burst into laughter. "So much for Tom's schemes."

Emily laughed, too. "One day he may make a fortune, but I don't think just now is the time. How do you feel about his developing it?"

"Doesn't matter how I feel," Pris said calmly. "I don't have any say in the matter. Daddy left him the house and property. He could start a leper colony there and I couldn't stop him."

"Oh," she remarked vapidly. "Well . . . I just wondered, is all."

"Daddy settled his conscience by giving me lots of money. Tom, of course, being the son, got everything that mattered. I really loved that house. I begged Daddy, and begged him, to let me have it. Tom didn't care about it—and look! Last month was the first he'd bothered with it in years. And for what? To sell it. To make money. He never cared for it like I did, but Tom had the Warden name, and when I married, I wouldn't. And if I didn't marry—no heir. Daddy felt the place would become more important to Tom as he grew older, but Tom is very insensitive." Despite the continued calmness of her voice, Pris's words were coming fast and the ice in her glass slipped and rattled often as she worked steadily on her drink. "Well, I certainly didn't mean to get started on that!" Pris's smile was lopsided. "Let's talk about you, Emily. Did you and Charles have a family?"

"A son."

"What's his name?"

"Steven."

"Steven Sinclaire. It has a nice sound, Emily. How old is Steve? What does he do?"

"He's thirty," Emily said, subtracting the year from Steven's age that would square up time sequences, should anyone bother with them. "He works for a company that makes fiberglass stuff. Bronner Fiberglass and Insulation."

"Oh? How nice." Pris yawned. "Where does he live?"

"In Indiana. The home office is in Pennsylvania, though, and since he's in line for a promotion, he may be living there soon."

"How lovely. Let me freshen your drink."

"I'm not done."

"Well, I am. Excuse me a moment." Pris left for the kitchen, from whence came the cozy gurgling of the Scotch bottle. "Does Steven have a family?" Pris asked politely upon her return.

"Oh, yes. A little boy of seven, a daughter five years old."

"Charming," Pris declared. "And he likes his job?"

"I think so. He deals a lot with building and construction, and he enjoys those things, at least."

"Still, no one ever really likes to work, do they?" Pris observed.

"Charles did."

"Charles would. I'm really sorry, Emily, that my introducing Alice to our group had such a devastating effect on you. I mean, causing you to marry Charles and all."

"It was silly of me to have let it matter so much," she said cautiously, wanting to keep the conversational trend going without getting bogged down in her marrying Charles Sinclaire. "But then, I guess being silly is a prerogative of youth."

"Probably that's why Alice appealed to me," Pris said meditatively. "There was nothing silly about her, and I was looking for something that would give meaning to everything. Know what I mean?"

"Yes, sure, Pris. And don't worry about it. Do you ever see Alice?"

"No. I haven't, now, for a long, long time. She just dropped out of sight. She never did come to the last Fall Fest, even though I invited her and she seemed so keen to go. It was as though she lost interest in our group—maybe her father took a bad turn just then, I don't know. I can't remember anymore. She taught district school for a couple of years, I think. Until her father died, and she went back to Boston—to Gilchrist's. Speaks well of her, doesn't it? I mean, it was the height of the depression when they took her back, and women weren't in a very favorable position just then, with so many men out of work."

"What happened to the old gang?" She folded her hands, resisting the urge to light another cigarette. "I suppose the depression ruined everything for everybody."

"It sure did. I heard about your father, Emily, committing

suicide and all—but believe me, he had a lot of company. Becky Levering's father shot himself. Evvie Thayer's father managed everything pretty well, but the Kings were destitute and Ginny Porter's father sold apples somewhere, or so I heard . . . Oh, you need a refill!" Pris exclaimed, seizing Emily's glass. "Off I go." She picked up her own on the way.

"Not so strong this time!" Emily called.

It was just as strong.

"What did everyone end up doing?" she asked, getting the focus back on their youth. "Did poor old Ginny ever find a husband?"

Pris snorted. "You should see him! Hasn't got a hair on his head—bald as an eagle. Glass eye, too. You're never sure whether he's looking at you or not."

"And Caroline King?"

"Oh, Caro. Spinster—who'd have thought it? Her brother Bob did well with Standard Oil, though."

"How nice. Tell me about the other boys. I think it's interesting to find out how they came along in life."

Tell me about Tim, she willed. Tell me about him.

"Well, Jacky Pollard, my old beau, is president of a goddamned bank, if you can believe it!" Pris giggled. "How he loved to pet!"

"And Evvie's brother?"

"Something dull, as I recall. Selling something for some company," Pris said vaguely.

"And Alice's cousin? Remember, that cute fellow from Amherst?" How nice it was to talk about Tim—even in so offhand a manner.

"Inherited his father's business, I think. Whatever that was—wherever it is. Ned Pettingill went into the theater, of all things."

"No kidding!" Emily exclaimed, letting the subject of Tim Bradley pass by as unobtrusively as possible. "Whatever did he find to do in the theater?"

"Damned if I know. But he really liked it, and he's stayed with it all these years. He must be a homosexual. Charles, I gather, was not."

"Not what?" she asked, caught off stride.

"A homosexual. I mean, you had a son and all—though I guess a man can be both. Charles was always a little odd."

"Not that odd!" Emily laughed lightly, looking for another place to steer the conversation while her thoughts went wandering. . . .

If Tim had his father's business, that meant he lived in Worcester. Not very far from Cape Cod, really. . . .

"What was Port Huron like?" Pris asked. "I mean, nothing in Ohio seems very interesting, Emily."

"Well, you're wrong." Quickly she took the conversational ball and ran with it. "After the hills and irregularities of Massachusetts, Ohio does seem awfully flat, but the quality of light makes up for it, and the colors in the air; the sky is so wide you can see for miles and miles." Pris, she observed, was not listening.

"Isn't it dull, living alone? I mean, that house of yours is so big. Isn't it spooky?"

"A little."

"I should think you'd try to find something smaller."

"My being there serves a dual purpose, actually. It gives me a place to live, of course, but even more important, my being there ensures the well-being of the place. A house deteriorates fast without someone to care for it. They're like people, that way."

Pris stared. "I didn't know you were a philosopher."

"Time takes its toll." She grinned.

"Do you suppose our family's house is dying, like a neglected old person?"

"I'm sure I don't know, Pris. It looks just the same, from the outside."

"Huh." Pris shrugged. "So, will you just go on . . . living at Kingsland?"

"I suppose so. Actually it belongs to my son Steven, but he won't be ready to live in it for a long time. And to tell the truth, I don't feel the need to go anywhere else, though I think I may do things a little differently from now on."

"What do you mean, different?"

"I'm beginning to feel like I'm treading water—and I think I've done it just about long enough."

"What else can you do?"

"I'm thinking of opening a shop in the barn," Emily answered, since Pris seemed to require it. "Remember our barn?"

"Sort of."

"Has a mansard roof, like the house, and a huge weather vane on it, in the form of a running horse?"

"Oh, yes! What kind of shop?"

"I haven't thought that far yet."

"Frankly, Em, I can't see you as a shopkeeper."

"Why not?"

"Well, it's sort of undignified, don't you think?"

"Better than being bored, don't you think?"

Pris looked at her drink, finished it, went into the kitchen and reappeared with the bottle in hand, from which she poured a generous belt. "Emily," she declared. "I'm so bored I could scream. I'm going crazy."

"Maybe you ought to get a job yourself."

"I've thought about it," Pris said. "But I'm utterly unqualified to do anything."

"Couldn't you learn?"

"Go back to school, you mean? Learn how to take shorthand and type and stuff? Forget it!"

"Do you think it's beneath you? I make fudge."

"Fudge! To sell, you mean?"

"Yes. Mr. Snow sells it for me."

"Really!" Pris laughed. "How droll!"

Emily restrained the quick reply that begged for release. "There's nothing embarrassing about honest work," she said instead. "And it beats boredom by a mile. I believe it was boredom we were discussing?"

"Oh, yes, boredom. Well, I'll tell you, Em, it isn't just taking menial work that's slowing me down. Naturally we must respect honest labor." Pris blinked earnestly, refilling her glass and Emily's too.

"Then what is it? What's slowing you down?"

"Darion. His new job doesn't pay very well—it's quite a letdown from his position at Hatfield, really. Naturally it hurts his pride, and one of our biggest problems now is how much of Daddy's trust we can use to pay the bills. Darion wants us to live on what he earns; he doesn't want to use the trust money at all. And since Daddy designated Darion executor, there's not much I can do about it."

"You could get a job," Emily interjected.

"I have a small allowance," Pris said, having not heard. "And that's all. Can you imagine the uproar I'd have to face right here at home if I took a job independent of my husband's judgment, as executor of my father's trust. . . ."

"Oh. Then your husband doesn't want you to work?"

"I love Darion very much," Pris said, without troubling herself to answer. "But I have a lot of trouble reasoning with him. It was a lot better when he was working at Hatfield's; he was a lot easier to live with, believe me. Now he says if I want more money, I'd better get out and earn it." Having contradicted herself completely, Pris burst into tears, and

Emily found herself wishing she had not come to Olney at all.

"That's a shame, Pris. About his job." For lack of knowing what else to do, she picked up her Scotch and drank it neat.

"It sure is. If Darion had been smarter, he'd be employed by the conglomerate. But he was loyal to Hatfield to the end, the fool. And I'm the one to pay for it."

"Gosh, Pris, I don't know what to say." In fact, she was rapidly becoming so tight that she could hardly speak at all.

"Olney was bad enough when we had position—when Darion was important. But it's intolerable now that we're nobodies. Here, Emily. Let's have a little more." Her hands shaking, Priscilla Warden Hunt splashed the Scotch liberally, and they both drank liberally.

"Maybe you should move."

"Darion won't. I tell you, Em. There's no living with the man. If only I'd married Jacky Pollard." Pris sighed. "Do you remember Jacky?"

"Of course. Why didn't you? Marry him?" Her thoughts were as disconnected as her speech, and she knew she had slipped irretrievably over the edge of sobriety. Too late, she told herself cheerily. Too bad.

"He jilted me," Pris said morosely. "I went off to Bryn Mawr and he went to Harvard and met a perfectly dreadful girl from Radcliffe. He ditched me. It was awful."

"Hell, Pris," she said soggily, watching the room tilt to one side, tip to the other. "You're not the only girl who ever got jilted."

"What would you know about it?" Pris snorted. "You were always so popular. You never had to bear that kind of mortification."

"Why, that's not true," she insisted, her mouth strangely filled up by her tongue. "Tim Bradley jilted me."

"Tim Bradley!"

"Yes. Alice's cousin."

"Huh," Pris said. "I always wondered why she changed her mind about marrying him. And now I know—how amazing! Tim jilted her for you?"

"No, no, dear," Emily slurred earnestly. "He jilted me. For her sake. He and I went out a few times—"

"Oh, well . . . a few times." Pris waved it away. "Nothing compared to what Jacky did to me. After all, we'd been going together forever. Jacky and I—"

"Hell's bells," Emily burst out, "Tim Bradley and I were lovers."

Despite her increasingly drunken state, Pris Warden surfaced long enough to focus. "Lovers! You devil, Emily! I never knew you were promiscuous."

"I wasn't. Tim was the first, and we only ever Did It once. I was a nice girl! I didn't deserve to get caught."

An alarm sounded somewhere inside her head. Did you say what I think you said? someone asked her.

"What did you say?" Pris asked thickly.

What have you done? someone screamed, and suddenly her body flashed hot, and then cold, and she was faint. Quickly as her crippled brain would let her, she tried to steer past this awful lapse.

"I said, I didn't deserve to lose him. He was such a good catch, Pris! Do you remember how handsome he was?" She struggled, hoping the expression on her face had not changed.

"Oh, yes. I do," Pris said with a sly smile.

"And a wonderful lover, too," she fumbled. "It was terrible, losing him to Alice. Of course, she was exceptional. Don't you think?"

"Oh, yes!" Pris agreed sweetly, falsely, sizing Emily Merrick up a little differently than she had before.

"Why do you think she never married him, once she'd got him away from me?"

"On account of their being cousins," Pris answered promptly. "She thought she could make herself just forget it, but she couldn't. So she broke it off. Too bad you didn't wait a little longer, Em, before seeking solace in Charles Sinclaire and the Ohio plains."

So many sibilants came out slushily, Emily noticed, trying to concentrate on one thing at a time. The expression on Pris's face, for one thing. Did it tell her anything? Had Pris caught on? Was she becoming so drunk that she'd never remember anything?

"I'm nearly dry!" she exclaimed, examining her glass. "Let's have another drink, Pris!" She could help the process along, couldn't she?

"I've never turned one down yet," Pris said rather grimly, and emptied the bottle into their respective glasses. "I'm awfully glad you're here, Em."

Somehow she must hide, and keep hidden, the spot where the placid surface of their alcoholic pond had been disturbed. Lead Pris away, keep her quiet and undisturbed so that there would be nothing to remember. Or maybe, she thought foggily, it would be better to rule the waters completely, so that any observable waves would be Pris's own. It would not be hard to do.

Fire one, she thought.

"Well, personally, I think your father is to blame for your troubles," she announced.

"Daddy?"

"Yes, your dad. I mean, Pris, he treated you like a child when he was alive. I mean, arranging a chaperon for you when you were twenty years old! A babysitter!"

Fire two, she counted with satisfaction.

"And then he caused you to be treated like a child when he died (fire three, she thought wickedly), forcing your husband into the role of a parent as far as money goes, giving Tom the house, as though you weren't capable of being responsible for it."

"You're so right!" Pris exclaimed. "I never thought of it that way, exactly, but I believe you've hit the nail on the head. Daddy believed I never grew up."
little while and soak up the world that was his, where he lived day after day, where he hid, so that I could never find him. But he couldn't even take that much time for me." Pris's face crumpled up, and her mouth drooped and her eyes filled. "He didn't love me!" she sobbed. "He didn't love me."

Oh, Christ, Emily thought drunkenly.
at his desk. That was all I wanted, Em. Just to sit there for a

"I thought he was so nice, too."

"Well, he wasn't. I remember, when I was really little, begging him and begging him to let me come to his office and sit

"I'm awfully glad you're here, Em. I just go crazy, for being lonely." With an enormous sniff, Pris regained a semblance of control. "Darion never talks to me anymore, and you can't tell me that he has to be on the road as much as he is. He's only trying to stay away from me."

"You must be mistaken, Pris." She felt around unobtrusively for her pocketbook, which she remembered putting beside the couch.

"He never makes love to me anymore." Pris drew her knees up and hugged them to her chest. "He must have a mistress somewhere. He must have! No man can leave a woman alone as long as Darion can ignore me unless he has a piece of ass hidden away somewhere."

"I'm sure you've only misunderstood him," Emily placated, scooching down, patting the carpet in a widening circle, feeling under it as far as she could reach. "Maybe you should talk to him about it."

No answer.

She looked toward Pris, an immobile, wrinkled, deeply breathing ball. Sleeping. Or unconscious.

At least she'd been spared having to thank her for the hideous evening. She would steal away to whatever room she could find, without disturbing Pris. She slid to her hands and knees, crawled around until she found the purse, crawled to the hall and felt her way along it, looking for a room with a bed in it. There was one . . . yes, and there was her suitcase too; Pris had run it in here sometime or other.

You are rather drunk, stupid, she chastened the creature who, fully clothed, sprawled onto the bed, wrapping the spread around herself. There are gaps in the evening you can't account for.

Forget about the evening, she retorted. You have other troubles. You have tomorrow, when you will have to listen to Pris hour after hour after hour.

"Oh, nuts," she said aloud, and slid sideways into sleep.

"Well, Emily, how are you this morning?" Pris was sitting at the kitchen table, neatly dressed, her face made up, her hair carefully beehived. But the ten-o'clock light undid her effort, its honesty revealing last evening's ravages in lines of pain beneath her powder.

She feels as dreadful as I do, Emily thought, ready to weep for the spear that someone had thrust clean through her head. She moved carefully to the table. "Have you got any coffee, Pris?"

"Oh, of course, dear. It's right over there." Pris pointed toward the counter without looking at it, thereby not having to move her head. Emily unplugged the pot and brought it to the table in order to avoid the struggle of having to fetch it another time. She poured a cup, sat gently down.

"I'm a little hung-over, I'm afraid."

"We did go at it rather enthusiastically, didn't we?" Pris remarked in gleeful rue. "But it was a fine reunion, wasn't it? At least, what I remember of it. Emily, anything I may have said about Darion—don't pay any attention to it, all right?"

"I don't remember your even talking about him," she lied.

"I don't either, actually," Pris giggled. "But that's the trouble when you have a little too much to drink. It's hard to remember anything. I'm so glad you're here! What a treat it is to share the morning with a friend." Pris gazed at her with fond, bloodshot eyes, and Emily could detect no trace of deceit in them. She really has forgotten, she thought with relief. She won't even remember that I told her Tim and I were lovers. Let alone that I got pregnant as a result. "How wonderful the coffee tastes!" she enthused. "And you're right. It is pleasant to have a friend to drink it with." There was a water stain on the kitchen ceiling.

"The plumbing leaks," Pris said instantly. "You were looking at that spot, weren't you?"

"Well, sort of. Just in passing, Pris."

"Plumbers are fearfully expensive, so Darion tried to fix it himself. I don't like to criticize his work, but I'm afraid that the spot is only one example of it. We could have hired a plumber, of course, but that would require using trust money."

If she remembers telling me about her father's trust, she remembers more than she's letting on, Emily thought, her relief ebbing fast.

"I'm so glad you're here, Emily," Pris said again, looking for more reassurance about Emily's mutual pleasure.

"Yes, I'm glad too, Pris." She poured another cup of coffee, wondering if there was any excuse she could find to go home tomorrow.

"I've got several things in mind that we might do later on, once we've got ourselves in some kind of shape," Pris said. "I'd like you to meet my friends, and Olney has a club that's very nice; I'll show it to you sometime. There's a Scandinavian restaurant only twenty-five miles from here, in Exeter, New York, that has a simply exquisite luncheon buffet. Darion will be coming in at about suppertime, but he'll have eaten on the plane. If we had a substantial lunch in Exeter, you and I, then none of us would have to fuss with dinner."

"Sure, Pris. Anything you want, as long as it's not just right away." The linoleum on the kitchen floor was as tired and faded as they were themselves, ladies past their middle years, growing old, no longer resilient. . . . She tried to steer past the melancholy thought. "I'd enjoy meeting your friends. And if the place you'd like to go for lunch is twenty-five miles away, it'll be midafternoon before we get back, which will be exactly right, because I'm sure, Pris, that I'll need to rest by then." (After which she would have to make conversation with Pris's husband, whose plumbing failures were only one example of his work. . . .) I've got to get out of here, she fretted. Soon as possible.

"Well," Pris said, "I'll call Nancy Stewart first. I've told her all about you, Emily, and she's dying to meet you."

"All right." The third cup of coffee was beginning to help. "Tell her late morning. I may be able to walk a straight line by then."

Pris laughed heartily, staggered to the phone. "Nancy?" She winked at Emily. "This is Pris, dear. My friend from Massachusetts is here and I wanted to bring her around." Pris paused. "Oh," she said, picking at a crack in the cabinet nearby. "When would be convenient, dear?" She listened. "Oh. Well. Better luck another time—right, dear?" She smiled, as though Nancy Stewart could see, and hung up quickly. "Nancy must have forgotten. Seems she's got her week solidly full—though she'll be at the club Friday. You can meet her then, she says. Just let me see what Harriet is doing."

It was awkward, and became excruciating as more and more of Pris's friends seemed endlessly, irrevocably busy. Why didn't she do this before I got here? Emily wondered. She could have spared herself the humiliation of being turned down right here in front of me. How awful for her.

She watched the morning pass toward noon through the cloudy kitchen window, until finally—oh, how long!—glancing at the clock over the stove, stained and grimy from the heat of the oven, Pris gave up.

"Well! By the time we get to Exeter, it'll be noon," she said cheerfully. "Why don't we just jump into our finery and toddle on out there."

"Sure! Let's!" she agreed with an excess of exuberance. Anything was better than sitting where she was, although her old, sober self was coming to life, and despite all her efforts, was considering the probability that Pris might not be a very safe person to drive with. You're stuck, kid, she told herself. You're just plain stuck with it. You'll have to get into that car and pray.

"Actually," Pris said as she drove, the freshening New York countryside pleasant once they left Olney, "Nancy Stewart isn't much fun at all. You'd find her dull."

"Nancy Stewart?"

"The first girl I called."

"Oh . . . it doesn't matter, Pris."

But it did matter. Pris pried open the wound, probed it, salted it. "I only called her because she was nearby. And Harriet is a perfect boob. And Betty McNichol! What a snob. Mary Harding? You'd hate her. I'm not especially fond of any of them. That's all there is in dear old Olney, though. Dull, uninteresting people. Pretentious snobs."

"That's a shame, Pris."

"It sure is. I feel I could have done so much more with myself if I'd had someone to do it with, you know what I mean, Em? If I'd had someone like you."

"It must be very tedious for you."

"It might have been better in Exeter, where we're going. It always made me a little cross, to think that Darion simply refused to commute, and because of that I never had a chance to find out if the women in Exeter suburbs, with more money at their disposal, would have been more interesting than the people in Olney. Here's the outskirts. You can see for yourself that it's wealthy."

It was, indeed, a pleasant, well-heeled little city and seemed vastly nicer than Olney.

"The restaurant is just up ahead." Low-eaved, a chalet in appearance, Scandinavian in name and cuisine, it was, as Pris had described it, elegant.

"Oh, there's Florence Myers!" Pris called as they entered. "Hi, Flo!" she trumpeted, trampling down the hostess on her way to the unfortunate older woman. Flo Myers, dining with another lady of her own vintage, looked up in alarm and did not introduce her companion even when Pris brought forward her long-lost friend from Massachusetts and waited for an invitation to join them at their table for four.

None was forthcoming.

"Pris, the hostess says that the table over there is ready," Emily urged, tugging at Pris's sleeve. "It's been so nice to meet you, Mrs. Myers." She smiled vacuously and dragged Pris away.

"Well!" said Pris. "Now that we've finally gotten rid of them, let's get down to the menu. The meatballs are out of this world, Emily, and I'll have a carafe of the house wine," she said to the approaching waitress.

Maybe I could call Steve, Emily thought as she ordered and watched Pris seeking refuge from her ills in the carafe and in a minute account of the triumphs of her now-grown daughters. I could call him and tell him to call me back and say that Kathy has chickenpox and Rick has mumps and Mari has broken her legs—both of them. . . .

Returning to Olney was, as she'd suspected, considerably more hazardous than coming out because of the wine imbibed by the driver and because Pris insisted on turning her head to look Emily in the eye whenever she spoke, forgetting that the road was rushing toward them, and other cars, as well. Gratefully they both made their way to their respective unmade beds, the dishes that had been in the sink yesterday still untouched, the garbage stinking in the sun, the living room dusty and airless in the afternoon light.

It's like being in a prison, she thought. Or a dream of Franz Kafka. You're caught and you can't get out.

She was aware of nothing more until Pris shook her awake. Daylight had gone.

"Darion's home," Pris said. "But he doesn't believe you're even here."

"Oh! Give me a minute to freshen up, Pris. I'll be out in a jiffy." Thank God she felt strong and refreshed after her nap!

"Good. Darion has just mixed the martinis. He's a whiz at them."

Her head spun at the very thought. "How is your ginger-ale supply?"

"Ginger ale!" Pris exclaimed, affronted.

"I need to dry out a little from the effects of last night."

"Oh, come on, Em!"

"I mean it. I'd get sick."

"No, you wouldn't."

"Ginger ale or water, sweetie," she said firmly, turning her back on Pris to punctuate her determination.

"Oh, all right," Pris sulked, and left.

When can I call Steve? she thought. Maybe early in the morning, except that the husband will be here. Maybe Pris will sleep late and the husband will leave early for work, and I can sneak into the kitchen where the phone is . . .

She changed into a fresh dress, straightened her hair, splashed cold water on her aging face. How sad, she thought in the mirror, that the prospect of meeting a man—any man—is so unexciting to you. Old age is rather unfun. You don't look all that old, either. Just a little fatigued, sport.

Maybe it would be different if you weren't having to meet Priscilla's husband, the failure, but instead, someone interesting, challenging.

Buck up, old buddy, she exhorted herself, and commanded herself to smile graciously as she entered the living room.

Darion Hunt rose from his chair, his hand outthrust. Stunned, Emily could only stare. He was a man of medium height and broad shoulders, with the erect easy carriage of an athlete. His dark hair curled in vigorous exuberance, his eyes and mouth were cradled in lines carved by laughter. His handshake was warm, his greeting without affectation.

"I'm glad to meet you, Emily." His voice was strong and filled the room. "I hope you can live up to the reputation you've acquired around here!"

"I'll do my best." She found herself standing there too long, staring at him, taking him in, soaking him up. He was not a failure, despite his misfortunes. He was neither inept nor insensitive, as Pris had portrayed him. He was magnificent.

Down, girl, she counseled herself.

"Here's your ginger ale, Emily," Pris offered. "She says she won't drink your martini, Darion."

"To each his own," Hunt said easily.

"She won't have any fun."

"She might, honey. If we give her the chance." Darion's voice softened as he spoke to his wife, became soothing, coaxing, gentle, as though he spoke to a child. His control over its range was astonishing.

"Pris and I had a rather gala reunion last night," Emily explained. "It's taken me all day to even be convinced that I belong to the human race."

"By all means, you must have ginger ale until you're fully recovered! If you care to change your mind, be sure to ask for crackers to soak up the swill."

They seated themselves expectantly.

"Pris tells me that you're traveling a good deal these days," Emily began politely. "Do you enjoy it?"

"Actually, I do. Pris and I have been anchored here in Olney for so long that it's great to get out and spread my wings a bit."

"I wish I could," Pris grumbled.

"Anytime, honey," Darion Hunt said. "I can get you a ticket whenever you want one."

"It'd be too expensive. I'll take a little something to freshen my drink," Pris said. "These are pretty weak."

"I'm not through with mine yet."

"Oh, Darion!" Exasperated, Pris reached for the pitcher, but more quickly Hunt set it on the floor by his chair, out of her reach. "Pris and I have an agreement," he told Emily pleasantly, his voice betraying neither strain nor reproval. "Neither of us drinks more than the other when we're having a cocktail together."

"He's really afraid I'll pass out before supper," Pris said bluntly. "But we're not having supper tonight, Darion, and I'd appreciate a refill now, please."

"When I get mine, you get yours," he said firmly, and

turned to Emily. "You're living on Cape Cod now, Pris says. In an old family house."

"Yes. An ark. Or an albatross, depending on your point of view. Actually, my son Steven owns it."

"However did that come about, Emily?" Pris asked.

"Do you remember my cousin Elizabeth Edgarton?"

"I'm afraid I do."

"Pris!" Hunt murmured.

"She's not being rude. She's being factual," Emily said quickly. "My cousin Elizabeth was a difficult person who hated men—all men, except my father, and apparently my son Steven. She willed Kingsland to him outright—much to my former husband's dismay." She laughed, happily picturing Charles's defeat at the hands of Elizabeth Edgarton. "You remember how pretentious Charles always was, Pris."

"Oh, yes. Ready, Darion?"

"Almost. Go on, Emily."

"The house is the biggest one in Waterford, excepting only the Wardens' place. And Charles, my former partner in life's voyage, coveted it from his first memory."

"Maybe that's why he married you, Em," Pris said rudely. "To get your house."

Startled, Darion Hunt glanced at his wife, then at Emily, silent apology in his eyes. "Come on, Darion," Pris nagged. "Bottoms up."

It seemed fairly clear that Pris had been working on the relief of her troubles while Emily napped, but Hunt was not aiding or abetting her relief now. He drank slowly while Pris waited, foot tapping.

"What have you both done to amuse yourselves today?"

"We went to a really good place for lunch," Emily offered.

"Where was that?" Hunt asked Pris.

"Exeter. Skandia Hause." She fidgeted.

"Oh, yes. It is nice."

"I was going to take Emily over to Nancy's, but she was busy," Pris said. "She had a million things to do; it was a shame, really. And Harriet! Well! You should hear about the runaround her decorating man's giving her! She was all tangled up, trying to straighten out the mess he'd left her in."

"Spring's a busy time of year, that's for sure," Hunt said noncommittally, watching Pris's gestures closely.

"And now I seem to be dry," Pris challenged. "Change your mind, Emily?"

Perhaps if she offered to share the remains in the pitcher

there would be less for Pris, and the situation would not get out of hand as quickly as it had last night.

"Yes, I think I will. Tell me where to find a glass." She smiled pleasantly at Pris and then at Darion Hunt—but she had not fooled him. "I'll get you a glass," he offered, unwinding from his chair, heading toward the kitchen.

"You might as well make a new batch, if Emily is going to join us," Pris suggested as he left.

"Don't bother!" Emily called. "I only want a little."

"Darion! Make a new batch!" Pris insisted, and they waited to see what he would do. He returned with a glass that she'd heard him pull out of the pile of dirties and rinse in the sink. He did not replenish the pitcher, and in exasperation Pris stalked out to the kitchen and splashed her glass with straight gin, filling it. Startled, Emily glanced at Hunt, who, she saw, was watching her.

"Pris says Olney has a rather nice club that you both enjoy," she said, hoping to hide her dismay.

"Rather drab members," he said, in his eyes the signaled reassurance that he could handle Pris. "Good golf course."

"Who's drab?" Pris asked, reseating herself, carefully not spilling even a drop.

"The people out at the club. I was telling Emily that they really are a little on the dull side."

"I'll say," Pris sighed. "All they ever talk about is clothes and parties. That was why I enjoyed Alice Bradley, Emily. Clothes and parties were the least important things in her life."

"Is Alice the one you knew as a girl?" Darion Hunt asked attentively. "If clothes and parties didn't interest her, what did?"

Surely he had heard of Alice Bradley countless times. Then, as Pris went on at length, describing Alice in terms and phrases that certainly he'd heard before—perhaps knew by heart—it became clear to Emily that he was playing for time, trying to space Pris out so that her drink would last longer.

"What I think we should do is go to the club now," Pris said. "And approach them philosophically. That's what Alice would have done, you see."

"How would you do that?" asked Hunt. "I mean, what sort of philosophical discussion do you think they'd be capable of?"

"Well, how about this? We could go over, the three of us, and ask if they believe in God. How's that for starters?"

"I think I need another drink," Emily said.

"Perhaps you could use a cracker, too," Hunt suggested. "Perhaps we all could."

"I'll get a box," Pris announced, struggling to get out of her chair.

"Oh! Let me! Just tell me where," Emily protested, desperate to keep Pris away from the bottle of gin on the counter. But Pris was too quick.

"Good as done." In the kitchen she topped off her glass; distraught, Emily looked to Hunt. He gestured, his hand flat: she was to do nothing. Silently they watched Pris stagger back.

"You forgot the crackers, honey."

"Well, you could help," she snapped. "You could share the work, Darion, instead of just sitting there and making me do all of it."

"I offered before," Emily said with very fraudulent brightness. "I'll offer again."

"Cabinet over the stove," Hunt said.

"Darion! Get them yourself! You're the host."

"I think Emily's able."

They argued about it while she searched out the saltines, and were still at it when she came back. Had Hunt picked a fight to distract Pris from an assault on the club? Miserably Emily wished they'd stop.

"You leave me in this desert all day long," Pris said flatly. "And you expect everything to be spick-and-span when you get back. A dish in the sink—I get a sarcastic remark. Miss the garbage one day, and it's a national disaster. But you know, Darion, when I sit here all day, bored and lonesome, my energy is sapped. I'm exhausted, perfectly exhausted. And you can't even get a box of crackers."

"That's why I wish you'd come on a trip with me sometime. It'd relieve the monotony."

Pris's smile was maudlin. "Thank you, darling. That's awfully nice of you. I'm going to kiss you, just for that." She sprang to her feet, and Hunt, on his own just as quickly, caught her as she crumpled. He nodded to Emily and carried Pris from the room.

She stared at the martini glass in her hands. Its gin content had been very low, probably Hunt's effort to keep Pris sober. Whatever could she say to him when he returned?

He was a big man, but he walked soundlessly into the room, seated himself in his former chair without fanfare. "I'm sorry, Emily," he said simply.

"How long has this been going on?"

"Quite awhile."

"Is she an alcoholic?"

"Yes."

"You mentioned you wished she went on your trips with you. Would you really dare to take her?"

"Not anymore. Five years ago, when I started the job I have now, I'd have taken her; she could have handled it then, and I suggested it then, hoping it'd give her something else to think about. She only came once, though. I keep offering, because she'd be hurt if I didn't. She'd take it as a loss of faith—which, of course, it would be."

"So this has been going on for five years?"

"Fifteen—though not so critically as this. No doubt you've heard of the infamous Warden trust?"

"Um, yes."

"It was set up some time ago, in the last year of Mr. Warden's life. He came to me; he was afraid that Pris was drinking too heavily and would take the same path that her mother had. He wanted me to control the trust so there'd be something left to take care of Pris, should she become incurable. Or to give to her as a gift, if she straightened herself out. I didn't have much choice but to agree—Pris would have drunk herself to death in no time. But it was a mistake. I became her father, you see, who didn't love her, who withheld what she wanted. In this case, money. A surrogate for love. . . ."

He ran a hand across his face, the gesture of a bone-tired man, then glanced at his watch. "There's a passable television program on. Would you like to watch?"

"Sure," she agreed. Certainly they couldn't sit around all evening analyzing Pris. She fastened her eyes on the tube, thought about the next possible move she might make.

At ten o'clock, Hunt stirred, stretched. "I've had a long day; I'm afraid I'm falling asleep. I hope you'll excuse me if I turn in."

"By all means, go!" she urged. "I have a book I can read."

"Are you sure?"

"Of course! But before you go, I . . . I wonder if you might help me."

He smiled. "Anything at all," he said, and she suspected he knew already what she would ask.

"I think I'd like to leave a little sooner than I originally planned."

"I understand."

"I thought I might call my son and go out to Indiana to

visit him, as long as my bag is already packed," she hurried on, hoping to fill the gap in her manners created by this quick, unexplained departure.

"I don't blame you," he said, eliminating the necessity of prevarication.

Guiltily she asked, "Do you think it'd help her if I stayed on?" The weight of depression smothered her as she spoke the impossible words.

"It wouldn't do any good, Emily, and might be pretty unpleasant for you. I wouldn't stay. It's no fun to watch a person annihilate himself. Or herself, in this case."

"Not much fun for you, either."

"Not much," he agreed. His eyes met hers, steadfastly unwilling to avoid the truth but equally unwilling to indulge in self-pity. "If you like, I'll take you out to the airport early, and you can call your son from there—or just go on back to Cape Cod, if you'd prefer." She hadn't fooled him even for a minute.

"I guess I just want to go home," she said, and found, to her horror, that she was ready to cry.

Considerately, Hunt looked elsewhere. "I don't think Pris will awaken before daybreak. If we were out of the house around five-thirty, you'd never see her. Leave a note, if you like, and I'll explain when I come home again."

"You end up with the dirty work."

He shrugged, as though he'd done so much dirty work already that another morning of it didn't matter. "I'll get you an alarm clock. Wait here a moment." He reappeared with a wind-up old clunker that would surely keep her awake the whole night, and silently she crept to the room she'd been using, quietly repacked her suitcase and prepared to flee with Darion Hunt at dawn.

Muffled announcements bellowed quietly from the loudspeakers, echoing in high corners, reverberating around corners. The airport was nearly empty, and the muffled noise seemed to fill it absolutely. The coffee shop that overlooked the concrete airstrip was just opening as they arrived; a waitress, looking as sleepy as Emily felt, shoved a menu in front of her and another in front of Hunt.

"We'd like coffee now," he told her. "We'll order when you get back."

The girl nodded and whisked away, the crepe of her shoes authoritative on the composition floor.

"I assume you'd like coffee."

"Quite!" She was so sleepy she could hardly think, now that they'd gotten out of the house without Pris waking up. Sleep had eluded her much of the night, held at bay by that damned alarm clock and her general malaise—and something else besides, to which she refused to give enough room for analysis, and now, having left without incident, her tension relieved, she was nearly overcome by her fatigue.

Probably your poor fifty-one-year-old face looks pretty overcome, too, she thought wryly, but there wasn't much she could do about that.

"How do you manage to look so fresh at such an unreasonable hour?" Hunt asked, smiling. "The rest of us look like we'd slept between the spring and the mattress—but you're like a goddamn flower."

"I don't feel like any flower." She nodded her thanks to the waitress. "Orange juice and a doughnut, please."

"No doughnuts." The girl scowled.

"Muffin?"

"No muffins, either."

"What would you suggest?" she asked sweetly.

"Toast," the girl answered with venom.

"Just what I really wanted." The girl was not amused.

Hunt ordered a huge breakfast for himself. "She doesn't bother you, I take it."

"The waitress? No, she doesn't bother me."

"Pris would have made a federal case out of it," he said. "I forget that not every woman would." A wistfulness stole across his face.

He is so sad, she thought, meeting his eyes, declining to politely look away. "Let me express my sympathy," she said softly. "I lived with an unpleasant situation myself for many years. I know what it can do to you—your perceptions of life and people . . ."

He looked up to his arriving cup of coffee, and did not reply.

"I suppose deciding you'll support yourself and Pris with your own money is your way of curbing her?" Emily asked.

"Yes. Doesn't do any good, of course. But it keeps her trust intact. I'm afraid if I started using it to repair the house and buy clothes for her and a decent car, that it'd be like a dam breaking. It's easier to just draw a line and stay behind it; I'm hoping that by providing her with no distractions, she'll surrender sooner."

"To rehabilitation."

"Yes." He glanced up quickly, surprised, perhaps, at the

quickness of her perception. There was a long, not comfortable pause as they drank their coffee.

"She mentioned wanting to move to Exeter," Emily suggested. "She seems to think she'd be happy there."

"Yes, I know she does. To swing it, of course, we'd have to live partially on the trust."

"And you think it's too late?"

"I know it is." He looked out the large, harsh windows, watching a small plane bounce in on the runway. "What I don't know is whether or not it would have made a difference a long time ago, when she first started promoting the idea. She'd run out her string in Olney; I figured she'd just do the same in Exeter—and it would delay her coming to terms with her illness. Aside from using up the trust. But you always look back on a decision and wonder if it was the critical one, if it would have made the difference. Did you ever get into that situation?"

"I'm afraid my hand was forced, beginning to end," she said, and was caught in the wave of impulsive confidence. "In order to protect my son, I pretty much had to stay married. There were no decisions to make until Steven was old enough to take care of himself. Protect himself."

"From whom?"

"From my husband." This time it was she who hid behind the distraction of the waitress, arriving with breakfast. Soon Hunt would leave, would go to the office, if he had one, or home to explain to Pris that he had helped Emily escape.

"Tell me about your house on Cape Cod," he said.

"What would you like to know about it?"

"I've been to Waterford, with Pris. I seem to remember a large place, nearly hidden behind the trees. Mansard roof. Tower. Is that it?"

"Yes."

"A big place for you to manage."

"Oh, Steven manages it. I only report to him. He lived in Waterford awhile himself, and worked there, and has useful connections among plumbers and electricians and carpenters. He calls someone, and presto! They arrive."

"Do you like Waterford?"

She laughed. "I never considered whether I like it or not. It's like your family; it belongs to you. How you feel about it is irrelevant. Which reminds me to ask you about your daughters—relative to Pris."

"You needn't ask," he said briefly. "They have dealt with

their mother in the only way possible. Just as you are dealing with her now."

Stricken, she stared.

"There's no alternative, Emily," he said, his palms up to suggest the paucity of choice. "There's no other choice, except what you are doing. What good would hanging around do, trying to bolster up the notion that everything's okay."

"I might suggest that everything's *not* okay," she said, and then remembered that she would do no such thing, in case an unpleasant scene would recall things better forgotten. Hunt saw it too.

He was fast enough, God knew. He was a marvelous man, she thought, and assented to the waitress's glum offer of a second cup of coffee, waited for him to excuse himself to go home, or go to work, to exit, to never come back, just when she'd found him.

"Did you meet Pris in Waterford?" he asked.

"Oh, no! We went to school together in Milton! I've known Pris since my first memory, and then, of course, we spent summers together in Waterford, and were roommates at Bryn Mawr."

"Bryn Mawr! I went to Penn!"

"Why, yes! Now I remember Pris saying so."

"Did you like Bryn Mawr?"

"Hated it," she said cheerfully. "But the Main Line is awfully pretty. I don't mean the mansions—which are stunning—but the countryside around there."

"Delaware Valley." He nodded. "Yes, I know what you mean. There's a special charm to it, isn't there? I used to row a lot on the Schuylkill—that was something special, too! Spring on the Schuylkill! Too bad it's not a more euphonious name. How can you write an ode to a river when words that rhyme with it are so drippy?"

"Like what words?" she giggled.

"Well, you have to invent them," he said with a straight face.

She burst into laughter and he chortled along with her.

"Did you ever go out to Valley Forge when you were there?" he asked.

"No, never did."

"Very pleasant. Very pleasant." He was smiling, with distant pleasure in his eyes, and the years had dropped away, revealing the young man he must have once been. Then he returned. "Would you like to tell me about Steven? Do you enjoy talking about him?"

"I'd bore you completely." She grinned. "Far as I'm concerned, Steven walks on water. He's grown straight and strong despite all the blows life has dealt him. There's no one I admire more, and the fact that he's my son has nothing to do with it."

"I take it your former husband is not his father," Hunt remarked diffidently.

"No." Something inside started trembling violently, because she was sure he knew it all without her having to say anything.

"I'm glad he's so decent a young man," Hunt said gently. "Your son, I mean. Somehow I get the feeling that he's made it all up to you."

Moved, she could not speak. He signaled for the check, relieving her of the necessity of hiding further. Together they walked toward the gate where her plane would board.

"Pris mentioned you'll be going to Albuquerque," she said as they took their place in line.

"Yes, day after tomorrow."

"She seemed to think you travel more than you need to."

"I know she feels that way, though it's not true. I suppose I'll have to get a job nearer home soon, if she gets any worse, but I've put it off because I like this one so well. It doesn't pay much, but it has a lot of challenge. The alternative is the Olney Gas and Electric. A friend can put me into accounting anytime."

"Is that as bleak as it sounds?"

"I'm afraid so." Olney Gas and Electric, and Pris, were his only future, it seemed, and quickly she looked away to hide her dismay from him.

"I'm going to open a shop," she confided, without knowing why.

"What are you going to sell?"

"I'm still deciding."

"Cape Coddy things, I hope."

"Oh, most definitely!"

"Fishnets and seashells?"

"Driftwood and baskets made out of seaweed."

"Cape Cod air in a bottle."

"Carved boats for the bathtub. Mermaids for the lawn."

The announcement for her plane racketed around them. She held out her hand without wanting to, feeling suddenly so lost and small that she ached with the agony of it, and wordlessly he took her hand in his own, looked straight into her eyes; the moment was mutilated again by the loudspeaker. A quiet shroud settled around them both.

"Good-bye," he said finally.

She could not say it, but could only look at him one last time, and then ran to catch her plane.

19

"It really stinks, Emily, and you know it," Pris raved. "Here I offer you the hospitality of my home, the renewal of my friendship, give of myself, as it were. And what do you do in return?"

"Really, Pris—" she tried to interrupt.

"What do you do? You sneak off with my husband!" Pris's voice became plaintive. "I needed you . . . and you ran away with Darion."

"I didn't either run away with Darion," she said loudly. "I left Olney earlier than I'd planned, and he took me to the airport, Pris, and that is all." That was not all—not by a long shot—but she had to gamble that it was all Pris knew.

"He's not the same anymore, Emily. He's a different man, and I can put two and two together."

"And what answer do you come up with?" She hated to ask, but surely Pris expected it.

"I conclude that something's going on. I think that the two of you are plotting behind my back, arranging time to see one another. Darion travels so much, I never know where he is. It'd be the easiest thing in the world for you to meet him somewhere without my ever knowing."

Clearly, then, Pris actually knew very little. She must be diverted. "If Darion seems different to you now," she counterattacked, "maybe he is. Maybe since he's seen how a sober woman behaves, he's having second thoughts about you.

Maybe he's thinking that life would be much more pleasant if you weren't drunk most of the time. There's nothing like comparison, Pris."

It was a low blow, which did not give her much satisfaction, but for the moment it worked. "Just what do you mean by that?" Pris demanded. "You'd think I was an alcoholic or something, to listen to you."

"Tell me you haven't got a drink in your hand right now, this minute."

There was a pause. "No, I don't have a drink in my hand. It's on the telephone table." Pris giggled.

"It's only four o'clock in the afternoon."

"So it's four o'clock," Pris said. "Pretty soon it'll be five o'clock."

"Why can't you wait until five o'clock?"

"I could if I wanted to."

"Why don't you want to, then? Why are you doing this to yourself?"

"I'm not doing anything to myself," Pris said stridently, her defenses slipping automatically into place. "Sometimes I get discouraged, is all, and things look a lot better after you've smoothed their rough edges with a drink or two. You know, Emily, being a woman is no joke. Daddy wouldn't give me the house, because I wasn't a boy. I hate being a woman. I hate it."

You're married to Darion Hunt, you fool! she wanted to shout. You should be on your knees thanking God you're a woman! She paced at the end of the telephone like a dog on a leash while Pris enumerated the ills of female-kind, more and more tense as she realized that this wreck of a person at the other end would believe neither truth nor falsehood, would hear nothing but her own voice, and if she decided that two and two did indeed add up, no amount of deceit would change her, nothing would stop her.

You never really thought you could go on seeing him, did you? she asked.

When she'd returned to Kingsland she'd unpacked; a great hollow space inside was growing, growing, and she made herself ignore it. She'd nibbled at her supper and slept fitfully, risen at dawn to watch the day break, moodily stared at her breakfast, paced around the house, picking things up, putting them down, listlessly making her way to the front door when its knocker rattled.

"Hello," he'd said sheepishly, looking foolish and hopeful and sad, there on the doorstep.

The great hollow space was swallowed up and her capacity for speech went with it.

"May I come in?" he asked. "Or would you rather I went away, Emily?"

"No . . . no," she croaked. She stepped back in welcome. Get hold of yourself, she instructed the inner Emily. He has come to you. He has come!

"Just stopping by on your way home from Albuquerque?" she asked with a straight face.

"Oh, yes. Definitely just passing through." He looked around the huge, anachronistic parlor, a relic from another age like a dinosaur or an anteater, and then he looked at her with eyes of love.

"Did you really believe I could just let you go?" he asked quietly, and the void of her loneliness filled up, and her heart too, and her awareness of him and of herself and of life in its very splendor; there were birds chattering in the backyard and a dog barked on Main Street and an infinity of flowers filled all fields everywhere.

"Darion." She heard his name ringing in her ears, in her soul too. She held out her arms and he came to her, gathered her up and the dream of Darion Hunt became the reality, warm and overwhelming, hungrily taking from her and giving back—giving life in its joy, in its exalting. She clung to him, close, closer, and they were as lovers in the tide of life, young again, strong again.

And vulnerable again, as only youth can be.

"I need you, Emily," he said humbly. "I thought I could spend the rest of my middle age caring for Pris; I thought I could accept a job in Olney, when the time for it came, and the approach of old age, taking it a day at a time—I thought I could do it all. I thought I was strong, stoic, able to take it. Now I find I'm not strong. Not anymore."

When he left the next morning, she knew that her loneliness would never have the same quality again because he existed, and he had touched her, and they had, together, affirmed the joy of life which she had not known for so many years. She would not be the same again, and apparently Darion was not the same, either, because Pris had sensed it, instantly.

"He doesn't respect me," Pris was howling into her ear. "And Jacky Pollard jilted me and I don't have any friends and Tom got the house and Darion's not nice to me . . . Oh, hell, Emily, you'll just have to excuse me. I'm too upset to talk to you anymore."

"Maybe if you took a little nap . . ." She stopped, because Pris had hung up already.

She went out into the kitchen to heat water for tea because she could not possibly answer the phone in one ring if she was this far away from it. She dunked the tea bag, watching the swirls of brown overtake the water's clarity, and wondered, about many things.

For instance: how could Darion have married such a girl as Pris Warden?—himself so strong, a personality so very intact, aware of itself, vibrant, while Pris was so weak.

Yet, she reminded herself, the Pris of long ago sparkled, laughed, and seemed confident, and joyous too. No, we don't change, she thought. And Pris hasn't changed either. It's only that different facets of ourselves emerge, once our lives have settled and we no longer need to attract and dazzle and lure. Pris, after all, always had gravitated to people stronger than herself, hoping, perhaps, to gain strength from them. She had always been weak, but her personality had disguised it well.

Not unlike Steven's wife, she reflected, in the matter of disguises at least. A girl who was popular in college, belonging to the best sorority, active, a leader, but despite the appearance of being a dynamic, onward-moving person, Mari was only a top-rank conformist, in college striving to fulfill the image of a successful woman on campus. Just as now she conformed to the image of successful wife to a rising executive, attending club meetings and the PTA and drinking midmorning coffee with the Right People. . . . We carry around a hidden person—maybe many people; we don't know they're there, they surprise us always—but we have not changed. We've only become what we truly were. . . .

In the library the phone rang. Carrying the cup of tea, she settled herself at Cousin Elizabeth's old desk and picked up the receiver. Across the room Kingsley Merrick smiled at her from his gold-framed portrait.

"Hello?"

"Anyway, I think it would have been a lot more polite to tell me that you wanted to go home. Don't you?" Evidently Pris had collected the pieces of herself and had reassembled them.

"I wasn't sure, Pris," she began, and then stopped. How do you tell the hostess that she was a tiresome drunk? "I just didn't know what to say."

"Do you know now? What to say, I mean."

"Yes, I suppose I do."

"Well, then. Go ahead."

She drew a deep breath. "I didn't want to stay in Olney and watch you kill yourself," she said.

"Really, Em, you dramatize so!"

"Well, passing out cold is a bit dramatic, don't you think?"

"Who passed out cold?"

"You did."

"I did no such thing. When?"

"The last night I was there. You kept filling your martini glass with gin in the kitchen when you thought we weren't looking."

"I certainly did not," said Pris. "And it's certainly beneath my dignity to discuss such hallucinations with you. Besides, you can't fool me. You're only trying to hide the fact that you wanted time alone with my husband. And very cleverly you got it."

"Getting out to the airport before you woke up was the only way I could figure how to get out of the house, Pris."

"You don't fool me, not for a moment. And don't think you can just have him, either."

Again the line went dead, but Emily did not move from the desk. Slowly she finished the tea, made herself live with the certain knowledge that she had contracted something fatal: the enmity of Priscilla Warden Hunt.

At the risk of sounding as pathetically self-pitying as Pris did, she did have to consider the fact that whenever she touched happiness, it turned to ashes.

She buried her head in her hands.

You marry a perfectly detestable person in order to rectify an error of judgment. You put up with him for twenty years so that Steven will be strong and able to fend for himself. You make yourself stay sane when the boy turns his back on you, that hideous year and a half after he learned who Tim Bradley really was, and after you get him back, you have to hand him over to Mari Crawford. You live alone for ten years, two of which were taken nursing your mother until she died, and now that you are ready to live again, you meet Darion Hunt, who can fulfill you absolutely—and you are going to lose him.

She picked up the phone in the middle of its single ring.

"Yes?" she inquired, sure and certain of who would be at the other end.

"You can't have him," Pris said, as though she had never hung up. "Don't think I won't fight to keep Darion. You leave him alone, Emily."

She could not let Pris's accusation pass without at least

nominal defense. To say nothing was to admit complicity.

"You don't have to fight to keep Darion, Pris. You can have him. He's all yours. He's always been all yours. He loves you."

"He does not love me and he never has," her voice went on spitefully. "But he's mine and he's all I've got. Don't you forget it. If you try to take him away from me, I'll spill the beans about you."

"Beans?"

"Beans."

"What beans?" she asked, trying to control her voice against the sudden sweep of anxiety.

"Why, dear! Did you think I couldn't remember? That I wasn't able to figure it out? That your precious son Steve is Tim Bradley's child? What else, dear!"

She knew, knew it surely, that she should make a smart remark, blithe and unconcerned, a remark that would throw Pris off the scent—but she could not.

She could say nothing.

"Your reputation won't be worth a shred by the time I get done with you," Pris ranted. "If you don't stop seeing my husband. And as far as your Steven is concerned, his career at Bronner Fiberglass and Insulation won't be worth a damn either. There or anywhere else."

She must do something!

"You're dreaming a situation up that doesn't exist, Pris. And if you insist on spreading lies about me, I shall be forced to suggest, to anyone who listens, that they had better consider the source."

This time it was she who hung up; calmly she walked to the kitchen sink and threw up.

Ah, Jesus! She wiped her lips, rinsed her mouth, cleaned the sink. Oh, Christ. All over again. We have to go through it all over again.

She looked out the kitchen window, across the smooth lawns that Steven had sown a dozen years ago, and the flowerbeds he'd planted in order to keep Cousin Elizabeth happy, and her tears spilled as she thought of his struggles with Charles Sinclaire and the awful deadening of his eyes when he learned the truth about himself. And then his determination to deal with it on his own, rejecting any help from her—in fact, rejecting her completely. And now the possibility that he would have to confront it publicly, as, of course, she would, herself. That he might be ruined, that he would reject her again, that she would lose him.

What would he do, should Pris shout it out loud?

Steven was not the sort of man to deny the truth. His style demanded that he work within its parameters. Yet she doubted strongly that he had ever disclosed his own personal history to Mari. She was not the sort of girl you confided such a thing to. She wouldn't know what to do or how to think, because the girl rarely thought about anything further than her own sphere of influence. And Steven's career at Bronner. That was something else again. F. X. Sattiswaite was the ultimate in old farts, without question. As so often happened, his personal ideas were narrow and hidebound, compared to fresh thinking of this day; high above the multitudes, men like F.X. controlled the financial destinies of thousands of people, were themselves brilliant, inventive, talented in their field—and yet their inner life had not matured at all. F. X. Sattiswaite would definitely avoid a man of illegitimate birth—even if he didn't know he was doing it. Illegitimacy, after all, was implicitly connected to illicit sex—the ultimate sin in the lexicon of men like F.X. And how many others, in high places, were just like him?

I'd rather my son didn't have to find out the hard way, she thought. . . .

The phone rang again, but she refused to answer it, stood with clenched fists and listened to it going on, and on, and on—Pris, surely. Anyone else would assume after five rings, six at the most, that no one was home.

She put the phone in a desk drawer, went into the parlor, put the *1812 Overture* on the record player, and tried to think. To think clearly.

They had covered the subject of Tim Bradley with silence, she and Steven. He'd wanted it that way—how typically male of him! To retire from thought the unthinkable! No woman could do it—but men could, she knew. They were masters at it. Now, like it or not, she and Steven could no longer treat the subject with silence.

It isn't fair, she wept. To have to pay so much, so repeatedly. But it was so, and crying was all she could do.

She went into the library again, removed the still-ringing phone from the desk drawer, broke the connection, and dialed Bronner Fiberglass in Arlington, Indiana.

"Steven Sinclaire, please," she told the operator, waited for the connection to be made. Steven, she thought, can you forgive me all over again? I don't think I could stand to lose you and Darion Hunt at the same time for the same old worn-out, dog-eared, moth-eaten mistake.

"Sinclaire here," the beloved voice said.

"Steve?" Her own voice trembled.

"Mom! What are you up to, calling in the middle of the day?" he chided, and then the edge of awareness slipped into his tone as it occurred to him, with the initial surprise over, that something was wrong.

"Steven," she said as calmly as she could, "I must see you."

"When?" It was like him not to ask why; he respected her and he knew that she would not make such a request without reason.

"As soon as possible."

"We'll be there in a month for vacation. I take it that a month is too long to wait?"

"Yes."

"And not private enough."

"That's right." They both meant that Mari must not be present, without either of them committing the disloyalty of saying so.

"Perhaps I need to check into the home office." It was in Pennsylvania. "Perhaps, depending on how critical it is, you could meet me in Boston when I'm on my way home."

"In a rather roundabout route." She smiled.

"Rather. You could take a bus, I think. Some of them come right out to Logan Field."

"Consider it done. Just tell me which terminal and when."

"You must be pretty desperate to agree to such a crazy scheme," he probed.

"I'm afraid I am, honey," she said.

There was a long pause. He knows, she thought. He knows what would make me that desperate.

"I'll get back to you later this afternoon."

"The phone might be busy," she said. "If I don't hear from you today, would it be all right if I call you there in the morning?"

"What in hell is happening, Mom?"

"I'll tell you when I see you."

"Hey," he said softly. "Mom? Whatever it is—we'll take care of it, okay?"

"Yes, Steven. We'll try."

As soon as she hung up, the phone started again, and she hid it again in the drawer and left the house and walked and walked in the spring sun.

The airport lobby was blessedly busy, blessedly impersonal, and she felt its very disinterestedness buoy her, give her distance from herself, give her the ability to greet Steven rationally and talk to him without hysteria.

There he came now, and her heart lifted as it always did when she beheld the son Tim Bradley had given her, tall and nicely built as his father was, with eyes deeply and clearly blue, as Tim's had been—yet now she was able to think of Steven's father without pain, because of Darion Hunt, to separate herself from those old wounds even though they were yet pursuing her. Yes, she thought, they will pursue us all our lives, Steven and I, and not even Darion Hunt can stop it from happening.

"Hi, Mom!" Smiling, happy to see her, Steven kissed her cheek and hugged her. "You're looking a little peaked, I must say!" Despite his jaunty words, his face reflected his concern. "What would you like to do? Where would you like to go? Want a bite of lunch? A drink?"

The very thought of alcohol repelled her. "Lunch. See if we can't find a table in a quiet corner."

"Nothing's ever quiet in an airport," he said. "That's why conversation is so private." He thrashed it out with the hostess, secured a seat where he wanted one, ordered a martini. "Anything at all?" he asked. "Ginger ale? Tea?"

"Iced tea." She smiled, soaking up his presence, hoping he would not notice. Perhaps it'll be the last time we'll be like this, she thought. Perhaps we'll never be close again.

"All right," he said kindly. "What's the problem?"

The waitress appeared, reprieving her. "Iced tea, a martini, not too dry," he ordered.

"I didn't know you were a lunch drinker."

"When in business, do as the businessmen do," he retorted. "Are you stalling?"

"I'm afraid so."

The waitress appeared, with the martini and the tea. Steven ordered lunches for them both, and Emily, her hands damp, squeezed too much lemon into the tea, laced it with too much sugar, stirred vigorously, laid the spoon down while he patiently waited, sipping his drink, watching her procrastinations.

She sighed, no longer able to put it off.

"Recently I've been in touch with a woman who used to be a girlhood friend of mind. Her name was Pris Warden then, of the Warden name and fame in Waterford."

He was not visibly impressed with the Warden name and fame—but he would not be. Not Steven. "And?"

"I hadn't kept in touch with anyone from my childhood; then Pris's brother popped in one day—he'd been looking over the family place . . ." She was about to go into detail about Tom, then saw by Steven's face that she was stalling again.

"The upshot of it was that she invited me—Pris did—to her home in central New York State, and I went. And discovered that Pris is a well-advanced alcoholic. And that her husband is an extremely attractive, extraordinarily perceptive, very decent man with whom I shared an almost instant rapport, first relative to Pris and her problem . . . later, more personally."

"How much later?"

"A few days. Darion followed me home."

"Darion."

"Darion Hunt," she said firmly.

"He ought to be an actor, with a tag like that." He smiled, probably hoping to relieve her very obvious tension.

"He surely should. He looks the part and has a wonderful speaking voice. I wonder if he sings," she mused, straying a little in the lure of her attraction to Darion and her reluctance to face the rocky road ahead.

Steven laughed. "Why, Mom! You're in love!"

Knowing that she blushed only made her blush the more, and busily she stirred her tea. This time Steven did not prompt her.

She sighed. Here goes, she thought.

"The first night I was there visiting Pris, we were alone. Darion was away on business, and Pris and I reminisced as, of course, one will do. The two of us had too much to drink, and because I didn't realize how far gone I was, I'm afraid I was a little careless as we reminisced, Pris and I, about the days when she and I were young in Waterford."

His face was impassive now, his knuckles on the stem of the martini glass growing white. He set the glass down, hid his hands.

"I didn't say anything outright, but I said enough to give it away—that you are not Charles Sinclaire's child. And Pris remembered the man who is your father." The look in his eyes made her want to weep, but she could not afford to—not yet, because the worst part hadn't been told him yet. "Well, I hoped my slip had passed by, that she wouldn't remember my having made it. But it was a vain hope. When

Pris realized that Darion had become attracted to me, she called me, and she says that if I take Darion away she'll tell everyone she knows everything about me . . . and of course about you."

"Who is she likely to tell?"

"Let's put it this way. She knows where you work, because I told her that, too."

"Sattiswaite," he said, summarizing in one word the problem at Bronner.

Oh, God, she mourned, that I ever went to Olney!

You would not have met Darion otherwise, she observed pitifully. "I'm sorry, Steve. I'm more sorry than I can say."

He did not look at her; the waitress hustled up with their lunch, and he waited until their sandwiches and salad were in place, the girl gone.

"How determined is this Mrs. Hunt?" he asked. "Is she the sort of person to make idle threats?"

"Yes, she is. But that doesn't mean she isn't capable of carrying them out."

"Maybe she'd do it anyway," he said. "Even if you didn't see Mr. Hunt ever again, maybe she'd tell F.X. anyway."

"Maybe. I threatened to reveal that she's an alcoholic if she said anything to anyone."

"Will that stop her?"

"I don't know. It must have bothered her a little. She's been ringing the phone at Kingsland ever since, perhaps to tell me how she doesn't have an alcohol problem and everyone will believe her. . . ."

He considered it, the lunch untouched. "I guess you'd better tell me what you and Mr. Hunt plan to do. Have you spoken with him since the lady threatened you?"

"Yes. I've talked with him long-distance. He . . . he's going to get a job that doesn't require traveling, so he'll be home all the time and she'll have no reason to suspect him of meeting me."

"That's a little hard on you, isn't it?"

"It's hard on us both."

"Did you ask it of him?"

"It was what we mutually agreed to do."

"Are you trying to protect yourself? Or me?"

"I . . . guess we did it to protect Pris," Emily said, her misery nearly uncontainable. Darion! Darion!

Yet he exists, she told herself. Your lives have touched, and both of you know the other is there. Neither of you will ever be alone now. "People in our generation don't take marriage lightly, Steven."

"People in mine don't, either," he reminded her.

"And Pris is ill. We can't just ditch her and be happy with ourselves. It won't last forever. Soon enough she'll be institutionalized and we'll be able to meet one another, Darion and I. It sounds cruel, I suppose. But that's the way it is."

He stirred up his salad, laid his fork down again. "What I want to know, Mom, is whether you and Mr. Hunt despite your concern for Mrs. Hunt, really came to this conclusion on my account. Because if you did, I think you should reconsider." His eyes met hers without flinching. "I can take care of myself. You don't have to keep her quiet for my sake."

Her admiration for his courage—always high—rose higher yet.

"I know you've been hoping for a promotion to the home office." She made herself say it, because there was no point, any longer, in ducking things they'd been refusing to look at all these years. "If Pris talks now, to F. X. Sattiswaite, you might not get it. And unless I miss my guess, you've never mentioned your origins to Mari—and not to Kathy and Rick either. Perhaps now you should. There's nothing to hide about your father, really. I can tell you lots about him. The more you all know, the less disturbing it will be."

"There's nothing I want to know, Mom." He said it firmly, without rancor, without expression, either. "There's nothing anyone needs to know. If the facts of my background are yelled from the rooftops, let them be. I can face that—I was prepared to face it ten years ago, if you'll remember."

"But—"

"We averted circumstance then, and we may avert it now, depending on your friend. If not . . . well, illegitimacy is a fact of my life. I see no need to decorate it with amusing anecdotes about my father, just to make him likable, or bastardy digestible. Or your mistake, thirty-two years ago, palatable."

The muscles in his jaw were tight, and for a moment he was poised there, on the edge of his anger and determination to control the uncontrollable; then he sat back and made himself relax. "Sorry," he said briefly. "I guess that sounded harsh."

"I'm the one who's sorry," she said wretchedly.

"We'll manage, Mom," he said softly. "You will, and I will, too."

"How about Mari?"

He winced.

"You never told her, did you?"

"No."

"Why not?"

"Well . . ." He shrugged in an attempt to appear lighthearted. "Being as how I met her in 1950 when everybody was so sexually moral, and being as how Mari was a Midwestern virgin, purer than which only the driven snow gets, it seemed easier. And it still does. I don't intend to rake up anything I don't have to—but not because I'm afraid it'll destroy me. I'm just not going to let it assume a more important position than it does. If my boss learns of it and I'm out on my ear . . . well, that's the way it is. There's other bosses, younger ones, that aren't hog-tied by the morals of their grandmothers. My wife will have to accommodate it as best she can, if it comes to that. The kids, I just don't worry about—nobody raised in this day and age is going to get in a lather about this kind of thing. So go your way with Darion Hunt if the two of you change your minds about any responsibility you might have toward his wife. I'd rather know you were happy with a man you can love and admire."

Quietly they sat; she dared not look at him. "One day I will marry him."

"I hope so," he said.

"Not now, though."

"It's up to you."

"And Darion. Pris needs him."

The edges of her sandwich were curling up from disuse, and she knew she could not eat it. "I have to ask, Steven, if you're angry with me. I've been very indiscreet."

"I'm sure you never meant to be, Mom."

"But you have cause to be horribly mad."

"I'm not."

She peeked up at him. "Honest?"

"Honest."

"He's a person you'll like," she quavered. "I look forward to the day I can introduce you."

He covered her hand with his. "I'll look forward to it, too."

"Thank you." She could not stop her tears. "Thank you for everything, Steve."

He handed her an unused napkin to dry her eyes. "My pleasure, gallant lady," he said softly. "My pleasure."

VII

The Nomads

20

"And then we joined up with O.T. and J.W.," said Ron Howland modestly, finishing his martini with a flourish, tapping the bowl of the cocktail glass gently so as to dislodge the olive at the bottom. Around the table eddied the clink and clatter of Newton's restaurant and lounge, and Steven swirled the contents of his own martini in a gentle whirlpool around his own olive, listening to the rising and falling voices of the other diners and their occasional eruptions of laughter, felt the gentle breeze generated by a hustling waiter who raced past with a hugely heaped tray. The waiter wheeled, deftly lowering the tray to a nearby webbed rack, lifted the lids off the steaming plates, and Steven watched, pretending an absorption in the waiter's expertise while evaluating Ron Howland's game with Mr. Sattiswaite, president of Bronner Fiberglass and Insulation. And the foursome he and Mr. Sattiswaite had formed with O. T. Brown and J. W. Corey, giants of the Midwest's construction industry and therefore large-quantity consumers of fiberglass insulation.

It did not look good. Not at all.

Across from him, Wade Roper yawned, sat back. "Just between us fellows," he said, "I don't think Bronner should be getting into fishing rods."

"Hah!" Ron Howland snorted. "You'll never help your

own situation thinking that way, Wade! Promotion-wise, I mean. You know how much Mr. Sattiswaite likes fishing!"

"What's that got to do with it?" Wade demanded with a wink at Steven.

"Why, he's an expert," Ron exclaimed with a straight face, earnest, sincere, his Company Man mask not slipping even fractionally. "He knows what makes good equipment and what doesn't. He wouldn't take Bronner into fabricating rods without being damn sure they'd be the best. Fiberglass'll make a hell of a good fishing rod. Whenever we get around to producing one. Mr. Sattiswaite says so. Just as it makes a hell of a good canoe."

"Tell it to Grummond," Wade said around his lunch.

They'd lost Phil Anders to Grummond. Between that defection and Pearly Benson's health, which had hustled Pearly off into early retirement, the office staff was wide open for alteration. And Sattiswaite had used that for all it was worth, getting ten times as much work from every man in contention for promotion. Well, soon the suspense would be over. The new organization would be announced anytime now—and since he was due for his vacation starting this afternoon at five o'clock, Steven was determined to have the answer to the issue of promotion before he left, even if he had to go to Mr. Sattiswaite and ask for it. Only a dunce would leave town with everything up in the air, the competition free to cut Sinclaire's throat while the selfsame Sinclaire enjoyed life in his hammock on Cape Cod.

God knew the competition was cutting his throat at every opportunity anyway! Good ol' Ron, out on the golf links with Mr. Sattiswaite every Saturday, fishing on Sunday, licking F.X.'s boots Monday through Friday—he'd never realized that Ron was especially interested in the insulation division of Bronner, and perhaps Ron had not known it either, before Pearly left. But it was a shortcut to the top, and Ron didn't care much how he got there or what his job would be, once he arrived. That was the kind of man Ron Howland was—and uncomfortably Steven was aware that the kind of man Ron Howland was seemed very often to suceed.

Wade winked again. "I think I'll have another cup of coffee, and maybe dessert."

"Well, then, I hope you'll excuse me." Howland pushed his seat back, gestured to the waiter for his bill, signed it. "Fridays are apt to be pretty busy. And today Mr. S. might be making his announcement. I'd hate to miss that on account of fooling around here at Newton's." The implication was needlessly clear: boys who got promoted didn't dally over lunch. They ignored him, pretending to study the dessert menu, and when he left, they, too, signaled for their checks, signed, went outside to the growing heat of the June sun, rambled back to the office.

"He's got it," Wade said.

"What makes you think so? His golf game?"

"Miss Hastings. She says she's heard it in the girls' room." Miss Hastings was Wade's secretary, a Bronner employee for twenty years, and if she had heard it, probably it was true.

Steven's lunch turned to lead. "Maybe Miss Hastings is wrong."

"Maybe." They turned into the entrance. "But I'll tell you this, Steve. If Bronner has come to the point that an ass-kisser can take the prize instead of the fellow who knows the job best . . . well, I think it's time I began looking for another company."

"Let me know your next place of employment," Steven quipped. "I may need a reference."

Roper clapped his shoulder and they parted at the stairs in the lobby of the Bronner Building. Steven habitually climbed them; since no one else would, he climbed them alone, as fast as he could, in an effort to burn off some of the caloric intake from lunch.

He slowed down at a landing where a window looked over the Pennsylvania countryside, far out beyond the urban-suburban sprawl to the gentle rise of the Allegheny Mountains. Moodily he stared out.

Was Ron going to get Insulation? That would be just a bit disappointing, if true! He had really enjoyed the challenges of that department, the very stuff of its material, which had put him in touch with the person he'd once been, a man who could, and had, worked with his hands, who'd earned the respect of men like Bob Casey (a man he'd a lot rather be respected by than a prick like Ron Howland).

The insulation division and its problems had kept him in touch with the practical, earthy aspects of men's lives that seemed so clean and kind after so long on the cocktail and expense-account circuit, the suburbs and the club. It took the curse off the corporate structure, which, no matter how well it paid, seemed to him increasingly hollow.

And had seemed so ever since Mom had dropped that little bombshell into his life: that Priscilla Warden Hunt might call F. X. Sattiswaite and tell him just what Steven Sinclaire was. As a result he'd had to back up a bit, put some space between himself and what he was doing in case it should all be taken away. The space had never been refilled.

It was true, what he'd told his mother. He was not going to let a simple fact over which he had not an iota of control dominate his life, and he would prepare, in fact had already prepared himself to cope with it.

The threat never materialized.

Now Mrs. Hunt was incarcerated in an institution, probably permanently; she no longer posed a problem. She had not, for several years, but in that time in which he'd had to square off, prepare to meet her threat—ah, in that small space he had lost the pace and rhythm and drive of the corporation man. How incalculable was that little hitch, that momentary stop for air which had made him an observer of his life and climb to the top—none of which had been taken from him, all of which had been in momentary jeopardy—the entirety of which had been rendered just slightly less important than it had been because he'd known, then, how easily he could give it up.

Sometimes it was definitely not to your advantage to be an observer of your own life! But now, regardless of how he felt about the overall aspects of his job, he would have to get the truth of the insulation business nailed down before he left. He had to find out, and soon, whether he'd be working for himself or for Ron Howland. Yes, he could manage to live without being a corporation man, he'd discovered. But would he be able to live with it? If Ron Howland got the job that Steven Sinclaire wanted and had worked for? Was there enough room in the same office for them both?

There was hardly room enough now, he observed dryly, as slowly he climbed the rest of the stairs, crept into his office before anyone could nab him on any problem that might interfere with his clearing his desk. Deftly he sorted through the unfinished business there, made notes to help his secretary should certain customers call about certain specs, or certain difficulties present themselves before he could get back to attend to them.

"Mr. Sinclaire?" His secretary peered around the door, which was always partially open to her (she had only to push her wheeled chair backward in order to speak through its crack.) "It's Mr. Sattiswaite on two-three," she whispered. "Do you want to call him back?" (Thereby implying that Sinclaire was so busy—and therefore so important—that he would have to make time later to talk to his boss.) "Or will you take it now?" (Thereby avoiding the impression that Sinclaire was so poorly organized he didn't even have his desk under control at four o'clock on Friday, with himself due to be out of town for three weeks.)

"I'll take it," he decided, and she nodded, went back to her desk, switched the call.

"Hi, there, Mr. Sattiswaite," he said into the extension. "I'm glad you called. Wanted to see you before I leave for Cape Cod."

"Right-o," Sattiswaite's voice said jovially in his ear. "Could you drop by now?"

"Sure.

"If it won't interfere with your shutting up shop, of course."

"No problem," Steven said; his voice had automatically slipped into the same convivial tones that F.X. used, he noticed wryly. He strolled out, his pace determined but unhurried (a man who knew what he was doing), and walked the length of the secretarial pool to the elevators, took one to the top of the building, to the executive suite where F. X. Sattiswaite hung out with the vice-presidents.

"Well, Steve!"

F.X., a heavy man, heaved himself out of his creaking chair, extended a hand over his paper-piled desk to shake Steven's. He gestured grandly toward an overstuffed leather seat. Sattiswaite was nobody's fool—but he was predictable. Had Mom's childhood chum ever got to him about Sinclaire's questionable background, Sinclaire'd be out. Since Howland had completed a foursome at golf, was Sinclaire in?

Suddenly he was sure—and suddenly very, very tired.

"Well, sir!" F.X. cleared his throat, as he always did after well-sir-ing. "We've been very pleased at the way you've dug right in and gotten things done around here, Steve. You've really helped to fill the gap Pearly left." Sattiswaite played with the array of pens on the desk. "Sales are humming, and I think your efforts have had a lot to do with that."

"Thanks," he said. "It helps that there's a building boom going on."

Ron Howland would have claimed full credit. Modesty does not pay, he reminded himself, yet it would not matter in this case. Sattiswaite had his mind made up already.

"Well, an increase in construction has certainly been a factor." F.X. nodded. "And I think your rather intimate knowledge of building and construction has stood us in good stead. Howland tells me you actually built houses, once."

"A long time ago," he responded easily, though mention of

Ron put him on his guard. "I worked with a carpenter, earning money to go to college."

F.X. beamed. "I earned my own way, too."

Steven began to feel heartened; predictably, Sattiswaite would look approvingly on a man who worked with his hands.

"Boise, Idaho, or Portland, Oregon. And Denver," Mr. Sattiswaite mused importantly. "What I'm toying with, Steve, is sending you to manage the Bronner offices in one of those districts. I can't think of a man better suited to dealing with contractors than you, and, frankly, the men we have there now need to be brought back to the home office, given a refresher course. If they can't catch on, requirement-wise, well, they can't complain they weren't given an opportunity. I like to think that here at Bronner, we give men the chance they deserve."

"There's nothing like the home office to give a man perspective," he agreed feebly. So much for predictability.

"I'm going to name Ron Howland head of our insulation division—I'll be doing that next week, when you're gone, but I wanted to talk it over with you first. You've done so much with insulation, yourself. I hope you feel you can work well with Ron. He recommended you very highly, and I thought his suggestion of putting you in the field, with people whose problems you can really understand, was brilliant."

"No doubt," Steven said numbly.

"I'd rather you didn't mention my ideas to anyone before you leave, Steve. There's at least five people in line waiting for each of the districts I've mentioned, and I'd hate to have them discouraged, knowing you could take your pick."

What bullshit!

"Sure, I understand."

"Why don't you talk it over with Mrs. Sinclaire and your family? Two boys, isn't it?"

"A boy and a girl."

"Fine," said F.X. vaguely. "See what they'd like, and think it over from the point of view of those districts and your knowledge of them. Check in with me first thing when you come back from your vacation if you will."

"Certainly, F.X."

Sattiswaite heaved himself up again, terminating the interview. Steven shook the required hand, rode the elevator down, made his way through the secretarial pool where the girls were surreptitiously getting ready to leave for the weekend, their hair combed and their lipstick freshened, busywork in their typewriters so that they would appear too pressed to take anyone's last-minute dictation.

His secretary looked up as she saw him coming. "Mr. Roper called," she said, glancing at her notepad. "And Inventory Control, wondering where your estimates are." He noticed that she carefully avoided mentioning his meeting with Mr. Sattiswaite, and her eyes, when they met his, were filled with concern. Did she, too, have privileged information from the grapevine?

"We sent the estimate down already, didn't we?"

"There's a question on the Dallas one."

It took fifteen minutes to straighten out Inventory Control, and it was twenty minutes before five when he called Wade Roper back.

"Any word?" Roper asked.

"No," Steven lied.

"Thought I'd drop by and toast your vacation."

"Sure thing."

Wade was very apt to drop in for a toast, at any provocation. He was in high spirits this afternoon, and entertaining too, helping to keep Steven's mind off his troubles until five-fifteen, when the empty office echoed his farewells, and then it was time to come to terms with the fact that he had, after all, been upstaged and outsmarted by Ron Howland.

He poured a finger of bourbon.

Why in hell hadn't he stood up and fought for his right to the insulation division? Asked why Howland had got head of Insulation and not himself, when he'd demonstrated his expertise, earning the respect of men he worked with in ways that Ron Howland didn't even know existed? Told F.X. that it was head of insulation or nothing? Pointed to his own record, which F.X. understood perfectly well was good, and had even said so!

Instead of sitting there agreeing that the boys in the districts needed refreshing!

Because, pal, it just doesn't mean enough to you to fight for it.

Perhaps it had better start mattering, he told himself. Before you're out on your ass altogether. Perhaps you'd better start fighting, soon.

He slunk lower in his swivel chair with another finger of bourbon, trying to edge away from his anger, his humiliation, away from the inalterable fact that Ron Howland had got rid of him. Once in the hinterland, a man tended to stay. There was no point kidding himself. The man he replaced in the hinterland—that man was as good as gone. Finished. He knew those men, and it was true they could be better. They would be brought back, found wanting, excused. One day he would be one of them, because if you were out in the field too long, you lost your leverage in the home office. And Ron would make sure it happened. Steve Sinclaire was competition he could do without.

He tried to relax, sit loose. Take things one at a time.

So, the Sinclaires were going to move again. They'd done so, a half-dozen times, working up to this position at the main office.

Mari would have a fit.

Boise, Idaho. Portland, Oregon. Denver, Colorado.

Unless he missed his bet, the family would enjoy Denver. Terrific weather, nice little city, and closest to the East Coast and to Cape Cod and his legacy and his mother, holding the fort there at Kingsland by herself and doing a damn fine job of it, too. She wouldn't be too happy either, knowing he'd be so far away!

The phone at his elbow rang; he knew who it would be. "Hi, honey," he enunciated carefully.

"Steve? Are you okay?"

"Yes, I'm fine."

"I thought you'd be home by now."

"Just clearing my desk, getting everything ready for vacation," he said cheerfully.

"The Stanley barbecue is tonight," she said. "Don't be too late."

"Okay," he agreed, tucking the bottle back into its customary hiding place, the bottom-right-hand drawer. "Be there as soon as I can." He hung up, swiveled around to look out his window as he tried to work up some zest for his impending holiday, tried to forget about the barbecue at the Stanleys' and the discouraging news he would have to break to Mari.

She'd take it like a trooper, of course—the transfer part, at least. She was a good corporation wife, uncomplaining, heroically setting up the family tent in one place, and then, on signal, dismantling it and setting it up in another, finding new doctors and new dentists, meeting new teachers, and serving on new committees.

No, the transfer she could handle, no matter what she thought about moving. But that Ron Howland had beat him out of Insulation—that was something else.

He dug into the bottom drawer again, poured an inch more bourbon, sipped it unhappily.

You are henpecked, Sinclaire, he told himself. You're afraid of your wife.

Not true, he replied. I have let her down, and she'll be disappointed. Rightfully so.

And angry, suggested his inner gadfly.

Get lost, he instructed it.

Wasn't it odd how traits buried deeply became rampant in maturity, reversing the character of a loved one to nearly unrecognizable proportions? He could not remember the Mari of today being present in the girl he married, yet he doubted that she'd deceived him. It was not until mid-life that her nascent drives and ambition, delayed by the role women were required to play, found expression at the bridge table or the club committee, or in his career, toward which she pretended only wifely concern in order to conceal her zeal.

When she learned that Ron Howland had gotten the job Steven Sinclaire was in line for, she'd have a hard time being nice about it!

Well, it would pass, and life would resume, and together they'd enjoy it, because under unstrained circumstances, they got along well enough. The problem was, of course, that given the kind of life they lived, in the places where they lived it, strain lurked around every turning, for everyone.

Sinclaire, you are in the wrong business, his inner voice pointed out. You are in the wrong place.

And yet the corporate enterprise was an obvious choice fourteen years ago when he'd made it, with the economy unlimited, expanding, business vying for college graduates. And himself busting to get married and get on with life. It was not a choice he'd questioned at the time.

And it was a little late to question it now.

He tucked the bottle back, sat a moment longer wondering if he'd miss his office or not, if he'd like the one in Denver better, or Boise, or Portland. Then he took the elevator down to the lobby of the building and slipped around the corner to Maxie's Grill, where he could grab a spot of coffee to fortify him for the drive home, for the Stanley barbecue, for the inevitable confrontation with his wife, for the complications of vacation in Waterford with suitcases, boxes, and bags everywhere.

And there were further complications, he saw as he drove into Wildwood Estates. Lying on the front lawn was Rick's bike, balanced upside down on its seat and handlebars, its back wheel lying on the grass, wrenches of varying sizes lined up beside it. The carcass on the grass was sure to irritate Mrs. White across the street, who was probably glaring at it right now.

He inched into the garage until the bristling chromium of the front bumper rested ever so gently on the back wall. The houses in Wildwood Estates had been built early in the fifties when designers were unaware that cars would ever be so needlessly long. Now, in the year 1966, a car would hardly fit at all.

It was cool in the garage, and quiet too, easing the headache that was beginning to catch up with him. Along the walls were rakes and shovels, and in the far corner, the Sinclaire power lawn mower, the demands of which he had learned to hate. The lawn! The suburban symbol of success!

Ron Howland had a terrific one.

He opened the car door carefully, so that it wouldn't bang into the concrete wall (the garage was not quite wide enough, either), pulled his briefcase out of the backseat, pulled the garage door down (it barely cleared the tail fins). The family room lay on the far side, half below grade too. The Pennsylvania split level had a lot going for it, including the cool family room, partially underground. It was carpeted wall to wall, with built-in bookcases and closets for toys and puzzles in which the kids were fast losing interest as they grew up. At its far end was a comfortable couch and two comfortable chairs for the viewing of television—the tube now surrounded by four cardboard boxes, packed with the things the family would take to Waterford for its three-week vacation. In front of it sat Kathy, cross-legged on the floor, disdaining the hundred-dollar chair placed nearby for her comfort. On the TV screen Della Street said to Perry Mason, "Do you really think she's innocent, chief?"

"Hi, Dad," said Kathy cheerfully.

"Hi."

He dropped the briefcase by the door, and stooping down beside his daughter, planted a kiss on her left temple. Kathy pecked his cheek and leaned against him without taking her eyes off the screen.

"You smell," she observed.

"Gosh."

"Of booze. Celebrating your vacation?"

"Yup."

Beside her lay her hairbrush. No doubt she had been busily brushing until her hair flew straight out, snapping; she'd read that a girl ought to do that every day. She'd read a lot of things recently about how girls should groom themselves, and the youngsters she ran around with all read the same stuff, too, all of them forcing one another into a precocity they didn't really have. At twelve years of age, Kathy was preparing herself for Life.

Perry Mason was in the act of trapping and utterly demolishing the guilty party, who now leaped to his feet from the spectator gallery of the courtroom, confessing his hatred of the deceased and his reason for having deceased him.

"Patio party tonight," said Kathy. The commercial had begun and her attention was no longer required.

"So your mother told me."

"At the Stanleys' house."

"What are the kids going to do?"

"Play Ping-Pong in the rec room, stuff like that."

Another serial appeared on the tube, rerun from past years, with Lucille Ball and Desi Arnaz. Kathy settled in for another half-hour happily, jovially spent, requiring nothing of her.

He went up to the kitchen, where a pot of something in the oven bubbled over, hitting the floor of the stove with a violent hiss. He turned the temperature down and mixed himself a highball, took off his tie, unbuttoned his shirt. In the backyard, the slates of the patio had turned soft and glowing as the lengthening shadows of the day turned it into something you'd see in an ad, with gaily potted plants defining its periphery, geraniums and petunias, he guessed. The backyard looked neat, and in this light the lawn was taking a velvet texture, the whole scene very nearly approximating the picture in the ladies' magazine that had suggested it.

He leaned against the counter, looking out the kitchen window placed in exactly the right spot, so that the happy housewife would have a nice view while she did whatever needed being done in the sink. Except Mari, he was quite sure, was not happy there.

He mixed a drink for her, freshened his own. A glass in each hand, he went back through the well-kept, dustless living room, up another small flight of steps which led to the three bedrooms over the family room, and then up another short flight to the master bedroom over the living room, complete with its own bath, his-and-hers closets, wraparound sundeck. The room was immaculate, carpeted and noiseless, and he felt very far removed from Kathy, down in the family room.

"Hi, honey," he called into the bathroom, where a sudden roar of water indicated Mari's rising up out of the tub.

"Hi, Steve! I didn't know you were home!"

She wrapped herself in a bath towel and peeked out of the door, clouds of vapor preceding her.

"How are you?" she asked in her usual wifely way—well-intentioned, a question that needed no answer. She pecked his cheek and nuzzled his ear when he hugged her.

"You smell of liquor," she complained as she slipped into her closet, which was almost large enough to serve as a dressing room. In there she dropped the towel and put on her underwear and robe and removed the ugly plastic thing from her head that looked like the pot covers his mother once used for leftovers in the refrigerator.

"Celebrating my vacation with Wade," he told her.

"How's he?"

"Fine."

He sat on the bed, undid his shoes, put his feet up, and stuffed a pillow behind him as he leaned against the headboard, watching Mari rearranging her hair. At thirty-five his wife was probably approaching her prime. Her skin glowed and did not yet sag. Maturity had made her lovely instead of just pretty, and she had acquired the accoutrements of self-confidence through the years, that removed all suggestion of her underlying lack of security.

"In a way I wish we weren't going to the Stanleys'," she sighed. "Sometimes Rosalie annoys me, just a little."

"Let's not, then."

"If we don't go, Rosalie will be mad."

"Let her be."

"And then she won't ask us next time. And then the next time—like next month—when the Murchisons have a cocktail party, they won't invite us because they'll think we had a fight with the Stanleys and won't want to get in the middle of it, and pretty soon no one will sit with us at the club and no one will serve on my committee at the PTA. The kids won't be included in the next splash party at the Harrises' pool . . ."

Should he tell her now? That she need not worry about these repercussions, because she wouldn't be calling a committee meeting in the fall. That they wouldn't be attending anyone's cocktail party, nor would it matter who would or wouldn't sit with them at the club.

"So I think we'd better go," she was saying, "because Rosalie is talking about starting a bridge club in September, when the kids go back to school. I'd hate to be left out."

No better moment would present itself.

"I'm afraid that you won't be here in September, Mari, so it won't matter."

She stared. "Oh?" There was a long miserable silence while he inspected the melting ice in the bottom of his empty glass. "Where now?" she asked.

"This time we have a choice. Boise, Idaho, or Portland, Oregon, or Denver, Colorado. Seems that the fellows in the Boise, Portland, and Denver offices need to be brought back for a refresher."

"But you'll die on the vine," she protested. "If you aren't here, in the home office, they'll just forget you!"

"Probably."

"You'll never get to be head of Insulation."

"I never will anyway. Ron got it."

"Oh, Steve!" she wailed, her face all pinched up in anger and disappointment. "You mean after all this time . . ."

"That's what I mean."

"But you're twice as good as Ron Howland. And I'll bet you never told Mr. Sattiswaite so. I'll bet you just sat back and let Ron Howland tromp all over you!"

"I sat at my desk and did the best job I knew how to do," he said tightly.

"But it's not enough!" she cried. "I've told you and told you, Steve, it's not enough. Why, if you knew what *other* men do to get promotions! I listen to their wives! I know!"

"I know, too, honey. But it's not the way I operate."

"Then maybe you shouldn't be in business," she yelled. "If it's too hot in the kitchen . . ."

"You'd better get out," he chorused glibly, sliding off the bed. "I'll be in our kitchen if you want me. Which I think is relatively cool this time of day."

"Oh, Steve, I didn't mean to hurt your feelings," she cried, but his stride did not falter, nor did he look back. She may not have meant to hurt, but she hadn't spared him, either, and this was a poor time to tell a husband that he was a failure, when failure glared, stared, laughed in his face.

Well, perhaps he'd be happier in a branch office. There'd be no one's ass to kiss there, and he'd be left alone, to pursue sales of insulation and write up specs. Actually, it would suit his temperament a hell of a lot better than the home office.

But would Boise, Portland, or Denver really be any different from here? They'd end up in the suburbs, and they'd belong to a club, and the lawn would have to be mowed, wouldn't it? Would he be any better off, or would Mari, or the kids?

He sat at the breakfast nook with another highball, watched the flowers out on the patio nodding in the late day.

Mari came in, her makeup in place, a determined look beneath it. "Well," she said, looking at the casserole through the oven's glass door. "Since I've got our contribution already made, we might as well go."

"No," he said.

"You said, not ten minutes ago, that it was okay," she argued, defensive and unattractive.

"That was ten minutes ago."

"Just because you're mad at me, there's no reason not to join the neighborhood fun."

"It's not because I'm mad at you. It's because these parties are dull as hell. You know it, and I know it, and since we won't be living here anymore, there's no reason on God's green earth why we should go to another one. Besides, we won't have any fun; we never do. Bill Hughes will complain about the pro shop, and Rosalie will work the conversation around to her sorority and her sister, whose husband is the mayor of whatever godforsaken city they live in." And Ellen Hughes would make another attempt to seduce him, as she did every male.

"Steve, we can't just sit here while a party we've been invited to is going on over there!" As though to add credibility to her words, the distant bleat of a man's laughter from the direction of the Stanleys' patio reminded them—unnecessarily—that the guests were gathering.

"Rosalie will be crushed if we don't go," Mari coaxed, her herd instinct swamped by threat of exclusion.

Kathy came up from the family room. "Isn't it time to go to the Stanleys'?"

"We thought we'd relax for a while first, sweetie," said Mari, hastily covering up the problems of her present. "Run on over, if you want to. We'll get there sometime."

"I'd better," Kathy said. "I hate having a party start without me."

"Tell Rosalie we'll be along soon."

"Okay."

Kathy went off, mulling over so unusual an event as her parents deliberately being late to a neighborhood get-together. Something—very definitely—was going on. Probably another argument—not an uncommon occurrence.

But to be late to a party on account of it?

She hurried away.

On the wall of the kitchen the decorator harvest-gold phone jangled, and Steven reached for it. "Hello?"

"This is Mrs. White, across the street," came the strained and tense voice. "And I have been looking at the bike in your front yard. I've been looking at it all day. It doesn't do much for your yard, Mr. Sinclaire, and it doesn't do much for my view."

"We'll take care of it, Mrs. White," he said with the politeness he was trained to use on elderly ladies. He hung up with uncharacteristic abruptness.

"Who was it?"

"Mrs. Goddamn White."

"I'll go move the bike," she said wearily. "Unless you would."

"I think Rick ought to."

"That would be nice, of course. But he's not home yet."

"He will be. Soon."

"I hate to make Mrs. White wait. She's old and unwell, and even if it's not important to you, it is to her."

Rick appeared at the back door, releasing them from the ongoing argument.

"Hi, Dad."

"Hi, kid. Your bike needs to be taken care of. Will you bring it around to the patio?"

"Sure," Rick said. "I'd be glad to, Dad. But I want to talk to you about that bike."

"Move it."

"I think I could put a motor on it. Easy."

"And put my tools back, please. And then wash up for supper."

"Okay, okay." Rick disappeared into the approaching dusk. Across the patio and the greensward of the neatly mowed backyard, smoke rose densely from the Stanley patio. Steven's drink was beginning to make inroads in his tensions, added to the alcohol he'd consumed at the office. The walls of the kitchen spun a little, the bricks behind the stove, the gleaming cabinetry top and bottom, bright Formica-sheathed breakfast bar. Across from him, Mari fidgeted.

"Let's not tell the kids until the end of vacation," she said abruptly. "They enjoy Waterford so much—why spoil it for them." Her eyes filled; impatiently she swept away her tears. "I'm terribly sorry for what I said, Steve."

And then he realized the extent of her disappointment, which he had not really recognized before because of his own. He felt ashamed, eager to make it up to her. "Okay, honey," he said softly.

Rick returned, water still dripping from the lobes of his ears and tips of his elbows. "I'm ready," he announced in his hoarsely adolescent bellow.

"Are you through with your drink?" Mari asked.

"Yes."

"We ought to be on our way, then. Don't you think?"

"Sure," he agreed spinelessly. After all, it'd be the last party here, wouldn't it? What the hell difference did it make? Why disappoint her further?

"There they are!" called Rosalie Stanley.

"We thought you weren't coming!" called Bill Hughes.

"Of course we were coming!" Mari called back gaily. "Didn't Kathy tell you we were coming, Rosalie?"

"Oh, she told me, she told me," Rosalie said, in the act of putting a tossed salad on the Stanley picnic table and covering it with a net umbrella to discourage the flies. Strewn around the table were casserole dishes with candles under them to keep them warm, and buckets of potato salad, heaps of pretzels, and assorted desserts.

"I'll see you later," Rick said hastily, disappearing into the Stanley family room, where the record player was going and the plinking of Ping-Pong balls could be heard.

"Here, let me make you a drink, Steve!" Jeff Stanley said. "Sit right here, on this chaise. Put your feet up."

"Sure." Steven stretched out, his hands folded behind his head. "I'm on vacation, after all."

"Lucky dog," said Dave Cameron pleasantly.

"The Potters are going to paint their house pink," John McClaine told the party. "How in the name of God can I sell my house if the one next door is pink?"

"Don't worry about it," said Jeff Stanley. "No one in Wildwood paints their house pink. We'll see to it, old man."

"I shall sleep at last." John raised his glass in appreciation.

"You going to move?" asked Jeff Stanley. "Is that why you're worried about selling?"

"You're moving?" Rosalie screamed.

"Transferred?"

"Transferred?"

"Transferred?" It echoed around the party, the counterpoint to all their lives.

Steven flicked a meaningful look at Mari, reminding her that they had decided to keep quiet until the end of vacation.

"No, not transferred," John McClaine said. "Though I'm ready for it."

"God knows he's worked for it," said John's wife. "We could use a nice promotion right about now. Pay for the orthodontist."

"Oh, you can't leave now!" Rosalie said exuberantly. "We need you for the bridge club."

"I'm really looking forward to that." Ellen Hughes nodded.

"Me too. I haven't played seriously since my sorority won the tournament," Rosalie agreed. "My sister—the one whose husband is the mayor—her bridge club is really going places, and here I sit, my game getting rustier and rustier."

"I don't like the way the pro shop is being run these days," Bob Hughes was saying. "And the lounge is getting so cliquey that you hardly dare go in there alone. Group-wise, the club is great. But you ought to be able to circulate, and soon you won't."

Dave Cameron, who was very good at assembling small groups around himself and anchoring them, smiled complacently. "Like always gravitates to like."

"I think I'll gravitate to that picnic table," Steven said. "It's a shame to ignore such good food."

"I'll join you," declared Ellen Hughes.

They left the patio group and walked together to the table, where they picked up plastic utensils and paper plates. "Bob's right," Ellen said, putting a small mound of everything in spaced dollops on her plate. "The club is getting to be unfun. Don't you think so?"

"I haven't been over for quite a while," he said, slinging some potato salad.

"Well, as a matter of fact, I've been looking for you there—and haven't seen you."

"Unfun, like you said."

"But don't you get bored, just sitting at home?" She smiled, and the suggestion behind the smile was blatant.

Everyone decided to eat, right then, the kids pouring out of the Stanleys' rec room, the adults heaping their plates, the kids throwing pretzels around and then going back inside while the adults settled back to drink some more, watching the fireflies beyond the patio lights.

Jeff Stanley got Dave Cameron into a debate on professional football, to which Steven listened while drifting far, far from sobriety; Ellen Hughes perched lightly beside him.

"Well, you and Mari must be about ready for a vacation," she said. Her voice was husky and low, and she wore a blouse which was unbuttoned a little lower than even casual summer fashion directed, and she leaned slightly forward as she smiled, so that he got a glimpse of her breast.

Instantly he was stirred, and looked away.

"Boxes and bales everywhere," he said. "If we just moved into my house on the Cape and lived out of a suitcase in the suburbs, we'd be a lot better off."

"It must be nice to have a house in such a desirable spot."

"Oh, it is."

"How did you happen to buy it?"

"I didn't, I inherited it."

"Oh! An old house?"

"Yup. Been in the family a long time. My mother lives in it, so I don't have to worry about the pipes freezing, and it's always there, waiting for us."

"I wish you had a picture of it."

"I do, of course."

"Well? Let me see."

"It's at home. In a photo album."

"That's too bad. You must bring it with you next time. Or you and I could just slip over to your house and take a look. Sometime."

"That'd be fun," he said, his face straight.

She smiled suggestively. "Yes. Wouldn't it. Or we could meet halfway." She got up, strolled off, probably expecting him to follow. He accepted another drink from Rosalie and stayed in the chaise. There was always an Ellen Hughes, in every suburb, bored and restless, unclear about the origin of her malaise, seeking a way around it with a man. Any man.

In time Mari materialized out of the fog of alcohol with an empty casserole dish in her hand. "I thought perhaps we ought to be on our way," she said, "since we have a long day tomorrow."

"Sounds like a good idea," he agreed with relief. "I'll get the kids." He headed for the Stanley rec room; behind him he heard Mari saying insincerely, "Thank you, Rosalie, for such a nice evening." It had not been nice; it had been dull and exactly the same as all the rest of the Wildwood parties, with variety in neither the guests nor the conversation nor even the food.

Wildwood was, indeed, in a rut, just as the Sinclaires were, and would more than likely remain in one.

They extracted the kids and made their way home.

He mixed two more highballs, followed Mari up to the room they shared.

"Not another!" she protested.

"We're nearly on vacation, after all," he told her, enunciating carefully because he was no longer sober. No matter what you intended to do, by the time you left a party—any party—you were pretty well stoned. You would awaken in the morning with a headache—you expected it.

"Besides, how'm I going to seduce you if I don't get you drunk?" He smiled, but watched her with sufficient intensity to warn her that he meant to have sexual intimacy tonight unless she objected strenuously.

"I saw you talking with Ellen Hughes," Mari said, as though his limited infidelity was sufficient to excuse her.

He was too inebriated to get riled. "But Mar!" he protested. "I turned her down."

"You mean she . . . propositioned you?"

"Honey, she always does. She'll give it away to whoever will take it."

"Disgusting," Mari sniffed.

"But I didn't buy. Honest. If you don't believe it, just try me." He grinned.

She glanced at the evidence. "You're impossible." She laughed humorlessly. She kissed him in acquiescence and disappeared into the bathroom, no doubt arranging her diaphragm and puttering around, hoping to outlast him.

But this time he wouldn't fall asleep, alcohol or no alcohol. It had been two and a half weeks since he'd had sexual intercourse with his wife, and Ellen Hughes had whetted his appetite. He was well aware that Mari escaped this aspect of marriage whenever possible—yet she'd never turned him down outright. Just played a waiting game, as now, peeking around the bathroom door to see what state he was in.

Pleasantly he smiled, waved, and she came out of the bathroom, naked, slipped into a pretty nightie which he suspected she believed disguised her lack of interest—and indeed, it went a long way! Against its black sheerness her nipples pressed like the noses of two eager puppies, and the darker mat of her crotch was seductively suggested beneath the black nylon cloud.

"I hate Rosalie Stanley," she said, reaching for the drink he'd brought her.

"Don't think about Rosalie Stanley."

"I can't help it. I just can't be aloof; I couldn't stand to be snubbed. And untouchable."

"Why not try?" he encouraged her. "In Denver or Boise or

Portland, if you got lonely and wanted to be touched, I could take care of it."

She glanced quickly at him and giggled. "Poor Steve! You've been waiting all night!"

"I sure have."

She finished her drink, slid down beneath the bed covers, patted the space beside her. "Come on, then," she said in gentle resignation. "What are you waiting for?"

"Just an invitation." He shed his clothes and crawled in, reached for the light and snapped it off. He would touch his wife tenderly, and he would tell her how pretty she was, and he would roll on top of her and penetrate her and he would come to climax, quickly or slowly, depending on what he believed she wanted him to do, but he knew she would not truly enjoy it, despite her compliance and expressions of pleasure, for he knew that Mari only believed she must fool him, and that in doing so her duty to him was discharged. It could have been better—but it could be worse, too, and so he accepted it as he always had, and came to rest beside her, his mind and body drained as the soporific of sex gave him the respite demanded and begged for by that day, and erased the loneliness within.

21

In the parlor of Kingsland the gold-leafed frame of the Mary Deems portrait caught the sun and relayed its reflection onto the opposite wall, and Steven contented himself with observing its brilliance as he listened to Mari, sitting in her pocket beside him on the velvet couch.

"Why, Claudia," she asked with earnest interest (Mari always had taken Claudia Marshall seriously), "are you planning to move to Waterford?"

"Well, we're thinking about it," Claudia assented. "We've

been a little upset about the tax rate at home." She nodded at Mom, whose chair was placed directly below the Deems portrait, and Mom dutifully nodded back.

"We thought if we modernized the plumbing now," J. Barry Marshall said, "we could move any time we want to. We came down, this weekend, to arrange for the work to be done."

"Wouldn't you miss all the activities that you're involved with at home?" Mari asked, for Claudia had impressed on them all, early in the game, her importance in the suburban Boston scheme of things. The girl was another Rosalie Stanley if ever there was one, Steven mused, but Mari had never seen it in the years that the Marshalls, owners of the old Elijah Merrick house, had been here on vacation.

"Well, one reason we wanted to talk to you today"—Claudia's smile was orthodontically perfect—"was that we've been going at it hammer and tongs, Barry and I—"

"That makes it sound as though we'd had a knock-down, drag-out fight, dear," J. Barry protested.

"Well, that's not the way I meant it, of course!" Claudia exclaimed, tossing her abundant shag-style hair. "And I'm sure they do know what I mean, Barry!"

"What it amounts to is that we think living here year round might have a lot of advantages," he said. "And some disadvantages. Have they got a bridge club in Waterford, Mrs. Sinclaire?"

" 'Fraid not," Mom said.

"It strikes me that there might not be much to do if we moved to Waterford," Claudia said. "And no one to do it with."

"I keep telling her that she won't have time to be bored—and then I said, let's go over and ask Mrs. Sinclaire instead of arguing about it." J. Barry nodded a deferential head in Mom's direction. "Do you get bored, Mrs. Sinclaire?"

Mom laughed, and discreetly Steven continued to watch that golden spot on the wall lest his eyes meet hers. Bored! With Priscilla Warden Hunt in a sanatorium? He dared not look at his mother, who had never been happier or less bored in her life—though social activities in Waterford had nothing whatever to do with it.

"There are lots of new people coming into Waterford," she said innocently. "Young people, too—not just retired ones. People like yourselves, sick of the suburbs and looking for an alternative. I haven't any doubt that you'd find pleasant friends, in time."

"Barry could work from home," Claudia said to Mari. "He thought if we moved down he could make the pantry over into his office." Marshall was an architectural consultant, flexible, virtually self-employed. "We could do the house over, too, I mean restoring it to its original colonial appearance."

"What a fascinating idea, Claudia!" Mari cooed. "People are really beginning to appreciate the value of that kind of thing. You could show the house, if you wanted to, as an example of how it really was."

"Humm. I'll bet we could, at that. What a good idea, Mari! But we're not even close to a decision about it. I mean, who could teach Junior his clarinet? He's really doing very well—but these refinements are hard to find in the country. We could always send him to private school, I suppose," Claudia went on, switching topics back and forth like a hot potato. "Still, it'd be good for him to learn the country way of life, and how better than at school? It's the drug thing that scares me," she said to Mom. "And the black people. And the crime rate. And the tax rate."

"You're so right, Claudia," Mari sighed.

Steven had a hard time picturing J. Barry and Claudia in the barn of a house that Barry's grandparents had bought so many years ago for their summer use. Sure as hell the place didn't have a shred of insulation in it! He cast himself out over the sea of his expertise: remove the clapboards (probably there was nothing between them and the inner plaster walls), fiberglass bats, horizontally trimmed . . . Vapor barrier? he asked. Why not? he answered. Sure as hell that house will never be sealed so tightly that condensation would develop. . . .

"I told Claudia you probably belonged to organizations," Barry said to Mom as the back door rattled and the sound of knocking came faintly to them. "I told her you probably belonged to the Women's Club and the Garden Club and the Historical Society."

"Not the Historical Society," Mom said with a shudder, no doubt remembering Cousin Elizabeth's fondness for it. "We do have a pleasant Garden Club. Every year we pot things and have a barn sale here, at Kingsland." (It was as far as Mom had ever gotten with her shop, which Darion Hunt had caused her to no longer need.) The back door rattled again.

"I'll get it," Steven said to Mari, and gratefully left the living room, made his way down the hall. Upstairs he could hear Rick arguing with Junior Marshall. Kathy's record player vibrated somewhere in the depths of the house, probably the billard room.

"Bob!" he shouted joyfully as Casey's bulk and breadth came into view through the back door. "Son-of-a-gun, it's good to see you! Come in!"

"Just on my way down-Cape," said Bob by way of refusal. "Thought I'd stop and see what you were up to."

He stepped out onto the porch and gestured grandly toward the yard. The grass was freckled with chips of red paint; the shutters he'd scraped and painted leaned against every available tree like time-tilted tombstones.

"Bitch of a job," Bob remarked amiably.

"That's for sure. But a nice change from the old desk at Bronner." They had taken nearly the whole vacation to do it.

"How's the world of big business?"

"It stinks," he said shortly. "And life in the living room isn't much better." (He had never cared much for the Marshalls.) "You'd be doing me a favor if you stayed and had a beer with me."

"I'll do better than that. I'll take you away. Matter of fact, that's why I stopped."

"Oh?"

"I remembered that you were a sailing buff. I'm going to Hobbes Hole to see something I think you'd enjoy. Wondered if you'd like to come along."

"What is it?"

"A surprise." Bob grinned, the crinkles around his eyes deepening. He was probably approaching fifty by now, but his body was that of a young man, his leathery skin ruddy and tanned.

Casey is probably in a lot better shape than I am, Steven thought as he whisked back into the house to tell Mari where he was going, excusing his departure with a wave at Mom and the Marshalls, who were still mulling over the feasibility of moving to Waterford (which they would never do, he thought, being too firmly attached to the pleasures of city and suburban life). Feeling like a boy again, setting off on an adventure, he climbed into Bob's truck just as he had in bygone years, listened to Bob's description of Waterford's building boom as they barreled down the mid-Cape highway and then cut south to Nantucket Sound and Buzzards Bay.

The outskirts of Hobbes Hole modestly appeared: a smattering of cottages, a restaurant, a Creem-Mee Freeze and a fish market, and then, the town itself, silver-shingled with the sunshine glaring on the white-painted trim of each building, hiding the shabbiness of so old a village. Between the houses was the wink of water; the road dived down to the harbor, where the masts of small sailboats created a minor forest. At the piers, powerboats with their tricky, often exotic names were tied, their occupants lolling on deck chairs, dressed opulently, drinking opulently.

Bob walked briskly to the wharf farthest away, which jutted massively into the cloudy water with a floating dock attached at right angles to its end, forming a T. The stony shore curved around closely, only thirty or forty feet away; directly across were more piers, clogged with pleasure craft.

Shading his eyes, Bob looked seaward past the jetties that formed the mouth of the harbor; Steven looked, too. And in the channel between the jetties was the largest vessel he had ever seen, gaff-rigged, her square sails filled with the gentle breeze, her masts majestically towering over everything in the harbor, tearing straight in with the tide behind her. A crowd gathered to watch, and Bob moved to its front. Steven followed, unable to take his eyes off the old schooner (for it was instantly clear that she belonged to another age, another time), her height and breadth becoming more and more impressive as she headed for the dock like a juggernaut. Was she under control? His heart quickened and the palms of his hands were instantly wet; then the ship veered smoothly, the sails spilling the breeze, slackening, billowing. She coasted parallel to the wharf now, still fast, silent. A man on her bow threw a weight, around which was wrapped thin line; it bounced on the splintered gray boards of the wharf like a meteorite from another dimension; quickly Bob snatched it, towed in the heavier line to which it was attached, and hastily fastened the line to a cleat nearby.

On the deck of the schooner the man ran his end around a belaying pin as the ship passed by the pier. There was a tensing, a tightening, and water sprayed from the rope, and the rope twanged and groaned and smoked on the pin and, abruptly, the ship, all seventy feet of it, stopped.

"Christ," Steven swore reverently.

"Monkey's fist," Bob explained of the lead weight, around which he wrapped the line before giving it back to the deckhand.

On her bow, in gold leaf, was inscribed her name: *Jenny H. Lawrence*. She was no longer beautiful because she was old, and her years in the coasting trade, for which she was initially built, had flattened her lines and spread them as a woman's body is broadened and spread from childbearing.

Her black paint was scabby and her brightwork dull, but none of these things diminished her. They were uniquely a part of her, made her even more compelling and more magnetic than if she had been young and slim, because of the vastness of her experience, the mystery of her past.

In the cockpit the captain, a short man with dark hair, shoulders broad as the ship itself and not a spare ounce on him, was pouring liquor for a small group, lifting his glass in a toast, his voice raucously booming over the harbor without his words being understood; his audience burst into applause.

"Would you like to go aboard?" Bob asked.

"I sure would," Steven sighed. To behold the world of sail! The world of lines and cleats and canvas and all the special and precise tools for the sailing of a ship, unique and without equal anywhere else than on the deck of a vessel rigged out for business. They stepped over the rail, avoiding disembarking passengers, who gave them only a passing glance of superiority because they had been part of something larger than themselves, something a mere sightseer could not be expected to understand.

"Casey! You old son of a bitch! How the hell are you!" Disengaging himself from the group at the tiller, the captain made his way to Bob's side. "For Christ's sake, why didn't you come aboard sooner? I didn't see you!"

"I was busy rescuing your monkey's fist."

"Jesus! And to think you're wasting your time building houses for fat-assed city bastards."

He was surprisingly young, startlingly drunk.

"I want you to meet a friend of mine," Bob said happily. "This is Steve Sinclaire. Steve, this is Eric Larsen."

"How the hell are you, Steve?" Larsen looked deeply at him, unlike the usual first glance of a man upon introduction. "You both can rescue me from this bunch of dudes, thank God. So long, folks. . . . Glad to have you aboard!" He waved to the group with whom he'd been drinking, and they waved back, unoffended. He led the way to the aftercabin, from the windows of which, because it was set somewhat below the deck, only the legs of everyone on board were visible.

"I thought Steve would like to see the ship. He used to do a lot of sailing," Bob explained.

"Not ships like this, though," Steven said quickly. "Only little ones like summer camps have."

Larsen reached behind a cushion and came up with a bottle. He helped himself to a slug and passed it over. "Have some."

"Steven's great-grandfather was a merchant captain," Bob said.

"No kidding! Do you ever sail now, Sinclaire?"

"When I can," he said, swelling foolishly with the pride of belonging, yet eager to steer the conversation into loftier considerations. "How did you ever learn to handle vessels this size?"

"Not at any goddamned camp," Eric laughed.

"Eric, here, is licensed to sail the seven seas," Bob said proudly. "He's been sailing all his life."

"I sure as hell have," Larsen said. "I quit school when I was fourteen and wandered around until I could find men who could teach me what I needed to know."

"There can't be too many people capable, and licensed, to sail a vessel like this one," Steven remarked.

"There are some," Larsen said. "The problem is that there aren't many vessels this size left."

"The *Jenny* used to sail on windjammer cruises in Maine," Bob said. "Barbara and I went on one, a couple of years ago. We really had a good time."

"Why's *Jenny* here on Cape Cod now?" Steven asked.

"Her new owner preferred it," Larsen explained. "He moved her down last fall. It's a longer season, and warmer. If he had any guts at all, we could even sail her in October. It's cold as a witch's tit on the water then, but the weather's generally clear. But hell, all the owners really want to do is turn a profit. They figure to sail her around as her own advertisement, and sell her to the first reasonable bidder. Which there ought to be more of here than in Maine."

"What about you?" Bob Casey said. "You can't kid me, Eric."

"Eighteen thousand." Eric sighed. "At least. Want to go in with me, Casey? I have four thousand saved."

"Oh, sure, sure," said Bob, leaning against the wall of the aftercabin, helping himself to the bottle. "Good summer?"

"We're booked for the rest of the season," Larsen said. "The ship's reputation is spreading fast, too. The goddamned wharf is apt to be filled right up with spectators if I come in at noon like I'm scheduled to do. Hell, they all try to catch the lines. One day they'll succeed, and they'll go whipping around that pin like a piece of spaghetti. Cooked. It's the truth," he said affably to Steven. "The minute a man looks at *Jenny*, he becomes a seafarer. Or claims his great-grandfather was."

"I didn't claim that. Bob did."

Larsen laughed. "It shows, anyway. I mean, that you like ships and sailing. It's something a man can't hide. Take him around, Casey, if you want." He yawned. "If anyone asks for the captain, tell 'em you don't know me. I want to catch a nap, and sure as hell, someone'll want something if they know where to find me. Christ, the sons of bitches want you to pee for them."

He left the aftercabin with a jaunty wave, and they waited until the passengers had all disembarked, sitting in the cabin with Eric Larsen's bourbon as though they owned the place.

All the worries Steven had ever had fell away.

"Ready to look around?" Bob asked after a long period of companionable silence.

"Sure."

They mounted the three steps of the aftercabin, walked halfway to the stern of the ship, and climbed down the ladder that dropped into the belly of the vessel. To the left was the galley, with a wood stove and a pump attached to the side of the sink. High on the wall above it was a sliding window through which food could be passed to the aftercabin. Compartments for storage lined the walls. Across from the galley was a lavatory with a pedal on the floor for pumping water into the closet and flushing it out again; down the center of the vessel ran a narrow hall with a pair of enormous beams bridging it about forehead-high. On both sides of the hall were closely packed minuscule passenger quarters. At the far end, toward the bow, another lavatory.

"And that is that," Bob said. "Except for the captain's and first mate's berth in the bow. "You have to hope for decent weather, because sure as hell there's no place to go and nothing to do unless its topside." He patted one of the bridging beams, wrapped round and round with sheets and stuffing, looked about affectionately.

Silently they listened to the old ship sigh and shift at her berth, heard the tide rustling on the other side of her hull, heard the voices of the departing passengers and onlookers on the wharf, their shouts and calls distant and sounding happy, like the cries of children playing at dusk. They turned to leave.

"I have five thousand," Bob said suddenly.

"What?"

"I have five thousand dollars," Bob repeated, and there was an urgency on his face, a hope, a dream. A long silence built between them, and the companionship they'd shared over the years filled in the void. "It'd be really something, owning a ship like this. Even a small part of it."

"That it would." He sighed, shifted gears. "I expect I'd better be getting back. Should we look in on Larsen?"

"No. He's probably sleeping anyway. I doubt that he spends much time in the sack when there's a voyage in progress. Or, if he's in the sack, I doubt that he'd be there alone."

"Quite a guy."

"Very moody, actually. Up one minute, down the next. But he can sail. Crazy as they come," Bob said affectionately, "but there's nothing he can't do with a ship."

They climbed back up the steep street to Bob's truck. Behind them in the harbor the small boats bobbed like ducks riding the swells, and the towering masts of the *Jenny H. Lawrence* became short and squat from the heightened perspective of the town's elevation. Far out past the jetty were channel lights and flashers and blinkers and bells and horns and the far, far distant lights of Martha's Vineyard. Hobbes Hole itself was just opening for the night of revelry to come, the evening Mardi Gras of summer in the sixties, and the air was cool now as they drove, both carefully saying nothing about Bob's five thousand dollars.

The stars, brighter here than ever they were in the city, followed them back to Waterford.

"Where were you?" She frowned. "I expected you back before this."

"Hobbes Hole isn't exactly next door."

She gnawed on her lower lip, said nothing.

"What's wrong?"

"Nothing."

"Come on, tell me," he coaxed.

"Well, once the Marshalls left, I got to thinking about going back home . . . and moving. It just got me down, is all."

"Don't blame you a bit, Mar. Let's have a beer and forget about it for a while."

"I'll take you up on the beer." Her smile was only a partial success. "I don't think we ought to forget about it, though. Vacation's nearly over. It's time we told the kids."

"I guess you're right," he agreed slowly. "And my mother."

"Tell me what?" Mom asked, coming in to the kitchen without their having heard.

"We'll talk about it when the kids come in."

"Oh." Mom looked from one to the other. "I think I can guess." She shrugged. "Onward and upward, right?"

"Onward, anyway," Steven said wryly. "Let's get that beer."

"Onward?" Kathy asked, popping in suddenly from the back door. "Onward?"

"Get your brother," Mari ordered. "We have something to tell you."

Just as her grandmother had done, Kathy looked from one adult face to the other. Quickly she ran back outside, and Steven heard her voice, thin and wavering. Rick-ee. Rick-ee. She was close to tears already. She did not have to be told. He tried to stifle the guilt, sipped his beer, tried to arrange his face into lines of calm confidence.

The children reappeared, looking cautiously through the kitchen's screen door.

"Come on in," he instructed them. "We have some things to talk about, and we might as well do it now."

Wary, clear-eyed, they watched him steadily as they seated themselves at the table.

"I'm being transferred," he said calmly, without apologizing for it.

"You mean we're moving again," Rick said stating the case clearly, as Rick always did.

"Yes. But this time we have a choice. We can go to Portland, or Boise, or Denver. How many people can say that?" He smiled with determination. "I don't have a preference. Do you?"

"Do we have to go, Daddy?" Kathy asked.

"One place or the other, yes."

"Do you really want to?"

"I really don't," he said apologetically. His discouraging setback at Bronner, which he'd avoided thinking about for three whole weeks, now like a prison sentence had to be faced, and he was ill-prepared. "But I don't have much to say about it."

"When are we supposed to go?" his daughter asked.

"I'm supposed to tell Mr. Sattiswaite when we get back which office I'll take."

"Why can't we just stay here?" Rick asked.

For an instant no one moved.

"Here?" asked Mari. "Be serious!"

"Here!" Kathy exclaimed, and turned to Rick.

"Yes, here," Rick said loudly. "At least we know where everything is, here. We don't have to learn everything over again. We know it already. We belong here."

Here. Why don't we just stay here? Steven asked himself, startled at the strength of its appeal.

Here, he repeated to himself.

And the masts and sails, the bowsprit, the halyards and transom and aftercabin of the *Jenny H. Lawrence* instantly became real, present—as real and as present as his own family right here in the kitchen. Longing rose up, poignant, sweet, strong, and hastily he worked on his beer, busily pouring more, pouring some for Mari.

"We could stay here with Grandma," Rick was saying. "Couldn't we, Grandma?"

"Well," Mom said slowly, "as a matter of fact, I've been thinking of moving, myself, and if I did, there'd be no one to take care of the house as it should be cared for. The house would need you, as a matter of fact."

"Why, you never said a word about moving, Mother Sinclaire!" Mari exclaimed. "Where are you going?"

"I'm not entirely sure yet." Mom hedged, and he was nearly certain that she had it worked out, in all its detail. "But a friend of mine lives in central New York State, and I'm thinking of going there."

"What will you do in central New York?" Mari asked incredulously.

"Get a job. An apartment. Do something different. I've lived here sixteen years, and I think that's quite long enough," Mom said briskly. "So you can just move in tomorrow."

"There, Dad," Kathy said happily. "It's all arranged."

"Over my dead body," Mari exclaimed. "Live in a place like Waterford? There's no future here! It's a crazy idea."

And again the image of the *Jenny H. Lawrence* rose up hugely, imperatively, and her shadow fell upon him.

I have five thousand dollars, he heard Bob say. It'd really be something, owning a ship like this. Even a small part of it. . . .

"Why isn't there a future?" Rick asked defensively. "What's so crazy about it?"

The fact was, if he cared to face it (and he had not, these three weeks), that all he had worked to achieve at Bronner had been rendered to rubble by Ron Howland; now he was on the treadmill of the lateral shuffle, moving sideways and no longer up—an extremely vulnerable spot to be in. He was nearly forty years old, and he had relinquished Waterford long, long ago, having found in it the strength of will and purpose that he'd needed as a young man, and then he'd willingly taken the paths commonly pursued in the fifties and now the sixties. He hadn't been particularly happy doing it, and Mari had not been either. But he was mature and experienced now, better able to assess and accept certain immovables—about his world, about himself.

Nowhere else, he thought. Nowhere else can you get what there is to be had here; if you're ready for it, you can learn wisdom as Waterford people have learned it, learn to live as they do, placidly, modestly, to be sure. For they were a people unhurried, hardworking, and able to take what life offered and make the best of it. They lived a life that he had been too young, once, to want—but now, perhaps, needed.

"Don't tell me you're considering it!" Mari exclaimed. "It's only the whim of an adolescent boy!"

"It's not a whim," the adolescent boy insisted.

The whole thing was impossible. But the house in Pennsylvania might well clear fifteen thousand dollars. And Kingsland was his own, free and clear. Bob had five thousand dollars; Larsen had four. . . .

"An honorable and traditional way to make money in Waterford is to rent rooms in the summer," Mom was saying to Mari. "And this house is certainly big enough, once a little work's done on it. Most Cape people earn money in a variety of ways, a little of this, a little of that. You can't support a family of four on the summer tourist business, but you could get a good head start with it."

"A guest house?" Mari was trying it on for size, seeing a new image of a new Mari, busily directing her own destiny, absorbed with the pleasant details of her business, contributing materially to the maintenance and well-being of her family.

"Look," he told the children. "There are no shopping malls or big department stores or corner drugstores where you can hang around with the gang and drink Cokes. There's no bowling alley or movie theater, and if we lived here we wouldn't be able to afford to go to the movies, anyway, because no one here makes much money."

"There's TV," Kathy countered. "There's the beach in summertime, and sailing and hiking and stuff."

"The kids aren't like the ones at home," he went on reasonably, though there was no reason in the world why he should be arguing the point, particularly with Kathy, whose present friends he did not like. "The kids here will be uncool."

"To tell the truth," his daughter said, "I'd sooner not have to be cool. It's a drag. If everyone is doing it, you kind of have to go along. But if no one is . . . why, you can be yourself, can't you?"

There was a tightening somewhere inside, a little quiver.

"Why, yes, baby. You can."

He glanced at Mari. "I don't believe this!" she protested. "You are taking it seriously!"

Was it possible their little girl would remain a child a bit longer, here on Cape Cod? For that matter, might his wife lay claim to her own personality, here on Cape Cod? Might he? And Rick: might he grow straight and strong and more in touch with himself than would be the case elsewhere?

"If we ran a tourist house here at Kingsland, you kids would have to help, you know."

"Sure," Rick said. "I'd take out the garbage."

"I'd make beds," Kathy offered.

"We could raise chickens," Rick said. "I'd build a house for them."

"A pig!" Kathy shouted. "A horse! A cow!"

A chance to sail. To sail a lot, go out far, farther than he had ever gone, to feel the wind and the list of the ship and the tingle of drying of salt spray on his skin.

To never, ever sit at the desk of an office.

To wear blue jeans in the middle of the week.

To once again watch the elms fuzz up greenly in the spring and reach protectively across Main Street in summer and turn yellow in the autumn.

To watch the sun setting over the bay, the coming of the black ducks in the fall and their going again.

To belong to Waterford, as he had before, to its people and their ways, which he had learned once to respect so deeply. . . .

"You're all crazy," Mari insisted. "We are not going to run a guest house. We are going to move . . . to Denver or Boise or Portland."

And the house in Pennsylvania would have to be sold. They would have money. If he and Mari were careful, there'd be ample for the refurbishing of Kingsland in its transformation to tourist quarters and enough to buy a share in the *Jenny H. Lawrence*—a big share. Was there a man in the world he trusted more or liked better than Bob Casey, who'd befriended him in his youth and who had been his only steadfast companion over the shifting years? Bob, who had helped to initiate him into the code of Waterford things. . . .

"It's just silly to talk about it anymore," Mari said. "Time for bed, kids."

Woefully they left, and he sat with his mother and his wife and his malleable future, his to shape, his to decide, his to risk if he could but persuade his wife to venture out of the safety of known harbors.

"Well, now." Mari smiled at her husband, at her mother-in-law. "Let's talk about your plans, Mother Sinclaire."

"Not much to talk about," Mom said unencouragingly. Mari was the last person on earth with whom she would willingly discuss her relationship with Darion Hunt.

"Well, then, perhaps you and I ought to discuss which of your choices we'd prefer, Steve," Mari forged ahead with determination. "Personally, I think Denver appeals to me the most."

"What should we do about the house?" he asked Mom. "I hate to rent it."

"You could only get summertime people anyway," Mom said "And they're notoriously careless."

"How much rent do tourists pay?" Mari asked, her cupidity overcoming her.

"Astounding amounts." Mom laughed. "A couple hundred dollars a week, I should think, for a place this size."

"A week?" Mari squeaked. "What if we rented rooms, as you suggested a while ago, Mother?"

Mom shrugged. "Perhaps fifty dollars a week. Per room. If there were parlor privileges."

"How many rooms?" Mari started counting on her fingers.

"Probably we could make eight on the third floor," Steven said, watching her closely. "One would have to be a bathroom, though. Or two."

"And if you used the billiard room yourselves"—as she had, herself, these past five years—"you could rent the entire second floor, too," Mom said. "And there's space over the kitchen, too. But probably you're right, Mari dear. Probably it's crazy. Steven, why don't we hire someone to walk through, every other day or so. To make sure the house is holding up all right in bad weather, and to discourage break-ins."

"It adds up to five hundred dollars a week," Mari said. "Two thousand a month, four thousand a season, not counting the end of June or the month of September. How much do you think we'd need, living in Waterford?"

"Well . . . not as much as we're used to." Steven shrugged. "Half, maybe. No mortgages. Lower tax. Simpler style. Life in Waterford doesn't require new clothes or a stylish car. Bob might know someone, Mom. I'll ask him."

"I'm sorry to spring my plans on you like this," Mom said apologetically. "But I didn't want you spending your vacation worrying about the house."

"Any more than I wanted you to worry about our moving west." He smiled. "So you like Denver, Mari?"

"I think I'd like Denver," she said slowly, parting with her four thousand dollars only with reluctance. "But after all, I've never been there."

"Tell you what," he proposed, forcing himself to speak calmly, nonchalantly. "Let's just go off by ourselves, you and me, tomorrow. No hurry. No rush. Talk it over, think about it without kids hanging around."

"Or mother." Mom grinned.

Mari looked from one to the other of them. "Why, sure." She smiled. "It'd be fun. Can we have lunch out?"

"Sure."

"There's an art gallery in Barnstable I'd sort of like to see."

"Then we shall see it. And ride around. And relax. And consider our options."

"Fine." She looked at Mom. "If you don't mind, Mother?"

"Who? Me?" Mom waved any inconvenience that a day of keeping track of Kathy and Rick might cause her. "Far be it from me to impede the onward march of the Sinclaires!"

Just exactly where the onward march might lead, of course, Mom could have no idea. But he was quite sure that regardless of the topics scheduled for discussion the next day, Mom knew perfectly well that Boise, Denver, and Portland would not comprise their entirety.

"Good God!" Mari exclaimed. "Would you look at that one!"

She had spotted the *Jenny H. Lawrence* right away—not a difficult thing to do, considering the ship's size, especially since he'd headed Mari toward *Jenny*'s berth as soon as they'd found a parking spot in Hobbes Hole.

"Pretty big," he agreed noncommittally. Together they stood on the pier, with the sounds and business of the harbor behind them. "Probably pretty old, too."

"Do you know anything about that boat?" Mari asked a harbor hand loitering nearby.

"Sure I do." The fellow grinned. "That's the windjammer *Jenny Lawrence*. Hop on board if you want. Everyone else does."

"Just like that?" Mari demanded.

"Just like that."

She hesitated, obviously eager to explore. "What do you think, Steve! Do we dare? Let's!"

"You know I like boats," he said cheerfully, seeing her safely over the gap between wharf's edge and *Jenny*'s deck. They looked up at the organized tangle of lines running to and from the masts, and made their way back to the cockpit.

"Look how big the steering wheel is!" she exclaimed. "And see this! It must be the compass. Oh, look, there's a room . . ." She crouched low enough to look into the aftercabin. "Oh!" she gasped. "I'm so sorry. We just wanted to look around. I apologize for having disturbed you!"

"Don't worry about it," Larsen said jovially from the cabin.

Behind Mari's shoulder Steven waved, then pointed to himself, put a finger to his lips, pointed at Mari.

"Come on in," Larsen offered. "I'll buy you a drink."

It was ten o'clock in the morning.

"A little early for me, thanks," Mari said, but went down the aftercabin steps. "This boat is really unique, isn't it!"

"Let me tell you how unique," Eric said happily, a man in love, interested only in talking about that love. "*Jenny* is nearly a hundred years old."

"Good grief," remarked Mari.

"But these ships are built to last a long time," he hastened to explain. "*Jenny Lawrence* used to haul bricks and lumber and shellfish up and down the coast. There were lots of ships this size that did that, and there always have been until now. They were called the Apple Tree fleet, and *Jenny* has hauled her share. Now she hauls passengers. Cabin space for thirty."

"Where does she haul them?"

"Oh, around." Eric waved generously.

"And if there's no wind . . ."

"We wait. *Jenny* doesn't have a motor."

"What happens when you're in a hurry?"

"We push her. With a yawl boat."

"Good grief," Mari exclaimed again. "How primitive!"

"There are advantages, though. Since she doesn't have an engine, she doesn't come under coast-guard regulations. *Jenny* is probably the only vessel afloat that could hit the high seas without an inspector at every porthole and three in each head."

"What's a head," Mari asked.

"The bathroom," Steven said, mortified by her ignorance.

"She used to sail in Maine, but the season there is longer," Eric barreled along happily. "I'll bet we can get an extra month out of her here on Cape Cod. She's for sale, by the way."

"If she's so wonderful, why is she being sold?"

Steven wished heartily that he had not brought her.

"A hundred years is a lot of years," Eric was saying. "There's a lot that ought to be done to her."

"Like what?" Mari asked.

"She should have a new suit of sail. That's very expensive. She should be recalked, and probably a lot of her planking should be replaced. The keel needs attention, and probably new rigging is in order. And the stem has a problem, I think."

Steven did not think he would ask about what sort of problem the stem might have.

"But naturally these things don't have to be done all at once," Eric explained, speaking quickly. "Like a house, you plan your course of repairs and additions and refurbishings." Eric was visibly more relaxed now, without any real reason for being, except the drink he held in his hand. "I think Bob Casey will invest a bit in *Jenny*, Steve. And if you came in with us, then the three of us could own her. That would be swell, don't you think?" he asked, giving everything away. "I've always wanted a vessel like this. Compared to four- and five-masted schooners, she's a midget, but one man could sail her single-handed if he had to. I could live aboard in the winter, and work on her, take passengers in the summer, haul lumber in the off-seasons. Sounds great, huh?"

Eric hitched himself along the bench, prepared to mount the three steps to the deck. "If you'll excuse me, I have an urgent date." He winked. "But just remember, folks, *Jenny* breaks even at half-capacity. And she's never only half-full."

With a nod he was gone, like St. Nicholas in the old Christmas tale.

Steven did not have the courage to look her in the eye.

"You want it, don't you?"

"Want what?" he asked guilelessly.

"The ship. This ship. You want to buy it, with the profit from the house in Pennsylvania."

"Well, the thought has occurred."

"What about the repairs that the captain has just finished listing?" she demanded. "They sound phenomenal."

"*Jenny* goes now without lifting a finger," he pointed out. "It's only a question of plowing profits back into her until she's had the things done that have probably been neglected for quite a while."

"If you could see yourself," she said softly, "you'd be scared."

"What do you mean?" he scoffed.

"You come alive, Steven. You come alive in a way I've never seen before. After so long together, to discover something about you that I never knew . . ."

"You've always known I liked to sail."

"This is different," she said in a small voice. "This is like you've found a mistress."

It was a remark he thought wiser to pass. "Well . . . I just wanted to show you something unique," he said. "A floating antique. Let's get a bite to eat."

"I think you wanted to trick me into coming down here," she said, undiverted by the thought of lunch. "I think you were hoping I'd be as swept off my feet as you are, if I got a look at this boat."

"I'd hoped that you'd see the possibilities, that's true. Once Rick suggested staying in Waterford . . . why, *Jenny* seemed like a natural."

"Don't pin it on a fourteen-year-old boy. You had it in mind when you came home last night, didn't you?"

"No, I didn't."

"You and Bob didn't discuss it? Really, Steve! How gullible do you think I am? You and Bob have been thick as thieves for years, and both of you are sailing buffs. Don't tell me you didn't plot it out with him, detail by detail, about getting me down here, letting the ship and Captain Larsen do the talking for you."

"Well?" he asked. "What do you think?"

"I am not persuaded."

"She's unique, you must admit."

"Yes, I'll admit that!"

He waited for her to mount the steps of the aftercabin, helped her back onto the dock, silently accompanied her to the car and opened her door, went around to his own side.

"You don't have to sulk," she said crossly.

"I'm not."

"You are."

He pulled carefully into traffic; Hobbes Hole thinned out and signs for the mid-Cape highway showed up.

"Where're we going now?" she asked.

"Home."

"See! What did I tell you! You are sulking. You just lured me to Hobbes Hole to show me that relic, and now you're mad because I'm not crazy about it."

He pulled onto the mid-Cape; halfway to Waterford she relented. "All right," she said, resigned. "Maybe you ought to tell me what you think can be gained by our living in Waterford. I gather you think there is a gain to be had?"

"Not materially, there isn't."

"Well?"

"Are you satisfied?" he challenged her. "With our life, the life we lead every day, with the people we know, with the things we do? Do you like the people in the suburbs? Are you happy with my progress at my job?"

"Oh, that." She sighed. She shrugged—he could see it out of the corner of his eye. "I'm not sure that buying a leaky one-hundred-year-old schooner is exactly the best antidote to the poisons of modern life, Steve."

He laughed. "You're forgetting the tourist business. It's supposed to tide us over until the ship shows a profit. I'd find a part-time job during the winter, enough to buy groceries, and the rest of the time we could work on the house, renovate it to accommodate tourists. Come summer, I'd sail on the *Lawrence* and you'd run the house, with the help of Kathy and Rick. I think it wouldn't hurt them to know their help was vital to us."

"No, it wouldn't hurt at all," she acknowledged. "I am a little concerned about Kathy's growing up too fast . . ."

"But it all hangs on your willingness to go into business for yourself, Mari. If you'd rather not, then there's no point discussing it further."

"It is a little frightening," she said. "I'd sooner not discuss it anymore. Not just now."

He let her out at the front of the house, drove around to the barn.

"Where've you been?" Rick wanted to know.

"I just wanted to show Mom something."

"What was it?"

"An old lumber schooner. Tied up in Hobbes Hole. Bob knows the captain; he took me down there yesterday to see it, and I took your mother there to see it today."

"Will you take me to see it tomorrow?"

"Sure—early, though. It sails in the afternoon."

"Where's it going?"

"Around." He smiled, copying Eric Larsen's nebulous but descriptive wave. "She carries passengers to Martha's Vineyard and Nantucket."

"Gee," Rick said. "A big one."

"Yup. Mighty big." Damn! Not many chances came and went like this one—but his hands were tied. The *Jenny Lawrence* was a gamble—just as staying in Waterford was. Too big a gamble to impose on his family without their wholehearted support, and Mari was essentially a very conservative person.

He looked fondly at the boy beside him, whose cooperation, he knew, was his for the asking.

"Did you talk to Mom about staying here, in Waterford?" Rick asked.

"We discussed it."

"Come to any agreement?"

"No."

"I wish she was more of a sport." Rick scowled.

He should defend her, he knew. He should not let such a remark pass without explaining that living in rural Cape Cod would be hard for Mother and it was natural that the idea should strike her as impossible.

But he could say nothing, because by now living in Boise or Portland or Denver, fighting to stay alive at Bronner Fiberglass and Insulation, was equally impossible. Feeling more burdened than he ever had before, he walked with Rick toward the house, sizing it up as he approached, thinking over what details a person would have to watch for if he were keeping an eye on it for its absentee owner.

Maybe Linc Sears would do it, he speculated. Irregularly employed, without family, extra time. A bit of a lush, was Linc, but not an article would be removed from the house by him or anyone else, not with Linc guarding it. No detail of maintenance would be overlooked, for A. Lincoln Sears had worked in carpentry and allied skills all his life. Could probably fix the plumbing himself, if it sprang a leak.

The trouble with old houses, Steven reflected as he let himself into the kitchen, was that you were always worried about plumbing.

In the parlor he could hear Mari and Mom talking—oh, Christ, to J. Barry and Claudia again. Why don't they just move in? he wondered irritably. They're wearing out the lawn, running back and forth from the old house to this one.

He glanced at Rick, who made a face. Poised, they listened.

"I like to think these things are ordained," he heard Claudia say, breathless with the awe of her predestination. "I mean . . . that both of us . . . both families of us . . . have the same idea. At virtually the same time."

"I'd have said so yesterday," Mari said. "When you were here. But Steve wasn't sure of this ship—whether it was available or not. I mean, talk about antique, Claudia. You've never seen anything like this boat!"

"Really," sighed Claudia. "To picture Steve on the high seas, just like his ancestors! Living in the same place as they lived! It's just too romantic."

"And if you needed help when Steven is out on the vessel, why, we'll be right here," J. Barry was saying. "Neither of you would have to worry about a thing."

"That's nice to know," Mari said. "Because the only way such a scheme would be possible is if I were to run a tourist home here, and there could be occasions when I'd need a man's strength and judgment, Barry."

"Tourists? At Kingsland?" Claudia repeated.

"It's a big house," Mari said. "We can pack in quite a few." She laughed gaily. "Naturally! Steve couldn't expect to support a family of four on profit from a windjammer—not for quite a few years. He'd need my help . . . and the help of the children. We'll pull together, each of us contributing our bit, doing our part."

"Really," Claudia breathed, her admiration abundant. "You are an inspiration to us all, Mari."

"Please excuse me for a moment, won't you?" Mom's footsteps came down the hall, toward the kitchen. "I thought you two must be around here somewhere," she whispered.

"I can hardly believe what I'm hearing," he whispered back. "She wasn't buying any of it when we rode home."

"She's buying now. Apparently Claudia and J. Barry have had an offer for their house—unexpectedly, and very high. They came over, bragging about it, bragging about their pioneer spirit, their independence—individuality. Perhaps Mari saw their pioneering as a challenge! Rick, dear, I see that the barn isn't shut for the night. Would you take care of it?"

Rick agreed, accepting his being gotten out of the way, amenable to anything now that he was on the eve of reprieve.

"You didn't say anything about an antique boat last night," Mom chided, her eyes merry.

"A recent stellar development." He grinned.

"I haven't had a chance to tell you—and I wanted you to know—that I won't be living with Darion when I go to New York."

"Why not?"

"It's a decision we've made, and will stick to, for as long as Pris is alive."

"I wish you didn't have so many roadblocks in your way." He'd met Darion Hunt, more than once. If there was ever a man good enough, right enough for his mother, Hunt was the one—yet Mrs. Hunt might live forever, pickled in alcohol as she was.

"The roadblocks don't bother us. Pris'll never come out of that institution, and all I want to do is be near Darion; I wanted to tell you how happy I am, how confident I am that the years ahead will be kind to us."

"Let me wish you the best of luck," he said, hugging her. "And if you don't mind, Mom, I would appreciate having a little myself."

"It could be the making of you all, living here," she said strongly. "But Waterford is changing, honey. Be prepared for it—be tolerant of it. Unless you are, it won't work."

She kissed his cheek and hurried back to the parlor, and he poked about the old kitchen with its black iron stove and little gas burner hidden behind it, old and dingy linoleum, smudged walls. It'd take some freshening up, that was for sure—but he'd leave the old stove in, lending authenticity to the mind of the tourist who wanted to stay in an honest-to-God old house.

He stared out the window, at the lawns he'd seeded himself so long ago, and the flowerbeds gone to weed, and at his son, who dodged behind a tree, lying in ambush for Kathy, who was appearing from the other side of the house. Would it be possible, he wondered, that if he and Mari could shed much of their accumulated load? Would the challenge of living by their wits, close to the land, their lives directed by the seasons and their thoughts by the tempo of those seasons as Waterford had done for generations—could it give them the answer to their restlessness and underlying malaise? He was aware, now that he let himself be, that he was in need of something he could not define, something he'd missed or lost, something that might be part of him again here, at Kingsland, here in Waterford.

Something that the *Jenny Lawrence* would make possible for them all.

VIII

The Promise of the Jenny H. Lawrence

22

Spring hesitated with its usual reluctance; the wind off the bay was still shrill around the edges, the water was still gray; the herring had not begun to come up the mill stream. Steven wiped his hands on the greasy rag that Roly Hall always left on the gas pump, and turned up his coat collar, shivering a little. But he did not bother to go into the shelter of the station, because another car was pulling up to the pumps. Without enthusiasm he saw that its driver was Claudia Marshall in her Ford station wagon, wearing slacks and a sweater and heavy gold bracelets. Her daytime makeup meticulously right so that she looked like a fashion model in the Sears, Roebuck catalog, sporty but utterly feminine.

She rolled down her window, and the hot air from the car heater warmed his face. "Hi, Steve!"

"Hi. Fill it?"

"Yes, please," she instructed. He prepared himself for the conversation that was sure to take place while the meter clanked and whirred and the pump delivered gas at thirty-five cents a gallon.

"All set for your party tonight?" she asked.

"At the rate Mari's going, we'll never be ready. We've moved every stick of furniture five times, trying to get it right."

"Really, Steve," Claudia said earnestly. "I was so glad when Mari told me that you two were able to entertain, at last. It must mean you're on top of your renovations. The gang is dying to see what you've done!"

"Mari's looking forward to showing you," he assured her. "She's been digging up all the artifacts and dusting off all the old furniture stored in the barn. She's got the parlor looking like something from a museum."

"The gang'll love it," Claudia assured him.

He edged the meter over to three dollars and hung up the nozzle.

Claudia gave him her credit card and he took it into the station, where Roly Hall and Linc Sears watched without offering comment, wrote up the receipt, took it back to her to sign. If she were aware of the observation by the old men, she gave no sign of it, waiting with an untroubled brow, listening to the radio in her car, a woman without worries who watched while the tradesmen of Waterford did her work for her.

She signed, looked up, smiled prettily. "Thanks!"

"Right."

"See you at your party."

He waved and turned away, working hard not to resent her, because it was not her fault that she and Barry were fresh and perky while the Sinclaires were exhausted. He worked on Kingsland nights and the days off he had from the Texaco station, and he and Mari had done everything themselves except for the plumbing, which Harry Mayo had reluctantly finished by Christmas and had charged so much for that Mari's whole first summer of income would be needed to offset it. The gang had better love it, he thought ferociously. Whoever in hell the gang is.

No other car was approaching. He went inside the station and sat down in the chair nearest the desk.

Roly Hall grinned and winked. "We were just sayin' that's a nice-lookin' car."

"Nice-lookin' girl, too," said Linc. "Nice tits. You could just about see 'em from here."

"Linc," he chided. "You were looking."

"If a woman rides around in this weather with a tight sweater on and no coat," observed Linc, "it appears to me that she wants someone to look. Glad to accommodate her." He waved his pint in accolade.

"Help yourself," Roly said, gesturing to the pan of Mrs. Hall's cinnamon rolls which she'd sent in that day. He liked young Sinclaire and was glad, now, that he'd hired him despite the mumbled complaints of some folks, whom he would not name, that Sinclaire, who probably did not have to work at all, was taking a job that one of themselves needed. He pushed the pan of rolls closer to Sinclaire, to show him the sincerity of his offer.

"Thanks," said Steven, scooping out a cinnamon morsel and perching on Roly's desk, ready to hop out in attendance on the next car. The discussion which, no doubt, had started some time before, continued.

"They have all the signatures they need to put it in the warrant, you know." Linc gestured widely as he was apt to do, having been drinking since this time yesterday.

"Put what in the warrant?" Steven asked.

"That damn article about that damn Lyceum Hall in Truro."

Steven nodded. For forty years the Lyceum Hall had served as a private residence in Truro, bought cheaply from the town of Waterford during the depression and floated across the bay on a barge. Now certain of Waterford's citizenry wanted it back.

"And we're supposed to give land for it, too," Linc said.

"Where?" Roly asked indignantly. "I didn't hear nothing about land."

"On the King's Highway, my dear," Linc mimicked. "Where else."

"The King's Highway?"

"Main Street, to you. The Historical Society wants to rename it, though. The Olde King's Highway."

"La-di-da," Roly said, crooking his little finger over the handle of the coffee mug.

"They're all the same," Linc said. "They're all bitten by the same flea. Damned if there isn't a fella from New Jersey who bought an old place on the beach. He wants it to look like it was about two hundred years old. He found this date in it—1760—and so he wants that everything should be authentic. Going to show it off to the Historical Society."

"You wouldn't know anything about that date, would you, Linc?" Steven asked with a straight face.

"Christ, no," Linc said, only the slightest quiver at the corner of his mouth giving him away. "I wouldn't say anything, even if I did, and ruin that poor man's fun."

"Good for the carpentry business," Roly remarked. "Who got the job restoring it?"

"A youngster from Rhode Island, moved in a year ago. Took the job from Casey, too. Underbid him."

They thought about the dislocations now being caused by Waterford's real-estate boom, and the little office was quiet as each man settled into the unoccupied conversational space. Once you got used to it, the gaps were pleasant. Until you did, you itched around and made a nuisance of yourself trying to fill them.

"The Lyceum Hall is supposed to be a public buildin'," Linc said, still worrying the subject. "That's why the public is supposed to pay for it. Everyone's supposed to use it for meetin's."

"What meetin's?" Roly snorted. "Ain't nothin' to meet about that I know of. Don't worry so! Everyone's much more hot and bothered about the police department." He glanced at his receiver-transmitter. "There's some folks of the opinion that the job of cop shouldn't be combined with the job of dog officer—and that it should be full-time, and that it shouldn't be me as has it." He chuckled, unconcerned about such insubstantial opinions.

"You must think that Waterford doesn't need a full-time policeman," Steven ventured.

"No!" Linc declared before Roly could speak. "It don't. Summers, yes. We hire on extra men for traffic and such. But all year? Hell, we've always managed. It's nice people moving here, not thugs. What in hell do we need a new police station and a new chief and two dozen Indians for? Do you know what that'll do to the tax rate?"

"Who said anything about a new station?"

"No one, yet. But they will. They think big. Where they come from, they can afford to."

Roly shook his head in resignation. "I dunno. Maybe the town is getting ahead of us. Maybe it's out of reach already. Population's nearly doubled in the last three years. Did you know that?"

"I certainly didn't," Steven said. Nor did he know about much of anything else. He'd kept his nose to the grindstone so closely this winter that he was aware of little besides the price of paint and wallpaper and two-by-fours, all of which were more expensive than he realized and were reducing his and Mari's savings more quickly than they'd planned. Thank goodness summer and the tourist season wasn't far away!

The bell rang, and he ran out to fill the tank of an out-of-state car—rarely seen during the raw spring of Cape Cod and almost never during winter. Indeed, winter brought work nearly to a stop, and only the long-standing friendship he'd had with Roly kept him employed now.

He checked his watch: good. Eleven-thirty. Quitting time for him. He'd been on the job since six, when Roly opened up, but his day was far from over. This afternoon he'd work on the last of the upstairs bedrooms. He'd made six new ones on the empty third floor (it had held only the water tank, in old days, and trunks and trash), and now he was taping and sanding Sheetrock, a laborious, time-consuming, and not always successful job for an amateur like himself, who'd done so little of it.

"I'll be leaving now, Roly," he said, ducking into the office momentarily. "See you in the morning."

"Right."

"So long, Linc."

"So long, Steve. Take it easy. I think we just shouldn't take it layin' down, is all," he said to Roly.

He shut the door on their interminable conversation and jogged downstreet to his house. He'd finished the bedroom to the right of the stairs yesterday, and hopefully it was ready for Mari's assault with paper and paste. An old house, they agreed, should be papered, even if the job was done badly by beginners. It would add to the charm, and they wouldn't be sleeping with their mistakes—mistakes that transients would never notice. He'd take another look at it this afternoon, in the harsh cruel light of the March day—but paper covered a multitude of problems. . . .

"Hi, honey!" Mari called from the parlor. "There's chowder on the stove."

"Great!" He helped himself. "Kids coming home for lunch today?"

"Nope. They'll stay at school. I was too busy today to have them running in and out!" She bustled into the kitchen with the old pewter pre-Revolutionary mugs of Mary Deems Merrick in her hand. "I wanted to have the portrait and the mugs more or less in the same place. I found a shelf out in the barn—a sweet little Victorian thing with scrolls and curlicues. We could hang it near Mary Deems's portrait. And I'd like to bring Kingsley out of the library and put him . . . somewhere. Somewhere in full view." She perched on the edge of a kitchen chair while he stirred his chowder. "Near Elijah and Mary, since he's their grandson. If you don't mind, Steve!" she added, remembering at the last moment that the ancestors she was moving so glibly around were his, not hers.

"Of course I don't mind," he reassured her. He'd have preferred to store them in the barn with their faces to the wall, but they had become very important to his wife. "I don't mind at all, Mar, except I'm not clear on why you're moving everyone. And everything."

"When you're through, I'll show you." Patiently she waited for him to finish the chowder; patiently she explained. "Everyone has heard all about Kingsley Merrick, the Great Person, so I thought it was foolish to hide him in the library. And the mugs are priceless as well as interesting, and ought to be on display near their owner. It'll be stunning, really!" Last night they'd hung the portrait of Elijah Merrick in the center of the parlor wall, and his wife Mary Deems (whom some records referred to as Molly) had been settled to his left. "And if we put Kingsley somewhere to Elijah's right—over the piano, maybe—everyone will be together."

"Why leave anyone out?" he asked, mildly sarcastic. "What's wrong with Augusta and Julia and Kingsley's old man?"

"His father?" she gasped, the sarcasm passing her by. "You didn't tell me we had a portrait of the first Kingsley Merrick!"

"Well, maybe it isn't," he said quickly. "There's no way of telling, after all. There's no name on it. And you wouldn't want just anyone masquerading as the Great Person's father."

"Oh, no, I certainly wouldn't!" she exclaimed. He followed her into the library, lifted the heavy portrait of Kingsley Merrick off the wall, and together they carried it into the living room.

"Tell, me, Mar, are some of the people who are coming tonight Historical Society members?"

"Why, yes, we all are. When Claudia and I joined, they did too." He held the portrait up and waited for her confirmation.

"A little to the left. It's been a lot of fun, actually. Mostly because your family is so illustrious, honorable husband. Your prominence rubs off on me." She bowed from the waist. "I've really enjoyed the people Claudia and I've met, and I hope you will too," she said anxiously. He had not troubled himself to meet Mari's new group; he'd been too busy, too tired, too uninterested. But perhaps, judging from what he'd heard at Roly's today, he should have been paying more attention. He drove the nail deeply to reach a stud, missed, drove it again, succeeding. "If they make you happy, honey, that's what counts. But tell me—is it true that the society wants to rename Main Street?"

He hung the portrait and stepped back to observe. The room, for all its size, seemed very heavily populated.

"Oh! The Olde Kings Highway!" she laughed. "Yes. In the old days, that's what the high road was called, and there are still so many old houses on it that we feel it would be very appropriate, Steve."

"What else do they have in mind?" he asked casually. "The society members, I mean?"

"They're interested in creating a historical district on Main Street someday," Mari frowned, as though thinking carefully. "But just now the society mostly concentrates on the preservation of historical things and places. Why do you ask?"

"I hear things at the gas station, is all. I wondered."

"Well, I certainly can't be expected to know what all the members are plotting!" She laughed lightly, and he suspected she knew very well. "What are your plans for the afternoon?" she asked. "Nothing messy, I hope, now that I've got everything ready for the group."

Even two stories removed, the plaster dust he'd raise from the new bedrooms would filter down and settle all over everything.

"No sanding," he promised. "I'll tape seams."

"Thank goodness!"

"Got paper for the little room?"

"They had to order it—I'm supposed to pick it up today. So I'll do it now, and then I'll go to the liquor store, and then to the market. I'll be back by four." She kissed his cheek and perkily sped off, her mind on the details of her party, which pleased and excited her, and uneasily he watched from the parlor window as she whipped out of the driveway, spraying clamshells as she went, happy as an adolescent girl preparing for the senior prom.

He picked up his trowel from the kitchen counter, climbed the back stairs, which had been used in plusher times by servants. On the second floor, above the kitchen where the maids had once slept, he'd created two bedrooms and a central hall, and two bathrooms connected to the rest of the second floor; the whole of it would be given over to guests this summer. They'd painted and papered everything, and once he finished the third floor, he'd work on the old billiard room downstairs, creating an extra bedroom for the kids, converting it to temporary summer quarters for the family. It was enough to make a man tired, just thinking about it.

He climbed on up to the third floor, inspected the room he hoped he'd finished yesterday. Not bad, he thought, opening the putty can and filling in an overlooked crater where a nail had been driven in. He moved to the room next door, which he'd prepared yesterday for another coat of Spackle. He'd throw it on, maybe work on the windows, which stuck a bit. It was all he could hope to accomplish today. He lugged the big bucket of plaster into the room, heard a commotion on the back porch.

He pried open the sticking window.

"Hello?" he called. "Who's there?"

The man on the porch looked up. It was old Eben Gray.

"You busy, Mr. Sinclaire?" he called. "I can come back."

"Wait a minute," Steven called back, replacing the lid on the plaster (it would dry out if you didn't keep it tight closed when you weren't using it). He clattered down the stairs, trowel in hand, opened the door. "Won't you come in, Mr. Gray?"

"Thanks," Eben said, looking around as he entered. The kitchen had not changed over the years, except for the installation of water instead of a pump beside the sink; its renovation had not yet begun. Eben visibly relaxed as he saw the old black iron stove, the cracked linoleum on the floor, and the mess Mari had left behind in her preparation for tonight's party. "I'm awful sorry to bother you," he apologized.

"No trouble. Won't you sit down?" He put the trowel in the sink.

"No. No. I won't be long." Still, it was hard for Eben Gray to come to the point, trained as he had been to pass pleasantries for an indefinite amount of time before getting down to business. That was the only polite way, and yet Mr. Sinclaire, with drying plaster on his hands and his work-clothes on, clearly had other things to do. "Have you heard about town meetin' next week?" he asked by way of preliminaries.

"Yes, I've heard."

"Read the warrant?"

"No. Roly Hall said there was something about a full-time policeman—I know that."

"Yup. So there is," Eben concurred politely.

"Linc Sears said there was something about the old Lyceum Hall."

"Eyup." The old man's face did not indicate his opinion about this matter, either. Clearly they had not yet hit on the object of this visit.

"I'm afraid I don't know about anything else," Steven confessed.

"Well, actually, that's why I'm here," Eben said hesitantly. "You see . . . well . . . it seems like they want a clam warden."

"Clam warden?"

"Yup."

"What does this clam warden do?"

"Well, I'm glad you asked that, Mr. Sinclaire," Eben said, relieved of having to come to the point unassisted. "It seems there's this idea goin' around that the town can cultivate the clams. They plan to section off the Waterford flats like we used to divide cranberry bogs—make it eight parts and close all but one, every year in rotation. That way there'll always be a nice clam supply. They'll charge money for permits, the town will make enough to pay for the clam warden, and we'll have more clams than we ever had before."

"Yes?" he asked, unsure of the drift of Eben's conversation, mindful of the work that waited for him upstairs.

Eben Gray fidgeted a moment. "To tell the truth, Mr. Sinclaire, me and the Mrs. depend a lot on those clams. We certainly don't aim to go on welfare—no, sir!" Gray drew himself up proudly. "But without them clams, I don't know how we'll make out."

"You can dig in one part of the flats, can't you?"

"Yes. But the permit limits you to a quart a week, at least to begin with—which is a good deal less than me and the Mrs. generally use. And if the clams don't look so good to the warden, he can close the flats altogether, and then we wouldn't have none. And what's more, Mr. Sinclaire, I think these people—conservationists, they call themselves—they believe you can grow clams like you grow grass. They seem to think that you put seed in the ground, water it, and commence mowin' in a month. The fact is, Mr. Sinclaire, the Lord only knows what makes a clam decide to grow, and where. Diggin' 'em never seemed to make much difference, one way or t'other. They're just there some years, and sparse in others. Of course, me and the Mrs. have money stashed away," he hastened on, "because, as I'm sure you know, there've been winters when the bay freezes over and you can't dig at all. But how long will that nest egg last, if we have to buy a lot of food all year long?"

"Yes, Eben, I see your point," he said. "It would depend, I guess, on how big a nest egg you had."

"Well, that's fact," agreed Eben. There was a long pause. "We rent our place to off-Cape folks in the summer," he explained. "Why, Mr. Sinclaire, did you know they'll pay fifty dollars a week, and it's only one room?"

"One room?"

"My place. It has one room. But still, city people will pay fifty dollars a week to use it."

"Do you mind if I ask, Mr. Gray, where you and Mrs. Gray go when your house is rented?"

The old codger glanced around cautiously. "Promise you won't tell?"

"I won't, no."

"Not that it's a secret," he said. "Not really. Roly knows and all, and so do a lot of other people. But the new folks in town—well, it might confuse them, Mr. Sinclaire. You'll understand, I know—you're one of us—but . . ."

"Go on. I won't say anything, and no one's home but me."

"We take our car into the woods by the old Warden mansion," he said. "You know that estate east of town that's been empty for so long?"

"Yes, I know the place."

"Well, there's a heavy woods grown up beside it, and we park there for the summer. I can still dig clams, because it's on the water's edge, and if it's a rainy day and we're feelin' a bit confined, well, we just go off for the day, takin' the house with us, like we was a snail," he said, pleased with his imagery.

"You mean you live all summer in your car?" he asked incredulously.

"Why, yes. But Roly knows where we are. He says its okay."

"Oh, sure, Eben. I'm sure it is."

"I didn't mean to take so much of your time, Mr. Sinclaire, or go on like this. What I meant to do . . . what I wanted to do . . . is ask you if you'd speak at town meeting against the clam warden."

"Huh?" he asked.

"Well, I figure the whole things rises or falls on whether or not the town votes the money to pay a clam warden. They'll argue that it's only temporary—that the town won't have to pay for the warden very long, because in time the clams will pay for him. But the fact is, Mr. Sinclaire, them clams won't pay, and by the time the conservation people have figured it out, the Mrs. and I'll be on welfare. And we'll do just about anything not to have to do that."

"Yes," he said thoughtfully. "I can see that you would."

"I'll speak against it, too," Eben Gray said. "But all I can do is say that from my years of clammin' I don't truly think they can be regulated like that. And somehow, Mr. Sinclaire, I don't think the conservation people will believe me. They'll take one look, and they'll say: what does this old man know about it?" Steven looked through their eyes and, indeed, saw an old man whose scrawny neck extended through a frayed collar too large for it; there were patches on his knees and elbows, and safety pins where his buttons should have been, clumsy boots, and stubble on his chin. . . .

"I'd be glad to tell the meeting what you've told me—about the clams. If you think it would help, of course I'll do it."

"I don't think it'd hurt, that's for sure," Eben Gray said. "And thanks."

Steven watched the old fellow shamble down the driveway, climb into his roomy 1952 Buick; the summer residence of Eben Gray lumbered away.

Thoughtfully he cleaned the trowel, climbed the stairs again, tackled the seam he'd left, smearing on the goo, smoothing it, spreading it, feathering its edges so that it would eventually be unnoticeable.

There was another commotion on the back porch, and again he opened the window, which, now that it was getting some use, moved more freely.

"Yes?" he called. "Who is it?"

"Don Slater," called the young man standing there. "And Greenleaf Stone."

"Wait a minute," he called back, replacing the putty lid and trotting back downstairs. He threw the trowel into the sink and opened the door.

"Hi, Don. Hi, Leaf." He'd known them both from days gone by at the Ace-High. "What can I do for you?"

"It's about the warrant for town meeting next week," Slater said. "Hate to bother you, Steve, but could we take a minute of your time?"

"Sure," he said, giving up on the third-floor bedroom. "Come on in. Have a beer?"

"Sure," they chorused, and accepted a seat at the kitchen table.

"Seems there's a problem come up," Slater began, "and neither Leaf or me knows what to do."

Steven was beginning to get the picture now. Town meeting and the preparations and hearings required by it had got the pot boiling here in Waterford, and because he had lived here so long ago, among the tradesmen as one of them despite the fact of residing here at Kingsland, he seemed accessible to people who had nowhere to turn.

No good can come of this, he thought. No good at all.

"Actually, Leaf and I—the problems we're running into are a little like two sides of one coin," Don explained. "Leaf finds that more and more regulations are being required as part of Waterford's building code—he's the building inspector, in case you didn't know—and I find that a lot of pressure is being put on the Planning Board to make building here in town, and living here in town, more and more difficult."

"You're on the Planning Board, I take it."

"Yup."

"Like what kind of pressure?"

"Picky, silly things for the most part, that make the new people feel like they're in control, and not us. But there's one that's really got us worried. And that's why we're here, Steve. In order to discourage the growth of business, because business encourages people to move into town, there's going to be an article to zone the south end of the Rockford Road for business, and you won't be able to do business anywhere else, unless you've already been doing it."

"How about people just starting out?" he asked. "They can't do business from their homes?" God knew that only by working for yourself could you depend on earning a living in Waterford!

"They've got to do it on the Rockford Road. But hell and damnation, Steve, no one even uses the south end of it. How're you supposed to sell anything if no one passes by? You know how dependent we are on tourists."

"You can see what's happening," Greenleaf Stone said. "Waterford is growing fast and the people who've moved here are retired, mostly, or in business already. So they won't get hurt. They think Waterford will be ruined if it gets any bigger. But in order to stop it from growing, they're going to make it impossible for people like us to live here. Or our kids. And somehow, Steve, it sticks in our craw."

"Yes, I can see that it would."

"So we came today to ask you to speak against that zoning article—and any of the rest you feel moved to oppose. You . . . well, hell, you're one of us, but you talk like they do, and they'll listen to you. And whilst they listen, the rest of the folks at the meeting who've lived here all their lives—maybe they'll be encouraged to stand up for themselves and try to defend the town and the life we have here."

They had never needed to do so before. The chances were good that they would be inadequate now.

He looked from one to the other of them, men with large, work-scarred hands and weathered faces the texture of old wood. Men yet in their prime who would age quickly because of the demands on their bodies that their labor required. Men who had worked out their own destinies, all their lives, in their own way. Men he had admired for years.

"I'll think about it, of course," he gulped.

"There!" Don beamed at Leaf. "I told you!"

"Thanks," said Leaf. "Would you run for selectman next year, too? You're the man I need there. Selectmen appoint the building inspector—and fire him, too. I think they're gunnin' for me."

"Sorry." He smiled wryly. "I'm not a politician, and I don't intend to become one now. I have too much to do."

"That's right, you and Casey aim to run that windjammer, don't you?" Slater remembered on the way to the door.

"We hope to," Steven said. "It's sort of a gamble, but we hope it'll work."

"Well, we wish you luck." Don thrust out a hand to shake.

Leaf Stone shook hands too, and they disappeared around the corner of the lawn. Soon the roar of an inadequately muffled engine soared and they took off in a cloud of blue smoke.

He took another beer out of the refrigerator, chipped the dried plaster off the trowel and dissolved the remnants under the faucet, went again to tackle the bedroom. The lid wasn't even off the can before the commotion on the back porch began again.

The window opened smoothly.

"Hello?" he called out.

"Come on down," Bob Casey called cheerfully back.

He glanced at his watch: two-thirty. Rather early for a builder to be calling it a day. He left the trowel behind, picked up the beer.

"Help yourself." He gestured toward the refrigerator with the can, and Bob found one, settling himself into the kitchen table with his feet on the opposite chair.

"How's everything?" he asked very casually.

"I don't know what in hell's going on." Steven sighed. "But if I climb those stairs another time, I'll cut my throat."

"Hm." Bob commiserated, savoring the first sip of beer. "Been a little busy?"

"All of a sudden no one but me is qualified to speak at town meeting next week."

"Oh?"

"Everyone seems to think I'm the only man in Waterford who both understands the town as it is and is articulate enough to defend it."

"Probably you are," Bob observed.

Steven watched Bob closely, beginning to see what was happening.

"There's a few that'll listen to reason," Bob pushed on. "A few that think for themselves, if they're given a point of view they didn't know about before. And there's always the old town, of course, who might not have understood what's been going on, or what the outcome of all these shenanigans will probably be."

"Bob . . ."

"If someone's there, able to speak loud and clear, without adding a lot of shit and garbage to confuse the issue . . . well, perhaps there's some hope."

"Bob, did you put Don Slater and Leaf Stone up to coming here this afternoon?"

" 'Twas a decision mutually reached," Bob said loftily. "I had nothing to do with it."

"I'll bet you didn't," he grumbled.

"Look, Steve, a lot of Waterford people trust you. They've known you since you were young, working here like everyone else. You never set yourself over anyone else. What better liaison do we have? If it's always going to be 'us' against 'them,' we'll lose, if not next week, then next year or the one after. Their portion of the population will grow far faster than ours. If there isn't someone willing to stand up and be counted on the side of common people, then there's nothing to stop 'em. We were glad to have 'em when they moved here—but now they're going to take Waterford away from us. Won't you help?"

"I will, of course," he sighed. "But tell me. How much good do you really think I can accomplish?"

Bob's face reminded him of the day, twenty years ago, that he'd hired a young boy to pick up the Pettingills' yard. "Sufficient, I hope." He smiled.

"Hi, Dad!" It was Rick, coming in after school. "Hi, Mr. Casey."

Bob waved. "Hi, pal." He tossed the empty can into the trash. "Back to the mines," he said. "Laying oak floor today." He saluted, left; the truck moved silently out of the yard.

I'm tired, Steven thought, and the day isn't over yet and the party (he was beginning to really dread it now!) had yet to begin.

Rick seated himself at the kitchen table, with half a dozen chocolate-chip cookies making crumbs everywhere and a huge glass of milk spoiling his supper.

"Well, you seem to be in a hurry," Steven said genially. "Where're you going?"

"Dan Sears. He invited me to his house."

The Sears boy had not done so before—nor, as Steven thought about it, had anyone else.

"I hope you can eat your supper, after a snack like that."

"I hope I can too," Rick said, unconcerned. "My stomach has never failed me before, though. Don't worry about it, Dad."

"I won't," Steven promised. "I'd never worry about it. But your mother might."

"Yeah. She might."

"It's her job," he said loyally, "to worry about what we eat. That's what mothers do."

"And dads worry about being able to buy it, right?"

He wondered if he and Mari had talked about their ailing finances just a bit too openly. "Yes, dads usually worry about funding."

"Except for you."

"Why except for me?" he asked, amused at whatever it was Rick would come up with next. "Pumping gas isn't exactly a highly paid occupation."

"Dan Sears says we're rich."

"He does?"

"Yup."

"Maybe because we're city people," Steven suggested. "Country people always think city people are rich. And we bought the *Jenny Lawrence,* too."

"No." Rick shook his head. "It's because we live here."

"Here? At Kingsland?" he asked stupidly. "Our family has always lived here."

"That's just what Dan said," Rick pointed out. "Our family has always lived here, and our family has always been rich."

"Hm." Probably a kid like Danny Sears would make such

an assumption, because Cousin Elizabeth always acted the part of a woman of wealth, and God knew that Charles had always behaved as though he were local nobility.

"Despite what Danny thinks, I'm afraid it just isn't true. If we were rich, we'd never take in boarders, would we, and I wouldn't be working at Roly Hall's filling station."

The chocolate-chip cookies were gone; Rick busily blotted up the crumbs with an assiduous fingertip. "They all think it though," he said at last. "Dan says so."

"Who does."

"The kids at school."

"What do they think?"

"That we're rich," Rick repeated as patiently as possible.

"Does it matter?"

"Yes, it does. It means I'm not like them. It means I'm like Junior Marshall. I don't even like Junior Marshall, Dad. I never have. And then Junior went and boasted about what great buddies we were, and the kids all backed away, because they don't like Junior either."

"Why not?" he asked around the growing dismay that his son was not happy.

"Stuck-up," Rick said.

"You said you're going to Danny's house. Is he willing to befriend you now?"

"I hope so. He and I were on the same wrestling team in gym and I showed him some stuff I learned last year. He's been pretty nice to me since then."

"With Danny Sears willing to be your friend, maybe the other kids will be willing to accept you now."

"Maybe." Rick moped. "I hope so. It's no fun always watching and never being part of anything."

He looked at the boy carefully, masking as well as he could the pain of knowing his child had been hurt. "Is that what's been going on? You're excluded?"

"Yes."

"You never said so."

"No."

"Why not?"

Rick shrugged, and into the long silence said, his voice strained, "We all wanted to live here. It was my idea, even. It was supposed to be fun. At first I thought it would change. When it didn't, I figured I'd just have to live with it. I didn't want to spoil things for everyone else, just because they weren't working for me." He picked up his glass and took it to the sink. "I'd better get going," he muttered, and hastened away, probably sorry he'd spoken at all.

The kid had been miserable all year, and his own father hadn't known it! He'd failed his son—just at the time of the boy's life when he needed guidance and encouragement most; he was on the brink of really worrying about Rick when he stopped himself. Rick was a good boy and there was evidence, after all, that his quarantine was at an end.

Don't borrow trouble, he told himself. Let it catch up with you.

And sure enough, in only a few hours it did.

Claudia and J. Barry Marshall walked in without knocking; it was their style.

"Well, we finally did it!" Claudia announced to the assembled guests. "I know you won't believe it, but it's true. Harry Mayo just got done connecting the upstairs bathroom. We can bathe again."

"And we can breathe again," quipped Karen Jackson. "How nice for you, Claudia! And the rest of us!"

"Oh, Steve," said J. Barry. "I wanted to talk to you about insulation. Here we are . . . winter's over, but the furnace just goes and goes and goes."

"You're lucky you even have a furnace," he teased. "They had pot burners in that house once."

"I'd take a Scotch and ginger ale, sweetie," Claudia instructed.

He led J. Barry into the dining room, where he and Mari had set up a temporary bar. "Spring is a long, long season here," he told J. Barry. "You're right. You should insulate."

"I suppose we could blow stuff in?"

"Sure. Or, if you were going to put new clapboards on the house as part of your renovation, you could take off the old ones and lay in bats from the outside. Wouldn't bother the interior walls that way, or be messy either."

"Claudia would have a fit, replacing the clapboards," Barry said. "They're antique."

"They sure are," Steven agreed.

"Claudia and Barry's house used to belong to your family, didn't it?" Cy Sherwin asked, coming into the dining room. A research chemist who'd lost his job, he'd come to Waterford, where he'd once spent summers in a beachfront cottage, long since washed away by high tides, and now he carved ducks more realistic than real ones, while his wife Barbara operated a craft shop in the garage, selling hideous quilts of her own making. Rumor had it that the Sherwins enjoyed a substantial stock income.

"I told Cy that our house was built by Elijah Merrick," Barry said. "And he didn't believe me."

"He should have." Steven smiled. They gathered the drinks they'd made and took them into the living room, where most of the party had gathered around the portrait of Mary and Elijah Merrick. "Barry's grandparents bought the house in the twenties. Until then our family—part of it—had always lived there. And, yes, Elijah Merrick built it."

"Personally, I've always preferred it to this place," Claudia said, accepting her drink. "Though I hope it doesn't hurt your feelings, Steven, to hear me say so."

"Of course not," he assured her politely, as though her opinion mattered to him. "My attachment to Kingsland is strictly personal. Appearance or value has very little to do with it."

"Well, Elijah Merrick was a sea captain," Claudia persisted. "I think that's very romantic! Much more romantic than being a coach driver. And Elijah's house has far more character than this one. Colonial houses are much more pure than Victorian ones."

"I don't know about that," Karen Jackson protested. "They're each so different that I'm not sure you can compare them. Both your house and this one are jewels, in my opinion, each in their own way." She smiled and nodded to Steven, as though to reassure him that Kingsland was not a white elephant.

"Perhaps you're right," Claudia reversed herself graciously and changed the subject quickly to one that suited her better. "Did you know, Steven, that once there was a formal garden laid out on the west side? I never realized that Cape Cod colonial people lived so graciously! We've found a sundial top, and old flagstones beneath the accumulation of soil that seem to have been little paths. We're doing it over this summer, putting in a fountain, planting flowerbeds."

"How charming," cried Mari.

"Junior is wild about the fountain." Barry smiled fondly. "He thinks he's going to sit in it all summer."

"We're getting a quarterboard carved, too."

"Quarterboard?" Cy asked. "Carved?"

"You know. One of those long pieces of wood with a curl up at one end and a curl down at the other, attached to old ships with the ship's name on it. People have been buying new ones and hanging them on their houses. You can use a ship's name, of course, or one that you've made up yourself. Ours shall be inscribed 'Kaptainsholme,'" she announced proudly. "Because that's what our house was."

"Kaptainsholme?"

"Spelled with a K," Claudia said. "Like they do in Vermont. When they name a ski chalet or something."

"Ski chalet?" He could hardly believe her stupidity.

"I've always enjoyed skiing," she said.

"There's no skiing on Cape Cod, luv."

"What's that got to do with it?" she asked blithely.

"It's darling, Claudia," Mari fawned. "A darling name."

"Was this house—Kingsland—built by a sea captain too?" Karen Jackson asked Mari.

"No. It was built by this gentleman." She gestured toward the grand piano over which the Great Man's portrait hung.

"It's not as old as ours," Claudia began.

"Beneath it are the foundations of the original Merrick house," Mari pressed forward. "Built in 1725. Where Elijah Merrick was born in 1768."

"Ours is—"

"And this place, Kingsland, was built by Elijah Merrick's grandson," Mari said proudly. "Maybe driving a coach isn't as romantic as sailing a ship, but Kingsley Merrick made a fortune running coaches to the gold fields in Australia, and another fortune right here in Waterford when he set up a woolen mill on the old stream west of town, to make cloth for the Union Army."

"In West Waterford?" Don Jackson exclaimed. "That's a new one. Where'd you pick that up, Mari?"

"I didn't pick it up. It's a fact."

"There's nothing there now."

"That's not my fault," she chided prettily.

Steven watched her, laughing and happy.

"Kingsley Merrick was an extraordinary man," Mari was explaining to the group. "He made two fortunes while he lived, and was close to a third, in South Africa, when he died. He founded the library, here in town, and promoted the educational system until it was so good that it outdid the private school, and he even got the two principal Protestant churches in town to unite. And you know how fussy people were about religion then!"

"Oh, yes!" They laughed as they considered the antiquated notion of the importance of religion.

"Elijah Merrick started a new religious society," Claudia chimed in, unwilling to let her place be usurped even by her friend Mari Sinclaire. "It was really a courageous thing to do, in those days. I think Elijah met his nemesis in South Africa too, didn't he, Steve?"

He disliked the position of oracle, dispenser of information. "I think so, yes," he said sulkily.

"You really know a lot!" exclaimed Karen Jackson.

"I lived here for a while with a cousin who had something of an obsession with this sort of thing," he answered suggestively—but no one caught the hint that perhaps they, too, caught in the flux of the twentieth century, were being obsessive about the stable, stationary past.

"Steven, do you know anything—anything at all—about the old Lyceum Hall?" Karen asked.

"The one that was floated across the bay to Truro?"

"That's it!" she exclaimed. "The very one!"

"No," he answered. "I don't know anything about it. They'd taken it away by the time I remember Waterford."

"There's a lot about it in the old records," Claudia said. "The town voted, after the War of 1812, to build a hall because they'd gotten into the habit of debates. A lyceum of sorts was held at our house all through the war."

"Your house?"

"Kaptainsholme," she said loftily.

"The Historical Society hopes that the town meeting will vote to move the old building back," said Karen.

"So I hear," he remarked laconically.

"You work for Roly Hall. Have you heard any comments from the locals about it?"

"You mean whether they're willing to pay for moving it, out of tax money?"

"Yes."

"Why should they want to, Karen?"

She frowned. "Because it belongs here. Because it's part of Waterford. The lyceum movement was important, too. An important part of New England's cultural heritage. It stands for our past. And the Historical Society could use it for their meetings and their museum, and in the summer it could be an information center."

"Why should the town foot the bill for the use of a private society?"

"The society is open to anyone. It's not a club, and the building would benefit the town and everyone in it."

"It would benefit people who are interested in history, and that's all."

"The Bicentennial will be here in a few years. It might get us government money. . . ."

"It's not a Revolutionary object," he argued. "Claudia just said it was built after 1812."

"But money aside," Claudia interrupted, growing agitated, "it would be good for people to get stirred up a little about their heritage. If they don't care about it, they ought to." The Marshalls deeply enjoyed enlightening the masses.

"Crap," he said. "People's heritage is their own business."

"Just because you aren't interested in yours doesn't mean that other people shouldn't be," she snapped.

His patience was thin by now. "Let's return to the subject at hand, which was your question about local feeling. I think it isn't favorable."

"We need at least fifty natives on our side," Claudia said. "Would you be willing to speak for it at town meeting?"

Everyone was watching.

"No."

He could sense Mari's dismay. He was nearly certain that she had assured everyone that her husband, scion of the house of Merrick, would work in behalf of history.

"Why not?" Claudia's voice rose in her disappointment.

"Because if the Historical Society thinks the building's so important, it should raise the money itself, instead of making everyone else pay whether they want to or not."

"Oh, shoot, Steve," she said persuasively. "The society tried that years ago—but they never seemed to get as much as they needed. Why, it'd take forever for us to raise enough—and with costs being what they are today, it's just about impossible. Besides, that wonderful building won't always be available. We have to act! We have to act now! You aren't as alien to them as we are. You could persuade them, dammit. And if we could muster up one hundred total votes, we'd have it."

"Look," he argued. "Waterford folks don't always agree with each other. But until now they've argued things out on the floor of town meeting and made decisions then and there, either on the basis of arguments they've just heard, or their gut response. Not a little pushy group packing the meeting."

"Nonsense," Claudia said briskly. "There's only one way to get anything done, and that's to organize."

"There's only one way that a town the size of this one can function as it was meant to function, and that's if everyone tries to understand the other fellow's point of view. Why have you come here, after all? You want to be part of a way of life different from what you left, isn't that so? And now you want to ram your ideas down the throat of the Waterford local, as you're pleased to call him. Ideas that may have been appropriate to the places you came from, but are apt to be wholly inappropriate here. If you insist on your own way, you'll destroy what you came here to find."

They stared, as though he had descended into their midst from another planet.

"Waterford's the way it is because it's been left alone," he argued into the silence. "It's been allowed its own course, and it can accommodate you all if you'll just let it be and take what it offers you."

"It's growing too fast for that," said Barbara Sherwin. "If we don't move to save it now, it'll be lost."

"If you impose your own values on it, you'll have killed it before it ever had a chance to survive."

Surreptitiously they glanced at one another.

"I brought my sketches," Wendy Lane said loudly, attempting to lighten the tone of the party which was falling into shambles. "Would you like to see them?"

"Oh, yes, please!" Mari cried in delight and despair, throwing Steven a look that demanded his silence. "I found an easel in the barn, Wendy! You can set up your stuff on it." Busily she propped it open and everyone gathered around. Steven, on the fringes of the group, drifted into the dining room to mix himself another drink.

"The gist of my book will be this," Wendy said, setting a charcoal sketch on the easel. "That on our really old houses—particularly the small ones, the Cape Coddy ones—each chimney is different. Its bricks are set in unique patterns, and often the shapes are different too. Each has a distinct personality." She set another sketch on the easel, and sure enough, it was different.

"You'll make a fortune," Barry predicted. "It's terrific, Wendy."

Actually the sketches were both artistic and interesting, and Steven found himself wondering why he had never noticed such craftsmanship on the old houses before. It was like the window in a cathedral he'd read about so many years ago he couldn't remember where—a little, insignificant window that made its church famous. . . . He thought about the little perfect window and then about other small attainments and achievements that approached perfection, like shingling a house well, or growing a rosebush, or sailing a boat. Blearily he mixed another drink, making it stronger this time, parking himself in a corner where he was out of the way and could observe the group, which in turn tried to avoid him while pretending not to.

Why did they insist on taking Waterford away? he wondered. Why!

By the time everyone left, he was stoned.

"Well!" Mari sat herself emphatically in a nearby chair. "You certainly were the life of the party."

"Full of joy," he agreed. When he looked at her, two Maris looked back, but proudly he noticed that he spoke quite clearly.

We seafarers know how to hold our liquor, he told himself, and nodded in self-agreement.

"What I think, Mar, is that it would have been really something to see that old Lyceum Hall floating across the bay to Truro. Maybe the Historical Society should take on the project of floating it permanently. They could make a tea-room out of it. Move it around on request, don't you know. Take tea and see the world." He giggled.

"All you can do is make fun of everything," she said icily. "You can't take anything seriously."

"Kaptainsholme," he said. "Do you believe that calling the old Merrick house Kaptainsholme deserves my reverence?"

"Claudia can call it whatever she wants."

"She surely can," he said, slipping on so many sibilants. "And she surely will, and it doesn't matter a hell of a lot. But to see you genuflecting over it is hard to take, Mar."

"You belittle things because you don't understand them," she retorted.

"Untrue. I unnerstand a good deal."

"You belittle Claudia because you don't like her," she said, not listening.

"You're right, for once. And you know what? I think it's a shame, Mar, that the ideas of a shallow show-off like Claudia Marshall mean more to you than mine."

She stopped short. "That's not exactly the way it is," she said slowly.

"Not exactly, maybe, but the fact is that you buy her opinions lock, stock, and barrel. Don't you?"

"I hope you aren't so medieval that you think a wife ought to parrot her husband."

"I think an intelligent woman ought to uphold a point of view with integrity to it, instead of one that works on appearances," he announced with drunken dignity.

"Well, then?" she demanded. "Let's have it."

"Have what?"

"Your point of view. The one with integrity. One, no doubt, you've picked up from Bob Casey while he makes a fortune accommodating the building boom."

"Below the belt, Mar." He wagged a waggish finger. "Waterford is changing, whether Bob Casey builds houses or not. Whether Roly Hall pumps gas or not, or Linc Sears swills his gin, or Eben Gray digs clams, Waterford is changing. Those folks are willing to accept those changes the way they've always done—by moving over and sharing what they have."

"Oh, spare me," Mari sneered.

"And I shall speak for them. They feel inadequate to do it, and they've asked me to help, and if you really want to know, I'm damn proud they have. I'll be their man at town meeting."

"You mean in public?" she gasped. "You're going to speak in public?"

"Yup. Best place. In public. Hardly pays to speak anywhere else."

"Please, Steve!" she cried. "Honey, please."

"But I have to," he tried to explain. "I want to. And I'm going to."

She watched him silently, then walked to the stairs. "Well, I guess that's that." she started up. "Thanks a lot," she said over her shoulder.

Gosh, he commiserated with himself. It was enough to make a guy feel bad. It was enough to make a guy think he needed another highball before retiring to the cold, unforgiving side of his wife.

In fact, it was enough for two.

It was a disaster.

"Folks who had to hire a baby-sitter and didn't—it's really on account of them," said Leaf, stopping by for two dollars worth on his way from one building inspection to another. "Why, if everyone had come who should have come, it'd be a different story."

"Maybe so," Steven agreed half-heartedly, slopping soapy water on Leaf's windshield, squeegeeing it off.

What difference did it make? They had lost.

"Thanks," Leaf said, pushing his two dollars into Steven's hand. "And thanks for doing what you did last night."

"Okay."

"Better luck next time, huh?"

"Sure." Except that there would be no next time, and they both knew it. The road was all downhill from here. He took the two dollars in, rang it up, whisked back out to await the next customer, thereby avoiding Roly Hall, who'd been sitting at his desk all morning pretending to be engrossed in paperwork.

Don Slater honked as he went by, and Steven lifted a hand in acknowledgment—a casual, lackadaisical gesture—a signal of recognition, really, rather than a greeting. For countrymen did not wave enthusiastically, nor did they greet one another loudly. Only people from the city did that.

It's gone, he thought with something like panic. Roly and Leaf Stone, Don Slater and Bob—even me, maybe—we're relics. How could we have let it happen?

How could you have prevented it? he asked himself. It was in the cards as soon as suburbia started coming here.

He clenched his fists in helpless anger—for it had seeped away, the life he had come to find.

You'll just have to adjust, he told himself firmly. It's better than Boise or Portland or Denver, isn't it?"

I don't know, he thought. Perhaps it is. Perhaps it's not. . . .

It was eleven o'clock, and he could no longer put off facing Roly. Reluctantly he headed into the office, pulled up a chair. Roly had forsaken his bills and receipts and was uncapping the pint of rye he always kept handy at the back of his tool cabinet.

"Have some?"

"No, thanks." They sat for a while. "What does a dog officer do?" Steven asked, for this was Roly's only official position now.

"Gets animals off the beaches mostly. They aren't allowed there. He coaxes 'em into the car with a piece of Mrs. Hall's coffee cake and takes 'em to the Animal Rescue League. Not very exciting," Roly said sadly, drank deeply, stared out the window. "There's an awful lot of folks who've taken town meetin' for granted all their lives. And still do. They didn't come. If they had, maybe things'd be different."

"Maybe. But everything here at the station will stay the same, Roly. Everyone will still come by. They'll still sit around, drinking your coffee and filling you in on the gossip. You won't notice. . . ."

Roly lifted wounded eyes to his. "They booed."

"Yes," he said. "I heard them. I'm sorry, Roly."

It had not happened before. Waterford, whether it liked what it heard or not, had always given its people uncluttered liberty to speak. But not last night. And to make it worse, when the booing and hissing was stopped by the moderator, the booers and hissers retaliated by not listening, by whispering to one another, not once looking up at Roly Hall, sweating on the stage of the school auditorium while he explained that if people took responsibility for one another, as they had done up to now, there was no need for a large police force.

At least they had listened to Steven Sinclaire, even if their vote had not reflected it. Only the Lyceum article lost, and it was surely the beginning of the end of Waterford as he'd known it.

"You really spoke good," Roly said. "I was proud, Steve. Really proud. Will that zonin' article about business hurt you?"

"No. We're already on the tax records," he mumbled, ashamed though not responsible that he was protected while the next man to work for himself was not. "If you aren't the cop, what will happen to Eben and Mrs. Gray if they're caught camping in the woods beside the Warden place?"

"Don't ask me," Roly growled. "I done what I could for 'em. Now I can't do no more. The clam warden'll get 'em if the new chief don't. We don't do things the way they want," he burst out. "It's their town now. Or will be soon. They might just as well run it the way they want, and do it now, rather than later. Eben will have to take his licks, just like the rest of us."

There were tears gathering in Roly's eyes, but he manfully blinked them away, pouring himself another drink. When he lowered the shot glass, they were gone.

"What'll you do now?" Steven asked respectfully, as one might ask a man recently widowed.

"I'll think about it," Roly said firmly. "Have some land in Maine. Maybe I'll go there. Cape Codders have always gone down to Maine when things get too thick. A lot of us own property there." He nodded, poured another shot; the bell rang, and he departed to fill the tank of the waiting car. Steven did not wait for his return because it seemed indecent not to leave the man alone with his reconciliations and adjustments and the relinquishing of his place.

He really hated to go home. He hadn't seen Mari last night; she'd left early, after the Lyceum article had been defeated, and had been asleep (or pretending to be) when he came in, and now, most certainly, there'd be awkwardness between her and himself, not only because he had balked her group and put her on the spot, but also because up to the time she'd left, she hadn't once voted to curb the inroads of the newcomers.

He fetched a can of beer from the refrigerator and wandered into the parlor, where she sat with Mary Deems, hemming curtains for the new bedrooms.

"It's a little early for that, isn't it?" she asked, nodding in the direction of the can he held.

"A refresher," he said, without apologizing for it. He sat silently beside her. What was he supposed to say? he wondered bitterly. Congratulate her for being on the winning side? On the side of people unable to see the fragility, the delicate balance of the little town they were ruining.

Just don't think about it, he advised. Let it alone. Maybe it'll work out better than you think, given time.

"What will the gang use for a clubhouse?" he asked ungraciously.

"The Historical Society headquarters, you mean?"

"Yes."

"One of our members has a very old barn that he thinks would move well. The society will have it hauled out to West Waterford and we'll fix it up and make it into a museum. The Lyceum would have been a lot classier . . . but . . ." She shrugged philosophically. "That's the best we can do."

"It's wonderful, what you people manage to salvage out of nothing," he said sarcastically.

Throwing him a dirty look, she stalked out to the kitchen.

He thought about it for a while, resting, relaxing with his beer, and wished he could find something else to concentrate on.

"Dad, could I talk with you for a minute" It was Kathy, home for the lunch break, peering out from behind her eye-covering bangs.

"Sure, honey," he said expansively, glad for a distraction. "What is it?"

"Well, Dad," she said, primly pulling at her miniskirt as she sat down, her bony knees clamped together. "It's something I've wanted to discuss with you for some time."

"Go on."

"Dad, I really wish you'd stop pumping gas at Mr. Hall's station."

He stared at her, trying to think of something to say.

"I mean, it's embarrassing," she said, speaking carefully, as though he were hard of hearing or not right in the head. "I mean, it's not as though you aren't smart enough to do something more . . . more . . ."

"Respectable?"

She frowned. "'Respectable' isn't quite it. Sometimes it's very definitely square—being respectable, I mean. But pumping gas, Dad! That's not exactly cool, either."

"What would you suggest?" he asked, glad he was sitting down, because he was suddenly feeling very tired.

"Uncle Barry Marshall works in Boston."

"Yes, I know."

"Mr. Jackson sells real estate."

"I'm aware of that, too."

"Mr. Sherman carves ducks. A little square, but at least his hands are clean. Look at yours, Dad."

His were very definitely not clean. The grime was so ground in that he'd have to grow a whole layer of new skin, but he had not considered it shameful before. In fact, he'd been a little proud of it.

"How about the *Jenny Lawrence*," he asked. "Is it 'in' or is it 'out' to own a windjammer?"

"In. Very definitely."

"My hands get dirty on *Jenny*, too."

"It's different, Dad," she said patronizingly. "You know it is."

"Honey, even if the *Lawrence* succeeded, I might want to go on pumping gas." It was impossible to be sure of her response because of all the hair covering her face in teen fashion.

"Oh, gosh, why?" she groaned.

"It keeps me in touch with people."

"You must mean the natives."

She said it as though she lived in Zululand among Pygmies with topknots.

He looked at her, wondering who she was, wondering where she'd gone and if she could be found again; he looked at her and realized that everything she could have learned from Waterford had evaded her understanding, and in consequence, he'd lost her. Somehow she'd slipped through his fingers, and the integrity he knew lay here, close to the land, was passing her by, too deep for her yet childish understanding, too subtle for her yet childish observation. Her friends were the children of Mari's friends, and their standards were hers. She had gone away.

Her face, unscored by years of experience or wisdom, was

clouding now, her mouth quivered; his little girl began to cry. "They make me feel like a worm," she said. "They keep calling you Tony the Tiger, like in the gasoline ad, and they call me pussy—like in a little tiger cat. And then everyone laughs. If it weren't for the *Jenny Lawrence,* I'd be cut altogether."

Did nothing ever, ever work?

"Is it square that your mother is going to run a tourist home here?"

"No, it's okay," she explained, wiping her tears, which disappeared as quickly as they had come. "Their parents all do touristy things. Everyone here does. But clean things, Dad. Clever things. Not dirty things that only ignorant country people do because they're too stupid to do anything else."

His face must have turned scarlet, because Kathy was backing out of the room. "I'm sorry if you don't like it, but that's the way it is," she flung over her shoulder, and her flat-soled shoes clattered on the stairs and her bedroom door whanged shut and he was left alone with her unhappiness. And Mari's. And his own. And, now that he remembered, Rick's.

We've blown it, he thought. We've blown it before we even started. No one is happy and we're broke and Mari and I don't even like what each other stands for.

Is that the lesson Waterford can teach you, Sinclaire? he asked himself bitterly. Come to the shore, live close to the land, get in touch with yourself, and discover that everyone close to you is miserable. And that the town itself is slipping away, its values eroded, only a shell left. Waterford, upon whose values he had planned to base his life.

Maybe, Sinclaire, you're all wet.

No, sir, he told himself back. It's not over. There's still a summer at sea with *Jenny Lawrence.* A summer of finding out what you're really made of, as only the sea can teach you. A summer to show Mari and the kids what working out your own destiny can mean. Hell, we haven't even started yet! Waterford isn't dead yet! There's still plenty left for us. And there's *Jenny Lawrence.* Soon the season would be upon them, and *Jenny* would be his.

He would just have to hang on until then.

23

The sun was benevolent, reflected off the water in countless prisms, its indolent warmth drawing from the old decking and new paint of the *Jenny Lawrence* a saltiness unimaginable anywhere else. His heart glad and singing, the breeze gentle on his cheek, Steven stood in the bow with a knife in his hand, ready to cut the anchor rope if necessity called for it. Nearby, Jerry Ferris, first mate, was poised to throw the monkey's fist; in the cockpit Bob Casey watched Eric intently, ready to do his bidding, whatever it was. In the aftercabin Mari and Barbara Casey tried to talk to each other and to the hostess-cook whom Eric had hired—a young woman who was entirely too good-looking to suit them. Climbing around on the ratlines above, Rick served as watch; Kathy leaned on the rail where she had been waving all morning, from Fair Haven to Hobbes Hole, to the cars that honked and the people who everywhere signaled vigorously, welcoming *Jenny*'s well-publicized first voyage of the season.

Proudly *Jenny* approached the Hobbes Hole wharf. Her new paint shone and all her brass fittings had been polished and little gaily colored flags adorned her stays: *Jenny* was a middle-aged bride who had become young again, with attendants holding her train and admirers throwing flowers. On the wharf waited her following of old as well as the uninitiated who'd been attracted by the promotions and advertising, and the press and the first week's complement of passengers. All thirty for a full house, a band of happy pilgrims seeking the oblivion of a week at sea.

"Eric," called Jerry Ferris with the monkey's fist, "I can't throw this damn thing without braining someone."

"Maybe they'll move back," Eric suggested calmly from

the wheel, but he turned to Bob and said something that Steven could not hear. Bob instantly disappeared over the stern; only moments later the motor of the freshly tuned-up yawl boat roared.

The breeze, gentle as it was, filled the huge sails; near—too near—the crowd on the wharf cheered and inched even farther forward, appearing to pay no attention to the harbor hand working his way to the front in hopes of catching the fist when Jerry threw it. There were people of every description, young and old, in shorts and plaid pants and knee sox and sunglasses, wearing odd hats and carrying peculiar parcels, all out to amuse themselves for their holiday.

Eric called to Jerry now, his words unintelligible, but his voice urgent. Jerry dropped the fist and jumped to the deck where the donkey engine was housed. With a sinking heart and an instant loss of faith, Steven saw Eric nod in his direction, but without hesitation he obeyed the agreed-upon signal, cut the anchor rope and stood aside as the chain tore through its hole, sudden and violent like a load of gravel sliding off a dump truck.

"Ready about," Eric called, and *Jenny* jibbed, her enormous spread of canvas traveling from port to starboard with a lethal crack; she zipped around on the axis of the anchor chain, began to edge up to the dock, while all around them the pale worried faces of Chris Craft owners watched, and on the wharf, the cheering became wilder. The donkey engine sputtered to life and pulled up the anchor, now no longer necessary for the prevention of disaster, and the yawl boat, like a sheep dog, harried *Jenny* to the dock, where she was snugged up to the old tires that hung there, tied fast by the harbor hand, who had made it to the front of the crowd at last.

Mari and Barbara, blithely unaware that the *Lawrence* had survived her first near-miss, came up the three steps from the aftercabin, waving at the crowd, laughing and, no doubt, feeling like celebrities.

"Ready for the press, ladies?" Eric made a sweeping gesture toward the wharf. "You pour, Arleen," he said to the girl he'd hired as cook. "I'll amuse. The ladies here will circulate and keep the party going. And the kids"—he winked to Rick and Kathy—"will direct the new passengers to the aftercabin, where Steve will rake in the money. Bob and Jerry will stand around looking nautical, and at one-thirty they will clear the deck. Hopefully we sail at two."

"Hopefully?" Bob asked.

"Weather permitting." Eric nodded. "Now, move!"

Steven took his place at the aftercabin table with the book of reservations and the strongbox and settled himself to meet the first group of paying passengers.

They came in all sizes and shapes, but in only one color: white. They made their way eagerly to the aftercabin, paid their money, listened while he described the table sittings for supper, the routine of the ship when at sea and when in port, the locations of the toilets and the drinking-water barrel with its dipper, the limitations of the generator and hence of reading in bed at night.

In the galley, which he could see through the connecting window, Arleen Patterson, Eric's newly hired hostess, was dispensing ice and beer from the forward locker, pouring highballs into paper cups with a friendly smile; she'd brewed a pot of coffee, too, for anyone who wanted it.

In the cockpit he heard Eric carrying on at a wonderful clip, for the benefit of the press. "The *Lawrence* is one-hundred years old. She was designed for use in the coast trade, taking goods up and down the Atlantic seaboard. Potatoes from Maine, shellfish from Maryland, iron from Pennsylvania, bullshit from New York." Laughter, joy, scribbling of notes by the press.

Steven assigned bunk space, refraining from calling the cubicles below staterooms (although Mari and Barbara always did), explained that the lavatories, nautically called heads, please, were operated by a foot pedal and were extremely delicate, so would *everyone* refrain from putting *anything* extraneous down them? He heard Mari outside, and Barbara Casey, talking knowledgeably to visitors while Bob circulated, making sure the press had all the information and alcohol it wanted. At two o'clock they left, except for Rick, excused from this, the last week of school, and the passengers and crew prepared to take up another life in another time, when weather and the tide determined the tempo of a man's life and ultimately controlled it. Rick busied himself with coiling lines, acting the part of cabin boy as he best understood it, while Steven sidled into the cockpit; Eric was drinking with a half-dozen passengers, showing them charts and explaining their hieroglyphics.

It was two-thirty, well past the hour of expected departure.

"Well, Steve!" Eric acknowledged his presence affably.

"Well, Skipper," he boomed back with equal affability, as though they were putting on a stage play. "How's it doing?"

"Yes, Captain," asked a spectacled man with a nautical cap. "When will we leave?"

Expectantly the other five watched, eyes bright.

Carelessly Eric looked to the landward side of the vessel, over the wharves and sheds and the town. "Not yet," he said, rolling up a chart. "Why don't you folks have another drink?" Pleasantly he looked in Steven's direction.

"Sure, folks," he was bound to say. "There's a whole section in the forward bulkhead full of ice and ginger ale for setups. Now that the press is off the vessel, I regret to announce that spirits are not supplied by the house except for truly spectacular occasions, such as a write-up in the Boston *Herald* or the ramming of another ship at sea."

Happily the guests laughed. "But since we're not on the high seas yet," Eric put in, surprising him, "help yourselves to the bourbon, Scotch, and rye, which you'll find in the first bunk next to the forward head."

"When the hell do we sail?" Steven asked after the guests had gone. "Why did you offer them our private liquor supply? They didn't pay to sit at the wharf in Hobbes Hole and drink themselves blind."

Again Eric glanced landward. "According to the friggin' flag flying over the post office, the wind is still steady from the wrong quarter. We can't buck the wind and the tide, too, Steve. Either we'll have to wait until the tide's strong on its way out, or hope the wind dies."

"How long will it be before the tide is right?"

"In about two hours. But I think the wind will drop before then, and the yawl boat can give us a push. Once we're on the other side of the jetty, we can sail wherever we want. Just be sure no one goes ashore."

"Half of them are there already," he protested. "And the other half will want to go pretty soon, if they have to sit around here any longer."

"Well, they'd better stay the hell aboard," Eric said mildly. "In case the wind drops. I don't want to sail into Edgartown harbor after dark. In fact, I won't. If the passengers are farting around Hobbes Hole and we miss our chance because we have to wait for them—why, old buddy, we won't go out at all."

"We have to sail today," he agonized. "We said we would."

"Sailor," Eric said severely, "nobody argues with the tide. You ought to know that."

"But—"

"The charm of a wind-driven vessel is that you're driven

by the wind—isn't that right? You're dependent upon the elements, not manmade power, for Chrissake. This is the way it is. This is the way it's always been. Now, round up those effing customers. Keep the booze flowing. If they're having a nice cocktail party, they won't care whether they're moving or whether they aren't. Find Arleen; tell her to start supper. We can always eat if there's nothing else to do."

"Okay," he assented grudgingly. It was true. If the passengers were eating, at least something was happening; the arrival of cooked food would reassure them that their welfare was being considered, even if the elements were uncooperative. And food might offset the tremendous amount of liquor being consumed.

The corridor below was so narrow that two people could not pass without one of them flattening himself to the wall to let the other by. He ducked the two padded beams running from one side of the vessel to the other, squirmed by various passengers until he reached Arleen's berth near the forward head. He knocked on the door, but there was no answer, nor did she answer his call. From within the lavatory the flushing mechanism sloshed and moaned as its occupant furiously worked the foot pump, but he was not cool enough to knock, certainly not to linger, waiting to find out if its inhabitant was Arleen.

He worked his way toward the galley again, and went topside to see if she had simply escaped his first search.

She wasn't there, either.

He was getting annoyed now; if he couldn't find her, he'd have to start dinner himself, and God knew he was a novice. He peeked down into the captain's berth, on the port bow; it was empty. That left the mate's; when he opened its hatch cover, Jerry Ferris looked up, his hands cupping the fair whiteness of Arleen Patterson's spectacular breasts. Unable to take his eyes off her, Steven tried to speak and could not find his voice.

"We need you in the galley," he croaked at last.

"Who needs me in the galley?" she called up, and laughed; in dismay, he realized that she was very drunk.

He summoned what he hoped was a commanding tone. "Never mind, honey," he called down. "Ferris, get your ass up here!"

Reluctantly Jerry came, scowling, dropped the hatch cover as Arleen snuggled herself into his bunk for an unworried snooze.

"I don't care a damn about your morals," Steven explained

as reasonably as he was able. "But I care about this ship and how she runs. We're due to sail soon. Arleen's supposed to fix a meal, and she can't, thanks to you. Stay topside, Jerry."

"Okay, okay." Jerry waved away his offense. "But she was pretty well boozed up when I found her in the galley, Steve. It's not all my fault." He went off in search of Eric while Steven approached the galley, starting the stove, fanning the flames until the dial read four hundred degrees, mixing cornbread, according to the directions Mari had printed, for the feeding of thirty people.

Up on deck he could hear the party in progress, Eric moving among the merrymakers, his voice joyful above theirs until he began calling instructions and the passengers erupted into farewells and cheers. *Jenny* was going out!

He slipped up to the deck to help cast off the lines, to start the yawl, to raise the sails, to watch the shore slowly, slowly slide away until they passed the jetties and the breeze caught them, drew them onward and *Jenny* was on her own—and smoke was pouring from the galley.

Clearly the cook was in no position to enjoy sailing, much as he'd have liked to!

He mixed himself a drink, got another batch of cornbread going, piled tossed salad by the handful on plates, and handed them up to the aftercabin through the connecting window. Rick, who was looking green, distributed them around the table, along with the silver. The chowder had been made already by Arleen and only needed heating; he managed not to scorch it.

"First sitting! First sitting!" He rounded up ten of the least sober, fed them, cut cake, already baked, put up another ten salads, another ten soup bowls, another set of silverware.

He hadn't felt so competent in years, so entirely capable, serene in facing the tasks that lay ahead, strong, confident.

"Dad," confided Rick, "I think I'm going to throw up." He disappeared into the head and stayed there.

Steven heated water for dishes and started on them, bracing himself against the surge of the ship; he joined the third sitting himself, lingering happily over his supper, talking to passengers. It was a well-fed, content, and cheery passenger load that watched as the *Jenny Lawrence* cruised into Edgartown at dusk, bearing down on the yacht-filled harbor like a great bird coming in to feed.

"Ready about," Eric called, and into an incredibly small pocket near shore the *Lawrence* dived and wheeled, her sails crackling, her bowsprit swooping above the deck of a nearby yacht, barely clearing it, while its owner crouched by its tiller, hands over his eyes.

"Cut," Eric called, and Steven severed the anchor rope, the chain slipping loudly through its hole and then abruptly stopping as the anchor hit bottom. The sails sagged as the *Lawrence* quietly headed up into the wind, drifting to the end of her tether. All around them in the beautiful harbor, power-driven craft coughed to life, lifted anchor, moved away. Night was approaching and the passengers would be ferried to shore to play, to shop at the tourist traps awaiting them, to sample the bars, to walk around the tiny, picturesque town that whaling captains had built. Laughter and music were already emanating from the yacht club, which hung out over the water.

"Jesus," Steven muttered to Eric as Jerry loaded the yawl for its first run. "Couldn't Jerry have pushed us in, instead of tearing up the harbor at sixty miles an hour?"

"We weren't going sixty." Eric chuckled. "Besides, I like to see all those worried faces, watching us from their million-dollar Chris Crafts, wondering if we're going to spare them."

"What if the wind shifts? What if something goes wrong? We'd never survive the lawsuits."

"We have no power," Eric reminded him. "It's up to them to keep out of our way. But nothing will go wrong. With a vessel this large, it'd take more than a wind shift in a sheltered harbor to alter her direction. She'll go where I tell her to go. Honest, Steve. Just relax."

"Should we furl the sails?" he asked. "Since we're here for the night?" They were enormous.

"Christ, no," said Eric. "We'd just have to raise 'em again in the morning."

"We just leave them?"

"Standard practice, believe me. We're all set."

"All right. Now that we're clear on that score, I want to speak to you about Arleen," he began.

"Mr. Sinclaire," interrupted a pretty woman, coming up the companionway to await going to town with the next yawl load. "I'm afraid the bathroom is plugged up."

"The head, you mean," chided Eric playfully.

"Oh, yes, the head."

"Which one?" Steven asked warily.

"Well, both of them, actually."

"There are nice restrooms at the Sunoco station," Eric suggested. "We'll fix up the toilets while you're ashore."

"Oh, thanks." She looked dubious, but whether she was

worried about the Sunoco station or the crew's ability to repair the facilities aboard, there was no way of telling. She climbed over the side and into the yawl.

"She probably plugged at least one of them herself," Eric said scornfully. "No matter how big a sign you put up, they'll try to flush down a Kotex every time. Well, old fellow, it's your baby."

"I know," he said gamely. "And after I unplug the heads, I'll finish the dishes. The life of a sailor."

"Where's Rick? He's supposed to help you."

"Asleep. He was seasick all the way over. I think I'll leave him."

"He's your kid." Eric shrugged. "But he's aboard to help, not to sleep."

"Slave driver!"

"The ship sinks unless everyone does their part," Eric said seriously. "And that includes everyone, cabin boy to captain."

There could be no doubt that Eric was prepared to go to the limit when it came to making *Jenny* a success. He was turning now to help the last of the passengers onto the yawl, which, despite the calmness of the evening, pitched to a different rhythm than the *Jenny Lawrence*. He was truly spectacular in his role, invaluable, gallant with the girls, well-met with the men, gracious, charming.

"If they're happy, and get their money's worth, they'll talk about the *Lawrence* for the rest of their lives," he said, waving to the passengers until the yawl headed in. They leaned together on the rail. "They'll talk about her to their neighbors, and their friends, and their business associates, and they'll throw more business our way than any advertising we could possibly scare up."

"Certainly they'll be happy, the way you're treating them," Steven observed. "You can tell me now, Eric, and I won't breathe a word of it—but isn't that why you made such a spectacular entrance into the harbor? To please them? Give 'em something to talk about?"

Eric laughed. "With a ship like *Jenny*, anything she does is spectacular. She's a spectacular lady." He patted her old scarred side. "She's quite a gal. She has an image to live up to, and so do I. Just now I shall go ashore and polish my reputation as a man who knows how to hold his liquor."

"About Arleen . . ."

"What about her?"

"She was too drunk to fix supper."

Eric frowned. "Where the Christ was she hiding?"

"Jerry's bunk."

"I'll straighten her out," Eric pronounced. "Later tonight, when she's sobered up. One more chance, I'll tell her. And I'll mean it." The yawl was sidling up to starboard now, returned from its last passenger load. "I'd offer to help with the dishes"—he grinned—"but it's bad for my image. You understand."

"Oh. Yes, indeedy."

"Have a ball. A bent coat hanger will probably do the job on the head. If you haven't figured it out by the time I get back, I'll help. And that's a promise. And, by the way, the bilge could probably stand pumping."

Over the side he went, landing lightly in the yawl boat, draped himself in proper attitude on the prow while Jerry chauffeured him ashore.

It took an hour and a half to do the dishes, a half-hour to pump the bilge, and forty-five minutes to unplug the toilets. Exhausted, he fell, fully clothed, into his bunk; at five o'clock he would pry himself out, ready to start up the stove, in case Arleen wasn't able, prepare bacon and eggs and toast and take on ice and steaks and fresh corn and, oh, Jesus, something for sandwiches. Above him, Rick breathed heavily, serenely uninterrupted in his slumbers despite Eric's commands to the contrary. Steven did not decide on sandwich filling because sleep overtook him; he did not hear the straggling return of the passengers, each cautioned to be as quiet as possible out of consideration for those who had retired earlier than themselves. It was not until dawn that he was wakened—by the pounding sneakered feet of Jerry Ferris running along the decks as he rinsed them off with seawater—to the new, soft clean day that awaited, full of expectation: a day with horrendous amounts of work in it, a day with the prospect of joy in it, a short sail over to Vineyard Haven and a day in town, and the day after that a long sail to Nantucket, the open sea, its vastness, its release.

"Out of the sack!" he called to Rick, bouncing the upper bunk mattress with his knees, and then he climbed to the deck for a shower of salt water from the barrel suspended for that purpose, felt the tremendous lift that came—and could only come—with the prospect of success wrested from the sea. Yes, *Jenny*'s promise would be fulfilled, because he and Eric would make it happen!

24

"Hell and damnation," Eric howled. "You should have called me. You knew the wind had changed, for Christ's sake! You entered it in the log." He jabbed at the page, at the entry: "LOG OF THE JENNY LAWRENCE TO VINEYARD HAVEN. 1750: Anchor near shore wind SW," and the entry that followed it, "0100: Wind shift to NNE."

The breeze had reversed itself, and *Jenny* was stuck in the mud.

Normally only Eric touched the log. It was the sacred prerogative of the captain, and Jerry Ferris had not only usurped that prerogative but also had not responded properly to the information he had observed.

Jerry stood his ground. "If you hadn't been so busy screwing around, Skipper, you'd have done something about it yourself, and we wouldn't be aground now."

"Shit and manure," Eric shouted. "You just leave my screwing out of it. Read this, instead." Insistently he pushed the logbook into Jerry's unwilling hands. "Go ahead. Here. This notice posted on the front cover."

"Night orders," Jerry read in an elaborately bored voice. " 'Call me for any shift in the wind that requires a course change.' But we couldn't change course," Jerry pointed out innocently, "because we weren't under sail."

"You bird-turd. Let me know from now on, okay?"

"Okay," Jerry agreed.

Eric prudently abandoned the discussion, since to belabor Jerry further was nonproductive, leaned his elbows on the roof of the aftercabin, scrubbed his scalp. "We'll just have to hope that she floats on high tide, is all. The passengers'll have to fend for themselves."

"Let's take them for a tour," Arleen suggested. Any relation that she had enjoyed, intimate or otherwise, with either the captain or his first mate, was forgotten in view of the present difficulty. "Bikes," she said. "We'll rent them. I'll make up a picnic for everyone, and we'll end up at the beach. This early in the day there'll be plenty of bikes—and it's a beautiful day for a ride. The Vineyard's flat—even city people can manage it, Eric. They'll love it, and anyone who doesn't want to go can spend the day in Vineyard Haven. Their choice." Vineyard Haven offered only limited entertainment and it had been explored the day before. "I'll make sandwiches—right now."

She grinned, and the three of them, all of whom had seen her in varying degrees of nakedness, admired her as she leaned back against the rail, the sun bright in her hair, her bare legs nicely curved, her waist small and her bosom a soft, upright, pert shelf beneath her blouse. It bounced as she briskly set out for the galley, and all of them sighed, her transgressions forgiven.

The girl was enough to awaken the lust in any man, and certainly sufficient to cause a captain to forget the compass at one o'clock in the morning. Steven sighed and looked at the near shore, which had been brought closer to the *Lawrence*'s 180-degree change of position around her anchor, and waited while Arleen, who'd been stoned yesterday but showed no evidence of a hangover today, fed the crew and the passengers, washed up the dishes, constructed a picnic for thirty people, and cajoled them all into the bike tour. Laughing and loving the whole idea, everyone clambered into the yawl boat and climbed onto the bikes Arleen had found for them; waving happily at the captain and crew, they took off like a flock of gaily colored geese. When the tide rose, the crew and captain took turns with the yawl boat in an attempt to haul, push, and coax the *Jenny Lawrence* out of the mud; the wind was still from the northeast, blowing toward shore, so that the sails were useless. The motor on the yawl began to stutter under the strain, and finally it quit altogether, casting a pall of silence on the scene.

The *Jenny Lawrence* had not moved.

"You know," Steven said to Eric, "a man could get discouraged under these conditions."

"Oh, hell. Don't let this get you down!" Eric waved it all away. "We'll hire the effing harbor tug. No problem, Steve."

"What about that?" He pointed at the yawl, where Jerry was poking at the motor.

"I'll go ashore now and find someone who can fix it. Have yourself a snooze until I get back."

"A snooze!" he exploded. "Goddamm it, Eric, we just paid to have that engine overhauled. If we have to keep tinkering with it . . ."

"Relax, partner." Eric's voice became very firm. "It needs a new motor—and new motors are very expensive. I'm sure we can get through the summer on this one. Not without difficulty, but we'll make it. Then we'll know how much profit there is, and how much of a new one we can afford. Nothing ever goes *right* when you sail. Come on! Loosen up. We'll make it fine. You just have to roll with it, you know that."

That was part of sailing, and its power, Steven told himself, watching Eric row away in the dinghy. To lie back and measure yourself by your ability to handle whatever it was the sea threw at you. Wasn't it?

Well, it would take a little while, he consoled himself. After all, he hadn't lived aboard a seventy-ton schooner very long. Naturally he had to condition himself.

Eric brought back a mechanic; a tug chugged alongside; the *Lawrence* was dragged out of the mud, the tug (*Harriet R.*, Captain Holms) paid, the yawl repaired by the mechanic. The ship was theirs again.

"I suppose I should check the bilge," Eric said finally. He made no move to do so. "I kind of hate to," he confessed. "It'll be bad. Stuck like that, her goddamn planking is bound to have worked and loosened some calking."

It was bad enough. There was three feet of water forward, and they took turns pumping for the rest of the afternoon until the passengers returned from the picnic Arleen had arranged so easily. The girl *was* good at her job, and worked like a Trojan when she worked at all.

"Oh, it was fun!" She waved off her accomplishment negligently. "Did you get unstuck?"

"Were we stuck?" asked a sunburned lady nearby. "I didn't know that!" She did not seem unduly alarmed.

"We have been stuck, madam," Steven confirmed, bowing from the waist, "but no longer."

"Well, I expect we'll be on our way sometime." The passenger turned away and did not even bother to spread the news that the *Lawrence* had been earthbound all day. After all, when you went nautical, time and schedules had to be put away. That was why everyone was here—wasn't it? You had to roll with it, didn't you? And if the following day's sail to Nantucket proved tedious because fog blanketed everything, why—who cared? Not the thirty inhabitants of the *Jenny Lawrence,* toughened by the sea and succored by endless highballs and beer.

It was, just as advertised, a week away from worry.

Nantucket.

Jerry's running feet on the deck above dragged him into consciousness; blankly he stared up. The sagging mattress above confirmed the presence of Rick, who had not moved so much as an eyelash all night.

Over and around Jerry's swabbing of the deck was the sound of the wind, and on the other side of the hull the waves lapped against his ear.

Wind! Wind, and they had a long day's sail ahead, back to Hobbes Hole! With a breeze like this, they'd be able to leave Nantucket's harbor with all the grace and dignity of which Jenny was capable; she'd lean into the wind and raise a wake and fly free as she was meant to fly! He had yet to watch her in a heavy sea.

Eagerly he squirmed out of his bunk and carried his sneakers topside. From the galley came bacon and coffee and baking-bread smells, and in the aftercabin the tableware gleamed, ready for the first sitting. The breeze made the rigging buzz and whine and raised whitecaps at sea; in the cockpit Eric was drinking coffee moodily looking at charts held down by stones.

"I don't like it," he scowled. "*Jenny*'s too old."

"Too old for what?"

"The damned wind. It's at fifteen to twenty knots, and I'll bet my balls it's going to get stronger. I'm not sure we should leave at all."

"Eric," he exclaimed, "we have to leave. It's Saturday. We're due back to the mainland this afternoon!"

His dismay rose: dissatisfied passengers would definitely not be good publicity.

"I *know* we have to leave, for Christ's sake," Eric grumbled. "And, let's face it, *Jenny* needs wind, and lots of it. Fifteen to twenty is great, Steve, but if it rises to thirty . . . Well, we'll have to go, I suppose. The sooner, the better. We'll weigh anchor after breakfast. Go ring the son-of-a-bitchin' bell. Let's get these lazy boobs on their feet, the shittin', effin', pimple-assed bastards."

Eric was upset; it took no genius to understand that!

He ran to comply, furiously clattering the hammer on the bell to awaken anyone silly enough to still be asleep and helped Arleen in the galley, then left her to struggle with the dishes and presented himself on deck to help cast off and sail out. *Jenny Lawrence* was going to leave Nantucket in style!

He started the donkey engine. The sails, which they had furled last night on the prediction of wind, slowly climbed the mast as the engine inched them up; when they were secure, the engine winched up the anchor chain. *Jenny* leaned into the wind, her sails taut, and rode out to sea with all her retinue and heralds, trumpets and cymbals—gulls shrieking their praise and the other ships in the harbor tooting and whistling.

Oh, wonderful ship!

The breeze tore at him, and he laughed at it, and *Jenny* sang and raced, and spray flew up, catching in the sun and falling back occasionally on the deck, which leaned in the list of the wind. Nantucket dissolved, and only open water surrounded them, wide as the sky, bright as the clouds that raced them. He would never get enough! Happily he accepted the beer that Arleen opened and thrust into his hand, and he leaned on the rail and dreamed himself into the days when sailing ships were the fastest conveyances known to man. They were abeam turning buoy bell number seven when Eric ordered the jib to be set. Rousing himself, he helped Jerry unfurl it and felt the ship leap forward. Eric was drunk by now, he guessed—knew it for a fact—because Eric should not have set the jib if he was worried about the wind. . . .

But no one needed to worry for long: the jib let go almost at once, its tatters flying out over the water like banners. There was nothing they could do about it while the ship was moving.

He accepted another can of beer.

Twenty minutes later, abeam the cross-rip light house, the wind rose yet higher, but *Jenny* settled into it comfortably and the passengers had settled into the beer, which helped to ease the stomach when in motion. The whole party was wonderfully happy, cheering, shouting, singing, exhilarated by the elements of *Jenny*'s drama without understanding the details. Proud and happy, he watched them from the cockpit where he stood with Eric.

"Enter abeam gong number fifteen. Compass 295 degrees," Eric ordered, and Steven set it down in the log, pleased that he'd been trusted to write in it. "Hold the wheel steady. I want to check the sails," Eric instructed, and left the wheel to take a closer look.

"Head her up into the wind!" he shouted back. "It's starting to rip! Head her up!"

Obediently he spun the wheel, and *Jenny* heeled; and there was a sound similar to lightning hitting a tree, and a cracking, a ripping, as the mainsail split and the foreboom let go. The main gaff fell, slashing the foresail top to bottom, and the ship paused, without power, and backed down on the trailing yawl boat.

The passengers, too surprised and full of beer to realize the severity of their situation, remained exactly where they were, thereby sparing themselves injury.

"Well, I guess we aren't going to make it to Hobbes Hole," Eric observed, calmly inspecting the tangle of lines, sails, and splinters that lay heaving up and down in the water beside them. In the face of disaster, he hadn't the power to think up the appropriate four-letter words. "We'll have to put extra lines on the yawl," he instructed. "Towing a water-filled craft isn't easy."

The passengers watched, discussing it all in unconcerned beery voices.

"Squash Meadow shoals are nearer than I like to think," Eric went on. "Get the sail and the gaff out of the water if you can; cut us loose if you can't. We'll try a port tack under the staysail."

They limped.

They wallowed.

Jenny's retinue had deserted her, and Steven was closer to weeping than he'd been in years when they accepted a tow into Vineyard Haven, since *Jenny* had no steerage and no power.

"How'll we get home?" asked the little bitch who'd plugged up the head.

He stopped himself from snarling just in time, steadied himself. It was a logical question, after all, and most certainly was the first he'd have asked in her place.

"I'm afraid we'll have to put you on the ferry," he apologized. "Wasn't exactly what we planned—but the ferry it is."

"Do things like this happen often?" she asked innocently, gesturing inclusively to the wreckage of the *Lawrence*. "It's so exciting! And interesting, too, watching you all cope."

"Oh, we're very good at coping," he assured her. "Part of seafaring is knowing how to cope! Let me assure you, by the way, that we'll be responsible for your passage to the mainland. And we'll talk to the harbor master at Hobbes Hole, so that he can notify anyone who's planning to meet you."

"I may sue," grumbled another passenger. "I'm going to miss my train."

But nobody offered commiseration or sympathy to the fellow who would miss his train. When you sailed right out of the twentieth century and back again, a paltry thing like a train schedule was beneath the notice of all but the most obtuse.

To the last passenger, even the one concerned with schedules, they refused reimbursement for the ferry and left with hearty handshakes and kisses, taking with them more than they had brought aboard.

For them, at least, the cruise had been an overwhelming success. For the crew, the captain, the owners, it was a near-disaster. It would take a week, at least, to fix the damage, a week they could earn nothing but would pile up indebtedness—indebtedness that would require a good part of the summer to repay, with little left for maintenance. . . . We'll do it, he thought doggedly. We'll make it, damned if we won't. It'll be a long haul, but we'll do it. And to that, he and Eric drank a toast.

IX

The Legacy of Jenny Lawrence

25

Steven turned onto the mid-Cape highway. It was Sunday afternoon and the rush of cars that would leave Cape Cod later in the day had not yet begun. The pace was leisurely, traffic minimal, and he was glad of it. *Jenny* and her complement had been late arriving at Hobbes Hole yesterday, and the crew, himself included, had partied long into the evening. So long that he'd had to do his chores today, and an eddy of ease was welcome after the frantic race to scrub the galley bulkheads where the ice and food were stored, to clean the heads and cabins, to change the sheets and bundle the old ones up for delivery to the laundry tomorrow. Running a windjammer was a lot of work, he reflected, but *Jenny* was going to make it. That was clear. Bookings were running high, every berth taken since their mishaps in the gale. With luck, he thought, the yard bills at Vineyard Haven would soon be paid, and then the profit would be theirs, to be used at their own discretion.

He found his head wobbling, shook himself awake, turned

on the radio of the ancient truck he and Eric shared while on the mainland. These parties, these late hours, would have to stop! He grinned, there by himself in the truck—for the parties spontaneously grew from the happiness, the joy, of people seeking a respite from the strains of contemporary life in the *Jenny Lawrence* and finding it. Their parties were celebrations, their happiness contagious, and he'd thoroughly enjoyed this bonus that *Jenny* had given him. This week the center of celebration was a dentist from Jersey City, who every evening when the ship had dropped anchor, had filled his washbasin with martinis for the well-being of himself and the crew, disdaining the usual tourist attractions of Nantucket and Martha's Vineyard. Ah! Domenic Bruno! A toast to an indefatigable perpetuator of parties! Bruno had hidden his copious liquor supply somewhere on board, refusing to reveal where, and all of them had spent a good part of the week looking for it. And all of them had spent a good part of last night drinking what was left of it. And Steven Sinclaire had forgotten that once they docked at Hobbes Hole his work load was just beginning. At this head-splitting hour he regretted yesterday's party that was still grinding along like a juggernaut in the aftercabin of the *Jenny Lawrence*, all because Domenic Bruno couldn't bring himself to leave, couldn't face his dentist's drill, his office, his telephone, his wife. . . .

He pulled off the highway and onto the county road in Yarmouth, past the railroad station where Cousin Elizabeth used to meet him when he was a camper on the way to Quivet, turned right onto Six-A, the old Main Street which would be called the King's Highway one day, he supposed. Low tide on the bay, he noticed, easily visible now because some of the elms that once lined the road had died and been taken away, opening the view. West Waterford wandered out to meet him, sparsely populated and as rural a spot as the Cape's North Shore could boast. And there was the mill stream, so narrow that a man could jump across it, and the barn that the Historical Society had moved there this spring. The museum that was to be housed inside was nearly ready, and today Mari was hosting a meeting to organize the grand opening. The changeover for tourists had occurred yesterday so that she would be free this afternoon, her house guests at the beach or wandering about in the shops that catered to them. Kingsland, itself open for business, was not the most logical place for such a meeting, but it was her chance, she insisted, to undo the harm that Steven had done in the spring at town meeting.

He sighed. She'd been furious yesterday when he'd phoned to say he wouldn't be home until now, and could not help her with her seating arrangements.

"It's just that you don't want to," she'd said icily. "If you really wanted to help, you'd have gotten here in time." (Which, he admitted to himself, would have been the case if he hadn't joined Domenic Bruno's party.) "You're still trying to sabotage me," she said. "But it won't work, Steve. The kids will help." (In fact, between Kathy and Rick, Mari did not truly need his help at all. It was only her way of trying to force him, by default, into her corner.)

He decided not to think about it.

The library and the lovely old church had come into view now, bright in the afternoon sun, and the low road down which was the old Merrick place, and then the driveway of Kingsland, into which he turned, carefully avoiding all the cars parked for Mari's meeting.

"Hi, Dad!" Kathy was waiting on the steps of the kitchen porch. "How was the trip?"

"Good." He stretched, working out the kinks collected from his drive, sat beside her in the cool afternoon shade. "How are things here?"

"Six rooms rented," she reported. "And all guests at the beach, just like Mom wanted. We've been making little bitty sandwiches with all the crusts cut off, and deviled eggs, till they come out our ears. And then I passed them around and listened to ladies ooh and aah over me. And now I'm resting."

He laughed. Perhaps there was hope for Kathy yet! "Where's your brother?"

"Hiding." She grinned. "He moved chairs this morning and then disappeared so he wouldn't have to make deviled eggs."

He looked around. He had no wish to go inside with a house full of people bickering over historic trifles. Perhaps he'd find Rick's hiding place and crawl in with him.

"Steve!" It was Mari at the back door. Was she still angry? he wondered as she came out onto the porch.

"Hi, honey." He stood at her approach, kissed her warily, waited for her next barrage—but she had forgiven him. "I'm so glad you got back in time!" she exclaimed. "I was worried you wouldn't! Come on in!"

"Heaven forbid."

"The meeting's breaking up," Mari coaxed. "Don't worry. No one will bite. There's someone here you've just got to meet. She's been telling us details about the West Waterford mills, and she's fascinating! Come on!"

She tugged lightly on his arm, led him through the kitchen. "How was the voyage?"

"Fine. Just fine."

"No catastrophes?"

"Not a one."

"Thank God!"

She dragged him through the hall and into the parlor, where the guest of honor sat in front of the window, teacup in hand, nodding attentively as an old geezer filled her ear earnestly and probably repetitively. The room was in a state of pleasant disorder, with chairs scattered here and there; people were picking up their belongings, wandering one way and another as they made their farewells. Everyone was speaking at the same time, and their words and voices drifted by him, remote and disconnected as he walked with Mari toward that day's fascinating speaker, Alice Bradley.

She was nearly an old woman now. She was wearing gloves and a hat, which gave her vintage away, and a white blouse with a bow beneath her chin, and a skirt too long for a short-skirted age but appropriate for hers. She was watching him calmly, without expression, and he didn't know if she was as dismayed at seeing him as he was at seeing her. He only knew that the very sight of her was devastating.

Alice Bradley.

About whom he had not thought in years.

She had not entered his mind even once in all the time he and Mari and the kids had lived here. She had not entered his mind in years, nor had the circumstances under which he'd first met her. And now they were rising from the grave in which he'd buried them, rising in all their untenable, unbearable impossibility.

She knew.

He was sure of it, in a way he could not have described. She knew who he was. She had known since that evening eighteen years ago, when he'd played canasta with the Bradleys in their summer cottage. Beneath his belt the crab that so long ago had lived in his vitals stirred, rolled over, came to life.

"Steve, this is Miss Alice Bradley," Mari murmured reverently.

"Hello, Steven," Alice Bradley said. Her voice wasn't old at all, but was the same steady, even, unhurried one he remembered. He was suddenly aware that he smelled of sweat and low tide and looked disreputable in his well-worn blue jeans and T-shirt with holes in it that positively reeked now with the rise of his body temperature. Nearby, Claudia waved the Historical Society program in front of her nose.

"Whew!" she exclaimed. "The mariner returns!"

Alice held out her hand, and he shook it. "Nice to see you again, Miss Alice," he managed.

Her green eyes were deep, and he was trapped in them, unable to look away.

"Do you already know each other?" asked Karen Jackson, standing next to Alice Bradley's chair.

"Old Cape people always know one another," Alice said. "They're always bumping into each other, in the most unexpected places."

"Here she is, a veritable seer," Claudia complained. "It took us hours, searching the town records, to find her, and you knew about her all the time!"

"I never told him that we were researching the archives," Mari said in his defense. "So he never had a chance to say anything. We were trying to find everything we could about Kingsley Merrick's mill," she said to him as he listened without comprehension and without caring. "There are some properties out there with unknown owners, and we were hoping to find one that the town could take for a parking lot near the mill site. That was when we discovered Miss Bradley. The titles to certain property out there were passed to her through her mother, who was Kingsley Merrick's daughter."

"And here you are, a Merrick," Claudia crowed. "You could have told us all about her."

"Not necessarily." Although her words were unhurried, Alice Bradley broke in quickly and firmly. "You see, there are two families involved. Kingsley Merrick was indeed my grandfather. But my mother, his only surviving child, married twice. Steven's cousin, Elizabeth Edgarton, was my mother's child by her first marriage, while I'm her child by the second, you see." Smoothly, smoothly did Alice Bradley lead them all away. "I won't bother you with the whys and wherefores, but the two families gave one another a very wide berth. It's not surprising that Steven wouldn't have thought of me. He's probably never even heard of me."

"But you already knew each other!" Claudia protested, then stopped when she saw at last that she was trespassing. "Old family spats are so intriguing," she babbled, trying to bridge the gap created by her gaffe.

Why had Mom never told him that Alice Bradley was a Merrick!

Because you never asked, you fool, he answered himself savagely. You never wanted to know anything, so you never asked, and even when she offered again, way back when she met Darion Hunt, you turned her down.

"See why I hoped you'd get back in time to meet Miss Bradley today?" Mari enthused, returning from the door where she had bidden a guest good-bye. "I wanted to surprise you, Steve!"

"Well, you sure did," he said gamely.

Miss Alice's eyes were gentle as she watched him. "They tell me you're in the coasting trade now."

"It's called windjamming." His voice sounded strange.

"Quite an adventure! Where do you sail?"

"Oh, just Nantucket Sound," he heard himself saying.

"Tell me where," Alice said chattily, and Mari pulled over a nearby folding chair.

"Here, Steve! Have a seat! I'll just leave you two for a nice little talk while I see everyone out. I'll be back when they're all gone."

Alice Bradley was the last person on earth he wanted to be left with, but he was still too stupid with shock to think his way around this impasse.

"Nantucket," said his voice. "And Vineyard Haven, Hyannis Port . . ."

"And Edgartown?" Alice asked casually, yet he was nearly certain that her words were not casually chosen. "Do you go to Edgartown?"

"Oh, yes, always," he said remotely.

"My niece Diana owns a cheese-and-wine shop there. You must look her up. It's called Vincent's. That was her husband's name. She divorced him recently—you do remember Diana, don't you?"

"Yes," he said, sweating, bound to the chair, to her, to her eyes, which held him with a purpose that frightened him. Yes, himself a man who rarely feared anything, was afraid now—he feared Alice Bradley as a man might fear the Lord, who held all the answers whether a man asked or not, who gave the answers whether a man wanted them or not.

"All the girls are married and have families. All of them are living in the suburbs, and surviving it so far! Doug is with Digital, doing very well. Surely you remember him—of course! He was your CIT wasn't he?"

"Yes."

"He's married and has two daughters. Unfortunately not all the news is good." Her eyes were veiled now, and unreadable. "Unfortunately Doug and Diana's parents are dead. They were in an automobile accident three years ago."

His ears were singing as he stared at her, and Mari's voice was far away as she said, close by his ear, "Well! How are you two getting along?"

Tim Bradley was dead.

"Actually, all of you have been invited for cocktails and dinner," Claudia chimed in. "Let's adjourn the festivities for now. Steve and Mari haven't seen one another all week," she said to Alice Bradley. "So let's leave them alone for a bit. Why don't you come back with me, Miss Bradley, and I'll give you a guided tour."

"I'd like that very much," Alice said. "I've never been in Elijah Merrick's house. We'll talk later, Steven. I hope."

"We're in the middle of restoring the house," Claudia explained, leading Miss Alice away. "So it's in a bit of a mess. But it's coming just fine. I really love the old Georgian places, don't you? Their lines are so pure."

It was as though all of him had caved in, leaving a void, empty like the huge parlor was empty now, its guests gone, echoing and without the spark that could warm it, himself cold, friendless. . . . Mari followed him to the bedroom that he'd made out of the old billiard room.

"Isn't she grand? She knows so much! She has Kingsley Merrick's papers and everything, and lots of information about mills that have been on the stream since colonial days. Go ahead and shower, honey," she instructed. "I'll tell you all about it later. I'm sure you'll want to rest before dinner."

There was no choice. "You'll have to go without me, Mar."

"What?" Mari frowned, dismayed. "I said we'd go!"

"You shouldn't have," he said, pulling the holey, rancid T-shirt over his head. "I've had a full week, and you shouldn't have committed me."

"Steve," she began as patiently as possible, "Claudia's counting on us."

"I'm not going," he repeated. "I'm bushed and I'm not going to sit over there and listen to Claudia's drivel." Wearily he watched the eagerness, the pleasure, the exuberance drain away from her face. "I'm sorry," he said more gently, trying to placate her without upsetting the fragile balance within himself. "I'm just not going."

Wordless in her dismay, she could only stare; recovering,

she leaped instantly into battle. "I've been patient with you, Steve Sinclaire. I've put up with your ideas and your priorities and I really think it's time you tried to be considerate of mine."

He peeled off his stinking jeans, stepped out of his sneakers, and pulled off his fetid socks.

"It was really embarrassing this spring when you went and spoke up for the townspeople—but I understood you felt it was your duty. It's taken me a lot of time to smooth it over. But now, as everything is getting back to normal, to just not appear for dinner when Claudia has made a special point to include you . . ."

He headed for the bathtub to turn on the water.

"You've become selfish and inconsiderate," Mari said, following him. But he was not listening; instead he was trying to contain everything, as though his guts were threatening to spill out and he had to hold them in, the least movement painful, perhaps fatal. He had to be alone, he needed time—yes, time to understand, to accept, to grieve for the man who was his father.

"And I'm sick of it!" Mari's face was ugly; her mouth was twisted in anger. "A marriage takes two people trying and caring about the things that are important, and you aren't doing anything. I'm sick of it!"

She stormed out of the bathroom and left him alone at last. He shucked off his shorts and lowered himself into the soothing, steaming water, lay back carefully, closed his eyes carefully.

For eighteen years everything had been pushed down and out of sight. And now it had returned. All his memories of Tim Bradley, who had done so much for him in so short a time, eighteen years ago. All the pain of learning who he was. Of relinquishing the man he knew Tim Bradley to be.

"If you don't come, there'll really be trouble," Mari said coldly, reappearing at the doorway. "And I mean it, Steve."

Bradley was gone; Steven had hidden from him and all his family; years ago his curt withdrawal, his enormous effort to make all the Bradleys believe he didn't care—all of it could have been undone in a single gesture, when you came right down to it—and perhaps, all along, he'd believed that if he did nothing to change the situation, the choice remained in his hands. But now it was beyond his control. The early-morning sail he had not taken with Tim Bradley; the letters from Diana he had not answered; the one letter he had written—to Doug—coldly damning so that none of them would pursue him: these decisions were irrevocable now.

Because now Tim Bradley was dead.

"I'm leaving for Claudia's," Mari said. "I'm taking the kids. You will please meet us over there when you've bathed and shaved."

She paused, waiting for him to agree, and he lay quietly in the tub, waiting for her to go away.

"See you soon," she said pointedly, and then left when he did not answer or look at her.

He listened to her rounding up the children (Rick noticeably reluctant, since he did not like Junior Marshall). He heard the car motor and then the pebbles on the surface of the driveway, grinding and crunching against one another, and then the sound faded away. Carefully he soaped up, rinsed off, got out of the bath, dressed, shaved, shook the pillow out of his pillowcase and filled it with socks, shorts, and T-shirts, slipped out the kitchen door and into the rusted old truck which, fortunately, he'd parked back here where it couldn't be seen from Kaptainsholme, should anyone be looking. He drove back the way he'd come, carefully absorbing himself with the details of the road, carefully closing his mind until he'd made it to the safety of the *Jenny Lawrence*, where he believed he could cope with his wounds in peace and where he discovered the party led by the dentist from New Jersey was still in full swing.

Damn! There was nowhere he could go to be by himself, to do what he had to do, to come to grips with something so deep that he hadn't realized it even existed! He crept forward, to *Jenny*'s bow, cluttered with lines and engines and the anchor chain; clutching himself against the growing grief and sorrow and the awareness of having lost something he had not known he possessed; he listened. In the distance were the gulls and the bells of a church; within was a weeping from a lost, forgotten part of himself that had been covered by the rubble of past years, rising from its grave, and he allowed it now to breathe as he had never done before, and the freedom and joy he'd experienced in Tim Bradley's presence came into focus, sharp and clear and fresh as the hour he'd first encountered it.

Tim Bradley was dead. He would never lurk in any shadow; never suddenly, unbearably reappear, his hand outthrust. Tim Bradley was gone.

"Look who's here!" A very drunk Eric spoke very loudly,

and an equally drunken Domenic Bruno from Jersey City said, "Who *is* here?"

"It's Steve Sinclaire, by Christ."

"Who'n hell is Steve Sinclaire?"

"Steve-sweetie!" It was Arleen, not quite as drunk—but not far behind. "Honey, it's so nice to see you again!"

"But who'n hell is Steve Sinclaire?" Bruno repeated petulantly.

"He owns this vessel, stupid."

"Oh, yeah? Why haven't I seen him before?"

"You did, you jackass. You sailed with him all week."

"By God, you're right." Leering out of the darkness Bruno's face came close to his own while Bruno himself inspected him. "It *is* Sinclaire."

"Bruno won't abandon ship while his washbasin is still wet," Eric explained.

"Hate to leave anyway," Bruno said sadly. "I have to be in the office at nine o'clock Monday, drill in one hand, spit cup in the other. What a life."

"Are you okay, Steve?" Arleen asked, finally observing his silence.

"Of course he's all right!" bellowed Eric. "The only trouble with this man is that he's sober. Come with us, Steve," he urged. "Back to the aftercabin. We only came out here to pee."

"Oh! I forgot!" declared Bruno, who busied himself over the stern, sprinkling the floor of the yawl boat below, which he did not see in the darkness.

What else, really, made any better sense at this point? He allowed himself to be led, his preoccupation unnoticed, bridged by the hilarity of the others. They toasted one another, sang of Bruno's good-fellowness, and hailed because the gang was all there, and drank to the days of Auld Lang Syne, and the moments merged into a predictable void until he awoke the next morning, the aching of his head so potent that he was forced to lie still and could not prevent everything from catching up, nor prevent the understanding of clarified consciousness that beneath the reasonable, patient, hopefully intelligent man he believed himself to be, lived the boy who'd been waiting, all these years, for Tim Bradley to seek him out, brushing aside his withdrawal, refusing his rebuff as only Tim Bradley would have known how to do, driving right on past the impossibilities of the situation to the possibility of what might be shared if two people willed to share it.

Unbelievable as it seemed, still he was sure of it. His devastation could only be explained by losing someone close—and Tim Bradley had not been close except in the secret heart of the boy Steven, who held him holy there, who had kept him close there because Tim Bradley was not a man you could hate. He was, in fact, a man you'd hoped perhaps (for twenty years) you'd see again. And knew now, you would not. His loneliness and pain rose up, and up, and he lost his way. . . .

"Up and at 'em!" Jerry knocked happily on the door. "Get your cashbox and your ass topside."

He wrenched himself back—or was it forward?—to the present. To this day. Monday already, because they'd lost Saturday to partying, which had caused him to be late home yesterday, Sunday. And now it was Monday, and he'd left his wife.

Good Christ, Sinclaire, declared the part of his head that didn't hurt. You'd better call her and try to make up before it's too late.

I can't make up, the sore and aching part of himself (irrespective of his head) answered. I can't go back. Alice Bradley is there. And I'm not ready to take on Mari.

Then you'd better call her before she comes to Hobbes Hole, someone practical advised. Or else you'll be in the middle of a showdown before you're ready for one.

He pried himself out of his berth, staggered to the after-cabin, where the sad remnants of last night's party tried to pull themselves together.

"Where's Bruno?" he asked.

"On his way to New Jersey. I drove him to the airport. At daybreak." Eric shuddered at the remembrance.

Steven poured himself some coffee. "What time is it?"

"Ten o'clock."

Jenny was usually onloaded at noon. Bob would be here then, to help put ice in the lockers and water in the barrel, bring in wood for the stove and foodstuffs for a week at sea, gas for the generator and donkey engine, and, to meet this week's emergency, a new carburetor for the yawl boat. Sinclaire's Monday chore, besides signing on passengers, was to take the thirty sets of last week's sheets to the laundry. He drank his third cup of coffee, nerving himself up to do it.

"Here's the strongbox and the reservation list, in case there are early arrivals," he told Eric. "I'll try to fight my way over to Wing Ling's now."

"Early arrivals can fry ice," Eric grumbled. "No passengers are allowed aboard until one o'clock, and that's final."

He piled the sheets in the truck, drove around the corner to the laundry and staggered in, found a nearby hole-in-the-wall restaurant which was open this time of day, though functionless. It had an enclosed telephone booth, and he lowered himself onto its ridiculously small seat, maneuvered the folding glass door shut, dialed the operator, leaned his head against the back of the booth where the oils of other leaned-back heads had dirtied the dimpled metal surface.

"Hello?" Mari said at the other end.

The operator asked if she would accept Steven Sinclaire's collect call. There was a long pause while Mari considered.

"All right," she agreed grudgingly. There was another long pause. "Steve?"

"Yes. How're you, Mar?"

"How'd you expect?" she snapped.

"How are the kids?"

"Oh, just fine. They do wonder a little when you plan to favor us with your company, though."

"Look, Mar . . ."

"It was a little embarrassing, going to Claudia's without you, explaining your absence this morning to Kathy and Rick."

"Well, I'm sorry about that, honey. But something came up. Eric called me just after you left," he lied, knowing no other choice. "So I came back."

"You just didn't want to go to Claudia's. You might as well admit it."

"I already have."

"You don't like my friends. You aren't interested in the things that interest me. And you went out of your way to make sure that I understood it."

He waited for whatever else she might dredge up to feed her justifiable anger; the little booth was becoming stuffy and his head hurt; he pressed it against the glass of the door, hoping its coolness would somehow reduce the tumult between his temples.

"Are you there?"

"Yes."

"I was afraid maybe you'd just gone to sleep."

"No. I'm not asleep."

"Well, then?"

"Well, what?" he asked, trying to summon enough energy to sound reasonably alert.

"Well," she groped, "I was waiting for you to defend yourself."

"No defense, Mar."

"It's not over, you know. We'll have to talk it out sometime."

"I suppose we will."

"Sometime very soon."

"Yes."

"Like next weekend."

"Maybe."

"Definitely."

"All right."

"I'll look for you then," she said firmly.

"Okay."

Somehow he dragged himself back to the *Lawrence*. Bob had arrived and was busily stowing things in the proper bulkheads, waving jauntily. He waved back, set himself up in the aftercabin, lined up the cashbox and the reservations, three pens, and a can of beer. He listened to the voices of his friends, busy about the ship, the sounds of Hobbes Hole, of seabirds and the ripples of the tide.

Mary Harrington and Dolores Demars arrived with their suitcases and sneakers, straw hats and raincoats, prepared for any occasion, they told him. They were secretaries in New York City; they'd been planning this jaunt ever since they'd heard about *Jenny*. They surely hoped that he'd arranged good weather for them! Beneath their coquetry they sized him up: sufficiently handsome, unattached, well-mannered, no doubt well-educated. The voyage looked better than ever!

He explained the ship's routine to them in a performance he could deliver nearly by rote now; entered their money in the books; heard them trying to get down the steps of the companionway without exposing more than decent girls wearing skirts should.

Moodily he stared out the window, waited for the next.

A couple from western Massachusetts, who had never left their children with Mother before.

A man from Indiana whose grandfather had done some sailing. Ran in the blood, didn't you know?

A couple of kids from Dartmouth, handsome and well-groomed as the sons of the rich seemed always to be.

A lady professor, who dressed like one.

A Nubile Young Thing, whose parents should not have let her out alone after dark.

A party of four middle-aged couples, who would be cliquey and loud, he predicted.

All eager to voyage out and beyond the periphery of their known worlds.

Their excitement failed to move him.

He gave the money to Bob for deposit; *Jenny* cast off, accepting a tow out past the jetty because the yawl boat's engine sounded a little rough, even with the new carburetor, and Eric decided not to use it any harder than he had to. *Jenny* wallowed until the helm responded to the breeze, and then she picked up speed, lumbered out to sea.

He leaned on the forward rail, watching, the exultation of getting under way escaping him as he labored under his load. How strange it was, to be so overtaken, overcome by such passionate sorrow. Beneath the surface it had lain there as did all powerful emotions: grief, or jealousy, anxiey or elation, instantly ready to leap into life while the passionless person who harbored it reflected nothing of it until it had struck. Now, he supposed, his sublimated self had emerged because it was safe, with Tim Bradley gone. Safe to yearn. To hope. To need, to grieve. Nothing could be done about it. The barriers he'd erected were inviolate now, they could never be torn down—by anyone.

The Nubile Young Thing was standing in the bow of the ship, her long hair streaming in the wind. She was wearing a jersey which the breeze plastered to her breasts, and like a figurehead, she pointed them seaward, clearly enjoying the sensation she was creating among the male passengers. In his isolation he laughed at her, at them all, at himself, a boatload of fools on vacation from a reality they knew they could not escape but would strive perpetually to avoid.

It was Ferris's turn to stand watch when they reached Edgartown, Sinclaire's to run the yawl. Efficiently he ferried the passengers and crew. He tied the yawl to Edgartown's pier when the last load was over; he would meet them at ten-thirty onward to ferry them back.

"Where're you headed?" asked the Nubile Young Thing.

"Nowhere special."

"Buy me a drink?"

"Not tonight." She could have been his daughter. "Another time, thanks," he said diplomatically, and quickly lost her in the melee that was Edgartown at dusk. The business district was a scrambling mass of searchers for happiness and souvenirs, roaming the streets, crowding the taverns, trying hopelessly for seats at restaurants. He walked through it and out to the residential end of town, miniatured like a fairy land. Its streets were narrow, its sidewalks narrow too, running past white-painted fences that neatly hemmed little lawns. The low-eaved tiny houses hunkered only a few feet away, and everything was overhung with the immense towering trees brought as seedlings to America one hundred years or more before by the whaling captains who built the town.

He cut over a block and walked back toward the harbor and into the throngs again, the same surging, excited, happy, hilarious crowd which he could bear now no better than before. He cut over and back to the quiet end again, his footsteps echoing behind him, and back to the waterfront, in and out of different worlds, back and over, up and back until he came across the object for which he had not been able to admit he was searching: Vincent's Cheese and Wine Shop.

There was a sign swinging over its front door, made of weathered wood with the name carved deeply. Painted beside "Vincent's" was a wedge of cheese and a goblet half-filled with red, indicating the business of the shop just as signs had done two and three hundred years ago—and more. He went past it and back, past and back again before he could look, standing across the street, letting his memories of Diana Bradley as a girl wash over him, the girl whose eyes were the color of green and brown pebbles at the bottom of a clear stream, whose voice was rich and full, who, as he remembered her, was slim and supple, her hair alight in the sun, blowing gently around her alert, fresh face. Through the distant window he saw the woman she'd become, a woman who was slim yet, he saw, laughing with a customer, turning to a shelf of wines, reaching for one.

They had shared first love, that quietly sequestered experience which could never be had again, and he had not ever written her as he'd promised. He'd dropped her just as he'd dropped Tim Bradley. Now she was here, in Edgartown. Now he knew where to find her. Could it be that, through her, the sense of irrevocability could be removed from his nightmares?

He turned away before his loitering became obvious and she might discover him, stole past the churches and the graveyards and houses beneath their old imported trees, all woven into the placid fabric of their own identity, his footsteps echoing behind him, hollow as he was, empty as he was, lonely as he was.

He walked and listened to the summer night and its sounds and the downtown revelry rendered insignificant and small by distance, and then met the passengers at ten-thirty as he'd promised, going through the motions of life at sea.

26

He watched Hobbes Hole drawing nearer, nearer, *Jenny*'s pier filled with onlookers because the *Lawrence*, for once, was on time. Generally she arrived hours after schedule, and he hoped Mari would assume that *Jenny* had maintained her usual erratic behavior, because then daylight would be gone before she'd think to come looking for him. The road would be dark then, and she wouldn't want to come alone; she might wait until tomorrow rather than asking someone to come with her. For tracking him down was an admission that the Sinclaires were experiencing marital difficulty, and Mari, being the sort of person she was, would want to keep it quiet. Assuming, of course, that Mari understood how much marital difficulty there really was—and she might not. He had not understood it, himself, until the shores of home approached and the strength of his decision not to go back had risen firmly, unnegotiably.

He could not stay away forever. There were the kids to consider, after all. Little as Kathy needed him, Rick surely did. And little as Mari liked him, she needed him, too. But he could not return to her. Not now. Not yet. There was no possibility of being able to cope with her trying ways and still maintain his own internal balance. There was no desire even to try. There was only the determination to hold off anyone's approach, especially here, until he had gained control of his life and could move forward again. There was only the determination not be to pushed. By anyone.

Anxiously he examined each face on the wharf, hoping that Mari's would not be there; it was not, and he permitted himself a moment to relax, to plan. He would perform the chores which were his alone to do because Bob spent Saturdays at his own work (the arrival time of *Jenny* being unpredictable). Then he'd fortify himself against the confrontation that he was sure would come, prepare himself to do battle with his wife, and temporarily, at least, free himself from her. Somehow.

"I thought you'd gone home already," said Eric in the darkness of the early evening.

"Shit and manure," he swore. "You scared the bejesus out of me."

"You should watch your habits," Eric said. "You're picking up bad language."

"Must be the company I keep," he grunted. "Take this, will you?"

It was a case of bourbon, and one of beer. Eric caught them on the other side of the gap between *Jenny* and the dock. "Christ! Are you going on a bender?"

"Looks that way, doesn't it?"

"Well?"

"Well, what?"

"Are you? Going on a bender?"

"No," he said. "I only want to look as though I am. I expect my wife is going to come tearing over here in the next couple of hours wanting to know why I've left home and how long I intend to stay away."

"And?"

"And what?"

"How long do you intend to stay away?"

"I don't know yet." He sat down on the deck next to Eric, leaned against *Jenny*'s generous side. "But if she thinks I'm on a bender, she won't push me. She won't be able to, you see, because I won't make any sense. She'll give up. She'll go home and I'll be safe."

"I haven't the slightest idea what you're talking about," Eric said. "But if you're going to play the part of a drunk, I think you'd better get started."

Silently they accompanied one another through a can of beer. "Why are you on board?" Steven asked. "Alone."

Eric chuckled. "Sometimes I like being alone. Sometimes I even like sleeping alone, which doesn't happen very often when we're at sea." Peacefully they drank. He opened two more cans of beer, sliding one in Eric's direction. He waited, listened.

"I see headlights down the wharf," Eric announced.

It must have been true, because the mast was lit and shining. Then the mast disappeared, and murmured voices told him that Mari had not come alone.

"Can you see who's with her?" he asked. Eric cautiously looked over the rail.

"Casey, I think." Who else would she turn to without losing stature?

"Steven?" Mari called from the edge of the wharf, peering into the darkness, searching the cockpit. It was tempting to stay low, except that Bob would come aboard hunting for him and he did not want to appear foolish, nor did he wish to humiliate the mother of his children. He stood up.

"Mari!" he bellowed exuberantly, as though he were drunk. But he was not. He'd known he'd need a clear head so as not to trip himself.

"Help me over, Bob, can you?" Mari asked.

"Sure," he heard Bob say; they scuffled around, inching their way to the cockpit.

"And what do you think you're doing?" she demanded.

He looked up at her towering height. "Where're the kids?"

"Barbara's at your house with them," Bob said gently, soothingly, as though Steven were fragile and possibly dangerous.

"What's going on, Steve?" Mari demanded again.

He patted the decking beside himself. "Sit here," he offered. "I can't talk when you're so far away."

"I didn't come for a long and intimate chat," she snapped. "I came to take you home."

"Well, I'm not going home, so you'd better just sit here while you can. The ship leaves day after tomorrow, you know. I won't be here forever."

He heard her sigh with exasperation before she sat as directed. Though he did not see them leave, he knew that Bob and Eric had discreetly moved out of earshot.

"I'm glad you got Bob to bring you, Mari." He slurred a little. "He'll make sure you're safe. I was a little worried about that."

"Huh," she grunted. "You must have thought I'd be coming."

"I suspected it, my love." Elaborately he belched.

"Steven!" Her voice was urgent. "What in God's name is wrong?"

"Nothing's wrong," he urged. "Not with me, anyway."

"And so there's something wrong with me?"

"Well, Mar," he groped, looking for an opening, "how would you like it if you came home from a hard week at the office and found your parlor filled with historically oriented finks?"

"I believe I told you the society was meeting at our house last Sunday," she said stiffly.

"You did that. You told me." He nodded. "Yes. Would you like some beer?"

"No."

"Some bourbon, then?" He gestured toward the case, bulky in the darkness.

"That's yours?"

"It sure is."

"You plan to drink it all?"

"Well, in the course of the summer. I'll sort of space it out. Maybe."

"When are you coming home, Steve?" she asked hesitantly, finally arriving at the conclusion he desired her to reach.

"Don't call us," he quipped. "We'll call you."

"It isn't funny," she stormed. "When are you coming home?"

"When those damn historicals are out of my goddamned parlor."

"But they're out now!" Mari cried.

"No, dearest." He turned to her, put a hand on either side of her head. "They're in here." He squeezed and then let go in case she, or Eric, or Bob would fear for her safety. "They're in your head, and they're in my house. How do you think it feels, walking into your own house, and there they are. Every effing Tom, Dick, and Harry that wants to run the show to suit himself. All the pricks that voted against you in town meeting."

Of course! It was a natural! Congratulations, Sinclaire, he congratulated himself. That was very good.

"They voted against me. There I stood, giving speech after speech, laying it on the line, spilling my guts, pleading the cause of justice, and they voted against me. They oppose me, and even now they destroy the Grail. Philistines, every one."

"Steven," Mari said, her voice low. "This isn't the time or

the place to discuss the Historical Society or town meeting either."

"Well, sure as hell I can't discuss it at home," he complained. "Because the parlor's filled with the opposition. And because your head is filled by the opposition. Can you deny it, Mari?"

"We've had this out before," she said coldly.

"But without a conclusion," he reminded her.

"And this is your conclusion?" she cried. "Sailing about all summer in this godforsaken tub?"

"Please, madam," Eric protested in the night shadow, not so far out of earshot as Steven had supposed.

"Shut up," she said over her shoulder. "Steven, I'm sick of this. I've humored you long enough. You come home with me and sleep it off."

"I'll come home the day you decide that I'm more important than the Historical Society," he said stubbornly, satisfied that she would never, ever find the scent now.

"Of course you're more important!"

"No, Mari," he said with exaggerated drunken sadness. "No, I'm not. You go home. Barry or Bob, here—will help you if you need anything. I'll call in every weekend."

"I don't believe this," she said angrily. "Are you walking out on me, Steven?"

"Nope," he declared. "I'm only waiting here on *Jenny* until you tell me that the coast is clear."

"Then you can stay aboard till she sinks." Mari's lips were drawn back in a sneer of anger, and her voice was thick in her throat; her leaving was abrupt, troubling the very air surrounding him as he crouched there, waiting for her to get the hell away. He heard the car start, heard it pull away. Heard the quiet of the night again. . . .

It was a relief to have her out of harm's way, unable to disturb him until he'd settled down a bit. Wearily he rubbed his tight temples, looked up at the stars. Eric returned and opened another can of beer, sat beside him in companionable silence.

"If you're waiting up for me, you don't need to."

"I don't ever sleep early." Eric shrugged. "I'd prefer company, unless you'd rather I got lost."

In fact it didn't matter much, one way or the other.

"You know," Eric began, "if you stay on the outs with your old lady, you can live aboard *Jenny* in the winter. We could fix her up and haul lumber."

"Christ, what do you know about lumber?" he asked wearily.

"I know there are buyers who are interested in a permanent and regular supply of number-one-grade, because I've talked to them. I think I can get eighty dollars a thousand; in order to pay expenses, I figure I'd only need to clear twenty."

"Come on, Eric!"

"I know *Jenny* could carry one hundred thousand board feet, and I know that the Small Business and Loan Administration would give us all the money we'd need to put her in shape."

"Well, that's very interesting, old buddy. But I can't very well discuss it, because I have no plans for next winter at all." In fact, he refused to consider anything more than a day distant.

"Well, it never hurts to know what the possibilities are, does it?"

"No, of course not."

"It'd be great," Eric said with enthusiasm. "You'd love living aboard."

"Perhaps."

"It beats living with a woman. Any woman."

He laughed. "Thanks for the advice, Skipper. I'll sleep on it."

"You're leaving?" Eric asked in disappointment.

"I guess so. I'm pretty beat."

"Okay." Reluctantly Eric relinquished the possibility of an all-night revel.

Steven did not sleep; he had not thought he would. He wanted only to lie in his bunk and let *Jenny* comfort him and listen to her night sounds and wait for dawn. It was all he could do. Yet, what would it be like to live aboard her permanently? he wondered, carrying passengers in the summer and lumber in the winter, his own man doing what he best liked to do—sail—and with it earn enough money to support his family until Rick got to be a man and became a partner in the enterprise, if it suited him. Quite a legacy for a father to leave his son. You can't give him Waterford, he thought, because it doesn't exist anymore. But you can give him *Jenny*, if he wants her.

You're dreaming, he told himself. It's only a child's fantasy protecting you from facing up to certain realities you'd rather not look into just now. It was true that many men made their dreams come true out of sheer determination—but sadly he knew he possessed no determination whatever, that he was cold and mortal clay, unkindled by any dream, unable to respond to one—indeed, to anything.

27

She was talking to a customer. If she saw him enter, she gave no sign. If she knew who he was, she did not indicate it. She and the customer continued to discuss the right sort of cheese to complement the right sort of wine, and uncomfortably he wondered if twenty years had changed him so much that he was no longer recognizable. Twenty years could do that, but it had done little to change her.

Perhaps, he thought, suddenly cold, she is ignoring you.

"Hi, Diana." He made himself speak quickly when she was finished with the customer, afraid that if he waited, another chance would fail to materialize. She stared at him, first without recognition and then with the startled acknowledgment of who he was.

But not with surprise.

"Steve . . ."

She stopped, motionless, as though unable to make up her mind—and then her chin came up proudly, her shoulders straightened. "Well, what a nice treat," she said without noticeable pleasure.

Her voice was the same, if a little lower than before, and therefore a little fuller. Her face was unlined, her body lithe—he made himself stop staring.

"At least you recognized me. I was afraid you wouldn't." He made himself smile. It was an effort, because he needed her so much without knowing why. It had taken two weeks to work up the nerve to come into the shop, and now that he was here, he was hideously afraid of her.

"Actually I expected to run into you sometime or other, ever since I heard you owned the *Lawrence,*" Diana Bradley said.

"Oh? When did you hear that?" he asked, hoping he sounded jolly and well-met. God knew he must not look it!

"At the beginning of the summer, I think" she said, her eyes steady, with neither warmth nor rebuff—with nothing. "When the ship first came into the harbor, as I recall."

The shop's bell rang, and she turned to the customer who entered, leaving him to mull over the unpleasant understanding that she had known all season where to find him, and had not attempted to even for old times' sake.

Why should she? he asked himself, fending off despair. What have you ever done to encourage her friendship?

The customer left and the shop was quiet. She stood stoically by the door. Clearly the ball was in his court.

"I met your aunt this summer. She told me about your place here."

Nothing. Panic began to grow.

"She told me about you and Doug and the girls," he struggled on. "And she told me about your parents. I was sorry to hear about it, Diana."

"Yes. It was quite a shock."

The bell rang again and abruptly she turned to help her customer. Empty and aching, he looked at the polished pine paneling and shelves, gleaming pewter mugs and trays, the rich wine colors in their bottles, the wrappings of cheeses in their cases, and wondered if his desolation and loneliness would ever stop.

The customer left, and she remained behind the counter where she'd received money for the purchase of brandy.

"So this place is yours."

"Yes," she said, looking up from a note she was scribbling to herself. "My husband and I started it five years ago."

"Your aunt tells me you're divorced."

"Aunt Alice loves to talk," Diana observed noncommittally, and was rescued by another customer.

Should he just give up? he wondered. Certainly she was putting him off. Perhaps because she'd been hurt in her marriage and didn't want to encourage a man. Perhaps because Steven Sinclaire had stood her up twenty years ago. Perhaps because she didn't want to be bothered, was uninterested in men.

The customer left, and only one chance remained. Miserably he knew he must take it. "Have you ever been aboard the *Lawrence?*" he asked, his breathing difficult.

"No, I never have."

"How would you like a tour of *Jenny*—in the morning before we sail?" he asked. "Would you enjoy that?"

"No. I don't think I would."

"Or a day sail, maybe. Over to Nantucket," he went on, hopelessly exposing his need. "You could take the ferry back. It's quite an experience, sailing on a schooner that large."

"I'm very much tied down here," she refused firmly, and did not hesitate to outstare him.

There was no way to avoid her hostility. "I guess you wish I'd just leave you alone," he said softly, and his face must have shown his hurt, for she looked away as she answered.

"You can't just walk back into my life, Steven. You're right. I wish you'd just get out."

He left, humiliated, defeated, fled to the nearest tavern. It was not filled to capacity yet, the evening being young. There was sawdust on the floor and fishnet festooned from the ceiling. Buoys and lobster pots were strewn around in the usual attempt to make the room a fisherman's haven, and Arleen Patterson was at the bar, as though she'd been there all along, waiting for him.

"You look awful," she said. "You need a drink."

"You're right." Heroically he entered the spirit of the occasion in order to keep himself in one piece. He put an arm around her and smiled. "I'm sure glad you're here, Arleen."

"You are?" She gave him a swift appraisal that tried to answer the question: What ails Sinclaire? A nice-looking, decent fellow who had never looked twice at her before, who'd seemed awfully moody lately. Gladly she took on the task of restoring him to his former self.

"Let me tell you the story of my life," she offered. "Now that you've asked."

He laughed. "All right."

"And then, when everybody's aboard, we can row over to Chappaquiddick and you can tell me yours."

"My what?"

"The story of your life."

"Oh, yes, of course."

"Or we could settle for a beach party, if you'd rather. Just you and me."

"Sounds swell," he said, and was aware that she'd moved closer to him, her breasts softly nudging him, a thigh slightly pressing his. It was good to know that when everything else had failed you, the Arleen Pattersons of life were there, generous and full-bodied, kind and amiable.

In that moment his devotion to her was boundless, and he put Diana Bradley Vincent and her rebuff behind him, and Alice Bradley and his fear of her, Mari and the things she dubbed sacred, Kingsland, Waterford, even Rick and Kathy and the *Jenny H. Lawrence,* and welcomed the refuge that was available just then. . . .

The dinghy rocked gently in the ebbing tide. The Chappaquiddick ferry hustled back and forth with ducks following and gulls circling above, laughing. All along the waterfront, owners of boats went about their interminable antlike tasks and he remotely observed it all as the dinghy sank below wharf level. Then, because his visual range was so rudely impeded, and because the sun hurt his eyes if he looked out across the harbor, he concentrated on Jerry Ferris in the yawl boat, tied next to him at the dock. From beneath his seat in the dinghy he brought up a bottle of gin, still encased in its paper bag the way rummies carried theirs, and offered it across the intervening space. Jerry helped himself, handed it back, went on patiently tinkering with the engine, tightening, cleaning, oiling.

He ought to row out to *Jenny* and pump the bilge, he told himself. Yes, he nodded. He ought. She was taking quite a lot of water these days. Not enough to be alarmed about, Eric often assured him. Certainly no cause for panic, but definitely cause for concern. If there wasn't enough profit to do the hull after this summer, they had better borrow, Eric thought. The ship could take only so much, only so long.

But the profits would be sufficient. There were always a hell of a lot of people aboard, and this week was no exception. Yesterday—Monday—he'd collected a hell of a lot of money from them. He hadn't kept totals; it seemed unnecessary. *Jenny* would earn the required profit—or she wouldn't—but she couldn't do more than she was doing already, that was for sure! On the other hand, if he didn't pump the bilge and *Jenny* sank, she wouldn't earn anything at all. Yes. He must go now, and man the pump.

He did not move.

"Hi!" called Arleen.

He turned, slowly, so as not to jar his head any more than necessary. On the now elevated dock, she looked down over the fullness of her very ripe figure and said, "Going my way?"

"If he's not, I am," Jerry volunteered, gazing up in admiration.

"I thought I might row out to *Jenny,*" Steven said, speaking slowly in case he slurred.

"Nice day for a swim off the ropes, don't you think?" she suggested.

"I sure do!" Jerry volunteered.

"I wasn't speaking to you," she said saucily. Apparently today was not Jerry's day. She blew him a kiss and climbed into the dinghy facing Steven. She was wearing a jersey tank top and her nipples showed plainly beneath the fabric; her eyes brimmed with teasing laughter. "How about it?" she said. "Unless I miss my guess, no one's aboard."

"How about what?" he asked, refusing to play her game. In fact unable. He definitely felt unwell.

She only smiled.

"I had it in mind to pump the bilge," he said belligerently.

"Okay. We'll pump it together." Expertly she slipped the mooring, turned her face up to the sun. "Nice day."

"Yes." It was awfully damn bright, but he decided not to say so.

"You work too hard, Steve," she observed as he rowed. "You're not having any fun."

"No harder than you."

"But I'm younger." She wrinkled her nose at him, to indicate that the years between them did not discourage her.

However, he was not interested in whether she was discouraged or not, because just now he was interested in nothing at all.

"When's the last time you ate?" she asked, scrutinizing him carefully.

"I don't know."

"Would you like me to fix you some lunch?"

"No," he replied sullenly. He did not want her concern, because he knew where it would lead, and knew he didn't have what it took to satisfy her. Not today. God, his head! He coasted to *Jenny*'s side, and Arleen scrambled up the ladder. She hung over the rail, waiting for him to follow. Behind them, at the wharf, the bell rang, and squinting over his shoulder, he could see a group of passengers—Mavis Myers and her three pals, it looked like from here—waiting for him. The standing rule had it that no fewer than four people would rate a ride, but that was not a problem for these ladies, who never went anywhere or did anything without each other.

"Sorry, Arleen," he called up. "I'm being summoned."

"Drat!" She grinned down. "Another time, maybe."

The bell rang again, and he rowed off. The yawl's ailing engine had simply quit on the way out of Hobbes Hole yesterday, and they'd barely made it past the jetties on the last of its momentum, catching the breeze of the open water just in time to avoid total wreckage. They'd tacked about Nantucket Sound until they could pick up the yawl and Jerry, and Steven had been diligently ferrying passengers six at a time to shore and back ever since their arrival in Edgartown last night. It looked tedious and unending and undignified, rowing and rowing and rowing, but it was exactly right for him, the rhythm of the oars locking his mind into their pattern. He'd deliberately volunteered to be officer in charge of the rowboat, because he'd rather thought it might be soothing—which it was, and between rowing and drinking there was just enough momentum to halt the process of thought.

He approached the wharf again, and Jerry steadied the dinghy while, chattering and giggling, the four women climbed in, settled themselves, happily enjoying the placid ride back to the *Jenny Lawrence.*

"Did you have good luck with your shopping?" Steven asked politely, and the girls did not hesitate to tell him of a sale at one gift shop and some wonderful stuff (not on sale) at another.

Yes, rowing was better than lying alone in his berth, which he'd done a lot of lately, looking up at the bunk above, the springs of which didn't sag because Rick wasn't up there sleeping. It was better than wondering what Rick was doing or what he was thinking or what Mari might have told him, if his son was well-or-ill . . . and missing Kathy, of whom he never knew what to expect—typical woman!

He'd lain in that bunk many hours, listening to the sloshing and groaning of the plumbing, the joy and laughter of the passengers, the occasional whack of an unprotected head on the supporting beams which passengers in their haste sooner or later forgot were there. Without interest he listened to the distant arguments of the crew (their patience wearing thin as the summer bore on), soaked up the ongoing, onreaching solace of the great ship itself while his sorrow and grief gradually diminished and his depression, probably exacerbated by alcohol, intensified.

Yes, perhaps tomorrow he'd better dry out a bit. It was already a little late today, but tomorrow . . .

He held the dinghy steady while the fat bottoms of the ladies disappeared over the edge of *Jenny*'s equally fat side, turned, set himself to rowing back, now facing *Jenny* as he went, *Jenny* whom he loved more than ever for her sustaining, silent wisdom, the quiet magnetism of her world, which had helped him in ways he could not measure.

He rowed, rowed; he glanced over his shoulder to make sure of his alignment—and saw her.

The oars were not locked, and he lost one, grabbed for it, nearly capsized. He could hear Jerry laughing as he used the remaining oar as a paddle, circled around the errant one to capture it, replacing it, to continue on his way to the pier.

"Quite a performance for the holder of a Golden Arrow," Diana Bradley remarked, looping the painter around a piling.

He must have looked awful; certainly he felt it, unshaven, foul of mouth, sweat-stained, hollow-eyed. Disregarding Jerry, he climbed onto the pier and with Diana walked past the ferry slip and away from the waterfront and its eternal business. The silence between them was strained, but he knew of no way to relieve it. The stillness of the sea surrounded them, and the huge old shingled places of the summer wealthy grandly watched from behind their great expanses of waterfront lawn. She stopped and turned to him; the top of her head came up to his chin, and her hair was spun in the sun with red sparks in its brightness.

"I hardly know what to say. I'm just awfully sorry, Steve, if I've added to the hell you've been going through." She met his eyes then, and hers were kind and tender as they had not been two weeks ago. "I've spoken with my aunt. She told me—about you and Dad."

He swallowed past the obstruction in his throat and past the knot of tension there, while Diana searched his face, going over every detail as though to confirm the truth of what she had learned. His legs were trembling, and he lowered himself onto the sand; she sat beside him. There was a long, painful silence.

"My aunt told me you haven't been home since she saw you at the Historical Society meeting."

"No. I haven't," he admitted, sweating all over, his guts quivering like jelly. But she only waited, clearly expecting him to say more. "I needed time," he made himself tell her. "I still do."

"I'm sorry. I didn't understand . . . anything." Her eyes filled, and she looked away. "My aunt didn't realize how it would affect you, either. Learning about Dad, I mean."

Her profile was nearly the same as it had been when she was young, her nose straight and still fine, her chin firm and her lips full. And now—now the barrier of years had been breached and the girl she had been spoke to the young man he had been and to the man he was now.

"Alice wants to talk to you."

"What about?"

"She didn't say. She just called me and asked me to find you when the *Lawrence* put into Edgartown—and deliver her message. To please meet with her."

"Do you think it's important?"

"I'm sure it's important to her. Maybe its important to you, too."

He thought about it.

"I don't think it would hurt, if you agreed to see her," Diana proferred. "It might even help."

He sifted sand through his fingers, felt its grainy warmth, smoothly, silkily running off his hand.

"Steven," she said softly, "perhaps if you saw her and talked with her you'd find you wouldn't have to run away any more."

He opened his mouth to speak and saw helplessly that he could not.

"I think it's time you found your father," she said levelly. "And faced him. Then he won't hurt you any more. My Aunt Alice can tell you about him and I think that's what she wants to do."

The moment hung heavily between them.

"He's dead," she said softly. "He's dead, Steven. He's gone. He was a good man, and he belongs to you. If you could accept him instead of running from your memory of him, I think you'd feel a lot better, about a lot of things."

"Is that what you think I'm doing?"

"That's what Aunt Alice thinks."

There was no choice, he knew. Whether Alice Bradley was right or wrong, he could not go on this way forever—in fact did not want to. Alice Bradley, perhaps, could help him to close this part of his life, write the concluding paragraph to it, and keep it within the bounds of manageable pain.

"All right."

"Will a meeting at my house be all right?"

"Sure," he said, aware that he would be very glad for the chance to see her again.

"I have to get back," she said. "The store starts to get busy right about now."

They walked in the direction of downtown.

"Tell me about yourself," he said. "You know a hell of a lot about me, and I don't know anything about you."

"There isn't much to tell. I was married young, and six months later my husband was drafted into the Korean War. We have two children—twins—born when he was overseas."

"Twins!"

"Honest."

"It must be hard when they're small."

"You're not kidding! And it was even harder when Paul returned. He was different somehow. A stranger to me, and he remained one. He went through college on the G.I. Bill, and then he taught school—science—and then I realized, a few years later, that he was on his way to becoming an alcoholic. Which was a real problem. It was the cause of our divorce, actually."

"Where is he now?"

"I'm not sure. I'm always afraid he'll show up, but he never has."

"You were very young, to have married a man serving in Korea."

"I was eighteen." She was nearly defiant, as though challenging him to mention that very little time had passed from between seeing him last, many years ago, and meeting her husband. Perhaps too little time. "The house I live in belonged to Paul's family, and they gave it to me, since the children and I had nowhere to go. And fortunately I was awarded the business." Deliberately she hastened her pace. "Running the shop is fun—I've really enjoyed it. Aunt Alice tells me you and your wife run a business too. Aside from windjamming."

"Mari runs it," he said, stifling the demon that rose to declare he ought to go home, if only to take the garbage to the dump.

I'll go when I'm ready, he told it. Let J. Barry go to the dump. It'd be a good lesson in humility.

The pier where Jerry still tinkered with the yawl boat was crowded with *Jenny Lawrence*'s customers who waited to carry their day's treasure aboard.

"My fan club." He pointed and grinned, and realized that for a long time nothing had seemed even remotely humorous. He turned to the woman at his side. "Thanks, Diana, for coming down."

"It's okay." She smiled, and her eyes met his the way he'd hoped they would two weeks ago.

"When would it be convenient to see your aunt?"

"Why not next Tuesday, when you dock in Edgartown. Come to the shop as soon as you can; I'll arrange to have her at my place, and I'll take you there."

"All right, then." With a wave that was nearly jaunty he left her, loaded the first contingent of customers, and headed out to their floating palace, and as he rowed he saw that Diana Bradley, barely hidden around the corner of a waterfront building, was watching his slow, steady progress.

She's watching, he thought as he rowed. She's watching and she thinks I don't know it. He saw her turn away and disappear into the crowd.

"What's for supper tonight, Skipper?" asked Richard Nelson from Wachuset, Rhode Island. "All this sight-seeing and gadget buying makes a man hungry."

"Have to ask the cook," he replied. "But my feeling is that we're going to broil steaks on the deck. With the help of a charcoal grill, of course." Appreciatively, they laughed.

"Who's the pretty girl you were with, Skipper?" asked Mrs. Nelson, teasing.

"Old friend." He meant to say it briefly, without expression, but found that he could not stop his grin.

"Cat that swallowed the canary, if you ask me," a passenger said to Mrs. Nelson with a suggestive nudge.

"Here we are," he said quickly, sculling an oar and easing up beside *Jenny*'s ladder. "Up you go."

On the wharf the bell rang again, and he was glad for its excuse that would whisk him away before any more comments could be passed. He rowed back, loaded six more passengers. Jerry, who was putting the finishing touches on the yawl boat, regarded him speculatively, perhaps a little slyly, said nothing.

She watched you, he reminded himself. She didn't want you to know it, either. She hid.

And suddenly he realized that he was glad.

28

He scrambled out of the now-functioning yawl, hurried off the wharf, eager as a boy. He dodged tourists and Islanders intent on making their money while the season, what was left of it, yet lingered: hurried, nearly ran until he once again stood in front of Vincente's Cheese and Wine Shop, paused to catch his breath, aware of the anticipation that chased in and out of hidden places within himself. It was probably inappropriate to feel so glad at the prospect of meeting an attractive woman, he reflected, yet the plain fact was that seeing Diana Bradley last week had made a big difference to him and he was, indeed, looking forward to seeing her again.

Tim Bradley had not haunted him. He'd slept better and had drunk less, without even trying to cut back. He was less distant with *Jenny*'s crew; his interest in the passengers was reviving. If not whole yet, surely he was on the way to being mended. She'd broken the spell, had Diana Bradley, and if she did nothing more he'd be eternally grateful.

More? he asked himself, heading for the door of the shop. You're a married man. What do you mean, more!

You know perfectly well what I mean, he answered himself, and let himself in.

She looked him up and down.

"I must say you seem just a tad better than you did when I saw you last."

"I'm feeling a tad better too." He smiled.

"Let's hurry—if you don't mind! My aunt got here on the ten o'clock ferry, and since it's nearly two now, she's probably worn a rut in the floor with her pacing."

"Nervous, huh?"

"I'll say."

"Is your house far?"

"Oh, no! Just a couple of blocks. Come on!"

Signaling her departure to the young girl who was her helper, Diana led him out the back door, into a small court-yard and around the side of her shop, onto the street. "If I go out this way, no one will stop me for a discussion of wine," she explained. "Poor Aunt Alice would never survive more delay."

He laughed. "I hope this interview lives up to her expectations. Whatever she expects."

"Don't worry about it." She glanced up at him as they hurried along. "I think she just wants to set the record straight. Just to feel better about things. The way you do already."

"What makes you think I feel better?"

"It's obvious!"

He thought it wiser not to suggest that it was she, herself, who had begun the healing process, rather than the prospect of looking at the past with Alice Bradley.

In fact, he had not thought of this interview at all, but only of ways and means to get off *Jenny* and over to Vincente's without the crew knowing where he'd gone.

"Did you have a good week's sail?" she asked, a little breathlessly since they were hurrying.

"Fine week. The motor on the yawl boat is finally working. If it lasts the season and we don't have to spend more on it, Eric and I—Eric's the skipper—we may even be able to pay ourselves a wage."

"Your own future must be more secure, then. With the *Lawrence* making out that well."

"Sure is."

"You'll stay in Waterford?"

He thought of his foundering marriage, the gradual, inexorable foundering of Waterford itself. Things he did not want to talk about. "I suppose," he said.

"Here's my house," she said briskly, easing them past his reluctance. She led him through the white-painted gate, up the front path.

It was a Half-Cape, two windows to the right of its plain front door, its eaves low and its roof broad, its chimney too large, too heavy. The antique window glass rippled in rain-bowed waves and its interior was unchanged from the original design of half-houses: an entry large enough to accommodate the front door, from which a staircase curled up around the chimney block; a tiny parlor took up the front of the house; a keeping room in back, now a pleasant kitchen with a fireplace and wide, gleaming board floors. A small lean-to had been added, probably for wood once, but it held a cot and a pine bureau and a chair now, he saw.

Alice Bradley waited for him at the kitchen table. She rose to greet him, her face urgent, and then sank back as though willing herself not to rush at him, not to swamp him or herself with emotion that did not rightfully belong to this moment.

"I'm going back to the shop," Diana told them. "I'll return in time to take you to the four-o'clock ferry, Aunt Alice."

"Yes, dear, thanks," Alice Bradley said without taking her eyes away from him, and he wished she'd look somewhere else. He watched Diana leave, waved to her when she turned at the door to reassure herself that all was well.

Beautiful, he thought. She is beautiful.

"I want to tell you, Steve," Alice said, "how sorry I am that learning of Tim's death has upset you so."

How much did she know? How much had she understood? "What makes you think I'm upset?" he countered, finding that he resented this woman, who was a virtual stranger to him—a woman who knew more about him than he knew about himself.

She looked at her hands and said humbly, "If my visit to Waterford was in any way the cause of your leaving home, I can hardly forgive myself."

"It's not the cause. It's only the excuse."

Quickly she backed away from a topic which was not her concern. "I was uncertain at the time whether or not you knew Tim was your father. That's why I approached so obliquely." Her voice became firm and brisk as she bore down on the object of the occasion. "I hope you'll forgive me for asking how long you've known? About him?"

"Twenty years," he said, reluctant still. "My mother told me after that night when I first met you at the cottage. When we all played canasta." He was being drawn in, despite himself. His curiosity nudged his reluctance aside. "When I met you then, in East Waterford, did you know who I was?"

"Indeed I did, the minute I saw you. Charles Sinclaire couldn't beget a son like that! Besides, I knew Tim when he was about the same age—the similarities are unmistakable. And I remembered that he'd seen something of Emily Merrick that last summer we were all in Waterford. There was no doubt in my mind, though it was quite a shock, believe me! And the more I've thought about it, the more I remember, and the worse I feel. Because I have to take responsibility for your situation. Both now, and . . . and initially. That's one reason I wanted to meet you today. To own up to it—to rectify it if I can, in some small way."

"What did you have to do with it?" he asked, aware that he had never tried to find out before—about any of it. Nor had he wanted to.

"Tim and I were first cousins. Our fathers were brothers. We were close of age, and as sometimes happens in such situations, we became deeply attracted to one another as we matured—an attraction neither of us ever acknowledged. Generation after generation of Cape Codders married their first cousins and thought nothing of it, but Tim and I lived in the twentieth century, and we believed consanguinity wrong. So we always hid our feelings, Tim and I. By not acknowledging them, after all, they didn't exist! But the summer in question, Tim talked his father into letting him spend time in Waterford fixing up the old Bradley place while I devoted all my energy in the attempt to get the better of that harridan, my beloved half-sister Elizabeth Edgarton."

"She was something of a witch, wasn't she?" he agreed.

"A vixen is more like it. For years she'd blacklisted me. She'd gotten everyone in Waterford to forget I even existed, just because her mother—who was also my mother—married John Bradley. Talk about unfair!" Her old eyes flashed.

"She was pretty successful," he pointed out. "I spent a long time at Kingsland with Cousin Elizabeth, and I never even knew she had a sister."

"I'm not surprised," Alice remarked grimly. "She was clever and good at manipulating people. But the summer in question, I was very much in the public view, and I challenged her openly and vigorously. I didn't care much for Waterford's summer set but I knew they were the key because I could influence the younger generation of that society. Elizabeth controlled their parents, but the people my age or close to it had minds of their own, and through them I believed I could break Elizabeth's hold on her precious group. In fact, I believed I could break up the group altogether!"

"Where did my father fit in?" he prompted.

"Well, he was a virtual stranger to Waterford. Generally he and Uncle David only visited us in the off-season because, even though they would have been included in the summer group, being rich and successful and all, they were fond of my father, and to run around with the very people who snubbed Dad and me went against the grain. So Tim was new in town. He'd just graduated from Amherst and was all set to occupy his seat at his father's office, just as he and his father had always planned. Yet the closer came the time for him to be caged up in Worcester, the more he dreaded it. That's why he asked his father if he might spend the summer working on the old family homestead, which badly needed attention. He suggested that painting it would be a sort of vacation after all his hard work at college, and the indulgent papa agreed. So there we were, thrown together more than we'd ever been. At first I was so busy with my own schemes I didn't pay much attention to Tim, and he, for his part, set out to enjoy himself for the summer. He'd met your mother, and probably, had things gone smoothly, he'd have gone around with her for the season—conceivably would have fallen in love with her; married her. Obviously he liked her."

He only shrugged. It was a moot point, after all!

"But in an unexpected turn of events, we came face to face with how we felt. I'd unexpectedly got a wonderful summer job, supervising the Wardens' daughter, which was exactly the right spot to be in, because Pris Warden was in the center of things, and through her I'd be there, too. Within a week of supervising the Warden girl, I had her in the palm of my hand. And in two weeks, Pris and I were at the bridge table with her maids! I was ecstatic after that first bridge game! I came home smug and happy, and Tim was there, as he was apt to be late in the day. Daddy was out in his bog puttering around, and I was so delighted with my success I hugged my cousin, as one will do when enthusiastic, and we ended up in an embrace that changed to something quite different—and the game was over. Unfortunately, by that time Tim already had been intimate with your mother."

"Did you know it at the time?"

"Gracious no! Certainly not! But I know for a fact that they didn't see one another from the time I became Pris Warden's chaperon."

"Why are you so sure?" he asked.

"Because once I was part of things at the Wardens', your mother was in trouble. Her parents wouldn't condone her hobnobbing with me while Elizabeth was ranting and raving at Kingsland, and they couldn't let her run around with Pris Warden, who was constantly at my side. Tim was forbidden to enter the house too, being a Bradley—and so she had nowhere to meet him, talk to him. By the time her suspicions were certainties, he was gone. He'd run off. And I was responsible for it," she said sheepishly. "And I ask your forgiveness—if not now, then sometime when you find it in yourself to give."

"In what way were you responsible?"

"Well—let me approach it this way: Until that summer we'd avoided one another because we were cousins. Then we decided to look the other way. We reasoned that cousins had married one another for a long, long time, so what was the harm in another consanguineous marriage? The only family weakness I knew of was a Merrick weakness, on my mother's side. And Tim, after all, was a Bradley. So I believed. And so, of course, did he."

He was alerted by the look in her eye, pinning him to his chair, electrifying him, telling him . . . telling him . . .

Prickles chased themselves from one end of his being to the other, and he met her eyes and made himself wait.

Alice sighed and leaned back, releasing him.

"You ought to know . . . you need to know that my Uncle David—Tim's father—was Kingsley Merrick's bastard."

He commanded stillness of his body, of his brain, hung on tight.

"Yes! His bastard, Steve. And the only person in the whole world who knew it was my sister Elizabeth. And when she learned that Tim and I had become engaged, she knew she could use it to force me to relinquish him, and to force me to give up my hold on Waterford's society, which I was on the eve of taking from her. Two devastating blows to the enemy—me—in one swoop. A bonanza."

Alice shrugged, and Steven was quite sure that she was having trouble composing herself. But when she spoke, the battle was over, her voice calm.

"Illegitimacy was a terrible stigma in those days, and Uncle David, who was kindly, decent, not particularly original—he'd have been crushed, if not ruined. I couldn't chance it. If he'd responded badly—suicidally, which wouldn't have been at all out of the question, not in those days of those moral values—it would have scarred Tim far more deeply than my breaking off with him. Not to mention that my own father would have been profoundly upset for all sorts of reasons! An old man, near the end of his life. . . . I broke off our engagement. I told Tim that I couldn't, after all, marry my own cousin and that he'd be doing us both a favor by leaving town as quickly as he could."

"And?"

"And he ran away to sea in the best of Cape Cod traditions, and eventually returned with Diana's mother to take over his father's business, and we picked up our friendship where we'd left it, before we'd let down the barriers. And you know the rest. He hadn't any idea that your mother was already carrying his child. I assure you, Steven, that he would never have deserted her. Never! He was a tremendously decent person, as well as a tremendously attractive one. But I thought you ought to know . . . *needed* to know, that he was a Merrick. A grandchild of Kingsley Merrick, same as me. And that puts you directly in line with Kingsley Merrick too."

"Do you think I care?" he asked brusquely. "Frankly, Alice, I've heard of the great Merrick all my life. Cousin Elizabeth venerated him to the point of nausea, and my wife is going to do the same, I'd judge, and I'm really rather sick of it."

"I know, I know." She fiddled with her coffee spoon. "He deserves better, you know. He wasn't a stuffed shirt, at all. My mother remembered him well, Steven, and she had good judgment. My father, too, admired him, not for the reasons everyone else does, but because my father, too, had very good judgment. They admired him because he was so unpretentious."

"Unpretentious!"

"And determined to force Waterford into recognizing the basic worth of people. So determined that he made it over into an egalitarian society, where an honest man stood highly, no matter what his rank. And he single-handedly put power into the hands of the laborer by giving West Waterford the economic advantage of a mill. Because of that, West Waterford people were able eventually to move to the town's center when the rich left. The poor inherited the earth after all. The town you know, Steven—it's his legacy."

He thought of that legacy, watching her, and tried to control the bitterness rising within.

"People like your mother never knew what Waterford was really like," Alice Bradley said eagerly. "Because she belonged to the summer society. But that was only the fringe; the summer people were the cash crop, and that's all they were. The town belonged to common, ordinary, humble people; it was run by and for them. It was the town Kingsley Merrick had envisioned."

"Until now."

"Yes," she agreed. "Until now. And that's another reason I had to see you. When I went back to talk to the Historical Society, I saw people I'd known from before—in fact, I saw quite a lot of them. They told me about you—about what you'd tried to do on their behalf."

"Can't win them all," he fenced.

"And so I wanted you to know that you were following a tradition and a legacy Kingsley Merrick left you through your father," she forged on. "A legacy Tim himself never knew about. But you—you know it all! It's in your bones. You were born to it."

The front door opened, closed.

"—and I hope you'll keep on trying. For myself, I nearly succeeded in following in my grandfather's footsteps. He caused the ranks of the wealthy to open and made room for the humble. I failed, because of Elizabeth, but in the end the depression did it for me! It simply closed over the heads of the summer people like the Red Sea, and they were gone. And the town belonged to its year-round population as it had before, and the balance Kingsley Merrick had set up was restored. That balance is in jeopardy today, Steven, as you well know. You mustn't give up!"

"Maybe fate will do a better job than I can do," he parried. "It did Kingsley Merrick's job for him, it seems to me. Once when West Waterford people moved to the center of town—once when the world went bankrupt. Maybe fate will do it again."

"Fate can be made to happen," she insisted. "Kingsley Merrick did it. And perhaps Waterford can do it again today—through you. Surely you must have thought it mattered—you can't deny that you tried, Steve!"

"No . . . I did try." He looked out the kitchen window, to the minuscule yard out back fringed with tall bushes. "But it occurs to me that I did it because I needed them," he mused. "It occurs to me that I'm no different from Waterford's new people—that I didn't want the town to change, either. That the only difference between us lies in the things we want unchanged."

Alice Bradley drew herself up. "Clearly you wanted to give Waterford folk the chance to remain as they were—and where they were, regardless of why you might have wanted to, or what you needed."

"It doesn't matter, Alice," he told her wearily. "The town is out of their hands now, and out of mine."

"But you can seize the next opportunity, can't you? And the one after that, and the one after that? Why do you think I came so far! Why do you think I've told you all this! Yes, I wanted you to know where you came from. I owed you that.

But when I learned what you meant to those people . . . well, I wanted to urge you to continue what you've begun. They haven't given up yet, Steven, and you mustn't either. No dream is dead, if there's someone left to dream it."

He met her eyes steadily and did not permit himself the relief of looking away nor the agreement that looking away would imply.

"I used the vision of Kingsley Merrick to gain my own ends, Steven, it's true. But in the process I worked for a goal bigger than I was, and I'm not ashamed of what I did. I was proud of my principles then, and I'm proud of them yet. I wanted to urge you—beg you if I had to—not to abandon them. They matter," she faltered, and looked past him, life's injuries and penalties suddenly engraved on her old face. "If they're abandoned now, then Elizabeth will have won."

Diana, whom neither of them had heard, appeared in the doorway. "Do you still want to make the four-o'clock ferry, Aunt Alice?" She looked from one of them to the other. "Or do you need more time?"

Alice rose stiffly from her chair. "I'm supposed to meet a friend for dinner in Hobbes Hole at six o'clock. I have to leave, whether I want to or not." There was a minuscule pause in which he believed she waited for him to urge her to stay. He said nothing.

"Well, then, Steven, let's take her to the wharf," Diana said brightly, to counteract the tension in the room.

"Have we got time to walk?" the old lady asked. "I'd love to stretch my legs."

"Sure," Diana said, checking the clock. "If we move right along."

He followed the two women, since the sidewalk would not accommodate three abreast. Like a eunuch, he thought, dodging other pedestrians. I need a turban and a spear. He thought about that with determination, because he didn't want to think about anything else.

At the ferry slip throngs of people milled about, and most passengers were already aboard.

"Well, I'll thank you and be on my way," Alice said. "It's meant a lot to me, to be able to meet Steven and talk to him."

Diana kissed her cheek. "I'm glad it worked out."

For himself there was nothing to say, nothing he could say. He shook Alice Bradley's proffered hand and in silence stood with Diana and watched the old lady disappear into the ferry's maw. Bells rang, horns hooted, people called, and the ship majestically backed out of its slip, turned, glided out into the harbor at the far edge of which the *Jenny Lawrence* rode at anchor, a mastiff guarding Edgartown.

"I've got to go back now and grab supper," Diana said. "I hate to just leave you, Steve, but I have to run."

Above them the gulls gabbled in the blueness of the late-afternoon sky and the voices of humankind on the docks and in the streets of Edgartown blended and were jumbled up. He had no wish to be alone.

"Can I walk with you?"

Warily, she nodded. "Sure."

They threaded their way through the crowd and, when it thinned, walked side by side. He was no longer feeling like a eunuch, he observed with another grin that he hoped she would not notice.

"Was it all right?" she asked. "Talking with my aunt?"

"Sure," he answered, vitally aware of the grace with which Diana Bradley moved.

She glanced his way. "You know what I mean."

"No. What do you mean?"

"Well . . . did you gain or lose? It sounded like a quarrel when I came in."

"We weren't arguing, really. I'm trying to come to some conclusions of my own, and she was pushing hers, is all."

"Well, I'm sure it meant a lot to her, Steve. Thanks for going along with it."

"My pleasure."

Her neck was long and slender; he could enclose it in his hands and hold her life at his fingertips if he wanted to. Her skin was smooth, her cheek rounded like a child's.

"I see Doug quite often. Would you like to meet him again. Talk to him?"

"I don't know," he said. "It rather depends on what he thinks of having a bastard brother, doesn't it?"

"Don't!" Diana cried, and stopped. "Don't say that!" she flared, and they stood watching one another while the occasional passerby edged around them. "Don't be so unkind to yourself," she said more gently.

"I only wanted to see your reaction. Without your having a chance to think it over."

"Did you doubt me?" She walked quickly away, and he had to hurry to keep up.

He waited, bided his time until she'd slowed down a little. "I never worried about my own worth. I'd had to slug that out with my stepfather for years, and once I'd won my battle for myself with him, illegitimacy couldn't alter anything. But other people sometimes aren't so charitable. Or can't be. It's something I need to test. I'm sorry if I offended you. But the fact is that we really don't know how Doug will feel, do we?"

"I guess we don't," she admitted.

"So if it wasn't fair, throwing a remark at you to see how you'd take it—well, I apologize. But it's the gut response that counts. The one you don't plan on and can't control. I've learned a lot about gut response in the last few weeks."

"Ah, Steven . . ." Her voice was soft; quickly she overrode whatever she intended to say. "Do you plan to tell your wife now?"

"Yes."

"Why? I mean, after all these years, what difference does it make?"

"Quite a bit, I should think," he said dryly.

They turned into her own front walk, through the fence gate to the door of the little half-house. The parched lawn looked cool now in the lengthening shadows of evening.

"Your neighbors will wonder about all the comings and goings at your house today," he remarked lightly.

"I'll say!" She laughed. "Usually I work and nothing happens all day long." She dug into her purse for her key, turned to the door, her back to him. "They'll have a marvelous time, my neighbors, speculating on who that handsome man was they saw coming home with me." Her eyes twinkled as she glanced at him over her shoulder, teasing because, after all, he was a friend from long ago, wasn't he? With whom such a joke might be shared?

And then her expression changed and the twinkle disappeared and her gaze shifted uneasily. She retreated.

"Well, thanks for walking me back," she stammered, pushing open the door.

"Aren't you going to invite me in?"

"Certainly not! What would the neighbors say!" she retorted.

"I suppose you have to get supper for the kids."

"Oh, no. They don't live here with me." She caught herself, instantly uncomfortable. "My daughter shares a pad—I believe that's what they call it—with three other girls," she said quickly. "David lives in a houseful of boys. They only come home to deliver their laundry. I have to go, Steve. My help's off at six o'clock."

How cleverly she'd arranged the impossibility of their spending protracted time alone!

"I'd like to see you again," he said, fighting fear. "How about that tour of the *Lawrence?*" he persisted—for he must. "Will you let me show her to you now?"

"I . . ." Helplessly she looked up at him, unable to answer, and he was reminded of deer in the woods, gentle, slim creatures with great eyes, shyly coming forward, instantly leaping back when alarmed. "Will you?" It was not a polite, casual question: it was an important and critical one, and his intensity communicated itself to her. She backed a step into the entry, and he followed.

"Have you been home at all since you first saw my aunt?"

"No."

"Why not?"

Her question was not idle, he knew, nor was she prying. "When I first saw Alice, I panicked. When she told me about . . . your father . . . his death . . . I found myself in the middle of something I didn't understand and couldn't control. And then my wife had the poor taste or timing or both to crowd me so that I had to get away from her. And once I was gone, I found I didn't want to go back. Is that what you wanted to know?"

She flushed but was not deterred. "You have children."

"Yes."

"Do you miss them?"

"Yes."

"And your wife? Now that you've been gone from her for a while, do you miss her?"

"Hardly." He reached out to touch her hair. "Otherwise I wouldn't be here, would I?"

She did not look away or draw back; her eyes were large and very clear, and he watched carefully, listened to himself—to her—looked deeply and saw that Tim Bradley's death, whatever else it may have meant, whatever else it had done, had freed them. Freed him for her, playing into his hands and hers, and now that he was freed, he saw that he wanted her.

He wanted her and he always had.

"About the *Lawrence,*" he said, and heard a glad singing start somewhere, felt its rise. "Would you like to meet her next week?"

"Steve . . . I just don't know . . ."

"You don't need to be afraid of me," he said quietly. "I

won't hurt you, or deceive you, or run away again. I swear it." And then he drew her to himself, raised her face to his, and kissed her lightly and then deeply, and more deeply, yet with great and terrible restraint, until she answered and her body became a part of his own, so well made for him that she was infinitely flesh of his flesh. He struggled desperately with himself as her own exquisite urgency betrayed her, gave her to him, and she became the girl he'd held in his arms twenty years ago. It required all his self-control to draw away.

"Good-bye," he said softly. "I'll be back."

"Yes. All right." Her voice shook.

"To take you on that tour."

"I'll think about it." She leaned against the door as though she had no strength left and watched as he made himself walk away.

29

How different Waterford looked, now that he'd been gone these few weeks!

Of course he was not the haunted man who'd left it. That, certainly, made a difference. But there was more. Seen with a clearer eye, Waterford itself was altered because of the elms. For the heat of the summer had finished what the beetles began: most of the elms were dead. Their bare branches let in sunlight—all of it—and now, in the harshness of August, the lawns were even browner than usual and there was more dust along the road, and the antique houses were exposed like aging women in the sun, their caked paint no longer covering their wrinkles. It was not enough, now, to dress up an old, plain house with shutters and wrought-iron railings and lampposts designed to look colonial, because the house itself was set so barrenly on its lot, an old hen without eggs to hatch, without a future, without purpose.

He stopped at Hall's Texaco for gas and the latest news.

"How's it going?" he asked Don Gray at the pump.

Don shrugged. "Can't complain."

"How's Roly?"

"Gone."

"Gone where?"

"Maine."

"When did he do that?"

"Couple weeks ago. The selectmen took his scanner. He's not important no more. So they took it away, sold it, put the money in the treasury. Fifty dollars. New police chief didn't need it."

"Rubbing it in a little, were they?"

"I don't know," Don said, his face impassive. "I don't take sides. I liked to keep out of everyone's way."

"So then what happened?"

"Roly said he'd had enough; that's all. He said he knew the scanner belonged to the town, but he just hated like hell to give it to those bastards who smiled when they told him to return their property. Said they'd got what they wanted and he just plain was giving up."

He paid for the gas, drove on.

He pulled into the driveway at Kingsland, where the maples, thank God, were still intact. After the pitiless glare of Main Street, it was like fleeing to an oasis. The porches seemed blessedly cool and shaded; a no-vacancy sign hung from the railing by the steps. The front door was open.

"Hello?" he called.

"Um, hello," said a stranger, sitting in the horsehair chair under Mary Deems's portrait, reading the Sinclaire newspaper, invading the Sinclaire house.

"How do you do," he said quickly, and walked down the hallway to the kitchen.

It was empty.

He hastened to the billiard room, where Kathie was watching TV.

"Daddy!" She jumped up, spilling her mirror and brush, girls' magazines and hair rollers, and flew into his arms. "Welcome home!" It was clear that she had not doubted the eventuality of his return.

"How are things here?" he asked, hugging her. "How's the boardinghouse business?"

"Great!" she enthused. "We're making lots of money. Is the *Jenny* repaired now? Is everything okay? We'd have come to visit you, but there was always something coming up on Sundays and Mom couldn't get away. And Saturdays, you know, are changeover," she said importantly, obviously very much part of Mari's enterprise. And his absence explained to her satisfaction. Mari had evidently kept his image burning bright, and he certainly did have to give her credit for that!

"*Jenny*'s repaired for the moment," he told her. "Where's everyone?"

"Mom's at the Marshalls'. Rick's at the Searses'."

"So you're all alone?"

"Someone has to be here, in case the phone rings or someone comes to the door."

It occurred to him that she was defenseless should the wrong person ring the bell. And Kathie was only . . . was it fourteen now?

"No one's ever had trouble, Dad," she said, reading his mind. "And we're wired to the dispatcher."

"Oh?"

"All we have to do is touch one of six hidden switches and the alarm goes off. Everyone's been hooking up to the system since the new police chief came to town. The switches ring an alarm and a cop comes right away."

Well, he could hardly fault that protection, could he? You never did know, anymore, who was wandering around the Cape. You couldn't depend on your neighbor to help you, because anymore you did not even know who your neighbor was. Surely his family was protected better now than if Roly still resided at his station!

"When's your mother coming home?"

"Pretty soon, I think. Aunt Claudia is having a meeting."

"Historical Society?"

"Not really. It's a meeting of a lot of people—some of them society members, who are making up new rules. This one'll really get your goat, Dad." She laughed at him affectionately. "They're inventing a historical district on Main Street. And for most of Waterford."

"And?"

"If they can pass it, you'll have to go before a committee and ask to change the color of your paint or whether you can build a garage or plant a bush or cut down a tree." She laughed. "Can you beat that? And there's hardly a tree left to cut—did you notice how many of them died this summer? You should hear Aunt Claudia! The elms in front of Kaptainsholme are dead, and you'd think they'd gone and done it on purpose."

"I suppose your mother is quite taken with the idea of a historical district?"

"I'll say," Kathy said dryly. He shrugged, and she shrugged too, and he decided not to let it bother him. It was not his concern. If Waterford ever approved such a thing, then Waterford deserved it. If Mari wanted it, he would not bother to argue. He had other difficulties to occupy him now.

Mainly Mari herself.

The kitchen door banged, and several footsteps later Rick appeared.

"Dad!"

The boy had grown in the month's absence, as a garden will grow, untended, in warm weather, and Rick was clearly going to be as tall as his Dad when he got done.

"Gee, it's good to see you!" Manfully Rick thrust out his hand, but the greeting turned into a bear hug, despite the determination of them both to keep the proceedings adult and dignified.

"I see you've been keeping an eye on the place."

"I sure have. The grass has about stopped growing by now, though, so my troubles are over. Say, Dad, what do you think about putting a flagpole in the middle of the yard? I think it'd add a lot of class. If we do it now, we won't have to ask anyone's permission. And you don't need to tell Mom I said so, either," he said to his sister.

"I won't! I won't!"

"Like you say, it's got class." Steven smiled.

Another banging announced the presence of Mari, and he felt his entire body tighten. He waited, facing the door.

"Mom! Dad's here!" Kathy called, lightening the load perceptibly. He'd dreaded surprising Mari, and hadn't thought of a way around it. Trust a child!

"Hello, Steve," said Mari calmly, crossing the floor to kiss his cheek. "Welcome home."

"Thanks." He smiled, not quite able to meet her eye. "Seems as though everything's under control here."

"Oh, yes, the kids have been a great help. We're doing fine." She nodded their way in approval. "But I'm sure they could use a lift, now that the *Lawrence* is taken care of. And so could I. Do you plan to stay in Waterford for a while, now that *Jenny* is fixed?"

"Well, she's afloat still." He smiled. "The season's not over yet."

The front door opened and closed, but no one went to answer it or to see who was there.

"Full house," Mari said, "so there's no need to go out. Unless the bell rings for the manager."

"Dad says he'll help put up a flagpole," Rick told his mother.

"Oh? I didn't know you wanted one."

"Just thought of it," Rick said blandly. "But I think the place would look good with a flag out there where the driveway circles around, don't you?"

"We'll get started a little later." Steven winked at the boy. "We can get a big jump on it before I have to go back to the ship."

"Maybe you could give up the ship for a day or two," Mari suggested pointedly. "You could join her later, say, on Nantucket. You could take a ferry."

"I could," he said, wondering if she was laying traps. "But I haven't arranged to do it. There'd be no one . . ."

"Bob. There'd be Bob."

He could sense her pushing, pushing, to see how far he would go to accommodate her wishes—yet how much would she wish for when she heard what he had to say?

"We could do most of it in a day, anyway," Rick was saying. "I could finish up during the week. I'm strong enough. Dad! Feel my muscle!"

The kitchen door rattled as someone knocked gently on it, and Kathy disappeared to answer, reappeared.

"There's a man outside to see you, Dad."

"Did you ask him in?" Mari asked.

"He didn't want to come in."

"Must be a native," Mari remarked dryly. "I'll get supper ready."

It was indeed a native, old Mr. Shaunessy.

"Hi, John," Steven said as warmly as he could, in case Mr. Shaunessy had heard Mari's remark.

"Hello, Mr. Sinclaire." The old man, holding his hat in his hand, was nervous. "I hope you don't mind that I . . ." He stopped, glanced around. "Have I interrupted your supper?"

He was reminded that country people generally ate early. "No. We haven't even started. What can I do for you?"

"Mr. Sinclaire, they took my keys away and I wondered if you'd ask if I could have 'em back."

"Who took what keys?" he asked, and then remembered

that Mr. Shaunessy had, for years, been custodian of the United Church.

"I'm sorry, John. I don't have much to do with the church."

"But your family's been part of it for so long, and you've known me, Mr. Sinclaire. The church board don't—and it seems, at least as far as I can tell—it seems they don't trust me."

He stopped, and the hurt in his eyes reminded Steven of Roly Hall's when he was heckled at town meeting.

"They—the deacons—said one of them would come down and unlock the church whenever I needed to get in. But, Mr. Sinclaire, that don't make sense. So the only thing I can figure out is that they must be afraid I'll steal candles and crayons."

"Now, John . . ."

"Huh!" Mr. Shaunessy barked. "I been custodian forty years. You'd think they'd trust a man with a record long as that. Nothing's ever been stolen while I've been in charge."

"Maybe it hasn't got anything to do with trusting you," Steven suggested. "Who are the deacons?" He knew the answer, of course. "Are they new?"

"Every last one," Mr. Shaunessy confirmed. "And so I was wonderin' if you could speak a good word for me. They don't know who I am but you do. I feel real bad about them keys. It's like someone thinks I done a bad job. Maybe if you told 'em I was a good janitor . . . They'd believe you."

"John, I don't think I can get them to change their minds, because I don't think it has anything to do with you. Not at all."

"You don't? Really?" Shaunessy asked, eager to believe it.

"No, I really don't. I think they like to feel as though they're in charge and not you. It makes 'em feel better to let you know who's boss, and taking your keys away makes them feel that way."

Shaunessy snorted. "They must be just a little small, Mr. Sinclaire, if taking one old man's keys away makes 'em the boss."

"Seems like it," he agreed. "But it's the way some of them operate."

Shaunessy's shoulders dropped, then straightened. "So be it," he said, and thrust out a horny, gnarled hand. "Thanks anyway, Mr. Sinclaire."

He patted John Shaunessy's back; the old man's sharp

shoulder blades rose in twin peaks, and his body was thin and frail.

"How are things going otherwise, John? Around town?"

"Terrible. Did you hear that they fired Greenleaf Stone?" Shaunessy asked as they walked toward his truck. "He let some young folks live in the house they were building before all the permits were signed. They couldn't afford to complete everything that the selectmen kept addin' onto the code; they'd hoped to finish 'em whilst they lived in the shell—but they was caught, and so Greenleaf was caught too. Used to be, folks who had to work on things slow-like could do it here. But not anymore."

The old man climbed into his old truck, started the motor, and sat a moment, listening critically. "Time I looked at the plugs," he said. "Sounds a little rough."

"Timing might be off," Steven offered, in the way of the countryman.

"It might. It might." Shaunessy eased out the choke, pushed it back, and the motor resumed its normal pace. "Can't run the town the way it's always been done if more and more people are going to live here, I suppose. Nothing's like it was, and maybe it just can't be." Shaunessy smiled sadly ahead, through the windshield, seeing the days of his youth and strength fading to memory. "But it sure helps, Mr. Sinclaire, knowin' that you're here. Knowin' that when something goes really wrong, you can speak up for us."

Steven waved deprecatingly and watched the truck rattle and cough exhaust as it left.

"Dinner's ready," Mari called. As he approached, she waited for him by the door. "And afterward, I'd like to talk to you," she said coldly.

"Good," he said, his tone an even match for hers. "Because there's a few things I'd like to tell you, too."

"You're illegitimate?" she whispered. "You're a . . ."

"That's right," he said evenly. "Mom had already become pregnant when she married my stepfather."

"But she seems so nice," Mari protested, her Midwestern, mid-century morality automatically rising in censure and chagrin.

"She *is* nice," he said calmly. "She made a mistake, is all. I knew about it a long time ago, but I'd never really dealt with it, never even thought about it. I just put it away, and Miss Alice Bradley brought it all back because my father was her cousin. I couldn't just stay here and let it overtake me, Mari. That's why I left."

"And now?" she asked. "How are things now?"

"Seem settled," he replied briefly, not at all sure how things were—or what things she meant, unwilling in any case to dissect them in her presence.

"You knew it when you met me?"

"Yes."

"And said nothing."

"That's right."

"Rather deceitful of you, Steve."

He shrugged. "That's how I was handling it, at that point. By avoidance. There's no point apologizing."

"Well, you don't seem very sorry," she declared, working on it, perhaps in order to have something concrete at which to vent her dismay. "It's the least you could do—be sorry for having tricked me."

It was not hard to hold on to his temper, because he understood she was looking for a target. "What do you want me to do?" he asked reasonably. "What do you want me to apologize for? Not being candid? Or for being illegitimate?"

It was a cruel question, because it put her in the position of having to excuse that which her heart could not forgive.

"It's parents who are illegitimate, really," she said pontifically, doing her best. "The children born out of wedlock have little to say about it. But I'm afraid I can't just shake it off, Steve. You'll have to give me time."

"Sure."

She was staring at him, as though he were different from the man she'd known five minutes before.

"What did you want to talk to me about?" he asked, reminding her that she'd asked for a confrontation even before he had.

"Well, I was going to take you to task for leaving like you did," she said feebly. "But now that you've told me why, the wind is gone from my sails. It makes what I've done seem mean."

"What have you done?"

"I . . . I was angry," she said, taking a deep breath. "I didn't care if you ever came home or not. I was going to show you that you couldn't just walk in here as though there'd been nothing wrong, and expect me to take it."

"Certainly reasonable," he said agreeably, and she glanced at him quickly as though surprised by his complacence. "How did you think you'd get even with me?"

"You always seem to like sex so well, I thought that I needn't feel I had to go along with it, because I didn't need to please you anymore. You haven't troubled to please me."

"Well, I suppose you have a point," he said neutrally. "I mean, if sex has been so unpleasant . . ."

"Not unpleasant. Just . . . not enjoyable for me the way it is for you."

"And perhaps you find it even more repugnant, now that I'm not quite the man you thought I was."

Her eyes betrayed the truth of it, though she looked away quickly. And while separate bedrooms would relieve him of having to deal with the fact that he no longer desired her, still, her rejection was more of a blow than he'd have believed possible, severing all the remaining lines of communication they shared. He turned away so that she wouldn't see that she had hurt him.

"Suit yourself, Mar." He shrugged. "Where the hell shall I sleep?"

"I took care of that," she assured him. "I bought us twin beds while you were gone."

"How swell of you," he retorted, and then stopped. There was no point in sarcasm. "If you don't mind, I'll take a room of my own—when one is available. Until then, I'll sleep on the couch."

"I do mind," she hissed. "It'd get around in a minute. I don't want everyone in town speculating on our sex life—but a lot of people have twin beds."

"By everyone in town, I take it you mean Claudia."

"One among many," she assured him.

"Well, I guess it's something you'll have to learn to live with, because I'm not going to share a room with a woman I can't touch." He sized her up. "And I take it that you'd prefer I didn't make love to you anymore. Am I right?"

She faltered. There was, after all, no reason to expect a man to stay around if such pleasantries weren't available to him—every woman knew that. If she denied him . . . "I really haven't thought it out completely, Steve," she temporized.

"Well, perhaps you'd begin to think as of now. I'll sleep on the couch until you come to a conclusion. Take your time, Mar. I'm in no hurry. Meanwhile, you'll have to excuse me. I've got a flagpole to put up."

Why are you so angry? he asked himself as he left the house, churning and hot. Nothing she's done or said comes as a surprise to you. Why are you so worked up?

Because I am human, he answered. Because she has turned me away—

"Look, Dad!" Smudged and grimy, Rick held up a large gold-leafed sign inscribed "KINGSLAND."

"Where'd you find that?"

"In the barn. I thought I remembered seeing it there a long time ago. I was thinking, Dad, that we could set the flagpole and attach an arm to it and hang this sign from the arm and maybe plant a bunch of bushes and stuff underneath it."

"Sounds fine."

"Here's a shovel for you." Rick grinned in invitation, and together they set out for the front lawn. "Why do you suppose such a swell sign was made in the first place?" the boy wondered, lugging it along. "I mean, it's perfect for advertising, but the house has never been used for tourists before, has it?"

"Heaven forbid," Steven laughed. "But the people who used to live here in Waterford did advertise—to each other. Everyone's house had a name—the more imposing, the better."

"Like Kaptainsholme?" Rick suggested with a straight face.

"Quite," he answered.

"Did you and Mom settle your fight?"

"What makes you think we were fighting?"

Rick shrugged.

"Must have seemed peaceful, with me gone so much of the time this summer."

"Dull," he said. "How about digging here?"

They sized it up: dead center of the semicircle formed by the driveway, and certainly the most visible spot. They began.

"But was it a relief—or not—to have no infighting?"

Rick glanced up, then back to the clod of earth and grass which he had pried loose. "I'd rather not say," he told it.

"Don't blame you."

They dug silently.

"The lumber yard is closed," Rick said.

"Probably."

"We'll need cement and a pole."

"Bob will have cement. He'd let us use some."

"How about a pole?"

"Seems to me Bob has a day-sailer with a hole in the bottom. Maybe he'd sell us the mast."

"Gee, Dad, do you think so?"

"We'll go over when it gets too dark to dig, and find out."

"It'd have real class." Rick sighed, and glanced up gratefully. They smiled at one another, and returned to their shovels.

30

"Oh, Christ," Eric swore. "A hurricane watch."

They were holed up in the captain's bunk while everyone else poked about in Vineyard Haven. The passengers would ring the bell when they wanted to return; until then, Steven and Eric had snatched for themselves two uninterrupted hours. Steven had napped and written a fatherly letter to Rick with further suggestions about the mast that they'd managed to set in concrete before he'd left. Then he called on Eric, glued to the marine radio. The bottle which Eric had been nursing all day contained yet three inches of amber poison. Disciplined as always, he would make it last until suppertime; now he had his ear to the speaker, listening to the distant voice in its endless repetition of bulletins. It was late August, the breeding season for hurricanes.

"How big is the storm they're watching?" Steven asked. "Do they think it'll be bad?"

"Lessening in intensity, they say." Eric passed a hand over his face, dug at his eyes. "Broad in any case, and coming fast. It's off the New Jersey coast now. We'll start feeling its effects tonight. I don't like it."

"Not enough time to get back to Hobbes Hole?"

"It'd be dark before we got there, for Christ's sake. I won't sail in the dark. Not with a boatload of passengers."

"What do you want to do?"

"I want to get rid of 'em." Eric's eyes were bleary. "I have a bad feeling about this storm, Steve. If it's going to do to us what I think it's going to do, I'd a lot rather no damn fool was around asking stupid questions. We'll have our hands full."

They'd have their hands full getting the passengers off, too. He shuddered to think of it. "The passengers aren't going to like being sent home," he hedged pleadingly.

Eric was not impressed. "I don't give a shit what they like. The ferry will run first thing in the morning, assuming the storm hasn't reached us by then. I want them on it."

"And if the storm has hit?"

Eric shrugged and refused to answer.

"I take it the bilge situation is no better?" Steven asked.

"It's worse."

"You think we'll go under?"

"I'm not sure how she'll take pounding on the pier," Eric said. "She's an awful old lady, and nobody's done her any favors. We'll be pumping till our arms break, and we'll be tying and retying lines, trying to keep her away from the wharf. We can't leave her out here at anchor."

"Which wharf?"

"One of those over there, by the oil tanks." Eric gestured in the correct direction, even though, deeply buried in the bowels of the ship, they could see nothing, and there was no point of reference. "I spoke with the folks that own 'em, and they said we could use their docks if need be. We'll have to push her over. After we get the passengers loaded onto the ferry. Take care of getting rid of 'em, will you?"

"Sure," he soothed. "Don't worry about them."

"I'm not," Eric said morosely. "I'm worried about the *Lawrence*. Get that bitch Arleen off, and Jerry too. He's more harm than help. I'll call Bob when I check out the ferry tickets. I think he'd better beef up our checking account in case everyone cashes in at once." Eric savagely rowed ashore to use the telephone, chewing furiously at his lip, the haggard lines in his face deep and harsh.

The bell on the wharf rang; a group of passengers, their arms full of packages, looked expectantly toward *Jenny*. They'd had dinner and a drink or two, they'd shopped successfully and enjoyed themselves, and now hailed their taxi. The yawl struggled to life, and he went after them.

"Hi, Steve," they called, untidily scrambling to their seats. "How's it going, Commodore?"

"I'm afraid there's bad news," he told them before revving up the motor, over which conversation was not possible. "There's a tropical storm on the way. I'm afraid I'll have to ask you to pack your bags and be prepared to abandon ship first thing in the morning."

"You're kidding!"

"We'll refund your money, of course. And pay for any accommodation you might have to get for yourselves until you can switch your plans, covering the nights you'd normally have spent with us."

"Oh, nuts," growled a woman. "Here I am, all set to party it up for the week!"

"Are you really serious?" asked another pretty passenger.

"There must be a law," a man muttered. "There must be."

"You folks are my responsibility," he reminded them as pleasantly as he could manage. "We're sailing an old ship, and it's not possible to know how she'll respond—or if she will. If you'd rather stay here in Vineyard Haven and wait, it's fine. But I think you'll have trouble finding accommodations—and I won't have time to find them for you."

Their sulky faces glowered and scowled as he turned the yawl's motor over and sped them to *Jenny*.

"Start packing," he said. "When I've got everyone aboard, I'll meet you all in the aftercabin, with your reimbursement and a ticket for the six-A.M. ferry."

"Six o'clock in the morning!" a woman scoffed. "Can you believe that? I haven't seen the world at six o'clock for years!"

They climbed aboard and he went back to the wharf, wishing the yawl sounded healthier. It was running, and it hadn't refused to start yet—but he was not confident that it could push a really heavy load, like a seventy-ton schooner, away from a dock in a storm. . . .

It took forever. Explaining. Cajoling. Dispensing checks like confetti. He was relieved that Eric had thought to call Bob about replenishing *Jenny*'s account as his balance dropped, dropped, and disappeared into the crater of negative numbers.

They began taking the luggage off at four in the morning, so that nothing would be left behind in the rush. The breeze was heavy, raising waves and blowing the tops off them, so that the bags were soaked by the time they were piled on the wharf. But the storm was taking its time, and the ferry would run.

Dawn attempted to lighten the sky as they awakened the passengers and fed them and lent them foul-weather gear on their trip to the steamship-authority slip. Then began the task of moving *Jenny* to the oil docks, a job made more difficult by the wind, which pushed her seaward from her anchorage in the harbor. The morning sky was unencouraging, the water brassy, more and more turbulent, tending to push the prow of the yawl away from *Jenny*'s stern until it finally quit altogether —fortunately only three feet from the dock. They pulled, hauled, tied, retied, rested.

"Here's the battle plan," said Eric. "The wind is blowing us away from the pier—and that's what we want, provided the lines hold. But if the wind changes—and that depends on where the eye of the storm is, and if the storm even has an eye—well, then we've got trouble. We'll have to try pulling her over to the opposite dock, so we'll put plenty of lines out now, and hope we can switch her over with the donkey engine."

"Sounds hopeless." He was tired already, just thinking about it.

"Shit and manure!" Eric shouted. "Have you got any better ideas?"

It seemed dubious at best, attempting to move a seventy-ton schooner with an antique donkey engine in the teeth of a storm, but what choice was there? He shrugged. "Lead the way, O Captain." They fastened lines and nailed down the hatches and hammered boards across the windows on the aftercabin. The fire in the galley stove was extinguished and the sails stored forward, and then they fortified themselves against the approaching calamity with a six-pack of beer and a fifth of bourbon. The whistle of the ferry had long since blown and the vessel departed, no doubt in Hobbes Hole by now. Vineyard Haven had brought its lawn chairs inside and lowered its flags, and every boat in the harbor was double-anchored and hog-tied. They could only wait it out.

They leaned against piles of life preservers stacked on the aftercabin benches.

"Ah! Beer," Eric cheered above the rising wind. "Just what I needed. Sinclaire, let's toast the storm!"

"What about the bilge pump?" he asked, opening a beer for himself. "Should we start pumping?"

"No hurry." Eric waved benignly. "We're okay for the moment. When the storm intensifies, we'll probably have to really go after it; we'd better rest now, while we can. Besides, I'm beat."

"I won't argue." He worked his way into the beer, made a deeper pocket in the life-preserver pile.

"We'll take turns. Half-hour each," Eric said. "And if we have to, we can do it together."

"Jesus, spare me," he laughed. "*Jenny* might as well sink and be done with it."

"She'd better not," Eric said seriously. He opened the new bottle of bourbon and chased his beer with a generous swallow. "It'd be a shame to lose her now," he said. "If only because living on her is so great. You'll love it, Steve, if you decide to do it. There's something about this cabin in winter that you can't match anywhere. Warm. Safe. Safe even from yourself, because everything is reduced to the most simple terms. You're clean, because *Jenny* is clean. You forget the rat race and how rotten people can be—how rotten they can make you be. You become worthy—if you know what I mean."

Such fluid, articulate, poetic expression also meant that Eric was departing into a state of inebriation.

"It stinks!" Eric waved the bourbon bottle. "They bring it aboard with them, the passengers do, and I hate them. Every one of those sons of bitches. Did you know that?"

"No. I didn't realize it. You hide it very well," he soothed.

"Did you hate them?"

"The passengers?"

"The rats, dammit! The ones running in the rat race. When you were in business, did you hate them?"

"I didn't love them. But they're not the problem, Eric. The biggest problem is that you'll turn into a rat yourself, in order to hold your own."

"There! Exactly what I mean! Were you ever afraid of turning into a rat, Steve?"

"I'd just got elbowed out of the job I wanted when I left Bronner. If I'd wanted to stay, if I was going to survive, I'd probably have had to elbow back."

"Well?"

"I never had to decide. Because we bought *Jenny*, instead, you and Bob and me."

"What if you do have to decide? What will it be?"

"No problem, pal. I'm in less danger of becoming a rat now than I've ever been, and so are you."

He wished Eric would not alternate sips of beer and swallows of bourbon.

"What makes you think so?" Eric demanded.

"Because of *Jenny*, really. Because you can run in the race and do a damn decent job without becoming a rat if you've learned what *Jenny* can teach—what I've been able to absorb just by living aboard her this summer. I think we're pretty well insulated from rathood. We'd be operating from a different base."

"I'm not insulated. And I don't think you are either," Eric insisted. "I think that we if go back to the rat race, it'll get us. *Jenny* has only postponed the inevitable."

"I don't think so."

"And besides that, we have one hell of a problem, Steve. *Jenny* isn't going to live forever."

"It doesn't make any difference," he insisted. "She exists. She'll always exist."

"I wish you were right. Because if she sinks, I'll be out in the race again whether I want to be or not. *Jenny* is my last chance. Not many women like her around." Eric passed a hand over his eyes, massaged his temples. "Christ, I've been pumping that bilge half the night, every night, it seems like."

"You have?" God only knew the bilge was high enough when he took his own turn. *Jenny* was in worse shape than he thought.

"She won't sink," Eric said fiercely, as though reading his mind. "I won't let her. If I have to spend the rest of my life at that pump, she's not going to sink."

"Of course not," he cajoled. Oh, Christ, Eric had to stay sober if *Jenny*'s condition was this bad! "We'll repair her this fall. We'll borrow, if we have to. We just have to weather this storm."

"Oh, yes, the storm," Eric said absently. "Yes."

"How much are you awake at night, pal?"

"A lot."

"What's the trouble?"

"I can't sleep, is all." Eric shrugged, but his face was suddenly deeply lined and the eyes of haunted despair peered out. "Do you know what it's like, not being able to sleep?"

"I guess everybody does, one time or another."

"I mean night after night, with no sleep in it?"

"No. Not like that."

"Pretty soon it's all you can think about," Eric said. "You get frantic. So you tell yourself that you'll just take advantage of being an insomniac. You'll damn well stay up. Do the things you want to do. Like to do. Must do. But you get tired. You get awfully tired. You want to rest, sleep, forget, but you can't. It's like there's dogs after you and you can hear their baying, like geese in the sky, and if you lie down for long, they'll catch up."

"And then?"

"Why, Steve, you don't know what dogs do when they

catch a rabbit?" He studied the bourbon bottle, picked at its label. He switched to an apparently unrelated topic. "I need a good breeze to get *Jenny* going."

"Yes, I know."

"But I'm murdering her. A good breeze is too much for her. It's this goddamned sound, Steve. It's Nantucket Sound. Its waters are murder, and they're tearing her apart. I'm letting the dogs catch up, you see?" His face was contorted. "Now, will you get your goddamn ass out there and pump, for Christ's sake?"

"I'm going, I'm going!" He struggled into his slicker. "But I sure as hell do wish you'd quit drinking while I'm gone."

"Consider it done." The Eric of old smiled up at him, breezy, profane, competent.

As soon as he battled his way through the door, the full force of the gale struck him, taking his breath away, shrill in his ears, blinding him. He paused to get his bearings, swept the water out of his eyes, worked his way to the forward portion of the cabin roof where the pump handle was, dutifully, mechanically pulling up, pushing down, pulling up, pushing down. He lost track of time, of himself; Vineyard Haven was no longer visible; only a few darker spots in the sweeping rain suggested the buildings closest to the waterfront. Near at hand, small craft bucked and leaped on the waves; farther away he saw one heading out to sea, torn loose from its moorings. The water pumped out in a steady stream, without even the least evidence of its level being lowered. He pulled up, down, endlessly, and wondered if the cabins were awash yet. There was no way to tell, and no way to find out with everything nailed so tight.

She will not sink, he told himself, pumping to the rhythm of the words.

She will not sink.

She will not sink.

His body was beginning to burn with fatigue.

She will not sink.

She must not sink, because if he couldn't live with Mari this coming winter, if they couldn't bear to be housed in together, then he needed to live with Eric aboard the *Jenny Lawrence*, helping to tidy her up for her next season.

If she has another, he thought.

Another boat whisked and bobbed across the harbor, and a dinghy crashed into the far side of the south dock. If the wind changed, and the small craft started piling up on the shore, there'd be hell to pay, for sure.

Eric came up to relieve him, and they took turns until the wind let up a little. He wasn't leaning against it quite so hard, he realized, and he stopped pumping, nearly unable to lift his numb, burning arms. He made his way around to the hatch door, checking the lines as he went. They appeared to be holding well. If the eye of the storm was approaching, everything would shift, wouldn't it? And the wind, for a bit, would work with them. They should be moving *Jenny*, allowing her to snug up to the next dock so she wouldn't be beaten against the pier here.

With Eric, he leaned wearily against the rail. "I'd judge, from the light, that the storm's lifting."

"It's changing," Eric said. "I don't know about lifting. Why don't you take advantage of it and get us more beer?"

"I was wondering if we should move the ship."

"Well, Steven, it's a gamble. I've had a change of heart about it all." Eric's voice and its tone told him that Eric was exceedingly drunk, though Eric's words continued to drop, fully shaped, from his lips. He droned on endlessly about how you could try to outguess a storm and probably be wrong, concluding that *Jenny* would stay where she was and that as long as the wind had let up a trifle, perhaps Steve would be a jolly effing good fellow and get some more cigarettes as long as he was going for a six-pack. Eric would pump while he was gone.

It was better than standing around wondering what the storm was going to throw at them next.

He jumped across the opening, closing, opening space between the ship and the dock and went down the sandspit on which the oil tanks squatted, monolithic, and on down to the center of Vineyard Haven, which looked small and insignificant and without vitality beneath the wide, unkind sky.

Most of the bars were open, he saw, packed to the very top with the holiday crowd, which had taken this opportunity to ride out the storm congenially. It was really not a hurricane at all, they insisted at the Sign of the Mermaid, where the appearance of a man from Beyond (himself) stirred all the others to thinking that they, too, should try their luck outside. He spent a lot of time advising them to stay where they were, and struggled to get to the bar. He was reminded of college days and college taverns, and the closer he got to the bar the greater was the conviviality of those who cared progressively less and less whether the storm ever ended.

Eric had long since made arrangements with the Mermaid's owner about storing his personal liquor supply, and surreptitiously the fellow put a dozen bottles of beer in a Jordan Marsh shopping bag while Steven lingered over a glass of draft, then tunneled interminably until, finally, he was at the door and could leave the humid, fermented air behind, exchanged for the higher humidity of the summer storm outside.

The wind was still slack, he noticed, but it was definitely coming from the opposite direction now. They had not experienced the clearing sky of an actual eye. Either it was not a hurricane at all, or its center was passing elsewhere. But sure as hell the wind had changed, and now the rain increased, and unless he missed his guess, the storm's intensity would pick up soon. Visibility was poor; he could barely make out the storage tanks as he looked for the dock and for the lesser hump of the *Jenny Lawrence.*

She was not there.

Impatiently he glanced over his shoulder at the way he had come earlier, to locate a boat shed that he was sure had been there before. He went over to it and started again, walking to the dock where *Jenny* ought to be. The rain picked up and brought mist with it, and the sea dissolved and the land withdrew. The pier lay before him, hanging out into nothingness, pointing its splintered finger to the sea, but the sea was void, without definition, without substance in the rising wind, and there was no ship.

Jenny was gone.

"Eric!" he called, hearing the futility of his voice.

"Eric!" he shouted to the uncaring sky.

"*Eric!*" His voice tore at his throat.

Beside the dock trailed *Jenny*'s lines. Clearly Eric had taken her to sea. He had used the change in the wind's direction to get out of the harbor. He had run away with her, like a dying animal heading to the wilderness. He had chosen to chance the open sea rather than pounding against a dock—but there was no chance at all. *Jenny* was unable to run before a storm—any storm.

The stabbing awareness and its shock backed him savagely against the unrelenting wall of certainty. Eric would die, and his sleepless nights would be over. He'd even explained why—and now the future that they'd all planned was over, too.

An upsurge of rocketing wind nearly pushed him into the water. He held up an arm to protect his face against the spitting, spiteful rain; slowly he walked to the sandy spit of beach covered with storm garbage now, and set the ridiculous

Jordan Marsh package down on the ground. It was drenched and soggy, and it fell apart, bottles spilling onto the stones; one of them hit a rock and broke, its froth blending with the spindrift.

The storm, having caught its breath, was rising and he was alone, without plans, without hopes.

Whatever it was that he'd been seeking in *Jenny*, whatever he'd found in her, would have to be sought elsewhere, found elsewhere if that was possible, and soon. Very soon.

He could not face the fetid bar, nor bear its confinement. The shops were shut, many of them boarded up, but he wouldn't have entered one even if it had been open. He had to have space, somehow, because he'd been thrown into the morass of facing up to his life, and perhaps, when he came right down to it, he'd been engaged in this struggle most of the summer. It was too much—too much to think about all at once; he needed some room to breathe and just to be.

Edgartown was seven miles away. It would take a long, long time to get there.

Grimly he set himself against the storm and made his way through the deserted town, a stranger on a desolated land inhabited only by himself. The whole of the earth was swallowed up in a vastness of rain and fog and wind, without a living soul to see whether he fell to the gound, exhausted, or to see whether the damp drizzle on his cheeks was rain or tears, and he didn't know himself if he wept or not on that unending, unwinding road to Edgartown, on which he, a pilgrim, had been set for reasons he no longer understood.

Jenny was gone, and her world with her, and it was hard to assess exactly what was left. There was one certainty: he no longer had the option of living aboard the *Lawrence* this winter, should he decide his marriage was over. *Jenny* no longer offered him home base.

Nor did Kingsland, his refuge for so many years. For Kingsland was occupied, and if he left Mari—or divorced her, or she divorced him—she would get it. The house was all he could offer by way of settlement. It was a legacy he would have to leave behind.

You have just learned about the rust and the moth, Sinclaire, he advised himself—as though he hadn't known already!

You have a son, a daughter, he reminded himself.

And, perhaps—just perhaps—you have Diana Bradley. If you can get to her.

A sheet of water rose up and arched like a plume and fell

on top of him. He stopped, dripping, suddenly cold with its soaking. Ahead of him the bloodshot eyes of brake lights glowed and a car door slammed, a man ran toward him.

"Jesus H. Christ, I didn't even see you until the last moment! Are you okay, mister?"

"I think so. Wet is all . . . but I was wet to start with." He tried to laugh reassuringly, but no sound came out.

"No day to be walking the Edgartown road. Can I give you a lift?"

"Sure can," he told the fellow, whose homely, honest face, lined with concern, peered out from beneath the bill of his dripping paint cap. Dressed in hip boots and a slicker, a rather scruffy slicker that probably leaked, he was clearly a year-round resident of the island. "Come on then. They're expecting me in Edgartown. I got to hurry," he urged as they climbed into the battered sedan and started on their way. "I'm on the emergency patrol," he explained. He drove steadily, without hurrying, so that no accident would befall him, so that he would be at the ready to beat back disaster when he arrived. He was clearly proud of his role in the scheme of island things, giving his best to ensure the well-being of tourists and of the newly arrived Vineyard citizenry, all of whom probably believed that the sum total of his existence was confined to considerations of their comfort. Who disdained him and would disinherit him eventually, if they had not already done so, as had happened already in Waterford.

Fool, he thought. What a fool, and then told himself to stop. Bitterness was not going to do a thing for him now, and it would do nothing to help the dispossessed either.

The windshield wipers beat their poor best against the onslaught of rain; there were no trees on the road, because the Vineyard was not given to trees. The car seemed to be going nowhere, with only the passing of the sandy verge confirming that they moved at all, the storm now a void through which they passed. Its refuse became apparent when they reached the edge of Edgartown, where the road was littered with twigs and leaves and an occasional branch. They came to a tree that lay across their path, pinning some electric wires that snapped blue sparks and stuttered.

"End of the line," announced his driver. "Sorry. I'll have to walk the rest of the way, and I guess you will, too."

"I've only got a block or two more," he said. "Thanks."

The Islander waved and headed down the street, intent on his errand of mercy.

He leaned into the storm again, walking down the rain-shining street until he reached Diana's little house. There were no lights in its windows, because the power was out, and it seemed suddenly lonely, suddenly empty, and it drew from the depths of himself a loneliness that he'd been able to avoid in his struggle to get here. The worst possible thing that could happen to him, he understood now, would be Diana's absence.

Jesus, she had to be home. She had to be!

Oh, God, he prayed even as he remembered his determination never to pray, never, ever to call upon that unresponsive, uncaring, nonexistent deity. She has to be there. She's got to be.

He knocked on the door of his asylum, waited a long, cruel time for it to open.

"Hi," she said faintly.

"Can you give shelter to this benighted fool?" he asked, his tone as light as he could make it. "Seems I'm out in the cold, windy world with nowhere to go."

"Oh. Sure," she said wonderingly, backed up, letting him into the entry, where he shed his coat.

"I was afraid you'd be at your shop."

"Most of us closed up." She led him into the front room. "What do you mean, you've nowhere to go?"

"It seems I've lost my ship." His fatigue and shock overtook him, and he had no more strength with which to make light remarks. "She's gone, Diana. I can't take you on that guided tour, after all." He felt tears near the surface, and he sank onto the couch that took a whole wall of the parlor. Through the kitchen door he could see the table where he'd sat talking with Alice Bradley. He rested his head on the back of the couch, stared up at the ceiling. "Eric took her out to sea. He took her and she can't make it . . . and he knew she couldn't."

Diana only watched.

"When the wind shifted. During what little eye we had, he sent me on a fool's errand, and when I got back . . . nothing."

She let out her breath, as though she'd been holding it the whole time. "Why did he do it?" she asked softly. "Why?"

"I guess he was at the end of the line." He looked listlessly in her direction. "And so am I."

She impulsively reached for his hand as every ounce of his energy drained away. "How did you get here?" she asked.

"I walked."

"All the way from Vineyard Haven, in this storm?"

"I got a ride, halfway."

"You must be awfully tired, Steve."

"Yes, I guess I am," he admitted, his eyes closing at the very thought.

"Stretch out, right where you are."

"Shoes," he mumbled, and felt them being removed and himself tipping sideways, stretching out. "I'm glad you were here," he sighed. The room rocked. "I don't know what I'd have done if you hadn't been here."

"I'll get you a blanket," she said, tucking sofa pillows under his head.

He meant to tell her not to bother, and then the rasp of wool was drawn over him, his body heat instantly caught and returned. Like a child he reached for her hand. "You won't go away, will you?"

"No," she said, tucking the hand beneath the blanket. "I'll be right here. Have you been home since I saw you last?"

"I am home." Silence entered the room as darkness when the shades are drawn, entered his body and battered mind and sleep, like an unexpected guest, arrived suddenly and took him away.

The house was quiet, with a stillness peculiar to snowstorms and electrical failures. The low, golden light of the distant candle coaxed him up, up from the pit of exhaustion into which he'd fallen, up, up into the present moment which he was unable to identify.

Across from him was a small fireplace, he observed, which, because the room was so little, was not far away at all. . . .

It was Diana Bradley's house, he remembered, and then he remembered *Jenny Lawrence* and Eric too, in a hideous, awful yawning of cavernous consciousness. Remembered the whole world of *Jenny Lawrence* which had sunk, like Atlantis. How desperate Eric must have been, he thought. I didn't really understand it, even though he told me. And yet if Larsen hadn't sunk *Jenny*, she'd probably have ended her days as a sun-bleached hulk in the mud of Vineyard Haven harbor. She'd never have survived pounding on the pier. She was hopeless the minute that storm headed our way, and Eric knew it. And in his desperation, committed himself to the only decision that made sense to him.

He lay quietly, trying to accept it. Then the sound of a page turning in the kitchen put *Jenny* to rest, and Eric too.

For he was in Diana Bradley's house. Just the two of them,

without lights or telephones. No one knew he was there, and no one would know until he chose to reveal himself.

Could he take up the girl Diana Bradley where he'd left her eighteen years ago? Would she let him? He remembered the kiss he had forced on her, to which she had so fully responded the last time he'd been in the house, and knew that he would try. He sat up and caught himself before he moaned aloud; he was stiff in every muscle and strained in every bone. He stretched cautiously, swung his arms, bent, pulled, edged his way toward the kitchen.

"Well!" She looked up. The candle cast her face in velvet.

He tried to smile past the upwelling of desire. "Have I been asleep long?"

"Awhile." She looked at a clock over her stove which wasn't going because the power had yet to be restored. "It's probably around midnight. You must be hungry!"

Quickly she slid from her chair and opened the refrigerator door, busied herself with an examination of its contents, which were dim now because there was no light inside. "I have a six-pack of beer." She glanced at him. "Would you like some?"

"Sure."

"And ham. How about a ham sandwich?"

"Later, maybe," he said. "It takes awhile to wake up."

"All right. We'll just see about it in a half an hour or so. Let's work on the beer first." She rummaged in a drawer and found a can opener while he seated himself at the table, moved the candle aside so that he would be able to observe any change of expression.

"Tell me about Eric." She passed him the opened beer. "I didn't want to ask you much before—you seemed so tired. Tell me why he would take *Jenny* out."

The beer was cool, smooth, wonderful.

"Eric wasn't the person he seemed," he said. "He always surrounded himself with people, but he was a loner. An unhappy one. Just before the storm hit he got talking about living aboard the ship so that he could avoid having to deal with life, and with himself. He told me he hadn't slept much all summer—he must have been exhausted, and all nerved up—running from something—he didn't know what. His thinking was confused."

"Do you believe *Jenny* would have sunk in the harbor, if he'd stayed?"

"Probably. She was taking a lot of water. Her seams

were surely working. We pumped all morning, and it never seemed to make a difference." Suddenly his throat closed. He did not want to talk about *Jenny*.

"Are you sure you aren't hungry?" she asked quickly, drawing him away from his sadness. "I can't get you anything hot right away, but we could build a fire." She gestured to the brick hearth, there in the kitchen. "We could heat up a can of soup or something."

"Not yet." He looked into the beauty of the candle flame, the blue of its center, the nimbus around it; his sadness eased, went away, and his desire returned.

He dared not reveal it—yet. Steadily he watched the candle, waited.

Into the silence she asked, "Have you been back? To Waterford?"

"Yes."

"What did your wife say?"

"She says I was unfair to have deliberately deceived her so long ago by saying nothing."

"Did you? Deliberately deceive her?"

"I suppose I did. I knew it would make a difference to her," he explained. "You don't ask for rejection, if you can help it. At least, I don't."

She hesitated a moment. "Is that why you never went to Dad? When you found out who he was? Were you worried that he'd turn you down?"

He took a deep breath, let it go.

"It never occurred to me to go to him—quite the opposite. It was imperative to keep away." *Now*, he thought. For in this instant it was just as imperative to make her understand—and now was the time to do it. Past the candle he met her eyes steadily. "And so I had to keep away from you, too, Diana. It's important that you understand that. And that you believe it." The moment hung between them, and then she pushed back her chair.

"Would you like another bottle of beer? I see you've finished yours. I'll have one, too." She spoke quickly, vigorously; her voice, always distinctive, was vibrant now. She dug two bottles out of the refrigerator. This time the caps escaped her, bouncing along the counter and onto the floor.

"Oh, damn!" She bent to retrieve them. "I never even asked if you wanted a glass. Do you?"

"No," he answered quietly, in an effort to put her at her ease—but she was not at ease, not at all. She reseated herself, still holding the bottle caps. She was wary, he knew, yet he must move forward, he must not let the past elude them. At its threshold they had lost sight of one another, and now, in order to cross it, they must regain those years and that time somehow. "Actually it helped a lot, knowing who my real father was. My stepfather was something of a tyrant, and when I learned that he had no real claim to my loyalty, I could free myself from him. And that was important. I'd have been crippled, otherwise. He was an awful son of a bitch."

She shook her head. "I didn't know that. How'd you get rid of him?"

"It's too complicated to explain. But what it boils down to was just not letting him exist anymore. My mother divorced him; my cousin gave me Kingsland instead of giving it to him, and I went my own way, without honoring his values. And so he ceased to be. Poof!" He snapped his fingers, as though Charles Sinclaire had evaporated.

"Where is he now?"

"I suppose he's just droning along at Sommerset and King, living in the Port Huron house, paying my mother alimony until she marries again—which, from the looks of it, will be a while."

"You and your mother have had to face a lot of misery. Doesn't seem fair, somehow."

"It strikes me that you've had your share."

She only smiled, a little wistfully.

"And my mother has found a man, and I've had *Jenny Lawrence*."

"*Jenny* compensated for everything?"

"She helped. My wife said it all: when I showed her *Jenny* for the first time, she complained that it was like meeting my mistress."

The word rose between them, unavoidably suggestive; the expression on her face changed, and he suspected that on his own there was the giveaway of concentrated intensity that rides a man when he is stalking his prey.

Her hand clutching the bottle caps tightened as she asked, "Have you ever had a mistress? A woman?"

"A woman, yes," he answered honestly, remembering Arleen Patterson. "A mistress, no." He continued to watch her, silently waiting for an answer to an unspoken question.

She looked elsewhere before looking at him. "We are a rather straight generation, aren't we?"

"Were you?"

"Straight? Yes. I was faithful to Paul."

"You haven't been married for a couple of years. Have you had a lover since?" he asked bluntly.

"No." They paid pointed attention to their respective bottles of beer. "What will you do, with your mistress lost to you?" she asked finally.

"I was going to think that over while I walked. Distinctly I remember wanting to figure out why the *Lawrence* was so valuable to me—what I'd found in her, whether it could be found anywhere else. Then the ride came along and I took it."

"And never came to a conclusion?"

"Well . . . I may have come to a conclusion that didn't require thought." His eyes held hers, and he refused to release her.

"You must mean . . . you must believe it can be found—whatever *Jenny* gave you—in another place," she faltered.

"Yes. I think it can."

In the silence, silence which no clock ticking measured, no voices tore, in which no motor hummed accompaniment, something hot and uncontrolled built up and reached out.

Quickly she jumped up, opened a cupboard. "Would you like some crackers with the beer? I have a fresh box up here somewhere." She turned to get his answer, and slowly he stood, pushing his chair aside, came around the table. There was nothing between them, nothing to separate them, nothing in their way. She closed the cupboard door and dropped the bottle caps on the counter, their tinny, tiny sound clear in the still room.

"I waited," she said; with difficulty she looked at him.

"I know. I'm sorry." He touched her hair, her cheek. "I couldn't come to you."

"Yes, I understand that now."

At her temple a vein lifted and fell strongly. He touched it with his lips; he drew her gently close, found her mouth with his own, and felt her tension. She was afraid. She was afraid, and he must help free her from fear.

"Was your husband unkind to you?"

"Sometimes. When he'd been drinking."

"You tighten up when I touch you. Do I remind you of him?"

"You're nothing like him."

"Do you want me to go away?"

"No," she whispered. "No." He ran his hand down her arm, back to her shoulder.

"Very soon now, it'll be too late," he said, and from the

deep of his being welled his need for her, his joy in her. Without taking his eyes from hers, he unbuttoned her blouse.

"Steve, I . . ."

He pulled the blouse aside. Her breasts, which he had never touched, were still youthful, firm, warm in his cupped hand.

"I don't know how to love a man," she said, her voice wavering.

"I'll show you." Her dark nipples were hard and tight, and when he kissed them they tightened still more and he heard the intake of her breath. "Is that little bedroom all right?"

"Yes."

He left the door of the lean-to open so that the candle would reveal them to one another when their eyes became accustomed to the dimness; he removed what was left of her clothing, stripped off his own, edged her gently back toward the narrow bed, to its edge, lowered her onto it, and because further discussion would do nothing to help, he parted her legs and covered her with himself and pushed inexorably into the hotness that awaited him so that he would not have to ask and she would not be called on to consent.

He hurt her. Oh, Christ, he'd hurt her, and so he knew it was true, that she'd had no lover—perhaps had not even known her husband for a long time. She was tight like a virgin, but ready for him nonetheless, wet and warm and full of need despite her fear. He could feel her urgency reaching out; he waited for her pain to ease and then to wane. He kissed her mouth and her eyes and her hair, the curve of her throat, and saw that her color was rising, her skin softly pink, glowing. She was a woman in need, a woman craving, a woman who did not know how to tell him, nor take what he would give.

"You have to trust me, Diana," he said quietly. "If you're reluctant, I don't blame you. But you have to trust me anyway. I'll help, but you're the one who has to let go and let me catch you." He kissed her without hurrying, the pounding in his groin an agony that he willed himself to endure; he kissed her until he could fairly feel her aching with his intensity; there was a mist of sweat on her skin. She held herself still—but it was with effort, he thought, and it was important, desperately important to break that control, demolish it so that there would be no restraint, no pride, no reservation. He must make her speak to him, he must make her admit that she needed him, he must make her beg, grovel if necessary. . . .

He tasted her mouth again, held her tightly, pinning her, every part of her, with every part of himself, immobilizing her, gambling on his certainty that the longer she would be unable to move, the harder it would be to resist the rise of her own lust. Already she was starting to strain against him, her breathing shallow, starting to catch in her throat.

"Am I hurting you? Am I too heavy?" His lips still touched hers as he spoke, and he felt as well as heard her breathless reply.

"No. You aren't too heavy. You don't hurt . . . oh, God . . ."

He drew back slowly, very far, as though to leave her.

"Don't!" Her eyes flew open, wounded.

"Don't what?" he asked softly.

"Don't—don't go away."

"Why not?"

She was silent, tears gathered, shining in her eyes.

"Why not?" He kissed her eyes closed. "Say it."

"I need you," she whispered. "I want you."

"Like this?" he asked, and slowly pushed in.

"Yes!" Her voice was thin, drawn from a far place. "Oh, yes."

Beneath him her bones melted and became part of his, her breath was caught, and he had her—he had her . . . he knew it! He watched the torment, the tumult, that he wrought. "Like that?" he asked, gently giving. "Like that?" he asked, cruelly taking, slowly, slowly—oh, oh, the burning agony of it!

"Yes! Yes!" she cried, over the edge now, past the self that feared him and what he could do to her; she shuddered in the quivering agony of arousal and she writhed and cried out because she could not help herself anymore, no longer in control because she was his, his own, part of himself, to do with as he willed for this moment, this hour, this lifetime, this eternity. He thrust deep and hard, and all his awareness, all his being was centered in the beating, burning, aching of their coupling. Distantly he heard her call his name and felt the tensing of her flesh, and within himself there was a rending, a tearing, as a tree uprooted from the earth, as a cliff falling into the sea, and from a distant place he heard himself cry out as he never had, compelled to give voice to the depth of his experience; from the deepest part of himself he was given over to the slam of orgasm that rolled across his whole horizon like summer thunder, and he lost track of himself, somehow, and then he returned, shaken and empty, lowered himself to her side, gathered her up. She twined her legs around his, clung to him, her face tight against the curve of his neck.

"It's been so long since I could fit with a man," she sighed shakily. "I can't get close enough."

He ran a hand across her hip and waist, felt her lips on his throat, felt the whispered texture of her skin, and knew that he could take her yet again, he who had believed the virility of youth was behind him.

"Even after I go back, Diana, we have to see one another," he said close to her ear.

"Yes." Somehow she moved closer yet, and he touched the curve of her spine and the fullness of her thigh, pushed her away to kiss her breasts and roughly pulled her beneath him.

"Yes," she urged, her voice a thread. "Yes," she cried, and he entered her again, found her ready, helplessly orgasmic, incredibly responsive, and he was sorry for the man she divorced who had not been able to unlock this part of her, glad for himself who had found her and her warmth and her openness as now she met him, aquiver in her eagerness, hot and deep.

Oh, Christ; the climax was drawn effortlessly from him, quiet, sustained, explosive, devastating. Shattered, he waited to be reassembled, and they were still for a long, long time.

"I wish we could go on all night," he confessed gladly. "I didn't know it could be like this."

"Me either. I believed it was all over for me, but apparently I've just saved it up."

"If only you understood how sorry I was, years ago—"

"Don't," she said, covering his mouth.

"Say you forgive it," he begged, taking her hand away.

"I forgive it," she said instantly.

"I loved you then."

"It's okay, Steven."

"I loved you," he insisted.

"I loved you too," she said softly.

"And I love you still."

"I love you too. I love you!"

He held her as tightly as he could, grateful, joyful, humble, exultant. "I have to start all over."

"Yes, I'm afraid so."

"Not only because of the *Lawrence*. Because of my wife too. I wouldn't have come here if my marriage were still in one piece. It's not, and I have to do something about it. I can't go on pretending that everything's okay. A lot of things haven't been okay for a long time."

"I gathered that." Her lips whispered over his throat, his chest; he felt a little nip, saw she'd raised a welt on his shoulder. "I've branded you." She smiled. "Wherever you go, everyone will know you're mine."

"They'll know anyway, because you're coming with me."

"No."

His elation and joy drained away, and in his nakedness he was cold. "You're not?"

"No, Steven." She pulled him to herself protectively. "I love you—you know it—and that's why I'm not going with you."

"I don't blame you for not wanting to leave the Vineyard or this house, or the shop," he said. "But I wouldn't expect you to—not all the time. Just part of the time," he urged. "And I'll come here, part of the time, somehow—I don't know how yet—I'll build you fires to sit in front of with me, and read you books, and bring you breakfast in bed."

She laughed shakily. "No. Let's just love one another now. Just now."

"And then?"

"And then you'll go back to do whatever you decide to do. But since you don't have any real idea of where you'd like to go or what you'd like to do or be, you have to go and find out."

"I'd like any decision I make to include you."

"I know you would. But it's more important for you to find out what you think is right for yourself. Don't you see?"

"No!" he said fiercely, clawing at the edges of the chasm of despair opening now beneath him. To have found her, after all this time! To have tracked her, pursued her, won her! "Why put us through it?"

"Because you have a chance to make a really free choice," she said, her voice low but steady. "You've lost all the ties you've had, except your children, perhaps, and soon they'll be gone, too. You're starting over, at the bottom. So much of your life has been conditioned by a secret you've been obliged to keep—by wounds you had no choice but to bear. Now that's not true. Now there's nothing."

"There's you."

"Yes. But that makes me an anchor." She was more beautiful than he had ever seen her. "If I come with you now, all the decisions you make have to take me into consideration. If I don't, every decision you make will come from the mainspring of yourself, and you'll see who you really are. It's the chance of a lifetime."

"I need you."

"I'm afraid you don't."

"I love you."

"Go find whatever it is you have to do," she begged. "Go find out what life requires of you. When you're done, we'll find out whether there's room enough for me. For all you know—for all I know—Waterford—and Kingsland—is where you belong."

He could only stare, defeated. "You really won't come."

"No."

"But you love me."

"I love you—and my not coming ought to prove it."

"You've got it all thought out."

"Yes," she admitted. "I had a lot of time to think tonight, while you slept. I've thought about a lot of things, ever since I saw you last."

"Like whether you'd let me make love to you?"

"Yes, that."

"Like whether you wanted to?"

"Yes." She touched his mouth. "And then, because we aren't the kind of people to take intimacy lightly, I had to think a lot about where it would lead, and where I wanted it to go—and where you'd need it to go. It's bound to lead us somewhere, and I'm willing that it should. But not now, Steve. Not yet. You've gone through so much, come so far . . ."

"And what if I can't find you when I've found what I'm looking for?"

But he knew the answer, saw it in her eyes.

She smiled. "Trust me," she said.

31

He called Bob from the Hobbes Hole dock, and then Mari. "Casey's coming to pick me up," he told the stranger on the other end of the wire. "I'll be home in a couple of hours."

"How did you and Eric weather the storm."

"Not so well."

"What's that supposed to mean?"

"*Jenny's* gone," he said, and hung up.

The day was intently bright and infinitely clear, as the day after a storm always was, and, hands in his pockets, he wandered the Hobbes Hole waterfront. Flotsam and jetsam lay in tangled heaps on the beach; the storm had not struck here as harshly as it had on the islands, though; and the destruction had been pared to the proportion of a nuisance. An empty bench looked out toward the jetty, and he sat on it for uncountable moments, and minutes, and perhaps hours, trying to make sense of things.

For how could he live in Waterford, which was being slowly dismembered by people who did not understand it? Was acquiescence to that destruction any different from running in the rat race and turning into a rat yourself? How could he live at Kingsland with Mari, running a boardinghouse with her while Diana Bradley was his mistress, while *Jenny Lawrence* and Eric rotted at the bottom of the sea. How could he do anything so totally lacking in commitment or integrity and still believe what he'd told Eric from the depths of his faith in life—that *Jenny* taught a man the wisdom of the tides, of the wind, of the water, from which he could move forward, whole and true, whether *Jenny* was there or not.

A shadow fell on the sand beside him, and Bob sat down on the bench. "Hi, pal."

"Hi. Heard anything?"

"I'm afraid so," Bob said. "I'm afraid there's wreckage washing up on Long Island that probably belongs to *Jenny*."

"There's always something being washed up in Long Island," he managed to say. "Maybe it doesn't mean anything."

Together they watched the sun dance in the harbor. "The insurance investigators are going to ask a lot of questions, I expect." It was Bob's way of seeking information without being direct about it.

"I wasn't there," he said, still looking out to sea. "I left to get beer, and the ship was gone when I got back."

"Any evidence that Eric untied her?"

"Plenty. The lines were lying slack, not frayed and not cut either. But he might have untied them in order to get *Jenny* away from the pier. Move her over. She'd have been pounded to putty where she was, once the storm started up again."

"They'll have a field day, I'm afraid."

"Let them," he said savagely. He watched a gull climb up the sky and drop a clam on the rocks of the jetty, dive to pull dinner out of the crushed shell. "Did you put extra money in *Jenny*'s account?" he asked. "Eric said he was going to ask you to beef it up."

"He didn't ask."

"He said he was going to telephone you."

"He didn't. But the bank did, yesterday afternoon. I transferred funds and put some of my own in. We're not overdrawn."

"I'll split it with you, Bob—what you put in. Soon as I can."

"Don't worry about it now."

"Why didn't Eric call, do you think?"

"Perhaps he was afraid I'd have time to get to Vineyard Haven."

Jesus! Talk about deliberate!

"I guess I wouldn't mention it to the investigators," Bob said.

"I won't. Doesn't mean anything, anyway."

Bob shrugged, and they sat watching the business of the harbor, and then, without hurrying, walked to the Casey truck.

"What are you doing to do now?" Bob asked. "I mean, now that *Jenny*'s gone, what'll you do for a living?"

"Been wondering about that myself."

"I wonder if you've thought about the building business. You're not green now; you're an experienced carpenter, and I wonder if you'd consider being my partner."

He did not look at Bob; he could not trust himself. "I'm afraid I can't."

"Why not?"

"I won't be in town."

"You're leaving?"

"Yes." There it was, fully formed, just as Diana had known it would be. "I'm rejoining the rat race."

"Come on, Steve. You've got to be kidding."

"I'm not."

"Why in hell?"

"I'd like to prove something, I guess." He looked at his hands, scarred, grimy. "Besides," he said, switching to a topic they could both get their hands on, "I don't particularly want to live in Waterford."

"Hell, Steve, it won't always be like it is now. All those new people have run before the storm and made it safely in, and they're eager to protect what they have. But it won't always be like this. Waterford will get to them, in time. Don't leave just on account of not liking it."

He thought of John Shaunessy, and Eben Gray, and the men who had come to him for help, and he wished he had not thought of them because it only made his decision harder. "I'm not leaving only because of that. Staying around is like saying it doesn't matter to me. And it does. And since I can't change it . . ."

"Running away won't change anything, either."

"I don't think I am running away. I think I'm choosing."

"Choosing what, for Chrissakes?"

"When I find that out, you'll be among the first to know." He grinned and watched the mid-Cape highway passing by, with scrubby little trees coming out to meet them and then hurtling backward as the truck sped on, and he thought about Waterford and its lesson in longevity, which only a place so old could teach: that it was not withering under the onslaught of people alien to it. Instead, it was accommodating the needs of people who sought refuge there—just as it had done these three hundred years, and more than likely would continue to, irrespective of whose needs they were—whatever Steven Sinclaire decided to do . . . or not to do.

"Damn that storm," Bob said unhappily. "Complaining about it doesn't help, but Christ, Steve! If *Jenny* hadn't sunk, you wouldn't be leaving Waterford."

"Well—she did. And I am. The first Merrick of Waterford lost his ship, too," he observed.

"That so?"

"Yup."

"What'd he do, then?"

"Started a new church."

"Huh."

They rode silently.

"The first Casey in Waterford shoveled shit in Kingsley Merrick's stable," Bob said at length. "Only, his name was O'Shea."

"Is that right?" He thought about it. "Must have gratified you, so many years ago, to see me shovel yours."

Bob grinned, without taking his eyes off the road. "For about two seconds, it did. But you weren't like the Merricks. You were yourself. Anyone could see that. In fact, everyone did."

"Huh," he responded in kind, his memories wounding him: carving a fraudulent date, Greenleaf whistling to the bird watchers of Linc Roly Hall, who in his entire career never issued a ticket. . . .

"Mr. Turner's resigned," Bob said.

"Who's Mr. Turner?"

"The fellow who was elected selectman this spring."

"Why'd he resign?"

"Too much work," Bob scoffed. "Seems he didn't plan on spending so much time at it. Says it's not good for his health."

"Hm."

"So the election has to be held again. In September."

"No, Bob. The answer's no."

"If you took his place . . ."

"It won't do any good. All it would accomplish is to buy time."

"Maybe time's all Waterford needs."

"I'm sure it is, Bob. But maybe it doesn't have to be bought. Maybe time—or fate—will do a better job than either of us could."

"I don't think it's that simple," Bob insisted. "I wish you'd reconsider."

They pulled off the highway and into Yarmouth, and on east of town to Waterford, where men with white cotton work gloves and plaid golf caps were nailing shutters onto the museum windows at the mill site. The leaves on the few remaining elms were beginning to suggest autumn, lusterless, without vigor, hanging unhappily over the road as they drove past the square old houses of captains, and those belonging to the Greek Revival, and the later Victorian ones, and then toward the mansard monstrosity that was Kingsland, the whole lot about to be preserved by the uniformity and call-to-order of a historic district, and he thought of that first Merrick, lost in space and time now, who built a house and lost his ship and started a renegade church. And the next Merrick of consequence, who amassed two fortunes and nearly made a third, who built the house they approached now, who reworked the town in the image he thought most proper—and of the descendant of the Merrick stableman, sitting beside him now, as much a part of the lore of Waterford as was Steven Sinclaire himself.

The sequence was interesting, he thought. He'd have to consider it more carefully, sometime.

"About the selectman's job . . ." Bob said, pulling into the driveway.

"What about it."

"I'd sure like to get a petition started, Steve. With your name on it. Won't you change your mind?"

He remembered Alice Bradley's face, her smile, her words: *No dream is dead, if there's someone left to dream it*. Perhaps she was right—but perhaps he need not be the one. Nor need he remain here, in order to dream. "You can start anything you want, Bob. But not with my name. I'm sorry; I've got things to do," he tried to explain. "And there's nothing I can do about Waterford that Waterford can't do for itself. Without me."

The flag flew from the mast in the front yard, the sign hung below; petunias drooped beneath. The gravel scrunched in the driveway, and on the front porch sat Rick, a rip in his blue jeans and mud on his T-shirt and a swelling lump beneath his eye. Steven left Bob without speaking, only holding his hand up to wave, and then turned to his son. "Gosh," he teased, "what does the other guy look like?"

"You may find out soon." Rick grinned. "Since the other guy is Junior Marshall."

"What in Christ's name for?"

"Well," drawled Rick, as though he'd been a country person all his life, "you know Dan Sears's uncle?"

"Linc?"

"Yup. Well, Junior was making some pretty raw remarks about Mr. Sears—he drinks quite a lot, you know?"

"Yes, I know."

"And Junior was saying things that Dan could hear, trying to make Dan feel bad, so I told Junior to stop, and he began giving me a hard time. So I let him have it."

"Settling things with a fight is apt to be a poor idea."

"You're so right." Rick nodded. "But Junior Marshall will think twice, Dad, before he tries to make himself big by making someone else small."

They looked at each other, man to man, there on the porch.

"You're not going to stay, are you?" Rick said.

"No."

"I'll sure miss you." His adolescent voice went hoarse.

"No, you won't." He smiled. "I'm only going as far as Boston."

"What are you going to do there?"

"I don't know yet."

Rick looked away, then back. "Can I visit you?"

"You bet. We both have a lot of things to learn yet, and I plan for us to learn them together."

"Maybe I could live with you."

"Certainly. If you want to. Or perhaps part of the time here, and part in Boston, if you'd rather."

"Gee, Dad! Do you think I could? Live in both?"

"I don't see why not. You belong here, after all."

"Yes, I guess I do."

"And you belong with me, too. I'll need you, Rick. Quite a lot."

"Me too," the boy said awkwardly, unable to say more or say it well, his grateful smile a failure.

It would not be easy, Steven thought. But it would resolve itself graciously if he was patient enough, enduring enough, sufficiently faithful to his own search. It would resolve itself, and at the end of whatever he found was the occupant of the half-house in Edgartown, and perhaps, just perhaps, another chance here on the land of his heritage for the boy beside him. Another chance for another Merrick, in whatever the town of Waterford had to offer in a time far distant from this one.

He hugged Rick briefly, released him quickly, and together they walked into the shadows of Kingsland.

Author's Note

Kingsland, This Is the House, and *The House of Kingsley Merrick* are set in a fictional town, inhabited by fictional families whose lives I have used, as authentically as my research would allow, to convey the times in which they lived: their customs, dreams, values, their response to the national heartbeat. For Cape Cod has always been directly affected by the developing, ongoing saga of American history.

Kingsland attempts to convey the customs and dreams of the twentieth century, as well as the impact of a particularly contemporary phenomenon—the flight of large numbers of our population to the sanctuary of a simplier way of life, an escape from a frantic, desperate destiny which, like a tidal wave, rushes toward a distant, unseen, unknown shore.

But the Promised Land is not empty. Living on it already are the men and women who have inherited it, whose values and essential simplicity have lent richness and texture to our American past and who have been its strength. And who are required to move aside as those in flight look for new answers to their lives.

The confrontation which is the background of this story could have been set in nearly any section of our country, because it is occurring everywhere. I have, however, located it on Cape Cod because that is where I witnessed it. The destruction of this tiny part of America did not happen as I describe it, for this is a work of fiction. But I have not invented the way of life that did exist on Cape Cod, a way of life deeply entrenched in the heritage of our nation. I have tried to preserve it in a web of words in order to make more tangible its values. For it is my hope that those values might be encouraged to flourish in the places where they yet exist, and that they might be regained in places where they have been destroyed.

For without them the Promised Land, wherever it lies, is lost.

Deborah Hill

ABOUT THE AUTHOR

Deborah Hill was born in Newton, Massachusetts, and grew up in Toledo, Ohio. She lived for six years in the Cape Cod locale that forms the setting for *This Is the House, The House of Kingsley Merrick*, and *Kingsland*, her trilogy about the Merrick family. Many of the characters and events in these books are based on real people and real happenings discovered through research into diaries, genealogies, records, and Cape Cod history, which lends her writing its tremendous authenticity. Deborah Hill was trained in philosophy at Villanova University. She lives with her husband and two sons in Vermont, where she is at work on her next novel.